BLAZEWRATH GAMES

BLAZEWRATH GAMES

WITHDRAWN

AMPARO ORTIZ

PAGE STREET
PUBLISHING CO.

PAGE STREET
PUBLISHING CO.

TO MAMI & PAPI.
I WOULD FIGHT ANY UN-BONDED
DRAGON FOR YOU.

Before the sport of Blazewrath was created, the question among witches and wizards remained the same: How can we keep our world a secret from humans who do not possess magic? This question did not have a long-term answer. In 1743, a dragon revealed itself to a Regular for the first time in recorded history. The dragon had not intended to disrupt the status quo of the magical community. It had wished to ask that Regular a different question: "Are you ready to soar?"

—*Excerpt from Harleen Khurana's*
A History of Blazewrath Around the World

CHAPTER ONE

DRAGONS ARE BETTER COMPANY THAN PEOPLE.
Not that I hate people. Some are okay.

People can't fly, though. Not with wings strong enough to break the shell of a dragon's egg, which is as hard as steel. Wings that double as weapons. Witches and wizards use fancy metal wands and even fancier potions to get off the ground. So what? Dragons don't need wands or potions. They can just *fly*.

Every two years, I watch them fly and fight for the Blazewrath World Cup.

No other sporting event is the home of dragon riders and their huge, badass steeds, hailing from the sixteen countries chosen to compete. Other sports have players who run. But they don't have a *Runner*, the only player without a dragon steed, who has to reach the top of a magically conjured mountain before they're blown away by a fireball or beaten to a pulp.

After today, that could be me.

For the billionth time, I sort through the stack of pages on my bed. Each one has a header that reads PUERTO RICO RUNNER TRYOUTS APPLICATION. I reread the first page:

Lana Aurelia Torres (Age: 17)
Application Accepted! Appointment: July 16, 2017 @ 1:00 p.m.
The Ritz-Carlton, Naples, Florida

*All candidates must possess an official birth certificate from Puerto Rico. If attending tryouts in the United States, candidates are required to participate in their current state of residence and none other. Previous track-and-field experience is preferred but not mandatory.
Training in martial arts is highly recommended.

Today is July 16. It's been four weeks since Blazewrath tryouts officially began. Now they're finally coming to Florida. Puerto Rico's former Runner, Brian Santana, got kicked off the team back in April. Getting fired is bad enough, but getting fired before your country plays *for the first time ever?* I would've cried. Thankfully, Brian's firing led to a broader search for his replacement, this time including Puerto Ricans living in the States. I'd switched from lamenting the loss of my country's Runner to celebrating the chance to take his place.

I don't have the "highly recommended" martial arts training, unless watching YouTube videos and hitting imaginary rivals in my bedroom counts. I used to be on my middle school's track-and-field team, but my grades started slipping, so Mom told me to focus on studying instead. Hopefully, I'm still fast enough to impress the International Blazewrath Federation.

There's a knock on my door.

"Lana, are you all set?" Mom asks. "I need help with the wrapping paper."

"Just a sec!" Thank God the door is locked. The ruby-red shirt and faded denim jeans I'll be wearing to hide my sporty clothes are still laid out next to my tryout documents.

"Okay. I'll be downstairs." Mom's footsteps echo across the hall.

Even though the coast is clear, I rush to put on my shirt and jeans. My brown hair flops all over the place, but after a few frantic brushes, I wrangle it into a decent ponytail. I slip on my black-and-white Adidas sneakers, the ones I run in every morning. Mom's used to seeing me in them, so she won't find it suspicious I'm wearing them to celebrate my cousin Todd's birthday. Besides, we're taking him to a wand shop. No need to whip out the stilettos and fringe.

I do a quick pirouette once I'm dressed. My meeting with the International Blazewrath Federation is in a mere *five hours*. Today I might become the new Runner for Team Puerto Rico. I might get picked to rep my beautiful island. The island I haven't visited in twelve years.

My smile fades. Twelve years is too long to spend away from home. The place where I became *myself*. Before my Puerto Rican father and my white American mother divorced, we'd lived in the mountains of Cayey. I would dash around our two-story house, its walls decorated in cracked coral paint, pretending to chase after dragons with Papi. He'd let me guide him through the endless greenery outside and the sloping, pothole-ridden roads. Our neighbors would catch me with notepads and purple pens, jotting down clues that would take me to the dragons' lair.

There hadn't been Sol de Noche dragons in Puerto Rico then. There was just a father and his only child, their feet running as fast as their imaginations.

Our imaginations were never as exciting as Blazewrath.

The Cup takes place in a different country every two years. I was only four when Papi let me watch my first tournament. He rearranged the furniture in our too-hot living room, barefoot and belting '80s rock songs, the windows open and the ceiling fan blasting. He demonstrated in theatrical lunges what the Runner has to do on the mountain and explained the offensive tactics each team's dragons could do. Two things engraved themselves in my heart:

The way my father's face lit up whenever a match started.

And how I desperately craved to be part of the matches myself.

Puerto Rico made me who I am, but Blazewrath is the reason I was born. It's my purpose in a life without my island. A life without my father, who's currently living in Brazil. He doesn't know I'm trying out. If I get picked for Team Puerto Rico, it'll be the best surprise of his life. If nothing happens, he'll never know what a disappointment I was to us both.

I grab the Whisperer on my dresser. It looks like a red sports watch and fits my wrist like a charm. I press the silver adjust button. "Samira? Can you hear me?"

"Affirmative! What's up?" she says. Tupac's "Keep Ya Head Up" blasts in the background. This Whisperer has *way* better sound than my phone. Thanks to magic, it lets me communicate with anyone from anywhere.

I'm not a witch, but being best friends with one has its perks.

"Just wanted to make sure the private wand-making tour is still happening," I say.

"Yup. I called the store again to confirm. I'll distract everyone while you sneak out for Blazewrath tryouts. I've already left my car in the store parking lot, so I'll slip you my keys. Then you act your booty off to convince your mom you're sick and can sit the private tour out."

I'm smiling wide again. "I owe you big-time, Samira."

"Make it onto the team. *Or* you could let me Transport to your house."

"You're not setting yourself on fire today."

She gives me one of her Olympic gold medal–winning sighs.

"That fire doesn't actually burn, Lana. Stop being extra. Also, I can get rid of it faster than before."

Now I'm the one who sighs. Samira's a great BFF, but when it comes to being a great witch, she's still a work in progress. She's not magically strong enough to perform complex spells, including the Transport Charm, which moves anything from one place to another. Her original plan was to Transport me straight to the Ritz-Carlton, but the last time she tried the spell, I was caged in blue flames for two hours. The flames didn't hurt me, but *two hours?* Come on. And since Mom's an OB/GYN, she's always on call from the hospital. Her car is off-limits.

Not that she'd ever lend it to me for this.

"We stick to my mother picking you up," I say. "It's a lot safer."

"Fine. Let's do it your boring way." I can picture her pouting in disappointment.

"See you in an hour, Captain. Again, I owe you."

"How about you admit *Law & Order* is the best show on television?"

Ugh, not this nonsense again. "Goodbye, Samira."

I tuck the tryout documents into my Wonder Woman backpack. It has this vintage-looking gold metal badge on it, which is shaped like the *W* on Diana's uniform. It makes me want to punch bad guys. Besides, Papi bought it for me last Christmas, so it'll give me some luck.

My phone's wallpaper fills the lock screen. It's a picture of Takeshi Endo, my favorite Blazewrath player. Two years ago, a fifteen-year-old Takeshi had been ready to represent Japan for the second time as his team's Striker. This photo is from a shoot without Hikaru, his dragon steed. He's in a brightly lit studio, wearing a simple white T-shirt and skinny jeans as black as his slicked-back hair. One of his sleeves is rolled up, exposing a lean bicep.

He's been missing for two years. No one has seen him since Hikaru's murder.

"Wish me luck, Takeshi."

I tuck my phone into my backpack and head down to the living room, where six different gift boxes, ranging from cufflinks small to dress shirt medium, have been dumped onto the velvet suede couch. The ivory wrapping paper remains untouched on top of my cousin's gifts.

I spot Mom near the TV. Leslie Anne Wells, the willowy Amazon in blue heels, with a couple of gray streaks in her brown hair. That's all I got from her. While she has her former ballerina poise and physique, I'm the proud owner of hips that could knock anyone out. My deep-brown skin wins me at least one look of confusion from strangers whenever I'm out with her. Like I can't be related to her because she's white. Sometimes I ignore it, even though I'm holding in swear words. Other times I throw knives with my glare and make them just as uncomfortable as I am.

Success rate for the latter is still at 100 percent.

Mom clutches the belt on her denim shirtdress. The words *Breaking News* appear along the screen with the photo of a man who's not really a man at all.

Silver scales cover his face. His whole body is made of them, but he hides them underneath a black leather trench coat and matching leather gloves. His eyes flash a bright bloodred at a surveillance camera. And he's grinning.

This is the man who was once a dragon. A Fire Drake from England, to be exact. His former rider, one of the few wizards to have a dragon steed, cursed him into human form. The curse stripped him of the claws that ripped hundreds of spines apart, of the fire that scorched innocents around the world. Twenty years have passed since the Sire's rider sacrificed himself to cast the blood curse. Twenty years of peace . . . until three weeks ago, when the Sire came out of hiding, broke into a dragon sanctuary in Athens, and fled with a Hydra.

"What's the Sire up to now?" I ask.

Mom dives for the remote control. I've never seen anyone turn off a TV that fast. "Another attack at a dragon sanctuary. There seems to be a new one every week."

I shudder. The Sire and his Dragon Knights, the fanatical followers who serve him, have been setting dragons free all over Europe. They'll probably move along to other continents soon.

What if he goes to Dubai? Sixteen teams are already at this year's host city for the Cup. Could the Sire's antics force the IBF to cancel it as a safety measure?

I *need* the Cup to happen. I've waited thirteen years for this shot at glory, at a taste of home. I can't wait a second longer.

"What's happening in that mind of yours, Lana?"

I clear my throat, fishing my phone out of my jeans' pocket. "Just thinking about Papi and how he's dealing with all this sanctuary drama. Let me check on him." Papi doesn't own a Whisperer, so it's normal phone calls for him. Thank God the time difference between Florida and São Paulo is only one hour.

The phone rings once, twice, ten billion times.

Papi doesn't answer.

I hang up and try again. He still doesn't answer. "*Why* isn't he picking up?"

"He could be in a meeting," Mom says as I shoot Dad a text to call me ASAP. "Carlos is better off than most of us, anyway." Mom sulks as she walks over to the gifts. "I told you both, didn't I? You can never trust something that much bigger than you with a will of its own."

I heave a sigh. "The Sire is a terrorist, Mom. He chooses to be this vile. Dragons aren't treacherous and terrible by nature."

Mom's hardened gaze flickers over to me. "And yet one tried to kill my daughter."

My groan could rattle walls. That happened when I was *five years old*. Papi had been a dragon-studies professor in Puerto Rico. São Paulo invited him to help with the adaptation process of the sanctuary's latest rescue, a female Pesadelo. She had been Un-Bonded, though.

Un-Bonded dragons are born without forming a psychic and emotional connection, known as a Bond, with a human rider. They consider humans a threat. Sometimes even food.

I remember Mom's screams as she watched from the other side of the spell-protected glass. Sometimes I hear them in my sleep. She might hear them, too. She's so concerned with monsters that she never noticed that her daughter survived a dragon attack with her little five-year-old legs. A daughter who realized on that fateful night she has what it takes to compete in the Cup. Maybe even win. All I needed was a team from my place of birth to be eligible for tryouts.

All I needed was the chance my mother would never give me.

"That was a long time ago," I tell her, "and it had been my fault."

"Please don't defend the indefensible." Mom glowers. "Dragons are capable of horrendous acts of violence. The Sire is proof of this."

"So are his Dragon Knights, who are humans."

"I'm not going to fight with you. Please help me wrap these gifts. We don't want to be late to pick up Samira and Todd." Mom swiftly takes the medium box and the wrapping paper to the dining-room table, where red scissors and tape await.

I swallow my cutting retort. She refuses to change her mind about dragons. She won't let me play Blazewrath. She won't care that the Sire could snatch my dream away. Tears fill my eyes. I turn around and wipe them away before Mom notices. It kills me not to have her support, but this is what life has been like for the past twelve years. She'll never change. Neither will I.

Maybe those staring strangers on the street are right. We shouldn't be related.

BOOM!

Something explodes behind me.

I jump back with flailing arms. Mom's screaming like it's the End of Days.

"Don't panic, people! I got this!" Samira Jones, BFF extraordinaire, stands in my dining room wrapped in blue flames. There's a halo around her puffy high bun. She looks like a Black angel trapped in burning spray paint. Samira whips out her wand, a copper rod with amethyst crystals on the sides, and aims a silent spell at the kitchen sink. Water glides out of the faucet in a straight line. It strikes the flames from the top of Samira's head to her camel-colored Nikes.

The fire coils inward, flickering like dying stars, then vanishes.

After she sends the water back to the faucet, Samira's eyes find mine. She's beaming as if she's won a billion bucks. She's about to say something when there's a soft *snap*.

The upper half of her wand tumbles to the floor.

Samira frowns. "Surprise . . ."

The dragon's historic reveal in 1743 marked the first recorded Bond between a dragon and a Regular. That dragon had been a Scottish Golden Horn. Dozens of other Golden Horns were born that same year, along with Irish Spikes and British Fire Drakes. All had Bonded with Regulars just hours after their births. 1743 is considered the beginning of a blended society that allowed for magical and non-magical beings to coexist under the protection of the same laws. However, there are those who still wonder whether dragons are worth trusting.

—*Excerpt from Carlos Torres's* Studying the Bond Between Dragons & Humans

CHAPTER TWO

THE INTERNATIONAL BLAZEWRATH FEDERATION HASN'T CANCELED my meeting.

I keep refreshing the email on my phone, careful not to flash the screen at Mom on the drive to Aunt Jenny's house. No new messages. No posts on social media. I squeeze the back of my neck. Maybe I'm overreacting? The Sire can't cancel the Cup. As long as the IBF is open to seeing me, my dream might still come true.

"Are you sure you're all right?" Mom asks me from the driver's seat of her Buick. "Do you need me to put those Monster X boys on the radio?"

"Oh God, not again," Samira whines in the back. She's clutching her broken Copper wand like a long-lost friend.

"It's *Monsta* X, Mom. Not Monster X." I'm not even cheering up at the prospect of K-pop. Who the hell have I become? "It's okay if you want to listen to the radio. I can't focus."

She nods solemnly. "Neither can I, honey, but that beast isn't going to ruin today for us. We need to stay positive for Todd. He won't turn seventeen twice, after all."

I stifle a groan. "Mm-hmm . . ."

Mom parks in Aunt Jenny's driveway, which is as white as the people inside the two-story, ranch-style house. My boiled eggs and grilled-cheese sandwich breakfast makes its way up my throat. Time to pretend I'm enjoying Todd's company while waiting to bail for my tryout. But pretending I'm enjoying Todd's company while freaking out over Papi's potential death at the hands of the Sire *and* the possibility that my Blazewrath career may end before it even starts?

That's pushing it.

"Go on ahead and say hi to everybody," I tell Mom. "Samira and I will bring the gifts."

Mom nods. "Perfect. See you girls inside."

Samira and I wait for her to disappear into the house. When she's gone, I turn to Samira. "What the hell am I supposed to do?"

She cocks an eyebrow. "What do you mean? Tryouts are still on, right?"

"Well, yeah, but Papi hasn't gotten back to me, and his sanctuary might be attacked next."

"What can you do about your father not responding?"

"Um . . . nothing?"

"Exactly. Now tell me something you *can* do."

My spirits are in free fall. Still, I guess I should find a way to make it through this infernal birthday party and get to that meeting at the Ritz-Carlton. Whether the Cup gets canceled or not, the meeting's still on. Tryouts will push me one step closer to my dream. I'm doing this for myself, but I can't forget this is for Papi, too. For our country. I can't let any of us down.

"Go to tryouts," I say firmly. "Do my best to make it onto the team."

"And we're back in the game!" Samira pumps a fist in the air.

I motion to her wand. "I'm getting you a new one."

She gasps, eyes wide and mouth hanging open. "You are?"

"Yeah. You're lending me your car. The least I can do is get you the fifth and *last* Copper wand you'll ever break." I give her a stern look. "Swear to me it'll be the last one, Samira."

"But I'm telling you for real, I can get the Transport Charm under control."

"Samira."

She slouches with a sigh. "Fiiiiine. I swear."

"Thank you. Now come on. Mom must be dying from boredom."

We pile all six gifts one on top of another, agreeing that I should carry them inside. When Samira and I push past the front door, I regret my decision to leave the car. Gold streamers hang from the ceiling in intricate bows. The gold balloons are shaped like magic wands. The ridiculous things are littered all over the place. Even the carpet's been decorated with a plaque-like banner that reads HAPPY BIRTHDAY, TODD! in gold letters. I'm sure there's a wand-shaped vanilla cake with gold frosting in the fridge. The candles are bound to be wand-shaped, too.

Todd Anderson, my oldest cousin on Mom's side, is *obsessed* with magic. He's not a wizard, though. None of my family members are. We're just a bunch of non-magic users. Or Regulars, as the magical community calls us. Todd hasn't gotten the memo yet. Nor does he understand he's turning seventeen. This party looks fit for a toddler.

"Jeez. Todd really likes himself a theme, huh?" Samira's tucking what's left of her Copper wand into the back of her jeans, trailing behind me.

"You think?" I walk into the dining room, hoping Todd left in a space shuttle to Jupiter.

Nope. The Boy King is standing next to my mother.

"Samira! So great to see you!" Todd says with the biggest grin on his face. He rushes over to Samira, wrapping her in a tight hug. Todd's gelled his nut-brown hair back today. He's wearing newly ironed khakis, a royal-blue dress shirt, and a matching V-neck cardigan. His cardigan has the Aster Prep logo on it, which is a Silver wand resting inside an open book.

This brat is going to a wand shop in an outfit that screams, "I attend an expensive private school with super-rich wizards and Regulars." Samira and I go to a school that's open to both wizards and Regulars, too, but Red Crown High is a public school. And I don't pretend I'm a witch because I hang out with one.

"Happy birthday, Todd!" Samira claps him on the back twice, but he won't let go.

I clear my throat. "Ahem."

Todd looks at me like he's just noticed I'm here. "Good morning, Lana," he says like he's greeting the common folk of his kingdom. He unglues himself from Samira and points at the boxes. "Are those for me?"

Oh no. These are for the Obamas. I'm sure they'll be super excited to get socks.

"Mm-hmm. Where should I leave them?"

"Don't worry. I got it." Todd scoops the boxes into his lanky arms. He power walks to the living room and dumps his presents in the same corner where Aunt Jenny always puts her white pine Christmas tree. Then Todd sidles up to Samira as I say a quick hello to my aunt and little cousins by the pool area, thanking her repeatedly for setting up the private tour.

"Oh, it's not a problem," says a flustered Samira. "It was actually Lana's idea."

Todd dismisses her with a wave. "Either way, thank *you*." His gaze finds me again. "How's that personal statement essay for Harvard coming along?"

"Great . . ." This isn't the time to tell anyone I haven't started writing that essay. What's the point? I'm not going to college if I make it onto Team Puerto Rico. And if I don't get picked, I'll skip higher education for at least a year. There's really nothing I want to study.

"You're so lucky, Lana," says Todd. "Schools snatch up minorities like wildfire. Once they see you're a Puerto Rican girl, your grades won't matter. But hey, if you need any help with that essay, you know you can ask whenever."

I hide my clenched fists behind my back, but I smile like I've trained myself for the past twelve years. "Thanks, Todd." The worst thing about being Puerto Rican with Todd as my relative is how often he reminds me I'm not like him. He acts like I'm family and a foreigner at the same time. As if it wasn't already hard to abandon my country against my will, in this new one I have to endure condescending remarks from someone who shares my blood.

I sigh in relief when Mom takes us back to her Buick. Todd's arm is melting into Samira's back. Her laugh is two octaves too high to seem genuine, but she's giving me that "Don't you worry about me" look, so I keep my mouth shut. Todd slides into the back seat with her.

"Birthday Mode is officially on, ladies!" he says. "Let's hit it!"

I buckle up and take a quick peek at my phone. Papi is still MIA.

Samira's advice cocoons me while I suck in a shaky breath. I should focus on the plan. Phase one is almost over. Today I still might become Puerto Rico's Runner.

I just have to survive the Boy King first.

SAMIRA'S RED COROLLA HIDES IN PLAIN SIGHT IN THE WAXBYRNE PARKing lot, six rows to the left of Mom's Buick. Samira slips me her keys while Mom and Todd lead the way. I hide the keys in my jeans' pocket. Samira quickens her pace to join a boring conversation about cravat patterns.

We head toward a grass-covered plot in the shape of a hexagon. We're smack dab in between the Naples Pier and Third Street South, where the only thing more stifling than the midday sun is the bustle at the Regular shops and restaurants. The Ritz-Carlton is a twenty-five-minute drive up north. It's 11:00 a.m. right now. I can totally make it on time.

A set of marble doors juts out of the grass. Waxbyrne's entrance is similar to the stairs that lead to a subway station. And much like a subway station, our destination is down. Magic keeps the store's underground network intact. It also prevents flooding and makes sure no harm is caused to sea life. I don't know why Waxbyrne is underground, or why the entrance is shaped like a hexagon, but there *are* stranger things in the world.

Mom turns to Todd. "Will the birthday boy do the honors?"

Todd pretty much floats toward the doors. "It'll be my pleasure."

Ugh, he's acting like he's never been to Waxbyrne. Regulars aren't allowed into the shop on our own, but Todd's wizard friends have brought him a billion times, though he's never taken part in their private wand-making tour.

Todd reads the two buttons on the side panels. One is engraved with the word ENTRANCE while the other includes the International Symbol of Access for shoppers with movement disabilities. The doors are enchanted to reveal a different entrance depending on which button a shopper presses. He jams the first button a little too hard.

Once the doors open from the inside, a gust of peppermint bark scent wraps all around me.

This is the best part about Waxbyrne. It smells like winter-season candy.

"Ladies first," Todd says to Samira, waving her forward.

"Why, thank you." Samira hooks an arm around mine.

We make our way down the steps together. Everything, even the walls, is built from the whitest marble. Not a single scratch or smudge on anything.

I'm halfway down when a witch's voice booms from invisible loudspeakers.

"Welcome to Waxbyrne, the world's premier wand shop! My name is Madame Waxbyrne, renowned wandmaker and owner of the greatest magical store in history. Whatever your magical skill level may be, we here at Waxbyrne have just the wand for you!"

Madame Waxbyrne's message plays on an endless loop.

In the entrance hall, the scent of peppermint bark hits harder. I take a deep breath, wishing I could lick the air. The receptionist's counter is dead ahead, with an elderly witch standing behind it and a younger wizard guarding the next set of doors.

The wall on the right is unadorned except for a gigantic logo that reads WAXBYRNE, a cursive script underlined with a thick brushstroke. That's supposed to be Madame Waxbyrne's own handwriting. Not that she's here to corroborate it. Waxbyrne is a chain of wand shops all over the world. It's the only business with an official license to sell wands from the International Bureau of Magical Matters, but that doesn't stop wannabes from cropping up in the streets.

"Who the hell wants to watch this?" Todd glares at one of the TVs mounted on the left wall. Each is tuned to a different channel. Mostly reality shows, but Todd's watching ESPN.

The camera pans to the same lean, black-haired boy whom I have as my phone's wallpaper.

I press a hand to my chest. "Takeshi . . ."

It's a rerun of the "Disappearance of Takeshi Endo" *30 for 30* episode. The footage is from 2015. Outside the IBF building in Tokyo, twenty kids smile up at Takeshi. He wears jeans and a white jacket with the Japanese flag emblazoned on the front.

Hikaru, the white Akarui dragon, is also smiling. His ivory feathered wings are tucked to his sides. Whenever he nods, the shorter crimson feathers atop his head ruffle a bit. He even pretends to blow kisses at Takeshi to make the kids laugh. Takeshi wraps up his speech to fervent applause, then the video cuts to him and Hikaru facing an off-camera interviewer.

"What do you hope these children will learn today?" the reporter asks in English.

Takeshi keeps rubbing Hikaru's chin. "The importance of compassion," he says in his gentle, kind voice. "It's like my late father used to say: 'We can make the choice to do good in this world, and no matter how impossible it seems, *that's* the right choice.'"

Todd sneers. "Focusing on this dragon vermin makes me sick."

I flinch. "*What* did you call Hikaru?"

Todd gazes down at me like I'm vermin, too. "My magical-history teacher's right. Mister Thompson says dragons and their riders have this . . . attitude. They think they're above us. And those Dragon Knight morons actually *worship* them." He shakes his head. "I don't care how long they've been here or how powerful they are. They're the worst."

Red bursts of light explode all around me. I can't smell peppermint bark anymore. I can't see anyone other than the wannabe wizard in his stupid Aster Prep cardigan. "You're confusing the Sire with every other dragon. Educate yourself before you run your mouth."

"*Lana*," Mom says. "Don't speak to your cousin like that."

I curse under my breath. Of course she'd think I'm the problem. No one can mess with her precious, Harvard-bound nephew. It hurts to know Mom will never support my Blazewrath dream, but knowing she'd rather take Todd's side than mine is the last twist of the knife.

I'm about to talk back to Mom when Samira snatches my wrists.

"Oh, look! The counter!" She drags me forward. While Mom's warning glare follows, Samira whispers, "Listen to me. You are *not* killing Todd Anderson today."

"He called Hikaru *vermin*," I whisper back with a growl.

"Ignore him." She faces the counter. "Good morning, ma'am!"

The witch looks up from her computer screen. Her name tag reads SALLY. "Welcome to Waxbyrne! How can I help you?"

"We have a private tour scheduled for today." Samira gulps, her expression guilty. "And, um, I'm here to buy a new Copper wand."

"Oh, you must be *quite* enthusiastic about reaching Silver." Sally hits a few buttons on her keyboard. The counter slides open in two halves. A glass bowl rises from within. It's filled with a sort of translucent, thinly grained dust. "Please place your hand inside to confirm your status."

Samira sinks her hand into the dust. Nothing happens at first. Then a fistful of dust flies up into the air, changing into a bright copper shade. The computer says, "Copper Wand."

Sally hits more keys. "Excellent. You'll turn Silver any day now."

"Yup. Any day." Samira's tone is as deflated as Todd's brain. Every witch and wizard starts out a Copper Wand. Their magic evolves as they grow older. Most stay Silver, though. Samira's little sister, Shay, is already a Silver Wand at fourteen. Having your little sister grow into her Silver abilities before you? Super embarrassing.

Even though breaking her wand was her own fault, Samira's doing me a huge solid by being here today. The least I can do is help her deal with my cousin's stupidity.

"Let's get you that wand." I put my hand on the dust pile. After a few seconds, the dust flies up again without changing colors. The computer reads aloud, "Regular."

The same thing happens when Mom's and Todd's turns are up. Mom is super chill, but Todd glares at the dust bowl as if he's pissed about being called a Regular.

Sally says, "Regulars must remain with their magical companions at all times. Paul will help you to Level Two. You'll meet your behind-the-scenes tour guide at the end of corridor six. Have a wonderful day!" She motions to the guard, who's pushing the marble doors behind him.

After thanking Sally, we get into the elevator, where each button is shaped like a wand. Its letters are written in the same style as the Waxbyrne logo:

Level One: Entrance Hall

Level Two: Copper Wands

Elemental Manipulation

Level Three: Silver Wands

Elemental Manipulation and Creation

Level Four: Gold Wands

Elemental Manipulation, Creation, and Destruction

Level Five: Staff Only

Once the guard shuts the doors again, Samira presses the Level Two button. The ride down lasts about five seconds. Another guard opens the doors for us. Instead of white marble, there are walls and tiled floors dripping in penny-colored paint. Customers are scattered throughout the store, which is really thirteen corridors that span from here to forever. Skyscraper metal shelves line each side of the corridors. All sorts of wands are displayed. Long, short, thick, thin, bedazzled, plain, you name it. They sit there, waiting to feel their future owner's presence.

"Remember the key to surviving Waxbyrne," Samira tells a slack-jawed Todd. "Duck."

"Watch out!" someone yells a few feet ahead.

I throw myself onto the floor. A swoosh echoes all over the place. More people fall down around me. When I glance up, a wand shoots into the middle corridor. It stops right in front of a russet-skinned teen witch wearing a coral dress and matching hijab. The girl gasps. The wand points directly at her, choosing her as its rightful owner. When she grabs the wand, the whole floor claps. An older hijabi sweeps her into a tight hug. This must be her first wand.

"I love it when that happens!" Todd stands up with shaky legs. It's like he's died and been reborn in the span of two seconds. *"Amazing."*

"Slightly dangerous, but yes. Amazing, indeed." Mom points to the corridor with a huge emerald sign, the number six painted on it. "The tour guide will be that way. We still have a few minutes before eleven-thirty, so if it's okay with Samira, we could walk around until your new wand finds you. Or would you like to wait until after the tour?"

"After is fine," Samira says. "How about we go check with the guide first?"

Todd rubs his hands together. "Sounds perfect."

Showtime.

While Todd hooks an arm around Samira's, I touch my belly and grimace. "You guys, I don't feel so good. I think I need to go to the bathroom. You go ahead. I'll catch up."

Todd doesn't spare me a glance. He's taking Samira deeper into the store. Samira sneaks me a thumbs-up, then pretends to be interested in whatever Todd's rambling about.

Mom looks me up and down. "We're not supposed to separate from Samira."

"Regulars are allowed to go to the bathroom, Mom." I bend a little, straining my voice to sound like I'm hurting. "If I don't make it, do the tour without me. I'll wait in the entrance hall."

She considers me for a moment. "Okay," she finally says, "but we need to have a serious discussion about how you behaved once we get home. Is that clear?"

"Mm-hmm. Bye."

I power walk away from Mom.

Holy crap. This is happening. I'm actually for real going to Blazewrath tryouts!

I weave past the endless stream of customers, getting closer to the cash registers and the Waxbyrne logo at the center of the marble tiles. The hijabi and her mother are waiting in line hand in hand. I offer the girl a quick smile. She offers me one, too.

BOOM!

I crash to the floor with a yelp. My left knee hits the tile hard, pain shooting up in one swift wave. Everyone drops like weightless dominoes. Some shelves slam right into each other. Wands are zooming around, either searching for their rightful owners or a way out.

Then a dragon's cries erupt from underground.

I serve the gods of wing and flame,

I live and die in their names,

Those who oppose will meet their ends,

May their blood be spilled as gods intend.

—The Dragon Knights' Prayer

CHAPTER THREE

THE BRAZILIAN PESADELO'S ROARS HADN'T BEEN THIS SHARP, THIS high-pitched, and they hadn't lasted this long. Back then, I'd frozen for just a second, then ran as her fireballs hunted me.

It's been more than a second, and I still can't move. My bones are weighed down with every unearthly note in the dragon's song of fury. How the hell did a *dragon* get inside the shop?

Customers scramble to the elevator doors. No one can Transport in or out of a Waxbyrne shop. Madame Waxbyrne, one of the few Gold Wands alive, has enchanted all of her shops to prevent anyone from breaking and entering. The guards are frantically pushing people back from the doors. The tallest guard slips past the chaos, beckoning the doors to open with a push of the button, but nothing happens. No matter how many times he tries, the doors won't budge.

BOOM!

The floor explodes behind me.

I'm launched a few feet ahead, screaming along with everyone else. This time, I land on my backpack, which cushions me from the fall. My knee is still throbbing. Wands keep darting across the room with ungodly speed. They smash into glass vases and bounce off the walls and even get stuck in the metal chandeliers. The piercing screams never end. As I'm sitting up, there's a sizzling noise farther ahead, as if something were hurtling flames through the tiled floor.

When I peer back, time stands still. "Oh my God . . ."

There's a huge, circular hole in the floor. The shelves that had once been standing in corridor four have now disappeared underground. The edges have been charred to a crisp, blackened and shrouded in graying smoke. Clouds of dust and debris are covering most of the area, but I still spot dozens of witches and wizards dangling off the edges, holding on for dear life. They're about to sink right into the hole, where the dragon cries out once more.

I scan the hole in a craze. There's no sign of either Mom or Samira.

"Samira! Samira, help me!" someone yells from the right side of the hole.

Todd.

He's driving his nails deep into the floor, clawing his way out, but he's slipping away. "Samira, please!" Todd's voice is the loudest of them all. *"Help me!"*

I bolt after him.

I crash into people running in the opposite direction, some knocking into me so hard that I almost lose my balance, but I'm flying through the terrified mass of customers. The graying smoke and dust cloud blinds me as I get closer to Todd. I swat at it and hold my breath, never stopping. When I find Todd, I drop to my knees and grab his wrists.

"I got you!" I start pulling him up. He's using all of his strength to lift himself closer to me.

BOOM!

Another quake strikes. It's stronger, longer than the first one. I'm launched forward again. I slam right into Todd's chest. We plummet into the hole together.

Screams rip out of me as I flail. Todd's screams are even louder. We slice through the clouds of smoke like bullets made of flesh and fear. I can't see how long I have left until I smash into concrete. Everything is gray and black and certain death.

Water breaks my fall.

I sink into a chilly, almost dead current. My screams die out as I inhale and swallow what seems to be water, as if I'm sinking into an underground lake. I can't see a damn thing in this cold darkness. I need to get back to the surface, where the ceiling lamps are shining bright. I'm kicking up as fast as I can. My chest is seconds away from bursting, but I push onward. When I break for air, I cough out every bit of water I swallowed, spinning around in search of Todd.

He's floating on his back two feet away, his eyes pressed shut.

"No . . . " I swim toward him at full speed. When I grab his shoulders, he doesn't even stir. At least he's still breathing. "Todd? Can you hear me?" I try shaking him, but he's out cold.

The nearest stretch of shore is six feet away. I hug Todd close, then swim toward the caramel-colored soil. Everything burns and begs me to stop. With deep, continuous breaths, I push Todd up onto the ground and settle beside him.

There are fir trees in front of me. The lake is more like a pit filled with water, twisting in a serpentine shape at the center of the room. Farther ahead, the fir trees lean side by side, doing their best to block the muddy, brown, cavernous walls behind them. One wall has a giant logo in black script. It reads LEVEL FIVE. This is the shop's lowest level.

And it's a dragon habitat.

Why the hell is there a habitat inside a wand shop? Habitats are supposed to be located far away from populated areas. What kind of illegal crap is Madame Waxbyrne pulling here?

The dragon roars again behind me.

I'm stiff as a board, cradling Todd with shallow breaths. If this dragon is Un-Bonded, it's going to strike once it sees me. Especially since it's already pissed off.

Remember what Papi taught you. No sudden movements. Stay down until the dragon tries to attack. They won't hurt you unless they think you'll hurt them.

I turn my head little by little.

I spot the scarlet horns first. Four on the left side. Four on the right. The two smallest horns protrude directly above the dragon's forehead. The rest jut out farther back. I swallow hard as the dragon stomps forward on its hind legs. Its scales are the color of molten gold, as are those spindly wings. And right at the center of its chest is a small, heart-shaped crystal.

Holy crap. This is a British Fire Drake. It has a crystal heart. It's not a real heart that beats and pumps blood, but it does make this Fire Drake different from its brethren—it can grant wishes to its rider. Fire Drakes, wish-granting or otherwise, are only supposed to be found in England, and yet here I am looking at one in Florida, hiding in the lowest level of a wand shop.

There's a guy standing before the dragon. He's about five foot eleven or so, with cropped black hair and a matching leather trench coat. His gloves are black leather, too. There's a large silver scale sewn onto the back of his coat. The same silver scale the Sire has for skin.

Oh. My. God. I'm stuck here with a Dragon Knight.

What do I do, what do I do, what do I do . . .

The Fire Drake opens its gigantic mouth, revealing a small spark creeping past its throat. The spark grows bigger and bigger until it's a fireball the size of a boulder.

The Dragon Knight raises his fist at the Fire Drake. He throws something at its chest.

A golden glow bursts to life upon impact, and the Fire Drake gulps down the fireball. It falls onto its side as the glow spreads all over its body. With an earth-shattering thud, the Fire Drake slams onto the ground, encased within the glow as if it's a shield. The dragon tries to writhe its way free, but it's no good. It stays down, moving slower and roaring louder.

That's not a shield. It's a Paralysis Charm.

For that spell to work on *any* dragon, this Dragon Knight has to be a Gold Wand: the only wizards capable of slaying dragons. He pulls out a bright golden orb from his coat's pocket. A smoky wisp glows from within the orb. He throws the orb at the Fire Drake's chest.

With a softer roar than before, the Fire Drake lies as still as a corpse. It's still breathing, but it's like the dragon's been hit with a second, and far stronger, Paralysis Charm.

The Dragon Knight isn't carrying a wand. Gold Wand or not, he shouldn't be able to channel his magic without one—or be able to contain spells inside objects. And he's *attacking* a dragon. He's not revering it or setting it loose like the Sire's henchmen are known to do.

My heart hammers as I ponder how to save both Todd and the Fire Drake.

This Dragon Knight is taller than I am. He's probably trained to fight everything under the sun. What if I can knock him out? I'd have to get closer. Even if I had a billion stones lying at my feet, my aim sucks so hard I'd end up tossing them in vain. If he's here to kill that Fire Drake, maybe I can get it to fight alongside me? Can we take this Dragon Knight down together?

Save the dragon, save us all.

When the Fire Drake stops roaring, the Dragon Knight pulls out a dagger white as snow. The blade isn't steel. It's . . . a claw. Or, I should say, claw bone. It's about the length of a police officer's baton but much, much thicker. The sharpened tip curves upward like a hook. The

Dragon Knight walks straight for the Fire Drake's chest.

He's not here to kill the dragon. He's going to steal its crystal heart.

I jump to my feet. "Stop!"

The Dragon Knight freezes. Then he slowly turns around.

I slap both hands to my mouth. His black hair is shorter now. His brown eyes have dark, heavy bags underneath. His skin is duller, too, and he's not smiling anymore. It's him, though. This is the boy who spoke to those kids at IBF headquarters in Japan about compassion. The boy who vanished after his dragon steed was killed two years ago.

Takeshi Endo, my forever favorite, is a Dragon Knight.

I drop my hands as I step forward, hoping for a different face, different eyes, and a different reason to feel like the universe has cracked into bits. "Takeshi? Is that really you?"

He says, "Unless you want to die, stay where you are. This isn't your business."

That's his voice. Low enough to make him sound older than seventeen, but soft enough to make anyone feel like they can trust him. I'm too dumbfounded to speak. Takeshi is a Regular. Whatever magic he's using, it doesn't belong to him, and he's ordering me to let him *hurt* a dragon. This is the same boy whose dragon steed was murdered by a Gold Wand. Now he's acting like dragons are disposable. And he's wearing the Dragon Knight uniform.

Takeshi walks up to the Fire Drake, raising his claw dagger in the air.

I run.

My clothes are sticking to me. My throbbing knee is killing me with every step. I still pump my arms and soar around the lake. I race toward the boy I never thought I'd stand against.

Takeshi lowers the dagger.

I tackle him before he finds flesh.

"Ugh!" Takeshi crash-lands beneath me. He loses his grip on the dagger. It rolls a good seven feet away, just shy of splashing into the water.

Before Takeshi can push me off, I lunge at the dagger as fast as I can. The stupid thing is heavier than it looks. I try to pick it up with one hand, but it clangs back down.

Takeshi seizes it in a flash. "You don't know what you're doing! Get *back!*" The kindness in his voice is long gone. Now there's only a cold, foreign slice of rage.

The Fire Drake roars the loudest yet.

Takeshi and I face the dragon together. The Fire Drake shimmers three times brighter. It's trembling, too, as if it's going to rip itself to shreds. The spell. The Fire Drake's writhing its way free of its hold. And it's not actually trembling. It's trying to spread its wings.

"Take cover!" I yell at Takeshi, but he's marching forward again, right to where the Fire Drake can kill him in seconds. "Takeshi, stop! You can't do this!"

The Fire Drake's wings fold out into the air, cracking the spell apart.

Golden shards shoot all over the place. I shield myself with both arms as the Fire Drake stomps the floor repeatedly. A few shards graze my skin. They leave tiny cuts that sting, but there's barely any blood. When the shower of shards ends, I find another fireball queued up in the dragon's mouth. It's aimed in Takeshi's direction. Which also happens to be *my* direction.

I snatch Takeshi's wrist. "Come on!"

To my surprise, he breaks into a run with me. I hear the blast of flames biting at my ankles. Heavy drops of sweat roll off my skin from the scorching heat. I push onward, dragging Takeshi like he's my shadow, then catapult into the lake. Takeshi dives in right beside me. We look up as a steady stream of fire darts above us. I hold what little breath I have left, but the fire doesn't stop. The Fire Drake aims its stream all over the lake's surface.

Everything within me is about to burst. I need air *now*.

One more minute . . . Just wait one more minute, and it'll end . . .

The fire stops.

I kick my way to the surface, gasping in the open again. Just as I'm about to sink back down, Takeshi rushes out of the water at full speed.

"Takeshi, *no!*"

My cry for him is useless. He's pulling himself onto shore where his claw dagger landed, while the dragon queues up a brand-new fireball.

Something rattles to the far, far left of the chamber.

Footsteps echo across the whole floor, as well as angry shouts. Dozens of security guards are dashing into the room, their Silver wands out and ready.

Takeshi has about five seconds before the Fire Drake burns him to raw bone. He grips his dagger tightly, whipping out another gold orb, and looks right at me. "The world you know is a lie," he says. "The world that's coming, that's the one you should believe in."

He smashes his orb on the floor. A gust of ashy-white wind swirls around him.

He's gone.

The fireball misses him by a split second. It scorches his footprints and the mark his dagger left on the ground, but still the Fire Drake keeps venting its frustrations. We both stare at the spot where Takeshi once stood, but only one of us has more questions than rage. The Fire Drake stops firing once the guards approach. It slowly retreats out of respect, not with the frenzied fear of an Un-Bonded dragon, and watches them pull me out of the lake. It doesn't try to attack me again as I lie on the shore. The real threat has disappeared.

"Are you okay, miss?" one of the guards asks.

There's so much I want to tell the guard, so much I want to ask him back.

Todd is stirring back to consciousness, swatting at the air and mouthing something I can't understand. He doesn't know Takeshi Endo is no longer missing—or that I've lost my shot at competing in the

Blazewrath World Cup.

Tears mix with the lake water soaking my cheeks. I'm wiping myself clean and holding in the swear words desperate to shoot out. It hadn't been the Sire who killed my dream. It hadn't been Mom or Todd. It had been the boy who was once all things good and right in this world.

"Miss? Can you hear me?" the guard says. "Let me help you up."

I sniffle, standing up on my own. "We have to get my cousin to the hospital. . . ."

Since its debut in 1965, the Blazewrath World Cup has taken the world by storm. Perry Jo Smith, British football legend and Silver Wand, founded the International Blazewrath Federation and began the tradition of handpicking which nations would compete every two years. Smith had been keen on including non-rider athletes in the tournament as well, which led to the creation of the Runner position. "Anyone can be a Runner," Smith once said. "You are not less because you do not have a dragon steed. We hope to encourage youth from all walks of life to try out for their country's team. It will be an honor for us to witness you thrive among marvels."

—Excerpt from Harleen Khurana's
A History of Blazewrath Around the World

CHAPTER FOUR

THIS ISN'T HOW I PLANNED ON GETTING FAMOUS.

For the past hour, all sorts of people have been trying to get a picture of me. Paparazzi. Newspaper photographers. Random Floridians who saw me when Waxbyrne's surveillance footage interrupted their programming. The Regular police had to cordon off the lot. Since the incident on Level Five involved a dragon and magic, this isn't their jurisdiction per se, but I'm grateful they're here. It's a straight-up circus, and I'm the main event.

The ambulance doors are shut. I'm sitting on a stretcher with Samira, who's flipping through her phone in search of Sire and Takeshi updates. Her parents are on their way. Mom's outside trying to get in touch with Papi, while Todd's been rushed off to the hospital.

I press my knuckles to my sore, stinging eyes. I stopped crying after leaving the shop, but that itchy redness still plagues me. The throbbing in my knee has faded to a dull ache. At least my clothes, hair, and backpack aren't wet anymore. The police allowed a Waxbyrne guard to use the Insta-Dry Charm on me. My minor cuts have been magically healed, too.

They won't let me go home, though. An agent from the International Bureau of Magical Matters is coming to interrogate me. The faster I cooperate, the faster I can leave.

"Unbelievable," Samira mutters. "Some people are talking about how hot Takeshi is. I mean, he *is* hot, but come on, world. The guy just tried to *steal a crystal heart*. He's all dressed up like a Dragon Knight now, and y'all are focused on his abs? I can't."

"Why would he even need the heart? It only grants wishes to the dragon's rider."

Samira puts down the phone, her gaze narrowed and alert. "Did you see those golden orbs Takeshi had? Not only were spells trapped inside them, but I think the *orbs themselves* were spells, too. Gold Wand magic in physical form, similar to Madame Waxbyrne's wands. Nobody in the magical community can trap magic like that." She grimaces as if she's about to say something unpleasant. "I think Takeshi needed to bring the crystal heart to a Gold Wand working for the Sire. Maybe they're strong enough to force the heart to perform magic."

It does make sense, I guess, except for one thing.

"Why have Takeshi steal it? Why couldn't the Gold Wand get it instead?"

"Because I think the wish is for Takeshi. I think he wants *real* proof of Hikaru's killer."

My eyebrows shoot up. Antonio Deluca, the Runner from Team Italy, remains the only murder suspect because he hates Takeshi. He'd also fled Edinburgh hours before Hikaru's body had been found. Only Gold Wands like Antonio have the magical strength to execute a dragon, but while everyone believes Antonio's guilty, no one can back it up with proof. The surveillance cameras at Hikaru's habitat had been torn apart with magic. The guards outside of the habitat had been struck with an irreversible Memory-Erasing Charm. If Samira is right, Takeshi's going after the one thing that will guarantee Antonio's imprisonment.

"He's only doing this for Hikaru," I whisper.

She puts her hand on top of mine. "Regardless of what he's after, Takeshi Endo is Dragon Knight trash. I'm so sorry, but he's canceled."

I should tell her she's right. I've seen this different Takeshi. This boy who hurts dragons. But if he's really searching for proof, he's just lost on his path to justice.

What if the boy in that Tokyo interview is still there?

The ambulance doors jerk open.

Mom stands between Mr. and Mrs. Jones, who both are gasping in relief.

"Oh, my sweet baby Jesus . . ." Mrs. Jones rushes toward her elder daughter. She crushes Samira in a rib-crumbling hug. "Are you okay?"

"Yes, ma'am," Samira says, even though her eyes are bugging out.

I giggle. While Samira's as tall as her father, she's a younger version of her mother. They have curly brown hair they tie up in buns, their eyes are the same shade of soft amber, and they have even more impressive hips than mine. Samira's a bit more slender than her mother, though.

Mr. Jones tips his New York Knicks hat at me. It clashes with his pressed button-down and khaki pants, but that's how he rolls. "Good to see you in one piece, Lana Lightning! You're an angel for what you did today. How are you feeling?"

"I'm not dead, so there's that," I say with a shrug.

"Oh, come here, you!" Mrs. Jones lunges at me, too. Her grip is strong enough to rearrange my spinal cord. "Thank the Lord you're both all right. I was so worried!"

"We're fine, Momma. Just a little tired," says Samira. She's still hiding her broken Copper wand behind her back. Looks like someone's not ready to fess up.

When Mrs. Jones lets me go, I gently pat Samira's shoulder. "You should go home. Get some rest. I'll call you after I wrap up with the bureau. They might not be ready for a while."

"Uh-uh," says Mr. Jones. "Leslie's with an agent right now."

He points to a thin white shield, rippling like ocean water. It blocks me from the onslaught of flashing bulbs. Mom walks through the shield, nervously running her hands down the front of her rumpled skirt. She lets out a quick yawn as she approaches.

"Todd has a concussion from the fall and a really sore neck, but he's stable." She looks directly at me, her expression somber. "Honey, your father is still unreachable, but I don't want you to panic. The bureau hasn't gotten word of anything suspicious at the São Paulo sanctuary."

I'm clutching my chest like it's about to explode. *Your father is still unreachable.* He could've misplaced his phone, but he's the most organized and put-together person I've ever met. I've already lost my dream. I can't lose my father, too.

"Good afternoon." A tall, blonde white woman walks up behind Mom. She's wearing an emerald coat and short cream pumps. Her silver badge has the acronym IBOMM engraved on it. The words AGENT HOROWITZ appear beneath the acronym, along with the tiniest Silver wand.

My jaw drops. "You're *the* Agent Horowitz. Living, breathing legend!"

Samira and I read an article about her in *The Weekly Scorcher*, a newspaper that focuses on dragon-related updates. She remains the only bureau agent who publicly identifies as a trans woman. She's also the bureau agent with the highest number of Dragon Knight arrests (seventeen total). One of her most famous captures was performed while *dangling off a cliff* in Cork, Ireland, when she'd snatched up six Dragon Knights at the same freaking time.

"Not sure about the legend part." She gives me a crooked smile. "I'm sorry to bother you on what I presume has been a difficult day, but I have a few things to discuss with you, Ms. Torres. I swear this won't take long."

"Of course," I say.

"Very well." Agent Horowitz pulls out her Silver wand, which is bedazzled with amber stones in the shape of triangles. "Ms. Torres. Ms. Wells. We should get going."

I rise from the stretcher with Mom's help, even though I can rise on my own. Mr. Jones holds out his hands for me, too. I take them and jump down to the grass.

"Call me as soon as you get home, you hear?" Samira says.

"Loud and clear." I give her a big hug and whisper, "And guess what I still owe you?"

"What?" she whispers back.

"Your fifth and last wand."

"*Pfft*. Worry about taking lots of pictures of the bureau. That place must be *ginormous*."

After I bid Samira's parents farewell, Agent Horowitz raises her wand overhead.

SWISH!

White light pours all over me. It vanishes a split second later.

I'm standing in the middle of a long, chandelier-lit hallway with walls of the brightest gold. I sniff twice. There's vanilla, chocolate, strawberry, and a little bit of red apple in the air. There's no furniture, no paintings or sculptures. There is, however, a massive gold door at the end of the hallway. It's shaped like a full moon, with a doorknob as big as a soccer ball.

"Come along." Agent Horowitz pockets her wand. "Our hosts are waiting."

I gape at her. "Wait, what? I thought we were going to the bureau."

"Not today," says Agent Horowitz as she struts down the long hallway.

Mom steps right in front of her. "Where are we, exactly?"

"Nowhere. At least not on any map you may recognize." Agent Horowitz turns to me with a kind smile. If she's planning on murdering us and dumping our bodies afterward, at least she's being nice about it. "Have you heard of the Other Place Charm?"

I gasp so, so loud. Oh. My. God. This is an Other Place. I, Lana Aurelia Torres, am actually for real in an Other Place right now!

"Yes," I say. "It's a spell that creates a location that can't be found. Not even by other witches and wizards. It's like a secret hideout or a private haven. They call it their Other Place. You can only access it if the witch or wizard owner invites you in." I tap the wall to my left. Sure enough, it feels sturdy and real, but it's not real at all. It's a figment of someone's imagination. This is one hell of a spell. "Is this your Other Place?" I ask Agent Horowitz.

"No." She sidesteps Mom. "The owner is behind that door. He's very excited to meet you both." She continues down the hall as if she's used to its every golden nook and cranny.

Mom snatches my hand as we reach the door. The steel knocker is a gleaming crescent moon coated in gold. A tiny, star-shaped viewer hangs above it. Instead of knocking, Agent Horowitz twists the huge knob. There's a soft *click*, then the door swings inward. There it is again—vanilla, chocolate, strawberry, and a little bit of red apple. Agent Horowitz makes her way into the brightly lit room, where gold walls and chandeliers appear once more. There's furniture inside, all darker than coal. Black-velvet chaise lounges. Black-velvet three-seater, demilune sofas. Even the coffee table in the center of the room is dark stained wood.

Three men sit in front of an unlit fireplace. I can't see their faces, so I keep moving forward, dragging Mom with me. Two of the men shoot off the sofa. The third stands up at a much slower pace, sipping something from a glass. Agent Horowitz stands beside the white man wearing a gray tweed suit and red tie. He's middle-aged and a bit plump, with graying black hair, blue-green eyes, and a smile large enough to restore anyone's faith in humanity.

My eyes bulge out of their sockets. This is the same man who unveils the Blazewrath World Cup during the opening ceremonies. The same man who carries the Cup toward the winning team at the end. Papi and I have seen him in countless press conferences, interviews, and even one baking reality show as guest judge. He said he'd eat anything with vanilla, chocolate, or strawberry on it. And he enjoys a red apple every morning.

President Russell Turner, the most powerful man in the International Blazewrath Federation, is smiling at me like we're old friends.

"Welcome!" he says in his British accent. "Make yourselves at home in my Other Place!"

I can't speak. Mom's grip on me tightens, but instead of reassuring her that this man isn't a serial killer from Leeds, England, I'm drawing a blank as to how to behave in his presence. And, most important, what I'm doing in his presence at all.

"Oh, don't tell me you're the shy type! I refuse to believe it." President Turner walks up to me, his hand outstretched. "Not after what I saw you do back there at Waxbyrne, Ms. Torres."

I stare at him, unblinking, still processing that he is, in fact, real.

"Excuse me, but who are you?" Mom has the ovaries to ask him.

"*Mom,*" I finally speak in my fiercest whisper. "Not cool."

President Turner laughs. He shifts his hand over to Mom instead. "Russell Turner, madam. I'm the president of the International Blaze-wrath Federation. Lovely to meet you."

Mom ignores President Turner's hand. "Blazewrath?" She makes it sound like it's filthier than any swear word. "If you don't work for the bureau, what are you doing here?"

"I've invited President Turner to join us," says the second man, who gets off of the sofa quickly. I can tell he's Indian from his accent, but I don't know which part of the country he's from. His skin is a lighter brown than mine, with brown hair that's been parted in the middle. He adjusts his navy blue suit jacket as he walks over to Mom. He seems ten years younger than President Turner, but he's far more regal in posture and stride. "My name is Nirek Sandhar. I'm director of the Department of Magical Investigations at the bureau. Pleased to meet you both."

Mom squints at President Turner. She finally shakes his hand. "Leslie Wells."

"Delighted, Ms. Wells. You've raised a splendid young lady, I must say. *Such* a brave soul." President Turner turns to me again. "Would you like to sit down for a bit, Ms. Torres?"

I nod over and over.

President Turner waves me over to the sofa. "Right this way!"

Mom releases me, thankfully. I match President Turner's steps as he makes his way back to Agent Horowitz, Director Sandhar, and the third man, whose face is now crystal clear.

I gasp the loudest I've ever gasped.

"What? You've never seen whiskey before?" The third man takes a sip from his glass again, this time slower. When he's done, he says, "Tastes like chicken."

President Turner chuckles, but I can't move a single muscle.

The third man, this tan-skinned giant at six foot five, with salt-and-pepper hair, a peach button-down shirt, baggy jeans, and dark circles under his even darker eyes, is none other than Manny Delgado, Team Puerto Rico's manager. The man who flips the bird at paparazzi like it's the reason he was born, skips press conferences to have longer naps instead, and has publicly sworn to only drink coffee brewed in his hometown of Ciales. I close my eyes and open them again. He's still here. I'm somehow in a room with Manny Delgado and President Turner, and I didn't even make it to Blazewrath tryouts. Not even my wildest dreams are *this* wild.

"Please excuse Mr. Delgado's sense of humor," Director Sandhar says, indignant. "He's only slept three hours, from what I gather."

"Two and a half." Manny plops back down on the sofa, his back to me.

"And does Mr. Delgado work for the bureau, too?" Mom asks.

"No, Ms. Wells, I'm very happy to say he does not," says Director Sandhar. "Mr. Delgado is the manager for the Puerto Rican Blazewrath team. He's in the States on official Blazewrath business, but he's been invited to this interrogation at President Turner's *insistent* request."

Mom's lips part, but nothing comes out. The last person she ever wants to meet is the man responsible for bringing the Puerto Rican flag to the Blazewrath field. "I see."

Manny puts his glass on the coffee table, then leans back on the sofa. "Can we get on with this thing already? I have to get to the hotel in time for my Monday shows."

"Always so patient . . ." Agent Horowitz puts a gentle hand on my back, leading me to the black-silk chaise to the left side of the room. We sit down together. Director Sandhar claims the matching chaise directly across from mine. President Turner and Manny Delgado sit shoulder to shoulder on the sofa, with Mom joining them at a snail's pace. She's studying everyone and everything like the whole room will explode at any moment.

As long as she doesn't go into full freak-out mode, I'll be fine.

Agent Horowitz pulls out her wand again, but this time, she also grabs a pearl-colored compact mirror in the shape of a square. There's an inscription in the boldest blue letters across the cover: Property of Agent Sienna Horowitz. She flips the compact open, revealing a silver screen made of glass. "Access request."

A robotic male voice speaks back to her, "Identification, please."

"Agent Sienna Horowitz, bureau ID number seven-seven-two-five-six-three-nine."

"Access granted. Recording mode on."

The mirror's glass cracks into three separate shards, each floating out of the compact. They linger around her like stalactites that have broken free of their cave's ceiling. At long last, the glass reflects everything in front of it, including me, and holy whoa, do I need a hairbrush. My *flyaways* have flyaways. Before I can fix the mess, the shards cast out a faint red shimmer, blinking in a synchronized beat. The Recorder is officially recording me now. I will go down in bureau archives' history as the only witness whose hair resembles a whole family of ferrets.

Agent Horowitz slides closer to me. "Lana, I'd like you to walk me through the day's events, starting with your arrival at Waxbyrne. Try to be as specific as possible."

I detail everything about my trip to Waxbyrne—the moment I saw the Fire Drake, when I realized my forever favorite was attacking it, those golden orbs with spells inside them. Mom either flinches or looks to the fireplace. She must be having a hard time with the fact that her daughter was in the presence of a dragon again. Hopefully, she's also realizing I *survived* again.

I wrap up my story with Takeshi's final message. "Just when he was about to Transport out of the building, Takeshi told me, 'The world you know is a lie. The world that's coming, that's the one you should believe in.' Then he vanished."

Director Sandhar's jaw clenches tighter than my knotted hair.

"Did you hear or see anything else that could better illustrate Mr. Endo's motives?"

"Not really, no. I'm sorry."

"Oh, you have *nothing* to apologize for, Ms. Torres." President Turner plays with his tie. "The Takeshi Endo I knew wasn't like this. I don't know who this boy is."

"He's the same boy you rooted for two years ago, only now he's realized what a carnival of shit storms life really is," Manny says unabashedly. "So he wants the crystal heart to maybe do something against his dragon's killer? I can't blame the kid."

"Thank you for sharing your much-needed perspective." Director Sandhar's tone drips with sarcasm. He's leaning forward, elbows on his thighs. "Ms. Torres, what about the Gold magic Mr. Endo was wielding in the orbs? What more can you tell us about them?"

"All I know is they were Gold and capable of paralyzing a dragon. Since Takeshi's a Regular, someone else must have given him that magic. I think the Sire is working with a Gold Wand. Has the bureau heard of a Gold Wand who can trap spells?"

Director Sandhar keeps a straight face. "Whoever's helping Mr. Endo is beyond what we're accustomed to, but we'll be pulling up every file we have on registered Gold Wands."

"What if this Gold Wand hasn't registered with the bureau?"

He flashes me a tight smile. "Then it's time we push them into the light."

Yikes. Now the bureau will be on the hunt for a rogue Gold Wand, along with a former Blazewrath superstar. An agent's job seems pretty stressful, but to pile all this onto it?

Agent Horowitz doesn't seem fazed. She's patting my back like *I'm* the one who has a dangerous to-do list. Bless her soul. "Do you have any questions for us?"

"Yeah." I lean closer to her. "Why is there a Fire Drake at Waxbyrne?"

Manny laughs. "Took her long enough. Go on, Sandhar. Tell her what you told me."

Director Sandhar scowls in his direction. "I'm afraid I'm not at liberty to discuss that with anyone other than Madame Waxbyrne. My apologies, Ms. Torres."

Manny clucks his tongue. "There you go, nena. Feel the burn."

I don't know which man to glare at the hardest. The one time I meet Team Puerto Rico's manager, and he's acting like a premium-level jerk. But Director Sandhar's brushing off the fact that a dragon is *living at a wand shop*. And what's worse, the dragon showed signs of having Bonded with a rider. Madame Waxbyrne isn't British, so there's no way the dragon is her steed. Dragons can only Bond with humans from their country. Something fishy is going on, and classified or not, I deserve to know why I almost died.

"But it's illegal." I speak a little louder. "Madame Waxbyrne is keeping a dragon that doesn't belong to her. That Fire Drake may have attacked me, but when the guards swept in, it stopped. The dragon is Bonded. Where's the rider responsible for its safety?"

"That's not for me to discuss." Director Sandhar nods to President Turner. "You're up."

President Turner stands with the speed of a boy who's been told he can leave school early. "Ms. Torres, after seeing the surveillance footage, I'm certain of one thing: You, my dear girl, are the bravest talent I've come across in a long, long time. You're fast, yes, but most important, you have a heart that beats for the right things. The whole world will know what you did today. They will know how fast, brave, and *good* you are."

If Agent Horowitz hadn't been tethering me to the real world, I'd think I'd entered the afterlife. Instead of God, the president of the IBF greeted me as I strolled through the pearly gates.

"Talent?" Mom sits on the edge of the sofa, all crinkled like she smells something foul. "Why are you calling her a 'talent'?"

"Because she is! Your daughter is one of the fastest young athletes I've had the privilege of meeting, even though her tryout didn't happen as initially scheduled." President Turner shrugs as he looks at me. "Ms. Torres, what you did at Waxbyrne proved a much better audition."

His words are an eighteen-wheeler speeding right through me. *This is why he's here?* Does he want to give me the chance to try out at a later date? Could my dream *really* still happen?

"My daughter hasn't signed up to play your atrocious excuse for a sport." Mom's laugh is a short, cold burst. "I'm sorry, but you've confused Lana with someone else."

"Stop it, Mom!" I press my palms against my temples, half regretting my outburst and half wishing I were somewhere far away from the mother who doesn't know squat about me. This isn't how I wanted her to find out, but I can't lie now.

She's watching me with a narrowed gaze. "What was that?"

I drop my hands. "President Turner's right. I did sign up for Blazewrath tryouts. I want to join Team Puerto Rico and play in this year's Blazewrath World Cup. I want to be a Runner and represent my country on an international platform. This is the only dream I've ever had."

Crickets. My mother is on a different plane of existence, seemingly grappling with reality. Even Manny's glued to her as if waiting for a bomb to go off. Mom, however, isn't detonating.

I gulp down. "Are you okay?"

"Does she look okay to you?" Manny says.

Director Sandhar shushes him, then addresses me. "If you'd like some privacy, we can—"

"The only dream you've ever had . . ." Mom repeats in a robotic voice. It's like she's trying out a foreign language for the first time. "Does that mean . . . you've *played* before?"

"No. There's just one dragon in the States. You need six dragons to form a Blazewrath team. And you can only play with a formal invitation from the IBF to participate in the Cup. They don't teach Blazewrath in schools or practice it anywhere else." I motion to President Turner. "Anyone caught playing amateur Blazewrath gets arrested and has to pay a high fine."

"That is correct," he says. "Blazewrath is illegal outside of IBF grounds and supervision for a variety of reasons, including several past incidents of non-rider Regulars who were known for baiting Un-Bonded dragons into playing with them. Most of those Regulars died, and the Un-Bonded dragons caused a lot of damage to private property. The invitation-only policy is one of the ways the IBF guarantees the sport is being played safely."

Mom nods. "Because dragons can't be trusted."

"They *can* be trusted," I cut in. "That Fire Drake was defending itself from someone who'd hurt it. The Pesadelo that tried to kill me in Brazil was Un-Bonded. I survived by outrunning its flames at five years old. You saw me on that surveillance footage today. I'm *way* faster now." I'm speeding through each word, but I can't stop. "Blazewrath is more than my favorite sport. It's the only thing that makes me feel like I belong in this world. Like I actually have a purpose."

Mom slumps in her seat, shaking her head. "Honey, *how* can you feel like you don't belong or have a purpose? Your parents love you. You have Samira's and her family's love. You're going to be a high school senior in two months. You're heading off to college next year."

"Am I? Have I told you what I want to major in?"

"Well, no, but you still have time to decide."

"I don't want to decide!" I snap. "I want to play the sport Papi taught me to love and to represent our island—our *real* home."

A shadow settles on Mom's expression, a storm that's yet to land. "I see . . . So everything I've done to keep you safe has ruined your life? Is that it? Have I ruined your life?"

I stare at her, unblinking. Of course she's ruined my life, but I love her. I always will. Even if living with Papi would've been *so* much better.

Mom isn't the worst person in the universe. She just did what she thought was right.

Now it's up to me to show her what the right thing was all along.

I'm sitting on the edge of the chaise, hands in prayer position under my chin. "You haven't ruined my life, Mom. You just made it harder for me to live my truth. I didn't want to tell you about my plans like this, but if President Turner will still let me attend tryouts, I'd love it if you could give me the chance to make my dream a reality. Ground me for lying and sneaking around. Take my phone and laptop and Whisperer and everything else. But please let me do this."

She studies me as if she's been sucked into a flurry of flashbacks— her screams back in Brazil, or the panic she must've felt during the Waxbyrne attack. Finally, she glances at President Turner. "Why are you really here, Mister President?"

President Turner slips his hands into his pockets, cocking his head in my direction. "I was hoping to formally invite Lana to join Puerto Rico's Blazewrath team as their new Runner."

I'm knocked back into a stiff, straight position. I wait for him to tell me this is an April Fools' joke, even though it's the middle of July. A few hours ago, Takeshi Endo had plucked my dream out of the realm of possibility and smashed it to smithereens. Now it's come back to life even more beautiful than before. I get to honor my island, my father, and myself, after all.

Then I remember that silver-scaled face on TV.

"What about the Sire?" I ask in a hushed voice. "His attacks won't cancel the Cup?"

President Turner's forehead creases. "Not at all, Ms. Torres. The Cup will go on."

"Trust me. He'll be caught in no time," Director Sandhar reassures me.

If the director of the Department of Magical Investigations promises me the Sire will be behind bars soon, who am I to believe otherwise?

The Sire is a force to be reckoned with, but I foiled one of his plans today. I can only imagine the level of badassery the bureau is capable of.

I turn to President Turner with the hugest fangirl grin. "So I'm on the team?"

"The spot is yours if you want it."

I lunge at him to shake his hand. "Yes! Thank you so much, sir. This is *amazing*."

"Lana is seventeen," says Mom. "In order for her to play, you need a parent's signature."

"Right you are, madam. Legal guardians of minors are required to sign their contracts."

Mom takes a deep breath. "May I see it?"

At first, I think the Fire Drake's roars have messed with my hearing, but when President Turner pulls out his plain Silver wand, I feel a little faint. I sit back down before I topple over.

The president flicks his wand twice. A yellowed papyrus scroll appears out of nowhere. It rolls down just inches shy of the floor. President Turner offers the scroll . . . *my contract* . . . to Mom.

I'm welling up, dumbfounded with the fact that my mother is taking this seriously. She's choosing to put my happiness before hers. I memorize the way she pulls her blue pen from her purse, the loose hold she has on it while she signs on the dotted line.

Leslie Anne Wells, my impossibly stubborn mother, has signed my Blazewrath contract.

I walk over to her, arms spread wide open. "Thank you, Mom."

She holds up a hand. "My signature is all the support you'll be receiving. I won't suffer through my only child putting herself in danger again. Go on and play for your real home. I'll be in the one you hate, waiting for you when you're done." She gives my contract to President Turner. "I'd like to Transport back to my car. I need to visit my nephew at the hospital."

I back away, my lips parted, but nothing comes out. Of course she'd never attend any matches or even watch them on TV. There's a difference between picturing something and having it drawn in bold colors right in front of you, though. Mom's choosing my happiness over hers, but she's also choosing not to be a part of that happiness. It's not that she doesn't fit in the equation. She just doesn't have the energy to try fitting in.

Mom follows Agent Horowitz out of the room. She doesn't say goodbye to me.

I rub my eyes over and over, refusing to cry.

"Ms. Torres, if you would like a moment alone, we won't mind," President Turner says.

"No. I'm fine. I, um . . . I'd like to sign now."

"Certainly!" President Turner gives me the contract.

I read it even slower than Mom. My obligations are in super-clear detail. So is my salary. Runners get $7 million. My eyeballs almost fall out. That's *a lot* of cash for someone like me, regardless of how well I live thanks to Mom's job. The money will be transferred to my account as soon as I put my signature on the page. Mom's signature means she agrees to have the money sent directly to me, even though I'm a minor. President Turner conjures a pen with his wand. I use it to sign my contract. Regardless of how financially stable my future feels, I still taste rotten apples in my mouth. This is supposed to be the best day of my life. There was supposed to be a choir of angels, dancing animals, a marching band, and free ice cream for everyone.

Instead, Mom's last words keep swirling like a tornado in my mind, slicing me deeper with each spin. I still have a mother, but why does it feel like she's gone forever?

Keep it together, Lana. You can cry when you're at home.

I hand the contract back to President Turner.

He flashes me one last smile. "Welcome to the Blazewrath World Cup!"

*Defining the Bond is both simple and difficult. The simplicity lies
in acknowledging what a Bond is: a personal relationship between
dragon and human, which allows them to feel each other's emotional
state through psychic communication. Younger dragons use images to
express themselves, since verbalizing their thoughts and feelings is
a more complex skill. The difficulty lies in the Bond's origins. Some
dragon-studies experts argue that Bonds are destined. A dragon breaks
out of its egg and searches for a rider because the universe has declared
it so. When one is taken from the other, the grief that ensues can lead to
wrath unlike the world has ever seen.*

—*Excerpt from* Carlos Torres's Studying the Bond
Between Dragons & Humans

CHAPTER FIVE

AFTER AGENT HOROWITZ TRANSPORTS ME HOME, I DRAG MYSELF
inside the house, where the silence guts me harder than I imagined.

Mom must still be at the hospital with Todd. She's choosing a
spineless jerk over me. And she's doing it on our last night together
until the Cup ends. President Turner has scheduled my pickup at 7:00
a.m. It'll be a top-secret Transport to Dubai, since the IBF won't release
a statement to the press about me joining Team Puerto Rico until we're
much closer to the opening ceremonies. I'll be on the other side of the
world, living my dream, while Mom goes on with her life. She's already

practicing. I'm the ghost of a girl she raised.

Papi wouldn't treat me like this. I can't leave for Dubai without giving him the best news of our lives. I can't leave without knowing why he's been off the grid. I won't sleep otherwise.

I unlock my phone.

Takeshi's photo is still my wallpaper. With a deep breath, I delete the photo and replace it with a plain blue screen. There are 172 Takeshi pics left. I start deleting them one by one, but seeing his face so many times doesn't soften the blow of making it disappear. I shove my phone into my pocket. Those pics can wait until my heart doesn't hurt.

Maybe I shouldn't call Papi alone.

I speak into my Whisperer. "Samira, can you hear me?"

Four seconds later, she's rambling back at me. "Hello, yes, obviously. How'd it go? Is the bureau pretty? Is it just like in *Law & Order: Magical Crimes Unit*? Are there marble statues of famous dead wizards every-where? Did they keep you in one of those rooms with the glass and the table in the middle and the crappy wall decor? Did you drink terrible coffee?"

"I didn't go to the bureau."

"You *what*? But they were supposed to take you there!"

This is it. I'm about to speak the words for the first time ever. Hopefully, they'll fill me up with everything Mom and Manny emptied me of minutes before. "My interrogation happened at President Russell Turner's Other Place. He wanted to meet me after watching the Waxbyrne footage." I pause for effect. "I'm the new Runner for Team Puerto Rico."

A saucepan clanks to the floor wherever she is.

"MY BEST FRIEND IS PLAYING AT THE BLAZEWRATH WORLD CUP, SHUT UUUUUUUUUUUUP! YOU ARE AN IMMORTAL SPORTS GODDESS!" Samira screams.

I laugh until everything hurts. I can always count on her to freak out when I can't do so for myself. "You think you can keep that fire a bit longer? I'm going to need it in a minute."

Samira's yells die at once. "Why? What are we doing in a minute?"

"You're helping me pack for Dubai," I say. "And we have to tell my dad."

SAMIRA AND SHAY TRANSPORT TO MY HOUSE TWENTY MINUTES LATER.

"Where do you want 'em?" Shay tucks her Silver wand into her jeans. She motions like a game show host to the two boxes of pizza Samira's carrying. She's the most adorable fourteen-year-old ever, especially in those low pigtails.

"Right here's fine." I lead her to the living room, where I've already set up my laptop and have the Skype window open. I help Samira put the boxes on the coffee table next to the computer. The smell alone is enough for me to know which is which. The top box is meat lovers, with cheese-stuffed crust for her and Samira. The bottom box is artisan spinach and feta for me.

Samira launches herself at me. "Congratulations, Ms. Runner!" I'm about to thank her when Shay joins in on the hug and pulls us all even tighter. The Jones sisters jump in synchronized glee, messing up my hair and destroying what's left of my eardrums.

When they finally release me, I plop down on the couch and start gobbling a slice. Samira and Shay sit down, too, and Samira confesses she's grounded for breaking her fourth wand, though her parents let her throw this mini celebration first.

"Cheers." Samira holds up her pizza slice like a wineglass. "To living the dream!"

I laugh heartily. "To living the dream."

We clink our slices together and stuff our mouths at the same time.

Shay points to my laptop. "So are we doing this?"

"We are." My laughter dies as I click on the Start Call button. Maybe Papi is nowhere near a computer, but trying won't hurt anyone. The screen remains black. I slide a bit closer to Samira, hoping her proximity alone will pump up my confidence levels.

A middle-aged man appears on-screen.

He has the same deep-brown skin, light-brown hair, and high cheekbones as me. The name tag on his violet polo shirt reads DR. CARLOS TORRES, BOND SPECIALIST. It's chipped at the left corner. He's sitting at his desk with a stack of folders and a map of the world's dragon sanctuaries. The misshapen star I'd drawn twelve years ago is still in the middle of the map.

"Finally!" I almost drop my slice as I lunge forward. "¡Hola, Papi!"

"Hola, mi amor. I literally just sat down to see if I could reach you." He rubs his face, as if trying to get rid of the exhaustion plaguing him. "I'm so sorry for not contacting you until now. We were transferring one of the male Pesadelos to the sanctuary in Roraima, and thanks to the Sire's latest attack, we had to turn off our phones as a safety protocol." Papi searches my face like he's cramming for a test. "Mija, a colleague told me what happened at Waxbyrne when I got back. He showed me the footage, and I'm *aghast*. How are you feeling? Are you hurt?"

"No, just tired. But I'm in great company." I move the laptop to show Samira and Shay.

"Hello, Mr. Torres!" They wave at him together.

Papi smiles at them. "Hello, ladies! I'm very happy to see you." He looks at me again, his expression heavy with concern. "Tell me everything, Lana."

So I tell him. Samira and Shay eat in silence as I recount the Waxbyrne attack, followed by the interrogation at President Turner's Other Place. Papi's eyebrows rise higher with each detail. When I finally get to the contract part, though, he's as mannequin-still as Mom was.

"President Turner gave you a contract on the spot?"

I frown at his incredulity. "He did. I'm on Team Puerto Rico. I leave for Dubai in the morning." A short, timid laugh escapes me. "I'm going to play in the Blazewrath World Cup."

I wait for the explosion of whoops and hollers. An even louder cacophony than the one Samira produced. Papi's cheers will screw up power grids everywhere and sink the whole world into darkness with its intensity. He'll call in sick tomorrow because he won't have any voice left.

"Mi amor, do you really think this is the right thing to do?"

The wind is knocked right out of me. My dream-turned-reality isn't giving Papi the joy we'd left back in Cayey. Feeling like a failure to one parent is crappy enough, but this sinks its teeth into me and tugs at my flesh ten times harder. This sport, this career, is meant to be our home and our safe place. We're supposed to be in this together.

"Why are you asking me that? Of course it was the right thing to do, Papi," I whisper. There's not enough strength in me to speak louder.

"I just feel like the circumstances behind your hiring are bizarre." He's shaking his head like he's solving an impossible math equation. "Why would Director Sandhar allow civilians unrelated to the crime scene into an official bureau interrogation? What does Blazewrath have to do with Takeshi's attempted theft? And what gives President Turner the kind of clearance to bypass security protocols *and* offer you the Runner position without putting you through tryouts? Manuel Delgado has even less clout than the president. So what's this truly about?"

His logic sinks in little by little. This whole situation *could* seem weird from an outsider's perspective. The back of my head is pounding something terrible. I massage it with little energy. "The president told me he saw all he needed to see in the Waxbyrne footage. He thinks I'm the best fit for Team Puerto Rico because of my speed *and* my bravery. You do make some valid points, though. I'm sorry I wasn't smart enough to see things the way you do."

"You *are* smart, mija. And you're the bravest person I know! You saved a Fire Drake. You stood up to the legendary Takeshi Endo, of all people." Papi blows me a sweet kiss. "My heart is so full right now. I'm more proud of you than you'll ever know."

I should be over the moon to hear he's proud.

But I can only focus on his disappointment for signing that contract.

"What do you think I should do?" I ask.

"Well, I suggest you keep your eyes open at all times. Be mindful of your actions and your words. Whatever's going on, you'll have to rely mostly, if not entirely, on yourself to grapple with it." His eyes crinkle as he smiles again. "I think you can still have fun and enjoy the company of your teammates. You'll be well protected from the Sire, too, so I won't worry about that. I'm only worried about the president's intentions."

"Speaking of the Sire," I say, "you need to get out of that sanctuary."

Papi taps a few of the folders, his expression totally calm. "Our new bureau security detail arrived before I got back. Director Sandhar sent dozens of requests for more agents. Apparently, the bureau wants close to a battalion at each sanctuary worldwide." He shuffles the folders from one side of his desk to another. "We'll be staying here."

"But you *can't*. The Sire and his Dragon Knights might strike there next."

"And when they come, they'll be stopped." Papi sounds much more okay with his potential death than my big mistake. "I can't abandon these Pesadelos. We're *so close* to a breakthrough with them all, but especially with Violet #43. She almost let me pat her nose yesterday before scurrying off. And we've been standing next to her without retaliation for a whole year now."

I cringe at the code name he's given the dragon that tried to kill me. Only Bonded dragons share their true names with their riders. Un-Bonded dragons don't communicate with humans at all, so they remain nameless. According to Papi, Violet #43 has been steadily improving, but he acts like she's more than a work responsibility. She's the reason he stayed in Brazil. It's like he's refusing to give up on trying to atone for what broke our family apart. Like he won't rest until she's no longer the dragon that almost took me away from him for good.

Nothing I say will get him to leave that damn sanctuary.

"Fine. . . . Just be careful, okay?" I say.

"Always have been."

We discuss what to pack for Dubai, calculating the best times to call him with updates, and reliving my trip to Waxbyrne. Papi watches the surveillance footage again while still chatting with me. He asks me all sorts of questions about the Fire Drake's behavior. He assures me the Fire Drake is a female, and that it's a Bonded dragon being kept away from her rider. He doesn't have any theories regarding their separation, though.

"I'll see if I can look into her case more," he says. "Usually Bonded dragons who are separated from their riders experience grief similar to losing a loved one. It can drive them to behave in self-destructive ways. The same applies to their riders, which is why I believe Takeshi's acting in complete disregard of the law. Each dragon species manifests this grief differently, but the Fire Drake managed to keep her composure until Takeshi's arrival. Her behavior seems to suggest she's in agreement with her current living arrangement."

"But why is she in a store? Why all the secrecy surrounding her rider's identity, too?"

The laptop screen goes black.

A crackling, static noise erupts from the speakers.

I sit up. Now the screen is stuck on that snowy image that usually means there's no signal.

Shay's phone is also flashing static. No matter how many times she presses the screen, it won't do anything other than flash the same thing.

I try muting the sound on my laptop, but it doesn't work. None of the keys do anything.

Samira and I look at each other. "Magic," we say together.

The static is gone.

Both the laptop and the phone show the same image again. There's barely any light, but I can see an onyx-tiled ballroom. The floor has scratches and strange spots in strange shapes. Headless stone sculptures of naked men and women encircle the ballroom. Uneven cracks and grooves mar their necks, as if someone ripped each head off. The camera backs up from the center of the room. When the next image comes into frame, I wish the camera had focused on something else.

There's a white man tied to a wooden chair.

Thick rope binds his arms, his ankles. It's the color of stars. He wears a black suit and navy blue tie, but his honey hair is all ruffled and knotted. The man seems close to my father's age. He's shaking and crying. He doesn't try to set himself free. It's as if he's already given up.

The man stops shaking and crying. Now he's a stiff, pale wisp of whatever he used to be.

"You must remember one thing above all else . . ." A man's voice comes from somewhere off camera. His accent is British, roughened by his harsh tone. "This is not your world."

My veins run dry. "It's him."

The Sire walks toward the bound man. Stardust scales cover the back of the Sire's head. His black leather trench coat looks heavy, but he's gliding as if it weighs less than a feather. There's the soft thud of his boots against the floor, the hissing intakes of breath, the growl rumbling past his lips. He stops once he reaches the back of the chair. The bound man starts shaking, but the Sire ignores his prisoner. With an otherworldly grace, he turns to the camera.

The Sire smiles like he's spilled the blood of all his enemies.

"You are living on borrowed time." He grabs the back of the chair, leaning forward, then runs a gloved finger over the man's cheek. "Agent Michael Robinson has twenty-five years of service to the bureau.

He's the third-highest-ranking officer in England. A quarter of the prisoners currently shacking up at Ravensworth Penitentiary have been his catches. And until today, he's been tasked with capturing me, like many who have failed before him."

I sink to the edge of the couch. To have the Sire as an assignment must make this man one of the best agents alive. Yet there he is, trapped.

The Sire smiles no more. "You do not send a worm to catch a god. This is not your world. This world belongs to the gods of wing and flame." He lets go of the man, the chair. "This message is for those who want to see Agent Robinson to safety."

The Sire waves to someone off camera, beckoning them forward.

Takeshi Endo appears on-screen. He's holding his claw dagger. He flanks Agent Robinson, and the Sire seizes his shoulder. His grip is tight, possessive.

The Sire looks into the camera. "Where were you when Antonio Deluca took Hikaru's life? Where were you when Takeshi mourned for this injustice?" He gives Takeshi's shoulder a squeeze. "You once knew this boy as your hero for the wrong reasons. He believed the lie you fed him. The same lie you feed the world every two years. That dragons are playthings. That we are better suited as your entertainment." The Sire shakes his head. "We are not your playthings. And this boy is now a *true* hero with a far greater cause. Are you not?"

"Yes, Sire," Takeshi replies. "Despite what the bureau would have you assume, I would never hurt a dragon. I will rescue those who have been deprived of their freedom." He pauses, drawing a bit closer to the camera. "This world belongs to the gods of wing and flame."

What. The. Hell. Samira and I were wrong. This isn't about catching Hikaru's killer.

He really *has* become a Dragon Knight.

"Indeed." A haughty Sire releases Takeshi's shoulder. He steps around the chair. "I hereby order the immediate release of all dragons held in captivity around the world, including the Fire Drake at Waxbyrne. I call for the demise of the Blazewrath World Cup. The Department of Magical Investigations will cease its efforts to stop me. *If* you refuse to obey me . . ."

In a blur of motion, the Sire lunges at Agent Robinson.

His sharp teeth find the screaming man's neck, then rip out his flesh.

Samira and Shay scream out together.

I don't have any strength left to. The horrors eat me from within, hungrier and hungrier until I no longer know what's left of me.

Takeshi keeps his eyes straight ahead. He doesn't watch as Agent Robinson's head hangs forward, limp and lifeless. He doesn't notice the Sire's whole mouth dripping in crimson.

A growl slips past the Sire's red smile. "It will be the last thing you ever do."

The laptop turns itself off.

So does Shay's phone.

The Sire is gone, Takeshi is gone, but their atrocity still clings to me.

Samira holds me. "We're all right, Lana. Do you hear me? Everything will be okay."

I nod because she wants me to, but I can only think of the man who was once a dragon, the boy who was once my favorite, and how they're killing my dream together.

Dragons had been scarce outside of Europe and Asia until the twentieth century. In 1968, Venezuela became the first Latin American country to produce a new dragon species, the mighty Furia Roja (see Chapter Seven: Dragons with Special Weapons). Other Latin American species appeared by the hundreds shortly after, most notably the Brazilian Pesadelo (see Chapter Thirteen: The World's Most Dangerous Dragon). The IBF first invited Central and South American nations to compete in the Blazewrath World Cup held in 1971. As of 2014, Haiti remains the only Caribbean country with a dragon species, but since they have one living dragon, they cannot qualify for the Cup. Perhaps someday the Caribbean will be the home of many dragons, too.

—*Excerpt from Harleen Khurana's*
A History of Blazewrath Around the World

CHAPTER SIX

MOM NEVER CAME HOME LAST NIGHT.

Not even after the Sire's video hit every single news outlet. Not even after I texted her to say Samira was sleeping over, then called to check if she got the text. Mr. and Mrs. Jones agreed after they heard my shaky voice on the phone. All Mom wrote back was, "OK." She was either at the hospital or at Todd's house taking care of him, like he's the one she birthed.

Samira and I are in the kitchen waiting for my Transport to Dubai. I eat the scrambled eggs and bacon she cooked, but my taste buds have been wrecked along with my dream. There's no way the IBF will ignore the Sire's threats. The last thing they'd want is more blood on their hands. Why bother hoping for an opportunity the Sire has burned into ruin? Not even Samira twirling around with a spatula in her Sailor Moon pajamas can put me in a good mood. Papi called me after the Sire's message, but his reassurance that everything would be okay fell flat.

The clock strikes 7:00 a.m.

SWISH!

President Turner and Manny Delgado are standing in my house's foyer.

"Good morning!" says President Turner, dressed in a burgundy suit and canary-yellow tie. It's a stark contrast to Manny's black button-down shirt and dad jeans. "You have a lovely home, Ms. Torres." He looks at Samira. "Hello, there! We've not been properly introduced."

Samira finally stops twirling, but she's still holding the spatula. "So nice to meet you, Mr. President. I'm Samira Jones," she chirps. "Lana's best friend."

"Your pajamas are *delightful*, Ms. Jones." President Turner gives her a big thumbs-up.

She curtsies like it's no big deal she's greeting the president of the IBF in her pajamas. God, I love my best friend. "Thank you kindly."

"Where's the whiskey?" Manny asks me point-blank.

I do my best to keep my voice steady. "There's no whiskey here."

Manny pouts. "Beer? Club soda?"

"Nope."

"*No* club soda? What kind of animals are you people?"

"Manny!" A mortified President Turner elbows him, then loosens up again as he nods at me. "Well then, Ms. Torres. All set for Transport?"

I gape at him. "We're still going to play?"

President Turner's enthusiasm dies a little, as if he's disappointed in me. "Why wouldn't we? Are you set for Transport? Or do you need more time to get everything sorted?"

I search for answers in Manny's face, but he just yawns. "What about the Sire's message?"

President Turner's cheeks drain of color. "The International Blaze-wrath Federation is cooperating with the Department of Magical Investigations in order to detain the Sire. Director Sandhar and his agents are highly capable of ensuring this threat's capture," he says. "Besides, twelve Dragon Knights were apprehended after last night's broadcast."

It's a good thing my knees aren't weak. Otherwise, I would've collapsed from shock. "That hasn't been on the news."

"Yes, it has." Manny holds up his phone. "Right before we got here."

His tone isn't dripping in sarcasm, so he's probably telling the truth.

"And the Sire?" I ask.

President Turner frowns. "He and some of his Dragon Knights escaped from the run-down mansion in Surrey, England, where they were hiding. The Un-Bonded Hydra from the Athens attack wasn't in attendance. It's possible the Hydra is no longer among their company. No need to worry, though. The bureau has several leads that will direct the task force straight to them." He attempts a warm smile. "I give you my word, Ms. Torres. The Sire will be stopped."

"Translation: Blazewrath is still on, nena," says Manny. "You coming or not?"

I'm dead silent. The bureau might have leads on the Sire, but what if they fail like Agent Robinson? What if I'm on the Blazewrath field while he's broadcasting someone else's murder?

President Turner's eyes are wide with panic as he steps closer to me. "This is your dream, isn't it? You *have* to play in the Cup, Ms. Torres."

I back away from him. Sure, I signed a $7 million contract, but Papi's warning is bursting in bright red clouds all around me. Maybe he's right. Something *is* off about this whole thing.

But I need that Blazewrath field.

"You're sure the bureau's leads are accurate?" I ask President Turner.

"Indeed. Don't be surprised if we hear news of the Sire's capture once we reach Dubai."

I look at Manny. He tells it like it is, so I ask him, "Do you think they'll catch the Sire?"

Manny doesn't miss a beat. "The Sire won't make it to tomorrow a free man."

Wow. Even Manny trusts Director Sandhar on this.

Samira doesn't speak, but she's giving me her fiercest "You better not" expression. I have no choice but to trust her judgment. It's definitely looking like the Sire will have spellbound handcuffs around his wrists sooner than he's anticipating. So will Takeshi Endo.

I tell President Turner, "I'm set for Transport, sir. Let me get my suitcase."

President Turner claps his hands. "Brilliant! Off you go, then!"

He and Manny wait downstairs while Samira and I fetch the carry-on. When we come back, President Turner offers to hold it for me, but I reassure him I'm fine.

Samira squeezes the life out of me. "Go win that Cup. I love you."

"Love you, too. And please don't visit Todd. That would only make him happy."

She laughs. I tell her I'm transferring two thousand dollars into her savings account so she can buy her last Copper wand and whatever else she damn well wants. Before she can decline the money, I roll my carry-on over to the door. I take one last look at the place where I've lived for the past twelve years—the place I never asked to move to—but where I grew to love Blazewrath more, locked away in my room with headphones on, scared that Mom would catch me. This is where she raised me without my father, never letting me see her break a sweat. She had no idea who her daughter was, but she fed me and clothed me and made sure I took all my vitamins.

She's not here to hug me goodbye, though.

She's not here to send me off down the path I've been sketching in my mind for years.

A tear slips down my cheek. I wipe it off.

Goodbye, Mom. I hope to see you soon.

President Turner whips out his wand. Manny moves to his right while I settle on his left.

White light engulfs me as I wave goodbye to Samira one last time.

I'M NO LONGER STANDING ON WOODEN FLOORBOARDS.

My Adidas land on something much softer, grainier, and less steady. I peek down at the ruddy richness beneath me. Naples sand is lighter, almost bleached, more like a prop instead of a natural part of the environment. I can't remember the sand in Puerto Rico's beaches. I'd spent most of my time in the mountains. But I do remember the heat, and the weather here reminds me of summertime on the island, sticky and humid and awesome for eating piraguas all day.

"Welcome to Dubai! Specifically, to Pink Rock Desert." President Turner aims his wand to what lies ahead of us. "And that over there is the Compound."

Sand dunes roll out for miles and miles. A boiling sun shines down on the deep ruddy richness. To my left, there's an incline with a rock formation at the top.

Right between the dunes is the Compound, which is a series of housing complexes for all sixteen teams. They look like steel bubbles splashed in white paint. The bubbles span from side to side in a horseshoe formation. They're as big as four-story buildings. There are no gates near the Compound, but it does have a bazillion wizard security guards. Each wears sporty clothes, not the suits and dresses bureau agents are required to wear.

None of them balks at President Turner's Transport Charm. Similar to Waxbyrne, no one can Transport into or out of the Compound, but it seems the surrounding patches of sand are fine.

"Local time is 3:17 in the afternoon. I believe we have hundred-degree weather today." President Turner waves me forward. "Ready to meet your teammates?"

My stomach somersaults twice. I'm about to meet the six other players and their Sol de Noche steeds. This will be the first time I'm introduced as a Blazewrath athlete. Little by little, the nightmare fades to the back of my memories, carving out a hole for the dream to reemerge.

Keep your cool. Be polite. Make them love you off the bat.

"I'm ready," I tell President Turner.

"Good. I'm starving." Manny plows through the sand.

President Turner and I follow him to the Compound, where the nearest guards bow their heads to the man who hired them.

"Afternoon," he says to every guard in sight. "Now, Ms. Torres, you're going to feel a lot better once we pass the shield."

"Shield?" I ask. Then a cold blast of wind slams into me. The area where the guards stand is magically air-conditioned. I can't feel the sun burning my skin anymore, either, so the shield must also protect from getting more than a tan. "Why am I able to go through the shield?" I ask President Turner. "Do I already have some sort of magical clearance?"

"Indeed you do." He motions to the sixth bubble on the left side. "That one is where you'll be staying along with your teammates. They're all expecting you."

There go those somersaults again. "Are any other teams already here?"

"Yes, they all have already arrived! You'll be meeting everyone a few nights from now, when Ambassador Haddad hosts a special welcome party for the teams."

Awesome.

Each house has a flag that designates which team lives where. Argentina, China, France, Portugal, Egypt, Puerto Rico, Zimbabwe, and Venezuela are on the left side. To the right side, there's Russia, Scotland, South Korea, México, Pakistan, Guatemala, Sweden, and Spain.

The entrance to the sixth bubble on the left is an oval door. Manny reaches it first, sliding a matching ivory key into the lock, then leaving it open for me to follow him inside.

White walls. White floors. White couches and settees and coffee tables and vases. Three white sets of double doors: one to the left, one to the right, and the last one at the very end of the lobby. There's even a white staircase at the opposite end of the main lobby, which spirals upward. It's the kind of white that haunts you at hospitals. At least the flat-screen TV is a newly dusted black. A modest tower of video games and DVDs has been set up on top of a white ottoman. There are plenty of books on the white shelves, including Harleen Khurana's *A History of Blazewrath Around the World*, which I devoured at the Red Crown High library in a day.

"¡Joaquín!" Manny calls out to the empty lobby. "¡Estamos aquí!"

Something clangs to the floor beyond the double doors to the left. There's some rushed chatter, too, followed by the double doors sliding open.

A man in his late twenties rolls out of the room in a wheelchair. Smiling at me like I'm a Girl Scout selling Thin Mints, he's dressed in jeans and a plain black T-shirt, but his Nikes are a bold neon green. He's a younger version of Manny except for his eyes. They're a more subtle green than his sneakers. Before his car crash three years ago, he'd been an international track-and-field superstar. I'd last seen him during the press conference announcing Puerto Rico's invitation to the Cup, his five-year-old son sitting on his lap and his adoring wife at his side.

"Joaquín Delgado," Manny's tone is lighter now, "my son, and your trainer slash coach."

I smile at Joaquín, who's stopped right in front of me. "Very nice to meet you. I'm Lana."

"Hola. ¿No hablas español?" Joaquín says.

"Oh, um . . . Sí. Un poco." Crap. I've been defaulting to English for the past twelve years. The only person I sometimes speak Spanish with is Papi, and it's a few sentences here and there. I can understand it just fine, but sometimes stringing sentences together is a bit of a pickle.

"It's okay. I speak both languages," Joaquín reassures me with a sweetness I've yet to detect in his father. "It's more than a pleasure to meet you, Lana. What you did for the Fire Drake was amazing. It will be an honor to train you these next few weeks."

I must look like a kid at the Disney Store. "It's *my* honor to train with you, Joaquín."

Manny gives Joaquín a one-shoulder shrug. "¿Y los demás? ¿Dónde están?"

"En la cocina." Joaquín waves to the room he exited earlier. "The rest of the team is in the kitchen, Lana. They wanted to give you a surprise. Ready to meet them?"

"Yes, of course," I say a little too fast.

"Wonderful. Follow me."

I leave my carry-on in the lobby. I'm the first to trail behind Joaquín, taking a steady breath that does little to calm my nerves. Manny and President Turner are whispering to each other behind me, but I don't pay attention to them. I'm about to *meet my human teammates*.

Joaquín enters the kitchen before me. The first thing I notice is the food. Most of the offerings on the L-shaped dinner table are just one big buffet for salad lovers. Baby spinach leaves. Kale. Spring mix. An assortment of toppings is displayed in sky-blue ceramic bowls. Other bowls have every single fruit known to man. Watermelon is the clear favorite, with four plates covered in triangle slices. There are glass jugs with a variety of juices farther down, but most are filled up with a slick green substance. I spot a huge pot of arroz guisado con habichuelas at the end. Half of it is gone. I suspect it's as delicious as it smells.

Six people stand at the end of the dinner table. The same six people whose names and faces I memorized since they were first announced as my country's team in a two-page spread in *The Weekly Scorcher*. They look exactly the same as they did two years ago. Three boys. Three girls. All clad in black activewear and black sneakers, which I suspect is what they always have on.

One of the boys has a white towel around his neck and a fistful of green grapes in his mouth. He's standing to the right, with brown skin that matches mine, short curly hair the color of wood, and wide-open eyes that are as dark as his clothes, as if I've just caught him in the middle of a prank. He chews at lightning speed and swallows even faster.

"¡Hola!" He makes his way toward me and offers me his hand.

"Luis García," I blurt out, shaking his hand. "Charger."

Luis's laugh is hearty, vibrant, and borderline contagious. "That's right." He lets go and points at me. "Lana Torres. Runner."

Wow. When a *teammate* says it, my new reality feels like home. "That's me."

"So I ate some of your grapes," Luis admits. "I'm sorry, but you have to understand. I can't be near grapes." He waves to the bowl and pretends to be in the deep throes of love. Or maybe he really *is* in the deep throes of love. "Nothing on this earth will ever keep us apart."

"He says the same thing about mofongo," Joaquín says. "We don't allow that dish in the team's diet, but trainers can eat all the mofongo they want. Sometimes twice in one day."

Luis slaps a hand to his heart. "Estúpido."

I burst out laughing. Luis joins me mid laugh, and we both sigh once the fit ends.

"There's still more food left for you," he says. "I only murdered most of the grapes. *And* the arroz con habichuelas." Luis puffs out his chest all proud. "We prepared you dinner!"

"*We*? I don't remember you doing much." Another one of the boys walks up to me, grinning and raising an eyebrow. He towers six inches over Luis. He's the darkest-skinned team member, even darker than Samira. His jet-black hair is cropped military style; his arms are massive, thick rods capable of pulverizing anything. "Welcome to the team, Lana."

"You're Héctor Sánchez. Keeper," I say before he can. "And our team captain."

Héctor nods. At nineteen, he's the oldest of us all, so it makes sense for him to be our captain. "How was your Transport here?"

"It was nice. And thanks so much for the welcome. Everything looks delicious."

"It is," Luis says. "Especially the grapes."

"Jesus. Get a new obsession," says Héctor.

"Bullying," Luis tells Joaquín, pointing straight at Héctor. "This counts as bullying."

The remaining boy and two of the three girls laugh behind him. The one who isn't laughing, fifteen-year-old Victoria Peralta, stands with her arms crossed. She's watching me like I've just spilled soda all over her white furniture. Victoria's the only light-skinned girl on the team, as white as my mother, but with peach lips and caramel hair straighter than a stick. She's even shorter than I am. I'm guessing five feet flat. Despite being the thinnest girl here, with a flat chest and small hips, she's rocking some ridiculous muscles under that black tank top.

I try breaking the ice with a smile. She remains stone-cold serious. Maybe she's not the smiling type? Or she could still be processing the fact that Brian Santana got fired?

Relax. She doesn't know you yet. Once she does, everything will be okay.

"Get used to these two bickering about nothing," says another girl. She's headed toward me with a spring in her step. Her skin is a golden tan, but her hair is an explosion of neon that could stop traffic from a galaxy away. The right side has to be the hottest pink known to the human eye. The left side is a dazzling purple. Unlike Victoria, this girl is all boobs and hips and bubble butt. "Hi. I'm Gabriela, but you knew that already, right?"

"Yes," I admit. "Gabriela Ramos. Charger. Just like Luis."

"Best Chargers ever." Luis drapes an arm over Gabriela. His right hand dangles from her shoulder. She holds onto his wrist, glancing up at him like a little sister admiring her big brother.

She flips her ponytail. "We are pretty dangerous."

"Debatable," says Héctor, who's pretending to look unimpressed.

Man, I'm going to love hanging out with them.

President Turner claps his hands once. "Come, come! You still haven't been introduced to your Blockers and Striker." He guides me forward to where the remaining team members watch me. Victoria still looks like she'd rather choke on glass than say hello. I pretend I can't see her. I don't think throwing a fit my first day here is the wisest idea.

President Turner halts right in front of the girl standing next to Victoria. She's the same skin tone as Héctor, making her the darkest girl in the room, but whereas Héctor barely has hair, Génesis Castro sports an Afro of nut-brown curls. For a girl whose sole purpose is to beat the living daylights out of the opposing team's Runner, she's as light as a yoga instructor, lean and chiseled without too much definition. She does have an impressive set of hips, though.

"Génesis Castro. Blocker," I say.

"Muy bien." Génesis gives me a quick wave. "Bienvenida, Lana."

"Gracias."

President Turner waves to the boy on Victoria's right. He's also light-skinned, with an angular face like an elf from a Tolkien book, but his super-straight hair is entirely bleached.

"Edwin Santiago. Blocker," I say. "Awesome to meet you, man."

Joaquín clears his throat. "Edwin doesn't speak much English."

"Oh." I flash through the interviews back from two years ago. While the rest of the team answered in English, Edwin spoke exclusively in Spanish, with Luis and Gabriela alternating as his interpreters. "Hola, Edwin. Es un placer conocerte."

"Igualmente, Lana." He speaks with the deepest voice out of all the boys. If I'd heard him over the phone without seeing what he looks like, I'd think he's a gigantic bouncer. Instead, the boy before me has the shape of a soccer player: strong arms, but even stronger thighs and calves.

"And this," President Turner says, "is Victoria Peralta. Striker."

I can't avoid her any longer. I try another smile, hoping to appear as friendly as I'm secretly praying for her to be. "Very nice to meet you, Victoria."

Victoria keeps her scowl in place. "Hi."

My smile is gone. Winning this girl over will be harder than I feared.

"Moving welcome, Victoria. I'm about to cry," Manny says as he wipes a nonexistent tear away. He claims the first seat at the dinner table. "Can we eat now? I'm going to eat now."

Nobody stops him from diving into the spring-mix salad bowl. He drowns half of his plate in ranch dressing, which has masking tape across the front labeled SÓLO PARA MANNY.

"Actually," I say, "I just had breakfast a little while ago."

Héctor nods. "Not a problem. We can save everything until you're hungry again." He's waving at the doors behind me. "Are you too tired for a walk?"

"Not at all."

"Perfect." He gives Joaquín a knowing look, a secret only they understand, then turns back to me. "Now let's go meet some dragons."

An egg is typically a dragon's first home. It can live inside that egg for weeks or months, depending on the species. Then July 2015 happened. On a hot summer's night, a newborn dragon rose out of the waters in Laguna Grande, a bioluminescent bay located in eastern Puerto Rico. There were no traces of dragon egg at the bottom of the bay. No evidence to support that the newborn had broken out of a shell. Marine biologists could only find a fissure in the lagoon's soil, which led to much-debated speculation that the island itself had given a dragon to its people.

—Excerpt from Julissa Mercado's article "Puerto Rico & Its Miraculous Sol De Noche Dragons" in The Weekly Scorcher

CHAPTER SEVEN

P API AND I HAD BEEN CONVINCED THE CARIBBEAN WOULD NEVER see another dragon.

The Haitian Tempête has been around for a decade now. He's the sole protector of the nation, flying around with his female rider in all of his eighty-foot-tall glory.

But he's not alone in the Caribbean anymore. Two years ago, a dragon as dark as night had been born in Puerto Rico for the first time. She'd soared into the sky at midnight, flames bursting from every inch of her, like a comet hurtling toward the stars. Hours later, she'd found her rider, the stone-cold serious Victoria, and waited patiently for her to accept their

Bond. Papi and I had called her a miracle. A gift from beyond. Now there are *six* Puerto Rican dragons, which all are competing with their riders in the Blazewrath World Cup.

And I, Lana Aurelia Torres, am about to meet them.

Breathe. Just breathe and do. Not. Pass. Out.

"Watch your step," Joaquín says as the elevator doors slide open. He and the other guys wait for the girls to get in first.

Victoria rushes to the back of the elevator. I trail behind Gabriela and Génesis, using them as my shields from Victoria. The guys file in one by one. President Turner's last in line.

He trips, then drops to his knees.

"Mister President, are you okay?" Joaquín beats me to it.

"Oh, goodness! My clumsiness knows no bounds." President Turner's laugh is as awkward as his attempts at getting up. Manny's quick to help him, though. "I think I need a bit of a rest, my dears. This old chap isn't what he used to be."

"Move along. I'll get him some water," Manny tells Joaquín. He presses the button to close the elevator doors without bothering to glance at any of us.

The doors snap shut.

"What did he trip on?" Gabriela asks Joaquín. "His own shoes?"

"Most likely," he replies as he presses the number-four button.

That must be it. There's nothing on the floor. At least the president didn't look like he was injured. Hopefully, his knees weren't banged up too bad.

The elevator stops. A loud *ding!* bounces off the walls. "Level Four," a disembodied female voice says above me. When the doors open, there's not a single trace of white ahead.

There's only pitch-black, uninviting darkness.

This habitat is dead silent. I can't even detect the dragons' breathing.

"Go ahead, Lana," says Joaquín. He's not the least bit concerned of something horrible happening. What if I trip and crack a bone in half? Or step on a dragon's claw by accident?

"You're sure this is safe?" I say.

"See for yourself."

How comforting.

No one speaks as I drag myself across the vast expanse of onyx. I'm on my own, hoping against hope I don't kick a dragon's leg. The floor isn't concrete but dirt. My sneakers slide across the grainy surface with ease. One step forward, stop. Another step, then stop. Hands grab at the nothingness, then I drop them again. I keep this up for what feels like forever. There's no sign of life anywhere near me. I feel like I'm playing hide-and-seek, and so far, I'm losing hard.

Then a faint glimmer of light shines straight ahead.

I squint at the light from a safe distance. It's a tiny spark, but it's not a spark at all. Smoke doesn't fly into the air above and around it. The flames don't fan anywhere. Instead, the spark is caged inside a shell, as if night itself has hardened into a giant, three-pointed star.

I'm staring at the tip of a dragon's tail.

There you are . . .

The first time I saw a tail like that, I'd been watching a livestream a local channel did for Victoria's dragon, and I hugged my laptop. Her steed, Esperanza, had been gracious enough to let cameras zoom in on her body. She'd even done a pirouette in the air. I remember falling in love with her, desperate to see her in person. Desperate for more dragons like her to fly out of the same bioluminescent bay. The other five dragons surfaced weeks later, and even though they all looked alike, I didn't lose my breath over them the way I had with the first Sol de Noche.

The dragon before me isn't Esperanza. Its tail is much thinner, less spiked and imposing. A male dragon. Little by little, the male's spine lights up in a fading, almost weakened glow, but the light isn't bursting out of his scales. There are no holes or crevices for the light to pour out of.

The Sol de Noche is on fire from within.

Like most dragons, a Sol de Noche can eject flames from a propeller in its throat. The propeller, the intensity of the flames' heat, and the speed at which they're ejected vary depending on the country of origin. That's pretty standard anatomy. Our dragons, however, can also wrap themselves in their flames and turn into massive fireballs. They can contract their flames to keep them close to their scales or push them out farther away to burn at a greater distance. Blazewrath fans are losing their minds. It's the first time a team with this kind of firepower will compete.

Only the top half of the Sol de Noche's body is visible, along with its eyes. Sol de Noche dragons have slits for eyes, thin and elongated, but bright as a daffodil's petals. They're glued to me, which is why I haven't moved an inch. I'm not sure what I can and can't do at this time.

A second light appears to my left, then another to my right.

Soon, I have six sources of sunlight surrounding me. None make any noise as they approach. They're seventy feet tall, with legs the size of four tree trunks side by side, but they're so, so quiet. All six Sol de Noche dragons form a tight circle with me at its center. Three males. Three females. Esperanza is directly behind me, the largest and shiniest one in the bunch. Her name means "hope" in Spanish, and yet she seems capable of ripping whole armies apart with a single claw. The males are a bit smaller but still super intimidating. Experts can tell them apart by the size of their tails and frontal horns. Males tend to have smaller of both.

Their frontal horns start glimmering at the base of the bone. The glimmer swirls up until the tips are little balls of sunshine. The fire then breaks free and floats toward the ceiling. Each ball presses against something stuck to the ceiling in different shapes, which become clearer upon contact with the flame. The balls expand until they mold into the shapes above.

The shapes are letters. When they're all lit up and shining down at me, they read, *¡Bienvenida a nuestro equipo, Lana!* It translates to "Welcome to our team, Lana."

The balls of sunshine keep dispersing into another shape that wraps around the message. It's an outline of some sort. There are several jagged edges, an imperfect drawing that I can't quite recognize, but it takes up the whole ceiling like a fiery mural. Little by little, that imperfect drawing becomes what it really is, burning even brighter than the letters.

It's a map of Puerto Rico.

My country lights up the whole habitat from above. The map is blank save for the welcome message scribbled at its center, which somehow shines even brighter now.

"Oh my God . . ." I haven't stepped foot in Puerto Rico in longer than these dragons have been alive, and yet their love for our land is fueling mine. It's a *part* of mine. And they're treating me like I'm one of them. I'm tearing up. Mom ripped me away from Papi because she'd been afraid of losing me. Now here I am, easy prey for these glorious creatures of magic and might, feeling more alive than ever before. Like I belong.

I take my time bowing at each dragon. "Muchas gracias."

All at once, the six dragons bow their heads in return. Their horns are still aflame. Inch by inch, the fire drops to the base of their bones again, where it flickers once and fades into nothing. The island on the ceiling is bright enough to keep us illuminated.

Luis walks over to the smallest female dragon. She lets him plant a kiss on top of her wide, huffing nose. "Lana, meet my lovely lady, Daga."

Dragons have never explained how their names come about—whether dragons choose them or if they're engraved deep within their consciousness. Not even riders are privy to this information. We only know their names are always in the language of their country of origin and, as some people believe with human names, they can provide a glimpse into their personalities.

"Dagger," I say. "That's what her name translates to in Spanish, right?"

"Sí. She's pure danger." Luis scratches Daga's ear. She unleashes an earth-shattering squeal of joy. One of her hind legs is even stomping the dirt. Oh yeah. Pure danger, indeed.

"This is Puya." Gabriela motions to the cringing male dragon standing next to Daga. He's inching closer to Gabriela as Daga squeals even louder, as if he's ashamed on her behalf.

"Puya," I repeat with a laugh. His name means "pointed stick" in Spanish. There's a dagger and a lance's pointy end working together as Charger steeds. Watch out, other teams.

Gabriela rubs Puya's cheek, which he relishes with a deep purr. It echoes throughout the habitat. Once it dies out, Gabriela says, "He's my best friend. *And* fashion stylist."

"I ride with her." Génesis waves to the female dragon opposite Esperanza. "Rayo."

"Ray of light," I say.

Edwin leans against his male dragon's chest, which has a thin silver birthmark right where his heart should be. It shimmers a little. "Este lindo se llama Fantasma," he says.

Ghost. "Me encanta." I tell him I love the name, and Edwin nods.

Rayo and Fantasma share a glance, as if telling each other a happy secret. So do Génesis and Edwin. It's like they're siblings who have a language only they're allowed to understand.

Héctor pulls out a whole handful of grapes from his pocket. He tosses them to his male dragon one by one. I've never seen an animal chomp down on anything harder in my life.

Luis gasps in sheer outrage. "You gave Titán my grapes?!"

"He deserves them more," Héctor says while Titán licks his lips. "Titán's the second oldest of the group. Esperanza," he waves to the dragon behind Victoria, "is the eldest. Daga is obviously the baby." He shakes his head as Daga keeps squealing. "We all Bonded with them in the same order they were born. So Victoria here was the first official member of the team." He speaks with such pride, and that statue of a girl just glares at me. "And now you get to close our ranks, Lana. We all are so happy to have you be a part of this family."

That last word kicks me square in the chest. These people and these dragons aren't the family I've been given, but as I stand surrounded by so much powerful magic, so much love for Puerto Rico, my heart weighs less than it did yesterday. Yeah, Victoria seems like she isn't cool with me being part of the team, but everything else feels like it suits me just fine.

"Do you have any questions before we get back downstairs?" Joaquín asks me.

"No. This has been incredible." I wave goodbye to the dragons. "Gracias otra vez."

They all bow at me again.

I follow my teammates to the elevator.

Victoria hangs back, though, falling into step with me. I'm about to ask her if there's anything I can do for her when she leans in super close.

"You better be ready to work, new girl." Not even lowering her voice can lessen her roughness. "Everything that happened today? Hold on tight to those memories. Special treatment is officially over. Tomorrow you'll wish you'd never come here."

She storms into the elevator.

I'm rooted to the spot, sinking into whatever's under this floor. There are six other faces before me, but I can only focus on Victoria's. She's still looking at me like I'm ruining her life, even though she legit just threatened me. Or maybe she's trying to pump me up for a grueling training schedule? Either way, I'm not Brian Santana. I'm not getting fired.

Ignore her ignore her ignore her ignore her.

"You okay, Lana?" Gabriela asks.

I answer her with a quick nod, avoiding eye contact with Victoria.

I stay silent as the elevator doors separate me once again from the Sol de Noche dragons.

They might actually be the least dangerous teammates I have.

WHEN I GET BACK TO THE LIVING ROOM, PRESIDENT TURNER AND Manny are deep into an episode of *Law & Order: Magical Crimes Unit*. It's the one where the Regular detectives find a kidnapped Copper witch in her Silver Wand uncle's basement. He runs away at the end of this episode and becomes their main villain for Season Seventeen. I only know this because of Samira. She puts up with my Blazewrath obsession. I put up with her love of *Law & Order*.

"All done with the habitat, I see!" President Turner rises without difficulty, but his hands are trembling a bit. "How did it go?"

I force myself not to stare. "Amazingly well."

He sighs in relief. "That's wonderful to hear, Ms. Torres." With a flick of his wand, he conjures a large golden envelope out of thin air. "Your schedule for the next two weeks is in here. Manny will serve as your guardian for the duration of the Cup, as you know, and this includes making sure you fulfill every commitment. However, you can always contact me if you need anything. Just press three on any phone in this house and it will connect you to me."

Oh wow. He's *that* easy to get in touch with? My teammates all nod, which probably means he told them the same thing.

I take the envelope. "No problem. Thank you so much for everything."

"Thank *you* for being here." President Turner looks at Héctor. "Your team is complete!"

Héctor gives him a high five. "Thank you for helping us, sir. Appreciate it."

"Russell? You have a meeting, remember?" Manny's tone kills the mood.

"Right. The meeting." President Turner glances down at his hands, which are trembling even more now, and he quickly hides them behind his back. "I'll be seeing you all at the welcome party in two nights. Have an excellent rest of your day!"

"You, too, Mr. President," everyone else says.

I don't say a word. His health problems aren't my business, but if he's overexerting himself or skipping meds or whatever, he needs to be more careful.

Once the president's gone, Joaquín says, "Any tour-guide volunteers for Lana?"

Gabriela's hand shoots up like she's in class. "We can do it!" she says, motioning to Génesis and Victoria. Only Génesis is nodding.

"Okay. Go on ahead, ladies."

Gabriela yanks me back to the elevator before I can side-eye Victoria.

THE HOUSE IS TEN TIMES MORE GIGANTIC THAN IT SEEMS.

It has a total of four floors, with one chamber in the fourth, which is the dragons' habitat.

All the dormitories are located on the first floor, hidden behind the double doors on the right side. The girls' dormitory is a sprawling suite with (wait for it) white furniture and marble walls. The floor's marble, too. So are the pillars. There's even a four-pole hammock in the office section. This place screams FANCY GIRLS LIVE HERE, but there are neon fabrics and feather boas on the right side of the room, where two of the four queen-sized beds have been arranged.

"This one's mine." Gabriela rushes over to the bed with the fabrics and boas. Her vanity is filled with candy-scented candles, makeup sets, brush kits, and wigs. Her *Sworn Magazine* cover from April is framed on the wall. She and Edwin are hugging each other as they smolder into the camera. They're both rocking all-black clothes and matching eyeliner. Gabriela has a mint-green wig on. Below their perfectly gorgeous faces, the headline reads, "Their Nation's Pride: How Gabriela Ramos & Edwin Santiago Are Putting Queer Puerto Rico on the Blazewrath Map."

"That was an amazing interview," I tell Gabriela. "I read it on my phone while stuck at dinner with my mother's family. Not even the soufflé could get me to stop caring."

She does a little bow. "Thank you. This bi girl felt immense relief coming out to the world. I won't speak for Edwin, obvi, but I sure felt like a champion." She twirls as she pretends to hold an invisible skirt. "And those *outfits*. I can't even describe how much fun that shoot was."

"It is a beautiful picture," Victoria says, staring longingly at the cover.

"And that's Victoria's side," Génesis says a bit too fast. She shows me the bed next to Gabriela's, which only has plain linen sheets. Victoria's wall is decorated with a note scribbled in super girly handwriting: *Sé el Sol en la Oscuridad.* It translates to "Be the Sun in the Dark."

"That's great advice," I say dryly.

"I know it is. Héctor said that to me when I was thirteen," Victoria admits. "He, Génesis, and I grew up in the same neighborhood in Loíza. He's always known how to make me feel better, but those words on the wall? They saved my life." She's as cold as a winter's breeze. "It's the last thing I said to my stepdad before I beat the shit out of him."

Oh crap. I'd been so busy wondering why she dislikes me that I'd forgotten about her past. While Héctor and Génesis have lovely families, Victoria comes from an abusive household. Her stepdad's in prison now, last I heard, but she spent most of her life enduring his rage. On her thirteenth birthday, he lunged for a vodka bottle, planning to break it on her mother's face.

Victoria grabbed it first.

The second her stepdad lost consciousness, Esperanza landed outside her house.

"Wow. That's intense," is all I can come up with.

"So were his bruises," says Victoria. "I'm still quite proud of them."

"This one over here is my bed," Génesis nervously cuts in. She's moved on to the left side of the room. Hers is the corner bed with a giant stuffed panda sitting on the pillows. She's got *tons* of snapshots of mixed-breed dogs and pit bulls on her wall.

I point to the dogs. "Are those all your rescues?"

"Sí. Bam-Bam and Boo are mine," she taps two of the pit bulls, "but the rest are happy in other forever homes. My sisters are running my rescue while I'm here, but I really miss them."

"What we're doing here is more important," Victoria says. "You change lives on a daily basis, but winning the Cup for our country will change lives, too. This will *save* lives."

I nod. "You're right, Victoria. I just hope we don't have to keep worrying about the Sire."

Victoria looks me up and down like I'm a squashed roach. "Obviously he'll be caught."

Something about the way she uses the word *obviously* makes me want to scream.

"Why don't we let Lana unpack?" Génesis grabs Gabriela and Victoria. "We'll be in the living room setting up movie night. Find us once you're ready."

They leave me to unpack alone. I check my schedule first. Scratch that: *two* schedules. Schedule number one is focused on training. I'll start at 5:00 a.m. and end at 4:00 p.m., which tires me out just by reading it. Schedule number two is all about official Blazewrath duties. The welcome party will be in two days. My uniform fitting and team photo shoot is in four. We find out the team brackets for the Round of

Sixteen on August 2. Opening ceremonies are on August 3. The Cup starts on the fifth.

I collapse onto my empty bed. The sheets are so smooth, it makes me feel like I'm floating.

This is my new home. This is my sun in the dark right now.

Hopefully, the world will be much shinier with news of the Sire's capture in the morning.

"In regard to the age limit for Blazewrath players, we owe that particular rule to dragons. Most Bond exclusively with teenagers, but when riders turn twenty-one, their steeds begin to show little interest in competing. All they want to do is lounge around in their bureau-approved residences and eat. I do not think this is out of laziness. I think they're just waiting for something more. A greater purpose than a game that pits them against one another."

—Transcript from 2007 radio interview with
Perry Jo Smith, IBF founder

CHAPTER EIGHT

THE SIRE IS STILL OUT THERE.

Before breakfast, I checked every news channel and website in the universe. Nobody's mentioned an arrest in the past twenty-four hours. They haven't mentioned Takeshi, either. Those bastards are still free, possibly kidnapping their next victim. There's been no official word on canceling the Cup, so my scheduled training carries on as if the Sire doesn't exist.

"This is how we'll tackle your sessions," says Joaquín. He and I are the only ones inside Training Room D, which has a track wrapping all around it. "First, we train here, then at the gym. We break for lunch. Afternoon sessions are for fight training with the Blockers on the simulated mountain in Training Room E." He pauses. "Let's see if you get that far today."

My morning is dedicated to jogging and sprinting intervals. Despite my intense sweating and flailing, Joaquín praises me every time I fly past the finish line. Then it's off to the gym on the second floor. The team exercises together here. Victoria tosses the occasional scowl in my direction as I do my leg raises, but for the most part, nobody bothers anyone. Lunchtime is pretty quiet, too. Manny doesn't join us at any point. He's probably hiding in his room.

Then it's time to fight.

When I walk through Training Room E's double doors, I'm decked out in protective pads for my elbows, knees, and shoulders, not caring about how ridiculous I look. My teammates already have their uniforms, which they're changing into back in their rooms. The only thing I've got that resembles what I'll wear on the field is a metal helm. It's black, of course, with a strip that's meant to protect my nose.

"Here," Joaquín says as I put it on. "It's been charmed to mold into your head's shape."

The helm is a few inches too big, fit for the Runner who came before me, then shrinks until it's a second skin. I knock on the helm's side twice. A tin-like clanging reverberates around me, but it's not too loud or annoying, and better yet, it doesn't hurt me. Standard helms are molded after what knights wore during the Middle Ages, but some countries take it a step further with designs that engulf your entire face. I'm grateful my team has the old-school version.

Manny finally shows up. He punches a complicated series of numbers into a panel beside the double doors. "The dragons will be with us shortly. Be ready."

The panel beeps twice, then the double doors slide open sideways.

Training Room E is a domed stadium. If I weren't looking at it, I'd think there's no way a stadium as endless as this one could fit inside our house. The Keeper's goalpost, where Héctor will stop the opposing team's Striker from scoring, is at the very end of the stadium. Just like in official matches, the goalpost is built in the shape of a thick, spiky dragon's tail. It's coiled tight, yet spacious enough to let the Rock Flame, the sport's official ball, through its center.

I gasp. The mountain is to the right side of the stadium.

On the Blazewrath field, there are two mountains, one for each Runner. We only have my mountain here. It's made of hardened, sparkling sand. The mountain almost reaches the chamber's skylight, with a curving, narrow pathway upward. The top is a flat, square patch of space, where an altar built from iron sits in the middle. My final destination. A Runner's job is to get an item called the Iron Scale to the top of their mountain before their opponent. Once the Iron Scale has been dropped off, the match ends, and that Runner's team wins.

"Mira eso. Se ve bien, ¿verdad?" Edwin comes up from behind me, asking if this place looks good. More and more footsteps loudly approach.

I've seen their uniforms before. And yet the second I turn, my breath abandons me. The suit's made out of thick black spandex, but the shoulders and chest areas are padded with metal that's been dyed to match the fabric. Right across the metal chest, engraved in white letters, are the words PUERTO RICO. The words shimmer a little. The players' last names and chosen numbers are engraved on their backs. Dark metal cuffs are fitted to the players' forearms. Four spikes protrude out of them. My teammates also sport the same helm as me, along with strapless, knee-high boots. I trust they're easy to handle thanks to a spell.

I've been expecting six athletes.

Instead, here are six warriors ready for the biggest battle of their lives.

"You all look *incredible*," I say.

Luis pats himself down. "I was much worse off the first time I came in here."

"He cried," says Gabriela. "A lot."

"So did you!"

"Yeah, but your sniffling was louder than hers." Héctor delivers the final blow.

Luis throws his arms up. "It was an emotional moment! What more do you want from me, man? First, you steal my grapes, and now you're calling me a sniffling crier?"

"No, señor. You just called *yourself* a sniffling crier."

"Positions, everyone," says a grinning Joaquín.

Victoria, Gabriela, Héctor, and Luis head for the main field. Edwin and Génesis run over to the mountain. I spot the Runner's mark at the base and jog my way there.

Blazewrath isn't a game where one can rack up points. It's more of a who-gets-there-first deal. It could take a Striker one minute to several hours to score. The longest match on record remains the 2015 quarter-finals showdown between Scotland and Spain. It had lasted five hours because neither Striker could get the Rock Flame through the goalpost. The Runner is stuck at the bottom of the mountain until that score is made, which especially sucks when the rival team scores first. Their Runner could be at the top by the time it's *your* turn to start running.

WHOOSH!

A gust of wind almost knocks me down. I flinch and shield myself, but the wind is gone.

The dragons have materialized inside Training Room E.

Actually, materializing might not be the right word. The dragons are outlines of themselves. Starker versions of the images you'd find in a coloring book. Swirls of dark smoke drift around each dragon as they fill up their scales with their natural blackness. Now they're flesh and bone. They stand in a semicircle formation on the main field.

"Whoa. They can use their magic to *appear out of thin air*?"

Joaquín nods. "They can Fade from one place to another."

Fade. That's a much better word for it. "How come the public doesn't know about it?"

"It wasn't until three weeks ago that they manifested this ability during practice. President Turner and the IBF don't know about it yet. I wanted to observe them more first." He taps his notebook with his pen. "A shame they can't Fade with their riders yet. We've tried several times, but so far, the dragons have only been capable of using this magic alone. Best to be patient."

I raise my eyebrows. Three weeks ago? That's right around the same time the Sire came out of hiding. Horrible things and wonderful things happened simultaneously. That's how the world works, but these specific things all involved dragons.

Relax. Maybe it's just a weird coincidence.

"¿Qué pasó?" comes Manny's voice from my left.

"Nothing. We were just going over the rules." Joaquín angles his wheelchair toward the edge of the pathway. His expression is as calm as if he's been discussing the weather. "Lana, you'll be waiting for Victoria to score behind that white line. Runners and Blockers must fight one another using a variety of martial arts, but most Blockers aren't as fast as Runners. From what I saw in your tryout application, you don't have any formal combat training, do you?"

"No, but I've practiced with videos on the Internet." Mom would've known something was weird if I'd signed up for classes. "I'll try to be so fast, they won't have time to fight me."

"There you go. Your main strategy will indeed be to outrun your opponents. They can't stop you if they can't catch you." Joaquín offers me an encouraging smile. "We're going to start as all matches start. Victoria will take the Rock Flame to the goalpost. Luis and Gabriela will escort her to the goal and defend her from aerial threats. Héctor will guard the goal. You, Edwin, and Génesis stay put until Victoria scores. For this first run, you won't be taking the Iron Scale with you. The dragons won't be throwing fireballs at you, either. We have to see how you do in hand-to-hand combat. The Blockers will pursue you once you reach the Block Zones."

I nod and mumble a quick "Got it."

Show them you belong here.

Fantasma and Rayo hover near the mountain, getting ready to attack me.

Joaquín uses a megaphone to communicate with Victoria, Gabriela, Luis, and Héctor. They nod to his instructions in Spanish. They mount their steeds at the same time. The dragons unfurl their wings together, soaring into the air in a straight line. Titán and Héctor dive toward the goalpost. Each rider steers by leaning and backing away from their dragons. Victoria's the only one who hangs on to Esperanza with one hand. She's holding the Rock Flame in the other.

Joaquín blows his whistle. The first part of the match starts now.

Victoria and Esperanza zoom across the field. Luis and Daga fly to their left, Gabriela and Puya to their right. Soon enough, Esperanza is sandwiched between her Charger teammates.

Joaquín pulls out a silver stick thing from his windbreaker's pocket; a blinking red button is perched at the very end. "Activating blasters." He presses it once.

The ground shakes. Three holes appear on each side of the field, like circles leading to the depths of hell. Instead of bats or demons, though, all that come out are long metal cylinders. The blasters aim to where the Striker and Charger dragons fly above.

Joaquín presses the red button again.

Fireballs shoot out of the blasters on the left. All three fireballs are flying straight toward Esperanza, but Daga and Puya crisscross between each other. They're batting the flames with their tails. The dragons are equally fluid and fast, weaving a thread out of shadows and rage.

With another press of the red button, Joaquín unleashes constant streams of fire from the blasters on the right. Victoria speeds up toward Héctor, but Luis and Gabriela whoop and holler as their steeds take turns opening fire at the oncoming flames. Daga and Puya push back the enemy fire, sending it back to the blasters that shot them out. Gabriela kisses Puya's neck, then leads him to the goalpost alongside Luis and Daga.

I let out a gasp. Victoria is standing on top of Esperanza's head. Poised and careful, she throws her arm back. Esperanza slams mercilessly into Titán. She's a freight train without brakes. Once the dragons clash, Victoria leaps into the air, swinging her arm forward.

Héctor also leaps up. He raises his arms to grab the Rock Flame.

But Victoria doesn't throw it. The moment Héctor jumps, she sinks back down. Victoria rolls under Héctor's feet, all over Titán's back, stopping just shy of his tail. She then tosses the Rock Flame at the goalpost with a primal scream.

The Rock Flame flies right through the goal.

"*Yes!*" I'm clapping like it's a real match.

Joaquín blows the first whistle for me. The second part of the match has begun.

My hands touch the sand, one knee bent. I've done this a million times. I won't even need to show these people how terrible I am at fighting because *they won't catch me.*

Joaquín blows the second whistle.

I fly across the sand.

Fantasma and Rayo dive for the mountain, but I'm focused on the pathway. It stays level for a few paces, then rises into a coil that fully wraps around the mountain. There are three Block Zones ahead—the only places where Blockers can dismount their steeds and engage me in combat. Their goal is to steal the Iron Scale attached to the Runner's belt, then toss it back to the foot of the mountain. Runners will have to go back and fetch it, losing valuable time. Block Zones are also where the Blockers' steeds are forced to stop blasting fire at me. Red lines mark their beginnings and ends on either side. The first Block Zone is the longest one, spanning forty feet, which is enough for any Blocker to drop in and deliver a beating for the ages. I blow past the red line, entering the first Block Zone with energy to boot.

Wings flap somewhere around me. Either Fantasma or Rayo approaches from the right.

All my strength is devoted to crossing that other red line. I'm halfway there, then closer and closer until it's only a matter of a couple of steps.

Edwin jumps right in front of me. He grabs my arm and yanks me back. My butt finds the ground first. Since there's no Iron Scale to steal from me, Edwin places both legs at my sides, trapping me where I sit. He stares at me like this is easier than he expected.

No. You're not going to beat me.

I slide under him, then push myself up to a standing position.

Edwin grabs me again, this time by my waist. He pulls me down before I know what's going on. When I stand, he kicks my legs from under me, sending me to the ground quicker. I aim a kick at his shins, but he evades it like a pro. Once I'm up again, I throw punch after punch at him, which he sidesteps effortlessly. He's not fighting me back. Every time I try to swerve and flee, he's there to drop me like a ragdoll. I lose count of how many falls I've racked up. Edwin sneaks in one last knockdown. I choke out a yell as I hit the sand, weak and sweaty and *done.*

I'm supposed to be faster than him. I'm supposed to not have time to fight him.

Edwin offers to lift me up, and I let him, regardless of how ashamed I am. He and I both search for Joaquín at the bottom of the mountain, where he's clicking a megaphone on.

"Okay," says a hopeful Joaquín. "Let's try it again."

I never make it past the first Block Zone.

Fourteen different attempts. All failed. Edwin is an unmovable force. I know I'm not good at fighting, but this is ridiculous. And I don't even know what awaits me with Génesis.

Manny's not even here anymore. He left at some point during my multiple defeats.

I sit on the sand next to Joaquín, deflating with every gulp of bottled spring water.

Joaquín waits for me to finish before speaking. "Génesis and Edwin will take you to their training room now. Outrunning the Blockers isn't enough. There'll be no more practice on the mountain for you until you can at least master the basics of repelling an attacker."

Oh, for the love of God. "I don't get to watch the rest of practice?"

"Not today, Lana. Go train with the Blockers."

Génesis, Edwin, and I leave Training Room E, but I'm the only one with my head down. I'm supposed to use my real uniform for practice soon. I'm supposed to run from real fire and carry a spot-on replica of the Iron Scale to the top of the mountain. This first day is baby food compared to what lies ahead. And yet here I am, sucking way worse than expected.

If I keep this up, I won't have to worry about the Sire threatening the Cup again.

I'll get kicked off the team before I even see the Blazewrath stadium.

The Bond always begins the same way. Soon after a dragon is born,
they invite a human to ride with them through psychic communication.
Once the invitation is accepted, dragon and rider are entwined for life.
But why do some dragons connect with humans while others refuse to?
This is where the theory of a destined rider-dragon Bond falls apart.
It would suggest that the universe has designed certain dragons to hate
humans. Or perhaps this is the perfect cosmic balance. Some dragons try
to kill us; others have been sent to keep us alive. The universe, it seems,
is playing a game of chess. We just need to figure out how long we have
left until checkmate.

—*Excerpt from Carlos Torres's* Studying the Bond
Between Dragons & Humans

CHAPTER NINE

FIGHTING ISN'T HALF AS FUN AS IT LOOKS ON TV.
    I have to accept someone else into my space. I have to study them and predict how they're going to move. I have to already know how to defeat them before they even try.

    Edwin and Génesis have zero issues with this. For most of the session in Training Room C, they have me doing slower, no-contact versions of their moves on the field. They show me how to properly place my feet and shoulders to deliver a punch. Then they have me using my elbows to strike even more invisible opponents behind me. I turn and hit, dizzying myself until I learn how to keep my eyes focused on a spot on the wall. Both Génesis and Edwin are hell-bent on having me build up speed and strength.

"Very good. Now let's try something different." Génesis gets in front of me. "Move."

Her fist shoots out toward me.

I squat way too fast, lose my balance again, and land on my butt.

"Try doing it like this." Génesis leans to the left and lowers her head.

I get back up. "Okay."

She sends another fist my way.

I squat even lower this time.

"You might injure yourself if you keep that up," says Génesis. "Let's go again."

An hour later, I can gracefully lean away from a punch. I can throw one in return, too, relying on my core strength and feet placement to get the job done. Edwin also takes his time showing me how to tilt my whole body to drive two quick jabs. Once the session is over, I drop to the mat, dripping as much sweat as the body is capable of producing.

"Tomorrow we practice grappling and tossing. Edwin will lead the session." Génesis puts a bottle of water and a clean, lavender-scented towel next to me. "No eres una causa perdida." She tells me I'm not a lost cause, which I'm choosing to take as a compliment.

I gulp down the whole bottle at once. "Did you two train in karate alone?"

Génesis points at herself. "Karate and kickboxing."

Edwin simply says, "Judo."

"Nice. So is Joaquín coming to tomorrow's session?"

"Most likely," says Génesis. "He probably stayed with the others today because he's been trying to get Daga to master one of the dive-and-turn techniques. She's a bit slower than Puya."

"What about Manny? Will he be here, too, or is he going to hide in his room all day?" I don't intend to sound bitter, but I can't help it. It's not so much like he's keeping a respectful distance from us so we can train in peace. It's more like he's doing his best to *avoid* us.

"He'll probably stay in his room," Génesis says.

What a wonderful guy. "Has he always been this distant?"

Génesis and Edwin share a look. While Génesis's expression suddenly shifts into a frown, Edwin seems even more serious than Victoria.

"Pues realmente no," he tells me. "Todo comenzó cuando Brian se fue."

This all started when Brian left?

"Why did he get fired?" I dare to ask.

"Because he punched me." Edwin speaks the words in English as if he's practiced them for people other than his teammates. "*Sworn Magazine?*"

My hairs stand on end. That waste of human skin hit Edwin after he came out publicly? I'm glad I never met him, then. I'm even happier I'm taking his spot.

Well, technically, I'm *sucking* at taking his spot, but it's still mine.

"Sí," I say. "Excelente entrevista. I'm so proud of you."

"Gracias." Edwin smiles. "Cuando trató de darme otra vez, lo dejé inconsciente." Edwin had knocked him the hell out when Brian tried to hit him again.

"Good. He deserved it," I say. "Manny was the one to fire him, wasn't he?"

"He called the IBF immediately," says Génesis. "Manny was so kind to Edwin and Gabriela, and he'd been such a warm soul to the rest of us, too. But then he left for London to meet with the IBF after Brian's firing. When he came back to San Juan, he wasn't the same man who treated us like his kids. He barely spoke, and he just . . . checked out."

That sounds more like the man I know.

After I thank Edwin for sharing his story with me, I clap softly. "So. Is it shower time?"

"Yes, please. You desperately need it," Génesis says.

I pretend to hit her with the towel, which makes Edwin crack up. Then I toss my water bottle at the nearest trash can, but it lands two feet away.

Now Edwin and Génesis are *both* laughing at me. Awesome.

"I promise I'll fight better than I throw," I say. "A *lot* better."

"I'm choosing to believe you," says Génesis. "Come on, Lana. Let's get cleaned up."

On the way to my room, Edwin and Génesis discuss everything from tomorrow's training session to their Doritos cravings. I'm still stuck on the man who went cold. There has to be a way to figure out the cipher that is Manuel Delgado. What happened in London? Manny hadn't been a fan of Brian, so something else must've rattled him.

Looks like my team's dragons aren't the only ones who can Fade away.

THE NEXT DAY, JOAQUÍN SPENDS MOST OF HIS TIME SUPERVISING MY fight training.

"You have to move faster." He states the obvious. I'm pretty sure he's regretting his decision to leave Manny upstairs with the rest of the team. Manny must be stoked to avoid my major fails again, even if that means standing in Victoria's insufferable presence.

"Lana? Did you hear me?" Joaquín says.

"Uh-huh . . . " I'm sprawled like a snow angel on the mat, bathed in sweat and self-loathing. This is the eleventh time I've fallen in an effort to run past Edwin. He's taking me down as if I'm a LEGO castle, easily breakable and scattered into pieces.

It doesn't get any better throughout the rest of practice. I'm sucking at maximum level.

Though, according to Génesis and Joaquín, I'm quite good at

punching and kicking. The trick is to punch and kick without exposing the Iron Scale to the enemy Blocker, which I don't know how I'm going to pull off, especially since I have no clue what the Iron Scale feels like dangling from my hips.

After that mess of a practice, I head to my dormitory to start prepping for tonight's welcome party. Festivities are still on schedule despite the Sire's silence. There's been some press coverage of Agent Robinson's funeral, but it's mostly been about his secret career. Turns out Agent Robinson was one of the bureau's best spies. Only a handful of agents knew about him until the Sire revealed he worked for Magical Investigations. It's like his life stopped right after he graduated high school, which was when he disappeared from the public eye.

There are also reports that Sayuri Endo, Takeshi's mother, has been taken to bureau headquarters for interrogation on her son's crimes. Most sites are speculating she's planning to come to Dubai and protest the Cup in honor of Hikaru. She hasn't confirmed or denied anything.

Whatever. My focus should be on the welcome party. I'm *finally* meeting the other teams.

I'll also spend time with President Turner. Hopefully he's feeling better. Not hearing from him since my arrival could just be a result of his super-busy schedule. But what if he's helping the bureau catch the Sire? How is he even capable of playing such a role in the case?

I could ask him tonight.

"So who's showering first?" Gabriela asks once we're back in our room. "I vote me, because I take the longest to prep and glam. I still haven't picked an outfit yet." She checks out a huge rack of clothes someone's left beside the office desk, where I'm currently firing up the computer. Joaquín said our team stylist won't be arriving until photo-shoot day, but she's sent over some options for tonight's event. "Do you ladies know what you're wearing?"

"Anything red," says Victoria.

Génesis points to a pale-green halter dress. "That looks pretty."

Gabriela takes it off the rack and hands it over to her. "Lana? What about you?"

"Oh, don't worry. Pick whatever you want, and I'll see what's left afterward."

Only Victoria stares at me like she suspects I've committed a crime.

"Okay. See you soon!" Gabriela disappears into the bathroom.

Génesis checks her phone. "Wow, so many missed calls from the animal shelter . . ." She power walks out of the bedroom, dialing at lightning speed. "Be right back!"

Victoria waves goodbye as she sifts through the dresses.

I open up Google on the computer. I could do a quick search for Sire updates. But I don't want to drag that negative energy into what's supposed to be a celebration. So I fire up YouTube instead. Watching Monsta X music videos will surely make me feel better.

"Why are you sucking so much?" Victoria stands three inches away. She's holding a pair of gold sandals along with a short red dress. "Is something distracting you from doing your best? Or have you always sucked?"

Is. She. For real? "What did you just say?"

"You heard me. What you did on the mountain was humiliating, Lana. And I heard you weren't any better today." Victoria sneers. "I don't get it. What makes you so damn special?"

This is the second time she's cornered me. I might not know what makes me so damn special, but she's the biggest coward in the world.

My smile is tight. "When was the last time *you* stood up to a Dragon Knight, Victoria?"

Her eyes shoot venom at me. "You're not getting paid to stand up to Dragon Knights. This team is talented. We *deserve* to be here." Her laugh is a brusque taunt. "The others won't say it to your face, but we all feel the same way. You're dragging us down. I will *never*"—

she gets closer to my face—"let you be the reason we lose. So get your shit together, and Do. Your. Job."

Victoria saunters over to her bed. She tries on the sandals as if everything's normal.

With clenched fists, I open my mouth, but nothing comes out. Do the others really feel like I'm dragging them down? Have they been pretending to like me this whole time? President Turner *did* handpick me, and not even Manny got to chime in. Is that the only reason they've been acting like they're cool with the girl who lives in the States joining the team?

They have no other choice . . .

A tear slips down my cheek. I sniffle and pat my eyes dry before more tears burst out.

Génesis storms back into the room. "Okay! What'd I miss?"

"Nothing." I scroll down the music videos, but I'm not in the mood for fun. Not even the prospect of the welcome party is exciting anymore. Not if I'm going with people who hate me.

I still need answers from the president. Namely, why did he offer me a spot on the team during a bureau interrogation? Manny's coldness and even Victoria demanding to know why I'm here . . . it all leads back to President Turner. Papi warned me to be careful of his intentions.

Tonight, I'm going to find out what they are.

Edward Barnes was fifteen years old when a Fire Drake flew out of the North Sea. The dragon found him on the steps of Foxrose Preparatory School for the Magically Gifted, where Barnes and his best friend, Russell Turner, were playing their usual game of cards. Barnes had never expected to Bond with a dragon, seeing as wizards are rarely chosen as riders, but the young Gold Wand immediately accepted the Bond and cheerfully flew away with his new steed. Even though only Barnes was privy to his true name, the world knows him as the Sire.

—*Excerpt from Julissa Mercado's article*
"A Cursed Life: How a Gold Wand Saved the World"
in The Weekly Scorcher

CHAPTER TEN

"THE DESERT SUN-KISSED GLAM LOOK IS OFFICIALLY conquered. What do you think?"

Gabriela puts me in front of the full-length mirror. She frames my face with her hands like she's voguing. Since she's wearing a million golden bangles on each arm, the room becomes a concert hall with the sounds of clanging metal. They match her gold pleated dress and heels.

My whole face is covered in makeup thanks to her, but it's so natural looking and un-cakey that it doesn't bother me. I'm rocking bronze winged eyeliner, which shimmers a lot. My outfit is a bit more laid back. I've chosen the ballet-slipper-pink crop top, matching knee-length skirt, and strappy mauve sandals that will let me bust a move if warranted.

"Awesome," I tell Gabriela. "You should do this professionally."

Gabriela is a ball of light. "That means so much, Lana! Thank you!"

There's no clear sign she's faking it, but Victoria's words still ring in my head.

Gabriela is just being nice not to hurt your feelings. Don't buy into it.

I give Gabriela a thumbs-up. "Sure . . ."

"We're done, right? We can go now?" Victoria crosses her arms by the door. Even though she's elegant in a belted ruby dress, her scowl sucks the charm out of her.

Breathe. Ignore her. Repeat.

If Génesis could roll her eyes any harder, they'd fall out of their sockets. "Yes. We're done," she says, gorgeous in her green dress and honey flats. "Lead the way, Victoria."

The guys are waiting for us in the living room, all wearing dress shirts and pants. Luis is the only one with a bow tie. It's bright coral, just like his shirt. Edwin is adjusting a silver earpiece to his left ear, which will translate anything spoken in English into Spanish. Héctor tells us we look beautiful while Joaquín and Manny emerge past the double doors. Both Delgado men are in head-to-toe black, but Joaquín softens the look with a smile.

Manny does a quick head count, then says gruffly, "Vámonos, mi gente."

The welcome party is right here in the Compound. An enormous white silk tent has been erected in between both rows of houses. Each house's entrance has a white carpet leading to the tent, where electronic music blares into the sky. Tons of security guards swarm the tent in polished black suits. Gabriela and Luis dance their way down the carpet. Héctor pretends to photograph them like a desperate paparazzo. Everyone laughs except me. Well, and Manny, too. He makes it to the tent's entrance first, parting the silk drapes aside for the team to file in.

The whole place is covered in comfy white couches. Some have green and black pillows. Others have white and red pillows. The four colors of the United Arab Emirates flag. Flowers have been arranged into intricate pillars on each corner. The flowers are light yellow with five petals, small and delicate. I see dinner tables with catering trays shaped like dragon claws, dishes from each of the countries represented in this year's Cup, and a separate stage with a photo booth. It even has a green screen and costume props.

To the left side of the tent, a large dragon sculpture has chocolate cascading out of its mouth. Assorted trays filled with fruit surround it. While I drool over the prospect of fudgy goodness, Gabriela gawks at those tubular glass chandeliers Aunt Jenny loves to collect pictures of on the Internet. They look like a bunch of elongated glasses of water have been glued together and somebody decided to call them art. The largest chandelier hangs above the DJ's stage, which is currently manned by a tall Black girl with short dreads. She's spinning beats like a pro.

"Holy crap. Is that Onesa Ruwende?" I point to one of the stunning Blockers from Team Zimbabwe. She's the only Blocker to have defeated every single Runner she's ever faced.

"That is indeed Onesa," an olive-skinned man says. He's standing next to Manny, with warmth in his brown eyes, sporting a navy kurta and white pants. "Welcome to the start of Cup festivities! My name is Asim Haddad. I'm the IBF's ambassador here in the city of Dubai and your host for the evening." He takes his time to shake everyone's hand. "Make yourselves at home. We have traditional cuisine from your country, as well as from the other participating nations. You can use the photo booth however many times you desire. We have a chocolate fountain over there"—he points to the dragon sculpture—"and the dance floor is always open."

"You don't have to tell me twice," says Luis.

Ambassador Haddad cracks up. "Please let me know if there's anything I can do to assist you. Enjoy your evening!" He claps Manny on the back. "A quick word, Mr. Delgado?"

Manny follows him to one of the couches, where a group of other IBF people are sitting. President Turner isn't among them. He'll probably be fashionably late. Maybe he'll show up even after all the teams have arrived. No big deal. I have all night to talk to him.

"We're the first ones here?" Génesis asks. "With the exception of Onesa, of course."

"We've failed our country already by being on time to a party," Gabriela jokes.

Héctor shakes his head, but he's smirking. "Come on. Let's go say hi."

"You go on ahead. I'll get some food," says Joaquín.

I follow my teammates on the way to the stage.

Onesa gasps when she spots us. She jumps offstage and hugs us one by one. God, she's even taller in person. And her amber eyes pierce through my soul. "Hello!" she chirps in a soft voice that clashes with her bulging biceps. "You all look amazing tonight. How are you doing?"

"You're Onesa Ruwende," I say. "You. Are. Onesa. Freaking. *Ruwende.*"

"Fangirl alert. Proceed with caution," Luis says into his shirtsleeve like he's security.

Onesa laughs her trademark husky laugh. "And you're Lana Freaking Torres."

I swallow hard. That name isn't meaning much, but she doesn't know about the mountain or the failed fighting sessions. She has no idea my teammates think I'm dragging them down. Tonight is about figuring out President Turner's real agenda, but it's also about burying the worst parts of me. Nobody can see me break. Especially those who *do* intend to break me on the field.

"So? *No one* can get past you." I gape at this wondrous girl with her wondrous track record. Well, her whole crew is incredible. Team Zimbabwe comprises mostly girls. Their only boy, Wataida

Midzi, holds his own as their Charger, but the girls are legends.

Onesa does a little bow. "I can't wait to see if we'll meet on the mountain."

"You're going down if that's the case," Gabriela says playfully. "Lana will smoke you."

"She'd better," a snide Victoria cuts in.

I'm about to say something when a boy's voice catches me off guard.

"Behold! An angel has landed on Earth!"

I recognize him, but still I turn around in shock. Seven white teens are approaching. The boy leading the pack is stacked like a wrestler, with lip and septum piercings. His hair is dyed the color of blueberries. Kirill Volkov, one of the Russian Blockers, beams at Edwin.

"Hello." The wattage of his smile is out of this world. "A pleasure to meet you, Edwin. My name is Kirill Volkov. I know your *Sworn Magazine* interview by heart. You're stunning both inside and out. If you allow it, I would love the honor of getting to know you better."

My jaw has never fallen this fast.

"¡Dile algo!" a giddy Gabriela begs Edwin to say something to Kirill.

But Edwin only blushes, his eyes darting from Kirill to the floor.

"Please forgive him. He's currently in distress." Artem Volkov, Kirill's twin brother, grabs Kirill's shoulders as if to restrain him. While Kirill has blueberry hair, Artem shaves his head and has a thick scar under his left eye. "He hasn't seen *The Little Mermaid* in three days."

"Four. It's been a difficult week," Kirill says.

Edwin laughs but still doesn't say anything. He just blushes even harder.

Kirill runs a hand through his hair to reveal his left ear. A blue earpiece has been carefully placed inside. "It's programmed to translate Spanish. I hear it in Russian."

I'm dead. It's such a small, simple gesture, but it's the sweetest thing I've seen in a while.

Edwin's still beet red, but he tells Kirill, "Gracias, chico. Me encantaría conocerte mejor."

He'd love to get to know Kirill better.

Kirill looks like he's won the Cup already. "You have excellent judgment."

"Let me remind you there are other people in front of you, Kirill," says a deadpan Artem.

"Really? I hadn't noticed," says Kirill. "Hello, other people!"

He and his teammates introduce themselves, but of course I know them all. Russia is an iconic team. They're the most physically intimidating athletes alive, mercilessly plowing through their opponents during the last Cup. They got third place because they'd squared off against unbeatable Japan in the semifinals. Also, every member is part of the LGBT community. Artem and their Striker, Kristina Ivanova, recently came out as bisexual. They're wearing pride-flag pins. Kirill was the first member of the team to tell the world he's gay.

When Kirill reaches me, he says, "If it isn't the Puerto Rican Bullet!" He leans in closer, suddenly serious. "Can I call you Bullet?"

"Only if I can call you Blueberry," I say with a straight face.

He winks at me. "Done."

"Are *any* of you going to dance?" Onesa asks.

So we start dancing. At first, it's all raising roofs and shimmies galore. When Onesa plays some old-school hip-hop, the dance floor becomes Swaying Hips Central. Kirill is giving Edwin some space, but Edwin shifts from dancing with Génesis to dancing with him. Victoria lets Luis spin her around for a while, then she joins Joaquín at the couch. Dancing must not be her thing.

Salsa music is playing when another team walks into the tent. Then another and another, until all I see are superstars. Argentina and Egypt make a beeline for the biggest couches. South Korea, México, Portugal, and China are in rapt conversation with one another as they strut to the food stations. Pakistan and Sweden arrive at the same time, sharing jokes with each other. Some of the Spanish players check out the chocolate fountain, along with Guatemala. France has taken control of the photo booth. They're snapping pics like it's an Olympic sport. Gustavo Pabón, the Venezuelan Striker, indulges in an arepa as he waves at me from afar. I wave back.

"I'm really thirsty!" Gabriela says over the music. "Let's get something to drink!"

"Okay!" I tell her.

She, Génesis, and I weave our way past the Swedish Chargers, who are singing ten times louder than Luis. Ambassador Haddad is sitting with Joaquín now. The Russian manager and trainer are also at the couch. I scope out Manny across the tent. He's alone at the bar, scrolling through his phone with a sour expression. His glass of vodka is almost finished.

If he drinks some more, he could spill some valuable secrets.

This is your chance.

"Excuse me, are you Lana Torres?"

I halt seconds before crashing into a white boy. He has dark-brown hair, hazel-green eyes, and a bit of stubble. He towers over me in his black The Skids T-shirt. Butterflies bounce all over my stomach. I'm standing in front of Andrew Galloway, Scottish Runner extraordinaire.

And Takeshi's best friend.

The last time I saw him, he'd punched Antonio Deluca on live television. They'd been in the press-conference room after Japan's victory two years ago. Takeshi had been giving his victory speech as team captain, and an envious Antonio clocked him in front of the whole world. So Andrew clocked Antonio right back. Security intervened before they could break any bones, but their fight had happened the day before Hikaru's murder and Antonio's disappearance.

"You're Andrew Galloway," I say stupidly.

"So I've been told for the past nineteen years," he delivers with a smirk. "If you have any name suggestions, I'd love to hear them. Unless they're nature or gemstone related."

Génesis and Gabriela laugh. I don't. Andrew probably knows about Waxbyrne. He might be hoping to fish for details.

Then he says, "Lana, do you like chocolate?"

Random much? "Um, yeah. Chocolate's great."

"Would you mind joining me over at the chocolate fountain?"

Yeah, I do mind. I have a team manager to corner.

"Actually, I need to check in with Manny real quick. It won't take long."

"Oh, this will be even quicker," says Andrew. "I promise." He's giving me major puppy-dog eyes. The dude even puts his hands together in prayer form. "Please."

Manny is still alone. He'll probably still be alone by the time I'm done with Andrew.

I blow out a sigh. "Okay . . ."

Andrew and I walk across the edge of the dance floor, where Luis is now grinding with Adriana de León, the Guatemalan Keeper. I ignore the thumbs-up he flashes me after noticing Andrew next to me. The path to the chocolate fountain is cleared, since the newly arrived Scotland is now the center of attention at the other side of the tent. Andrew motions for me to skip ahead of him. The dragon spills liquid chocolate to the stone base below, where a rich pool of dark milk swirls counterclockwise. I grab a white metal skewer and stick it into a slice of honeydew. Then I dip the slice into the pool, rolling it all the way around so it gets extra coated.

Andrew puts three marshmallows on his skewer. "Time to live dangerously."

I jump right to it. "So what do you want?"

"A full beard, mostly. Mine doesn't grow all that much."

"Right." I pull the honeydew out of the pool. He smiles as I bite into my slice, relishing the mix of decadent gooeyness and punchy sweetness. "For real. What's this about?"

Andrew takes his skewer out, placing the first marshmallow inches from his lips. "This is about saving the world. And I can't do that alone." He tugs the marshmallow free with his teeth. After he's done chewing it, he says, "You've seen the Sire's video, haven't you?"

The wind is knocked out of me. "Yeah . . ."

"And you've met my best friend, too."

My eyebrows are a hard-pressed line. "He's not the boy you remember."

"He's still a good person, trust me." Andrew lowers his head, lost in his thoughts. His sigh could devastate even Victoria on her chilliest day. It's the sound of someone who nourishes himself with a steady diet of longing. "This is all for Hikaru. I can *feel* it."

Great. He's fallen into the same trap I did. "Good people don't steal crystal hearts and murder bureau agents. I get why you think he might have ulterior motives, but he's doing *terrible* things, Andrew."

His gaze hardens. "I know him. You don't."

"No, you *knew* him. That boy is dead. He's not coming back."

I hate myself for tearing up. I hate that I have to argue with Andrew Galloway. I've been his fan since I first saw him race past Blockers in the 2013 Cup. I cheered when he punched Hikaru's suspected murderer. The last thing I want is to make him feel like crap.

"You're wrong," he says sternly. "He's trying to save the world, and we have to help him."

I fight the urge to ask if we're secretly filming for a prank TV show. The boy I met at Waxbyrne doesn't want to save *anything*. "What are you talking about, Andrew?"

"I saw what you did at Waxbyrne. You saved that Fire Drake without a second thought. Now I'm here to ask you if you're willing to save more lives."

I shouldn't talk to him. He's still grieving Takeshi's loss. He's not thinking clearly.

"How do you suggest I do that?"

"Blazewrath means a lot to me, but I want no part in a tournament that will result in the death of innocents if it carries on." Andrew checks for eavesdroppers again. "The IBF is being reckless and proud because the wrong people are putting the heat on them. They don't care about a terrorist who's releasing Un-Bonded dragons. What they *do* care about is us."

I take a step back, breathing hard. He shouldn't be this right. Of course I want the Sire gone, too. How does this guy think he can ensure the Cup goes on *and* lives are saved?

"What's your plan?"

"You and I need to stand in front of a camera during the opening ceremonies and express our desire to have the Cup canceled. We need to show solidarity with the Cup's protesters and the sanctuaries doing their best to protect themselves." Andrew's starting to smile again. "Once the world sees us fighting back, they'll join us. Others will see their new favorite girl, the most Googled human being this week, and they'll stand beside her."

I'm hearing every word, but there's only one thing reverberating through me.

A loud, sharp thing: *No.*

"The Cup *needs* to happen, Andrew. This is my only dream in life."

Andrew rolls his eyes. "It's a lot of people's only dream in life, but—"

"You don't get it. This is about more than winning a Cup." I stab another honeydew slice with my skewer, but my appetite's gone. Andrew gets to go home and fit in just fine. He doesn't have to think about being an outsider, not even on his own team. I could tell him this, but what's the point? He's never going to understand. "I won't ask for the Cup's cancelation. Pitch me a way to catch the Sire, and I'm all in."

Andrew raises an eyebrow as he draws nearer. "We stop him by ending his killing spree."

"And how do *you* know he'll really stop killing once the Cup is canceled? You cannot be this naive!" My voice rises with each word. Maybe speaking louder will make the message pierce his thick skull. "Besides, if you protest, it could backfire."

Andrew looks behind him. Nobody's coming. "How do you mean?"

"We're Runners, Andrew. We could look like traitors for telling our teammates what to do with their dragons. We'll even be traitors to our *countries*. You know how beloved this sport is. It's an institution bigger than the two of us."

"Our voices can change that. You're their golden girl now. You were brought here so you could shift the conversation in the IBF's favor. They won't fire you for speaking out. They need you running up that mountain."

Wow. He thinks I'm a publicity stunt. I'm here to make people forget about Hikaru's death, Antonio Deluca's disappearance, and Takeshi Endo's new allegiance to a tyrant. I'm the syrupy antidote to the Sire's threats.

I'm not a Runner. I'm not a Blazewrath player. I'm a tool.

"What do you say?" a tense Andrew asks.

"No." I push my shoulders back. "I'm choosing to resist in other ways."

Andrew's mood sours at once. "How?"

"For starters, *talking* to President Turner. He told me the IBF is cooperating with the bureau. Chances are he knows more than we do."

"Won't do a thing, lass. Guarantee it." He waves to the couches. "Do you see him here?"

Crap. President Turner is still nowhere to be found.

"Besides"—Andrew's voice is at an all-time low—"Edward Barnes and the president were best mates. Turner has known the Sire for years.

I highly doubt his hands are completely clean if the bureau's up his arse about his past."

Double crap. The Sire's former rider *was* President Turner's best friend, which means he knew the Sire when he was still a dragon. Knowing someone doesn't make you guilty of their crimes, but what if there's some truth to what Andrew's saying? President Turner could've even been on the Sire's side before he unleashed his chaos.

I gasp. "London . . ."

"What?"

"Nothing." Whatever Manny saw or heard in London rattled him enough to change his whole personality. Could it have been related to the president's association with the Sire? Did Manny stumble upon something he wasn't supposed to know?

Stop it, Lana. There has to be some logical explanation to this mess.

"Earth to Lana?"

I clear my throat. "Please don't boycott the Cup. It'll make you a pariah among the teams and their steeds. And *please* don't treat me like your bargaining chip."

Andrew's deep frown could break the thickest iceberg. "That's not what you are at all."

"Save it. We're done here." I toss the uneaten slices into a trash bin behind me, then place the skewer on an empty dragon claw tray. "Have a lovely evening."

Andrew's a wall in my path. "We're not superstars, Lana. We're not heroes. We're just prisoners in the biggest cellblock in the world. Your silence is going to keep us all locked up."

I swerve past him.

Manny isn't at the bar anymore. I do a quick sweep of the tent, but he's gone.

Thanks, Andrew . . .

Zimbabwe arrives as I plop down next to Gabriela on the couch.

Onesa jumps offstage and races to hug Wataida Midzi, whose indigo suit complements his dark skin. She hugs the rest of the girls and beckons them to the dance floor.

"What happened?! Tell me *everything*," Gabriela prods the second I sit next to her. "You know he's single again, right? I read that he and Chelsea Reid broke up a few weeks ago."

I take the water bottle Gabriela offers me. Even if I *did* trust her, I don't want to talk about Andrew anymore. "He just wanted to thank me for saving the Fire Drake."

Victoria's staring at me like she knows I'm hiding something.

I down the whole water bottle and head back to the dance floor. Génesis and Gabriela follow me with wide smiles. I lose myself among the future winners and losers of a game that hasn't even started yet. Tonight, though, we're neither winners nor losers.

And yet I feel like I've lost a game I never signed up for.

The Brazilian Pesadelo remains the most feared dragon species of all time. This fear is largely attributed to the fact that no Pesadelo has ever formed a Bond with a human rider. In 1986, the species gained further notoriety due to the tragic burning of a children's hospital in São Paulo, which was the result of three Un-Bonded quarreling over a meal. The venom laced in their fangs is also cause for distress. Once bitten, the victim suffers nightmarish hallucinations that last anywhere from forty-eight to seventy-two hours. But even though this species has a terrible reputation, we mustn't turn our backs on it. I strongly believe the Pesadelo can be nurtured into a peaceful coexistence with humans. Who knows? Perhaps a new species will come along and frighten us even more.

—*Excerpt from Carlos Torres's* Studying the Bond Between Dragons & Humans

CHAPTER ELEVEN

"**P**LEASE TELL ME I SHOULD'VE PUNCHED HIM," I IMPLORE Samira.

She's coughing up a thunderstorm. Even with her oversize Lauryn Hill hoodie and Sailor Moon pajama pants, she's the poster child of discomfort. I think I made things worse by fessing up to what happened at the welcome party. Manny went back to the house minutes before I left Andrew behind. President Turner never made it to the party. According to Ambassador Haddad, he suffered a medical emergency, but the president insisted we shouldn't worry.

It's the morning after the party. While the team eats breakfast, I'm in my room thinking about President Turner. How am I not supposed to worry when he's clearly hiding something?

"Andrew's not terrible enough for you to punch," Samira finally says. "But he's still terrible."

Samira blows her nose on the fifteenth Kleenex. "He could've approached you differently. Asking you to protest the Cup is kinda desperate, but he meant well." She takes a beat. "I would've joined him if he had a better plan."

"Samira. Did you forget the part where he asked me to turn my back on my team and my country? Also, and I cannot stress this enough, he thinks Takeshi Endo is a heroic soft boy."

"Can you blame him? They were best friends. I think Andrew's clinging to the memory of someone who once meant a lot to him. That's normal."

"Nope. That's delusional."

"Dang, girl. Give him a minute to grieve."

I throw my hands up. "He's had two years to grieve. *You* even canceled Takeshi the other day! Why are you defending him now?"

"I'm not defending Takeshi. He's still canceled. Andrew needs more time to realize he should cancel him, too." Samira sneezes. "He'll come to his senses when he's ready."

Ugh. This is so not how I hoped this video chat would go.

"You're obviously going to the doctor today, right?" I change the subject.

"You know it. I was fine yesterday. Stupid germs."

I suck in a drawn-out breath before ripping off the Band-Aid. "So . . . how's my mom?"

Samira frowns. "She's not good."

I should let it go. Whatever's wrong with her isn't my business until I get back home. Still, I ask, "What's going on?"

Samira says, "It's Todd. Your mother and aunt have been fighting with him a lot lately."

I sit up straight. "*Fighting?* But Todd's their favorite human ever."

"Your mother told him where you are. He wants to blast you to the press for being a Blazewrath player. For your"—Samira does air quotes—"*betrayal.* Your mother's convincing him to forget about you, but he *called* me yesterday, Lana. He found my number."

Thank God I haven't had breakfast yet. I would've puked all over this desk. "Please tell me you didn't answer that flaming piece of guano."

"I did," Samira says with a groan. "Todd kept on telling me how awesome he thinks I am and how grateful he is that I took him to Waxbyrne, despite what ended up happening. And he wouldn't stop mentioning that teacher he fanboys over at Aster Prep."

"Ugh. That Mister Thompson guy?"

"Yup. Apparently, Mister Thompson advised him to surround himself with people who could bring him peace of mind during this *difficult situation.* Todd said I was one of those people. He wants to hang out soon, but I told him I was incredibly ill, which wasn't a lie." She shudders. "He didn't use to creep me out this much. Now he's kinda pushing it, isn't he?"

"Don't answer his calls. He's dead to you, do you understand?"

She takes her sweet time in replying. "Okay. I mean, I *do* feel bad for him."

"You shouldn't. He's the worst." I wish Todd would visit me in Training Room C. Beating him up sounds like the best antidote for a bad day. That little scumbag might be reeled in now, but he's going to break loose. He'll have my name in his mouth for weeks. Maybe even years.

My mother wants him to forget me.

Samira might think she's protecting me, but she's just erasing me from the family tree.

I'm ruffling my hair in an attempt to not punch a wall. "Listen,

I gotta go, but please get to the doctor, okay? And let me know as soon as you get your new wand."

Samira coughs one last time. "Pinky swear. Have a good one! Love you!"

"Love you, too."

After signing off, I check Todd's social media accounts. There's nothing about me on any yet, so Mom and company have been doing a good job of keeping him under control, but that jerk's a ticking time bomb. I make a mental note to cyber-stalk him every single day.

I should probably look up President Turner, too.

Thousands of links pop up after I Google him. A 2007 article from *The Weekly Scorcher* stands out. A reporter named Julissa Mercado wrote a piece about Edward Barnes. It details Barnes's life as a child and teenager in Leeds, where he met his best friend and schoolmate, President Turner. The article hits all the beats regarding the Bond between the Gold Wand and the Sire, who found him when he was fifteen. A section toward the end jumps out at me:

The Sire didn't show signs of disdain for humans, particularly for wizards, until Barnes moved to the U. S. as an adult and joined the Department of Magical Investigations at the Bureau. It's possible the disdain had always been latent, but it was public knowledge by the time Barnes had celebrated his capture of Grace Wiggins, an American Regular and dragon supremacist. Barnes had caught 'the Headhunter of Alabama' hours after her notorious beheading of three witches outside of a church. Barnes's official report of the case mentions how Wiggins told him she'd killed the three witches in honor of dragons. They were meant to be a 'sacrifice to the gods of wing and flame.' The Sire had not been present during her arrest. It marked the first time Barnes went on a mission without his steed.

Right after Grace Wiggins was sent to Ravensworth Penitentiary, Barnes and the Sire reunited for one last assignment. Details remain classified. However, there were whispers they ambushed another Gold Wand, but they failed to bring him into custody. The next day, the Sire slipped out of Barnes's estate in New York and burned down his old house in Leeds. His parents, grandmother, and younger sister had been inside the home during the fire. They were pronounced dead at the scene, leaving Barnes with no surviving family members. The Sire carried on with multiple burnings throughout the country. He also flew to France, Belgium, and Germany, specifically to areas where Barnes had either visited or lived with his late family. The death toll reached hundreds in less than a week. Over the course of six months, an unstoppable Sire went on a rampage around the globe, taking lives both Regular and magical.

It's common knowledge that only a Gold Wand possesses the magical strength to take a dragon's life. What remains unknown is the reason why Barnes chose not to kill his former steed, or where he spent the last six months of his life prior to completing his dragon's curse. Many have speculated Barnes had been collecting the ingredients. The contents have remained in obscurity except for one: Barnes's blood. On December 19, 1997, Barnes's body was found outside the grounds of what was once his childhood home. A bloody dagger and an empty cauldron were the only things in his possession. The Sire's transformation took place as he was scorching a countryside residence in Perth, Australia. Soon after the curse changed him, he fled the scene and hasn't been spotted since.

There's a photo with President Turner, Edward Barnes, and the Sire in his dragon form. They're posing in a forest clearing. Both boys wear their uniforms: emerald blazers and pants, with golden ties and matching vests. While President Turner has always been chubby, Barnes was a lanky guy. His curly reddish-brown hair looks ruffled on purpose. He flashes the camera a winner's smile. The Sire gleams in his ninety-foot-tall body. He's a mighty beast dripping in diamond scales. President Turner has dead eyes. There's a quiet scream for help in his pursed lips.

I keep searching for more articles. One calls President Turner completely ignorant of the dragon's curse and its contents. He'd passed a lie detector test using a Truth Charm. He hadn't known where Barnes ran off to after his family's death. The picture in the forest clearing is the only one with all three together, and he looks super uncomfortable.

What if he'd known how evil the Sire was all along? What if he knows something about the curse, too, and he's tricked the bureau into believing otherwise? The only reason he'd have for hiding that information is to prevent the curse from being replicated.

Manny's voice blares through the intercom. "Lana, I need you in the dining room." He sounds like he's been chain-smoking for seven days straight, but the fact he's even acknowledging me is huge, let alone that he's asking to see me.

Maybe this is my chance to trick him into spilling the tea on London? I send a silent prayer for alcohol to be in Manny's proximity. That'll definitely make my job easier.

I rush to the dining room.

Manny's the only one there. He's yawning as he types something super fast on his phone. There's no alcohol around, but there's a small ice-blue box with a matching bow on top. A note on ivory paper has been placed next to it.

I sit on the chair to Manny's left. "What's up?"

"President Turner wants you to have this." Manny slides the box over to me.

Whoa. So this is from the *president*? "What is it?"

"If you open the box, you'll see."

I roll my eyes as I untie the bow. It slips off without hassle. When I open the box, my eyes grow twice their size. There's a cake inside. It's a square delicacy, covered in frosting the same color as its packaging. The piping consists of white buttercream that resembles dragon scales. They're tiny enough to pluck free with my pinky. The scent of fresh strawberries lingers in the air, but since there's none on top of the cake, they must be its filling.

I grab the ivory paper on the table. There's a message for me:

Dearest Ms. Torres,

My apologies for missing you at last night's welcome party! I was looking forward to celebrating you joining Team Puerto Rico, but a slight health complication prevented me from attending. Here's a special treat to make up for my absence. And don't worry about calories! They've been removed with a Vanish Charm just for you. Enjoy!

Your friend,
Russell Turner, IBF President

My stomach turns. Is he assuming I'm worried about calories because I'm an athlete, or because I'm a girl? Either way, President Turner is sending me *apology presents*. He's referring to himself as my friend. Maybe he holds me in high regard, but this feels . . . calculated. He *wants* me to feel special, and I have no clue why.

"Did the others get cake after joining the team?" I ask Manny.

He lowers his phone, side-eyeing me. "What does that matter?"

So they didn't. Looks like I'm his favorite. I don't deserve that label, and even if I did, it's a clear conflict of interest. The thought of being this important to a president with a past that links him to a terrorist unsettles me even more.

As much as I should focus on training, I can't think about anything else until I figure out what the president's deal is.

"If you stare at that cake any harder," Manny says, "it'll turn into dust."

I scowl at him. He might tell me about London if I'm clever enough, but he'll never fess up to whatever this cake really means. If I want answers, I have to find them elsewhere.

I push my chair back, ripping the note into pieces. I toss them into the nearest trash bin.

"What are you doing?" Manny's tone is alarmed enough to sound like he cares.

I pick up the kitchen phone and press the Intercom button. "This is Lana. There's calorie-free cake in the kitchen for you all. A treat from President Turner. Come get your slice."

I hang up and sit back down.

Manny's eyes bore holes into the side of my face. Then he storms outside. Hopefully, he'll tell President Turner I'm not accepting this gift or anything else he sends me. I'm not supposed to be the IBF's favorite. I'm not their puppet or tool, either. My teammates have been training far longer than I have. They deserve way more than a small share of cake, but it's a start.

Besides, I'm going to need all the help I can get to find out what's really going on.

I'VE NEVER SEEN ANYONE EAT SO FAST.

Luis is a human vacuum cleaner, devouring his slice in a matter of seconds. He's moaning like it's the best cake he's ever had. Héctor and Edwin poke fun at him, but they're also gobbling up their slices in a joyous frenzy. Either they haven't eaten cake in a long time, or this is really the most amazing dessert they've come across. Génesis savors every bite as if it's her last. Gabriela takes selfies with her plate, checking every picture with military-grade precision. She loads up the best ones to her social media accounts, then digs in, grinning the whole time.

Victoria hasn't touched her plate. She's watching everyone in silence, but especially me.

"I can save you that slice for later if you're not hungry," I tell her as kindly as possible. This is my chance to get her on my side.

"I'm good." She eyes the cake like it's stuffed with rat poison.

I hold back a sigh and cut my slice into more manageable bites. The strawberry filling is rich and gooey, dripping all over the plastic fork. The cake itself is vanilla, which isn't my favorite, but the filling packs it with the perfect balance of tart and sweetness.

My teammates are talking to one another in rapid Spanish, delighting in their gift.

"Doesn't food like this cost hundreds of dollars?" says Luis.

"Thousands," I clarify. "Gold Wands are the only ones who can perform the Vanish Charm, which is why calorie-free food is in such high demand around the world. My best friend isn't capable of magic like that, even if it's just destroying calories."

"What a special gift," Victoria says sarcastically. So she knows this isn't normal, too, which might make her hate me more. Like I had something to do with being treated this way.

I'm about to change the subject, but Héctor beats me to it. "Your best friend's a witch?"

"Yeah, she's a Copper Wand. Her name's Samira."

Luis poses with a hand under his chin. "Is she cute?"

"Ay, por favor, Luis," Edwin says. He pretends to puke on his empty plate.

I laugh along with everyone except Victoria, who gives a reluctant half smile. Once the laughter dies down, I set my fork aside and look over each of my teammates, saving Victoria for last. "So tell me about home. What's it like to be the first dragon riders on the island?"

For a split second, Victoria lights up like a whole park full of Christmas trees. Then she quickly shifts back into her usual sour expression, as if she's angry I made her smile. She pulls her chair closer to the table. "People treat us better than rock stars," she speaks in the softest voice. "They mail us letters and gifts to the San Juan house. They want selfies whenever we're out and about. Someone got a tattoo of my *autograph*. We get haters, too, but the love is louder."

"So much louder," Gabriela says with a nod.

"My life sucked so much before Esperanza found me," Victoria continues, "but she made the bad things go away. I had to move out of Loíza because the bureau needed us in a bigger house, so I did feel shitty about leaving Héctor and Génesis behind, but a week later Titán found Héctor right down my street. Rayo landed on Génesis's doorstep the week after that."

I pretend I'm hearing their stories for the first time. Gabriela recalls how Puya had found her in her southern hometown of Ponce. She'd been getting a crown braid done at a hair salon when Puya landed in the parking lot. Edwin and Luis had Bonded with their steeds after wrapping up a school day. They'd been studying at the same high school in Carolina, but had never spoken to each other. Fantasma startled everyone when he landed outside the school gates; same with Daga a week later. Héctor had been rereading one of his favorite *Black Panther* graphic novels when Titán found him. Génesis is the only one who'd been asleep during Rayo's arrival.

They also tell me about relocating to dragon-friendly housing in San Juan with their families. Victoria and Gabriela both brought their moms, Edwin brought his grandparents (they raised him on their own), and the others brought both of their parents. Each family lived in separate houses, much like the Compound residences. It was only when President Turner invited them to compete in the Cup that they all lived under the same roof without their loved ones.

"Has President Turner always been chummy with you or strictly professional?" I ask.

Héctor says, "He's been a mix of both. Nowadays we see less of him, but when we used to train back in San Juan, he would fly in almost every weekend to watch our progress."

"Was he alone, or did he bring staff along?"

"Always alone," says Génesis. "Why?"

"Just wondering." I take a bite of cake, licking the sugary sweet frosting off my lips. "What was it like when he first invited you to the Cup?"

My teammates take swift and animated turns discussing President Turner's invitation. Back in December 2015, he'd flown them to IBF headquarters in London. He'd gotten a private jet for them, along with a five-star hotel stay and extra days for sightseeing. That had been Edwin, Victoria, and Génesis's first time on a plane. None mention anything unusual about the grand gesture or the president's behavior during their trip. Luis even refers to him as "a fuego," which is an expression used to compliment someone on their awesomeness.

I shrug. "Did any of his gifts feel like too much from someone who's basically a stranger?"

"You're asking a lot of questions, Lana," Victoria butts in. "I think it's only fair we ask you some, too. Why haven't you returned to Puerto Rico?"

I sit back, arms hanging limp at my sides. Where the hell did *that* come from? "My dad lives in Brazil. I don't have any family left on the island," I reply with a dry mouth.

"Bullshit." Victoria's definitely not the whole park full of Christmas trees anymore. "Your mom has enough money to buy you a plane ticket. You could have reconnected with your roots if you *really* wanted to. And before you feed me some line about 'your roots go wherever you are,' it's not the same thing. People who think that are trying to justify their indifference."

"Victoria. Stop." Héctor's tone is stern enough to scare even the most rebellious of souls.

I don't know why he's stopping her. He feels the same way.

Victoria says, "You can call yourself one of us, Lana. That's cool. What bothers me is knowing how much it means to our fans to see our flag in the Blazewrath World Cup, and the person who gets to be our flag bearer during the opening ceremonies hasn't touched Puerto Rican soil in twelve years." She pauses with a sneer. "By *choice*."

The room shrinks three sizes smaller. Everyone starts talking at the same time, mostly in Spanish, but I can only see the ice-cold girl challenging me yet again. All I want is to annihilate her low opinion of me. The harder I try to defend myself, the quieter I am. I *could've* visited Puerto Rico. Mom hadn't stopped me, but she never suggested it, either. I didn't ask because I'd figured she'd be pissed. She would've seen it as another betrayal.

I rub the back of my neck as pangs of guilt shoot through me. The memories I hold dear aren't of the island itself. They're about me and Papi doing what we love in the place he loves the most. I hadn't spent enough time in Puerto Rico to understand it as more than the backdrop of my wildest dreams. It's not enough to be a part of this team to confirm I *am* Puerto Rican. It's not the same to read about and see pictures of a place rather than to be in the thick of things.

I hoped I'd be accepted as a team member, as another Boricua, once I got here.

But my roots will always be deemed too shallow.

"Lana? Did you hear me?" Héctor's voice is sweeter than honey. "You *are* one of us."

I'm welling up with every breath. *Why* is he so determined to lie? Does he not see how easily I can see right through him? "Whatever . . . I, um . . . I have to practice . . ."

I'm out of the dining room in a blur. I catch a few voices calling my name, imploring me to stay, but I jog to the elevators before anyone can stop me. My sobs grow louder as I press the button to get to my room, wishing I could hit Delete on this whole morning instead. I'm not fast enough to outrun the Blockers. I'm not good enough at fighting them. I'm not Puerto Rican enough to raise the island's flag high during the opening ceremonies, or to wear the Blazewrath uniform. Victoria's approach might not have been the kindest, but she has a point.

I don't belong on this team.

Extensive research has failed to provide a justification as to why dragons seldom Bond with witches and wizards. The most popular theory among magical-history buffs is the complicated relationship between the two species prior to the Reveal in 1743. There are recorded instances of European dragons engaging in open hostilities with the magical community. Most of these hostilities had been enacted to defend habitats and/or protect their eggs. Another popular theory involves dragons steering clear of those with the magical ability to wipe them out. This suggests dragons can choose with whom they Bond, which invalidates the destiny theory. If proven true, dragons have been in complete control of their fates (and their magic) all along.

—Excerpt from Edna Clarke's Magical History
for Regulars, Twelfth Edition

CHAPTER TWELVE

WHEN I ARRIVE IN TRAINING ROOM C, MY FIGHTING EQUIPMENT
is right where Edwin and Génesis left it, waiting for me to pick it back up. Chances are both Manny and Joaquín are skipping my practice to watch Victoria act like she's the best thing that's ever happened to the universe. I couldn't catch what the rest of the team said to her as I left. A part of me wishes I had.

I sniffle. *Nobody's* watching me cry today. One humiliating experience is enough.

"Hey!" Edwin bolts into the room. Génesis is hot on his heels.

"¿Estás bien?"

"Mm-hmm . . ." I lie on my back with a deep sigh. My peace is over before it could begin.

"Don't dwell on what she said, Lana. Victoria can be . . . too much." Génesis stands next to me. "I'm sure she was just trying to understand you better, but her methods are terrible."

"I don't want to talk about it."

Génesis frowns. "That's fair. Let's get you ready to fight. We're covering a lot today."

Edwin offers me a hand.

I glare at it. My heart isn't remotely near the vicinity of wanting to *pretend* I'm fighting someone. Not after Victoria swept the floor with me. Not after President Turner's fishy apology cake. I'd thought of myself as worthy because I was born on the island. I'm worthy because I'm fast. The Waxbyrne incident proved it, but I'd been running with a purpose then.

I had something to protect.

I sit up straight. The hole inside makes me ache for Training Room E. If I'm going to call myself Puerto Rico's Runner, I have to put that title on myself and live up to it. I can't wait for Joaquín or my teammates to tell me I'm ready. I have to *show* them I'm ready. All I need is something to protect. I don't belong on this team, but I still want to.

And I will.

I make a beeline for the exit.

"Where are you going?" Génesis asks.

"You wanna fight?" I say. "Meet me on the mountain."

I march like a soldier, out for blood, on my way to Training Room E.

JOAQUÍN IS JOTTING SOMETHING ON HIS NOTEPAD AS I APPROACH.

Manny's nowhere to be found, most likely hiding in his room doing absolutely nothing. The dragons must still be in the habitat, either sleeping or lounging around until they're called for practice.

I halt in front of Joaquín. "I'm running up the mountain today. I need the Iron Scale."

He looks up, his forehead creased. "Excuse me?"

"The Iron Scale. I need it." I point to the mountain. "To practice."

Joaquín puts his pen down. He sighs like I've exhausted him. "You're not ready."

"Yes, I am. I just need the Iron Scale to protect. Give it to me."

The elevator doors open behind me. The rest of the team files into the room, all wearing matching expressions of "What the actual hell is happening?"

Joaquín waits for them to surround us, then says, "You haven't been cleared for the mountain, Lana. Go back to Training Room C. We'll discuss your next steps later."

I don't move.

Joaquín waits for me to get lost, but his shoulders slump lower and lower, as if he's losing hope of getting me to the track. "You really think you can do this?"

"I know I can."

"And you'll stick with my method if you fail?"

"Absolutely, but I won't fail."

Joaquín lets out a laugh, then heads for the elevator.

No one speaks to me at first. Then Edwin offers to practice tossing with me while we wait. Of course I say yes. He gently helps me put on my protective pads, then guides me through the basics—how to stand, where to put my hands and elbows on the opponent's body. I do everything he tells me. I'm acing every single command, too. This is much easier than yesterday. Or maybe I'm just better at listening today. Either way, I'm going to kill it on the mountain.

When Edwin finally tries to get me to toss him, Joaquín returns. He's carrying an ivory bag with an IBF logo stamped on it. "This is yours," he tells me.

I snatch the bag at once, pulling out the gray object within. The Iron Scale. It's not a real dragon scale. It's a finely cut triangle with a smattering of gray dust all over it. There's a small round hole on the top left corner, which is where the carabiner loops through. A Runner's belt is supposed to hold the carabiner in place. The same belt Joaquín is handing over to Génesis, who starts strapping it around me. Of all the things I'm required to do as Runner, none have felt more powerful than this. This object is my responsibility. It's the reason why I matter in the game. I needed fire, so Joaquín brought me fire. And, in a way, so did Victoria and President Turner.

Now all I have to do is burn.

I hook the Iron Scale to the carabiner. At first, I'm a bit out of sorts, thanks to the shift in weight on my left hip. The Iron Scale forces me to lean to the side.

"Use your core muscles to steady yourself," Joaquín says. "It'll be harder to keep your momentum once you run up the mountain. Most Blockers land in front of the Runner, but sometimes a Blocker will land behind them. They'll come directly for the Iron Scale. Those are often the most dangerous Blockers."

True. During the last Cup's semifinals, while Andrew sped through that first Block Zone, one of the Blockers from Sweden dropped inches away from his back. Andrew had whirled around just in time to kick him down, but the Blocker did manage to snap the Iron Scale away from the belt. He and the Blocker fought for a while, with the latter eventually failing to stop the former from exiting the Block Zone, but I still remember how hard I screamed at my laptop. I won't be able to scream my way through this now, though.

Joaquín says, "We'll play a normal match. Lana, you'll enter all three

Block Zones. You still don't have your suit, so the dragons won't be firing at you. The Blockers, however, *will* attack you without mercy. Got it?"

I nod. "Loud and clear, coach."

"Good. Everyone, please call your steeds in here so we can get started."

My teammates close their eyes. Héctor and Luis both press a finger to their temples, too.

The Sol de Noche dragons Fade into the room ten seconds later. Their bodies are outlines of their whole selves once again, filling up with their natural dark color in slow bursts. Smoke coils all around them, but it's gone by the time their bodies are back to normal. Now they're six gorgeous marvels spreading their giant wings and wagging their flame-tipped tails.

Daga squeals gleefully as soon as she sees me. I pat her nose twice, which makes her wiggle her butt. Everyone laughs. The other dragons settle into their positions like the rest of us, totally focused on the fake match. They're as determined as their riders to get the job done.

But none are as determined as I am.

Joaquín blows his whistle.

The first half of the match begins. Luis and Gabriela escort Victoria to the goalpost. Luis flanks her left; Gabriela takes the right. Joaquín activates the blasters, which shoot never-ending fireballs from below. Luis steers Daga into whipping some fireballs away with her tail. Gabriela, on the other hand, is guiding Puya closer to Esperanza and acting as her shield. The male dragon takes most of the blows, without breaking formation. It helps Esperanza get to the goalpost unscathed. Victoria tosses the Rock Flame, but Héctor kicks it back to her. Victoria is relentless, though. After six different tries, she gets the Rock Flame to fly through the goal.

Joaquín whistles again.

I race up the mountain.

Fantasma is on me within seconds. I pretend he's shooting fireballs. It fuels me to sail across the mountain faster. My breathing is under control, so the path upward is a breeze.

When I reach the first Block Zone, Edwin jumps down in front of me. I swerve around him and wait for him to grab me.

He pushes me to the ground instead.

I fall on my chest but push myself up in a heartbeat. Edwin flips me over his shoulder, sending me down again and grabbing the Iron Scale. I latch onto his wrist. With another swivel, I drive my knee into his stomach. Edwin doubles over with a yelp. I squeeze his wrist tighter and crash my back onto his chest. Then I put everything I have into tossing him over my shoulder.

Edwin flips onto the sand on his back.

A gasp bursts out of me. *Holy freaking crap!* Edwin Santiago is flat on his back, and *I put him there.* He's not holding the Iron Scale anymore. It's still safely hooked to my belt.

I bolt out of the first Block Zone.

It's a tighter race for that second stretch of mountain. Génesis and Rayo stalk me on the way up. Luckily, the second Block Zone is shorter than the first. I enter seconds before Génesis smashes her elbow into my ribs. I wince but dodge her constant blows. Then she tries to clock me with an uppercut. I grab her arm and flip her over my shoulder. She's down just like Edwin. I catch her groaning as I cross the line that divides the Block Zone from my freedom.

Keep going, keep going, keep going.

The race continues for the third and final stretch of mountain. The last Block Zone is the shortest one. Once I cross the line, Edwin swoops in from the left. We dance our usual dance until he seizes my wrist. Before he can flip me over, I do the same thing Génesis did to me and elbow his ribs really hard. He's caught off guard long enough for me to flip him instead. Once again, down and out. I rush off before he tries to lunge at the Iron Scale.

The last patch of land is an uphill sprint unlike the rest of the mountain. My whole body seizes and throbs and begs me to stop, but I push through the pain. I run out of the last curve, then lunge toward the stone dais right in the middle of the mountaintop. The circular base has the exact outline of the Iron Scale carved into its center, a mold fit to hold the artifact in place.

I slam the Iron Scale onto the stone dais's center.

Fire shoots out from the Iron Scale, right toward the ceiling. The flame is harmless. The only thing hurting me is the swelling in my chest, the soreness in my ankles worsening because I can't stop jumping up and down. My throat burns from all the screaming, too. The crap I'd endured this morning is still flowing in my veins, but this winner's rush is more powerful.

I beat Edwin and Génesis. I made it to the top of the mountain.

I'm the Runner my country deserves.

"And Puerto Rico wins the game!" Joaquín laughs into his loud-speaker. He's clapping and cheering wildly along with my teammates.

Including Victoria.

I CAN'T SLEEP.

Despite leaving it all on the mountain, I'm more energized than ever. I'd made it to the top every time Victoria scored. How am I *not* supposed to be fired up about my first taste of victory?

The other girls are passed out in our bedroom. Even with their mouths slightly open and a few snores here and there, they look like Disney princesses. It's almost midnight, and they're taking our early wake-up call to heart. Tomorrow's our official team photo shoot. It'll be a long day split between snapping pics and sweating it out during practice.

Not that I mind. I *finally* get to wear my uniform.

The anticipation for tomorrow coupled with today's success? My whole body's vibrating so hard, I'm about to fall off the bed. Usually, I watch music videos when I can't sleep. I grab my headphones and head to the living room. Wouldn't want to start World War III because of my loud singing. Once I'm downstairs, I sink into the couch and search YouTube. The longer I scroll endless thumbnails, the more I crave to stick with Blazewrath content. So I open up BlazeReel, a website that features all sorts of Blazewrath-related videos. Most of the suggestions on my homepage are past matches. There's a handful of press-conference footage, along with fan-made compilations of funny moments with the players.

Then there's the Takeshi and Andrew interview.

It's an appearance they made in 2015 on *The Jeffrey Hines Show*, a famous talk show in England. The taping occurred two weeks before the last Cup.

I press Play. It starts with bleached-blond Jeffrey Hines doing his usual stand-up opener, flaunting a flamingo-pink suit, and then it dives into Takeshi at the ten-minute mark. He's in olive Dockers and a white pressed shirt, waving and smiling at the audience. He even stops to take selfies with fans while Jeffrey pretends to throw a jealous fit. Eventually, Takeshi sits down with Jeffrey on the ruby-red couch. They clink their coffee mugs together and compliment each other's outfits. They bond over their mutual love of French bulldogs and chocolate truffles.

Two minutes later, Jeffrey tells Takeshi he has a special surprise for him.

Andrew walks out with a basket of chocolate-truffle boxes and a wicked grin.

While the audience bursts into applause, Takeshi holds the sides of his face in an adorable display of shock. Andrew rushes over to the couch. He has Converse sneakers on, faded denim jeans, a Queen T-shirt, and a black blazer. He kneels in front of Takeshi, handing him the basket like a peasant offering his month's earnings to his king. Takeshi puts the basket on the couch, then sweeps his best friend into a hug. Jeffrey joins the audience in wild applause. When all three sit down, I'm smiling so hard my cheeks are starting to get sore.

I force a cough. No more smiling for me.

"Glasgow's own Andrew Galloway, everybody!" Jeffrey proudly announces.

Once the applause dies down, Jeffrey jokes about Takeshi and Andrew's vacation challenge, which is what they call the trips they take each other's moms on. Jeffrey pulls up a photo of Andrew and Mrs. Endo posing in front of the Magic Kingdom. Then the screen shows Takeshi and Lucy Galloway standing in front of the Eiffel Tower. Ms. Galloway is the spitting image of Andrew, except for her light-brown skin. Whether it's Andrew and Mrs. Endo flying over Mykonos in a helicopter, or Takeshi and Ms. Galloway eating at a restaurant in Barcelona, toasting with mason jars labeled ANDREW'S TEARS, the crowd breaks into joyous squeals.

Jeffrey says, "How do a Runner from Glasgow and a Striker from Sapporo become BFFs?"

"We met two years ago during the previous Cup," Takeshi says. "It was at the welcome party. I was speaking with my teammates, and in comes this guy asking if we wanted his autograph. He said it would be worth millions because of the countless shampoo commercials he'd end up booking." He can't resist a giggle. "Andrew and I bonded over our mutual love of the sport and dragons. Then we realized we had more in common than we thought."

Andrew chimes in. "We're both only children. Single mothers raised us. Different circumstances, of course. Takeshi's father stayed optimistic throughout his fight with cancer. That's a strong man if I've ever heard of one. Mine isn't worth a damn."

"You never met your father, did you?" a solemn Jeffrey asks Andrew.

"No. All he gave me was the inability to tan. I'm just red all over."

"Has he tried to look for you now that you're famous?"

"No. We're not in each other's lives. Never will be." I've heard him speak of this a million times. His Silver Wand mother raised him alone, living off a music teacher's salary and as many piano lessons as she could book. Since Andrew's a Regular, his dad must be a Regular, too, but that's all we know about him. Andrew taps Takeshi. "This man's father? Hero."

Takeshi bows his head. "I'm very proud of him. I only hope he's half as proud of me."

"Oh, he most certainly is!" says Jeffrey. "How long has it been since he passed?"

"Twelve years. He died when I was five."

"His funeral made headlines because of Hikaru, correct?"

Takeshi nods. "The day we buried my father was the same day Hikaru found me. Everyone from the factory where my father worked as a custodian attended the funeral. The whole neighborhood was there, too. But when a dragon swoops in uninvited, you're bound to raise a few eyebrows." His half smile breaks me and mends me at the same time.

Andrew taps his fist on Takeshi's thigh. "The youngest dragon rider to have Bonded with his steed right here."

"Yes, I do believe that *is* the record to beat," says an astonished Jeffrey. "Five years old!"

A blushing Takeshi says, "Hikaru saved my life. That last year was difficult for my family, but my father kept telling his silly jokes and reading me sci-fi novels. His cancer spread from his brain to his chest and lungs, and all he wanted to do was make me laugh." He crosses one leg over the other, squeezing his knee with both hands. There's an unfamiliar slowness to the way he moves. "My goal is to leave a legacy of helping others believe in themselves. No matter what you do, there's always the opportunity to find happiness somewhere. My father taught me that."

I'm crying.

I'm crying just like I did the first, second, millionth times I watched this video. Takeshi Endo had once been a boy and the whole sun at the same time, shining too bright for the rest of us. It took a British talk show for me to see him as a human being instead of that untouchable figment. It took an attempt on a Fire Drake's life for me to see him as an untouchable figment again, but this time, the dreamer who conjured him spun a boy from the darkest nightmares. Revisiting this video helps me see what Andrew still thinks is there: a hero.

Samira had been right. This is going to take Andrew a long time. There are too many memories, too many good things about the boy who no longer shines for anyone or anything. Even though he needed to hear every word I said, I could've been kinder to him at the welcome party. We're still fighting for the same thing. We just have different methods.

What if he can help me figure out the truth about President Turner?

I launch the BlazeReel Live app, which allows users to broadcast from wherever they are. Andrew uses the app to either give terrible life advice to his fans or to provide ridiculous reviews of what's on his plate. That little green dot appears next to his avatar. He's still online. Chances are he won't see my private message for a while, since he's probably swamped with DMs. This is still less awkward than speaking to him in person or even calling him at the house.

I reread my message before hitting Send:

Hey, Andrew. Just wanted to apologize if I offended you last night. That wasn't my intention. Regardless of how I feel about your offer, I really do admire you.

Also, I've been thinking about what you said regarding President Turner. Something's definitely off. He even sent me a cake to apologize for not coming to the party. As if I'm the reason he needed to go in the first place. I know you told me he's using me for publicity, but I can't stop wondering if there's more behind his actions, especially considering his past with the Sire. What do you think about teaming up so we can crack his code?

Ten seconds after sending it, two green checkmarks appear at the bottom of the message.

Which means Andrew's read it. I tap my foot over and over as the "Andrew is typing" notification appears. His message pops up on-screen:

water under the bridge, Lana. thanks for reaching out. means more than you'll ever know. now let's go find out what the president is really up to. what's your plan?

With a relieved sigh, I type my response:

I don't have one yet. Any ideas?

none. i've been watching an American reality tv show all night. my brain is fried.

Oh, you poor thing! JK I'm seeing him tomorrow at the photo shoot. What if I ask him about the Sire and how close they were? He might lie his ass off, but his face won't.

very true. text me later tomorrow with your findings. it'll help us form an actual plan.

I definitely will. Have a good night, Andrew. And thank you.

I'm smiling as I stretch my back. All signs point to an understanding between opposites. Maybe even a friendship. It's too soon to tell, but it feels good to be on the same page.

Jeffrey Hines 3@The_Jeffrey_Hines
Fire is one of the main reasons why humans fear dragons. Whether you
wield magic or not, you can't help but be transfixed at the sight of a
stream of flames emanating from a dragon's mouth. This is why all eyes
are on the Sol de Noche dragons for this year's Cup.
2:41 AM · May 23, 2017 · Twitter for iPhone

Jeffrey Hines 3@The_Jeffrey_Hines
Not only will this be their first time competing, it'll also be the first
time the world will witness fire in a different way. Will they eject
flames like every other dragon? Or will they rely more on their ability
to cover their whole bodies?
2:41 AM · May 23, 2017 · Twitter for iPhone

Jeffrey Hines 3@ The_Jeffrey_Hines
So many questions, folks, but at least we know this: Team Puerto Rico's
Runner, whoever they are, will definitely be the least-talked-about player.
2:42 AM · May 23, 2017 · Twitter for iPhone

—Transcript from a thread on Jeffrey Hines's Twitter
account (@The_Jeffrey_Hines)

CHAPTER THIRTEEN

THE NEXT DAY, THE DRAGONS' HABITAT IS TURNED INTO PHOTO-Shoot Central.

I haven't been up there yet, but Joaquín says there are huge blinding lamps, reflective panels that could shield us from alien attacks, and lots of monitors surrounding a single laptop. Ambassador Haddad is expected to arrive at 8:00 a.m. with our photographer and team stylist.

President Turner is supposed to be here, too, but Manny isn't giving us much hope.

"He could sit this one out," he says during breakfast. Manny sits directly across from me, filling up a bowl with cranberry-and-coconut cereal. "Russell hasn't been feeling well."

"What's wrong with him?" I keep my tone soft and warm. No need to freak Manny out.

He mumbles, "Don't know," and eats his cereal.

"Did he have any medical problems leading up to the Cup? Or is this sudden?"

"Finish your breakfast, nena. It's getting cold."

"Aren't *you* worried?" I wave to the others. "I'm sure we all are."

"He did seem pretty tired after his fall," says Gabriela. I could hug her. "Is he okay?"

Luis shrugs. "Maybe old age is catching up to him."

"Or maybe," Manny's eyes are tightly narrowed, "this isn't something you should focus on. You have a big day ahead. *Eat.* I don't wanna hear you complaining about lunchtime later."

I swallow my tongue and pick at my veggie omelet. Héctor chimes in with a swift change of subject—the weather, of all things—officially letting Manny off the hook for now. My target is President Turner. If he doesn't show up, I'll hit Manny with everything I have until he spills.

I keep my mouth shut all the way back to my room. I change into a plain T-shirt and jeans, while the other girls put on their uniforms. Gabriela takes care of everyone's hair and makeup. She styles us with the so-called Clean Starlet look, which includes pink gloss and voluminous mascara on our real lashes. We're all in ponytails except for Génesis; she's rocking her Afro.

When I arrive at the habitat, the dragons have already been positioned in front of the trees, the lights shining down on them. Their scales are gleaming even brighter. While most keep their cool as their riders approach, Daga wags her tail and stomps the floor in total joy.

Ambassador Haddad and two women are standing near the monitors.

The woman closest to him is as dark-skinned as Génesis, an Afro-Latina straight off the runway, but she's much curvier and older than my Blocker teammate. Fiftysomething, I'd wager, and somewhere between a glorious size twelve and fourteen. Her black hair is knotted up in a crown braid, and she stuns in a fuchsia dress with matching heels.

"¡Buenos días, mis amores!" she bids us a good morning with the kind of smile that befits a mother upon reuniting with her kids.

"¡Buenos días!"

The team takes turns hugging her. Even Victoria is the embodiment of warmth in her presence. Once the hugs are done, the woman waves hello to me, but it's the wave where she only wiggles her fingers. "Lana, mamita," she calls me in a raspy voice, "my name is Marisol Cabán. I'm your stylist. It's my pleasure to help you with your uniform today."

Yeah, I like her already. "Thank you so much. I can't wait to try it on."

"And we can't wait to see the whole team in their suits at last," says Ambassador Haddad. He turns to the other woman. "This is my daughter, Noora, your photographer for today."

Noora, who seems to be in her early twenties, is wearing a comfy dress I believe is called an abaya. Like her hijab, Noora's abaya is sable colored, but its neckline has fine embroidery in the deepest ruby thread. The designs are flower petals and the leaves attached to their stems. She's much thinner than Marisol, but together, they're a tag team of elegant powerhouses.

"Nice to meet you," I say to Noora.

"Delighted, Lana," she replies. "Hello, everyone."

"Hello," the team says.

Noora turns to Marisol. "You can get her dressed while I work on solo portraits."

"Perfect. Come, come. Take me to your dormitory, Lana."

I'm walking toward the elevator with Marisol when the doors open. President Turner bursts into view.

He's in charcoal gray today. His hands aren't shaking, and he's perfectly balanced as he walks into the habitat. "Good morning! My sincerest apologies for arriving late!"

"Mr. President!" I wave hello. "I'm so happy you could—"

"Oh, come! You can have your little chat later." Marisol yanks me forward with the strength of a Spartan warrior. "Let's get you in that suit."

"See you in a bit!" President Turner gives me a quick nod. He then bolts for Manny, hugging him and whispering something in his ear.

The elevator doors close before I can read his lips.

"UNDERWEAR ONLY, MAMITA. CHOP-CHOP."

As I'm tossing the clothes on my bed, I wonder what the hell President Turner whispered to Manny. It could've been something important. Maybe even Sire important.

I'm standing in my sports bra and panties. My stomach clenches. Mom's the last person to have seen me like this. She'd been zipping me up in a floral lace jumpsuit at Dillard's. "Aunt Jenny loves you in jumpsuits," she told me as I flung off the stupid thing. "She thinks they make you look more mature. I happen to think she's right." Naturally, I've hated jumpsuits since then.

I heave a sigh. She must still be dealing with her favorite nephew's stupidity, but that shouldn't make me feel bad. She chose him just like I chose this tournament. Besides, she's probably done a billion things to forget I exist. Why should I care about what's happening with her?

"Why do you look like you're about to knock me out?" Marisol backs away from me.

"Oh! No, I don't want to knock you out. Sorry."

"I come from a family of boxers, in case you want to go at it."

I can't resist a laugh. "It's just my, um . . . Never mind." Great. Mom's not even here, and she's *still* getting to me. This is a fitting, for God's sake. I have to act professional.

Marisol is quiet, but I know she's judging the crap out of me. "You sure?"

"Yeah. It's okay. Can I see my uniform now, please?"

Marisol *tsk-tsk*s me. "Tell me the truth, Lana. Are you angry?"

I gulp down. "Not at all."

Marisol studies me like an aunt whose job is to butt into your business, suggest how you should live while also acknowledging you're free to choose for yourself, then get offended when you don't do *exactly* what she suggested. "Here's a tip. You'll need that fire on the field, so keep it. Let it simmer until the time comes to burn them all. Be careful not to burn yourself away, though. That kind of fire could take you, too."

Burn myself away? I never thought of it like that, but she's right. This bitter little pill Mom force-fed me doesn't always come up to sabotage me. When it does, it has the power to derail me. I can't afford that. Mom is living her life. I'm living mine, just like she told me to. That should be enough for me to let it go. It might not be enough at the moment, but it will be.

"I'm fine, Marisol. Really."

"Mm-hmm . . ." Marisol pulls out a Silver wand from her dress's pocket. Well, at least I *think* her wand is Silver. I can't see the metal because of all the crystals attached to it. They're translucent little balls of light, mirrors to the world around them. Usually, witches and wizards don't bedazzle their wands this much. Either Marisol had this specially ordered, or the wand had already been designed this way, which would make it even more of a rarity.

"That's not a Madame Waxbyrne design," I point out.

"Good eye. No. It's not."

"But she's the only one who can sell wands legally. Where did you get it?"

"She's the only one who can sell to the *masses*, but there are other licensed wand-makers. They just can't serve the general public. Only wealthy and well-connected people have access to their designs." Marisol raises her wand. She's transfixed by it, as if she's never seen such beauty. "I bought this wand from one of Madame Waxbyrne's former classmates at Iron Pointe."

That's the top wand-maker academy in the world. It's hidden deep within the Swiss Alps. Madame Waxbyrne had studied there long before she became one of its professors. I've only heard of one other wand-maker who went to Iron Pointe—Julia Serrano, a Puerto Rican Gold Wand. She'd been the first Puerto Rican wand-maker to attend Iron Pointe in the late sixties.

"Was it Julia Serrano?" I ask.

Marisol lowers her wand, glum as a funeral attendee. "No," she whispers.

Well, that was ominous. "So . . . who was it?"

"That's not why we're here." She flicks her wrist in a jarringly quick motion.

POP!

A clothes hanger appears out of nowhere. It hovers right beside Marisol like a balloon, bobbing up and down. My uniform is on the hanger. The metal chest with its white stardust letters and my country's name on it faces me. The dark cuffs have the same four spikes as the rest of my teammates' uniforms, too. Marisol has even summoned my boots. With a flick of her wand, she turns the uniform around, showing me the back. TORRES is splashed across the middle in matching letters. The only thing missing is my number.

"Let's get you into this," says Marisol.

I let her take the uniform instead of ripping it off the hanger myself. This is history in the making. I'm about to wear a Blazewrath suit with my last name on it. Marisol takes her sweet time unzipping it, relishing every inch of her impeccable design, then holds the suit toward me, back first. I slip in one leg, then the other, until I'm fully clothed and Marisol's zipping me up.

I sigh in relief. It's not squeezing the life out of me.

"Raise your arms," Marisol orders.

I do as she says. The suit is a second skin to me. Even the metal is a weightless, cozy addition to the spandex. Marisol tells me to bend, lunge, and squat. I'm able to move without trouble. When I add the boots, everything feels even better. I can run for days. Marisol puts me in front of the full-body mirror. I'm every bit as stylish and fierce as my teammates, but not nearly as physically strong. Thankfully, I have them to do all the intimidation.

"For our final act, I need a number," Marisol says.

I scrunch up my face, then hang my head low. Victoria's criticism stings yet again as I stare at Marisol's wand. She's about to put a number of my choosing on a uniform that others from the island could wear in my place. Kids who've spent their whole lives where I only spent a handful of years, too young to remember what makes it irreplaceable. Reaching the top of the mountain proved to my teammates I deserve to play alongside them. But this number, this suit, will show the world I'm taking this spot from those who know their island better.

"There you go with that fire again." Marisol's eyeing me like I'm a juvenile delinquent in the making. "You can rage at the walls and the planets, because raging is normal and fun, but don't let that rage eat your heart for breakfast. You're not on the menu, mamita. You shouldn't let things consume you to the point where you can't tell what matters and what never should."

Easier said than done.

"What if I can't stop the fire?" I whisper. "What if it kills everything I am?"

"Only you can answer that."

Her words are fists to the gut. Of course I'm angry. I'm *furious*. But I'm not just the girl without a home. I'm not just the girl whose mother won't fully support her. The girl who wishes Takeshi would somehow be good and righteous and heroic again, that President Turner would own up to whatever he's scheming.

That's all I'm going to be if I don't keep my crap together.

There won't be anything to fight for, anyone to stand against, if there's no me left.

So I think of a number for my uniform. A number those kids I'm taking this opportunity from will remember me by and chant on the streets. I could stick with my birthday—November 7. That might be a little played out, though. Then I remember there are thirteen of us total on the team. I don't have a home, but I have people who remind me of the one I want.

I tell Marisol, "Twelve."

"May I ask why?"

"I'm playing with the strength and agility of my twelve teammates as my fuel to keep going. I'm carrying them all with me so I can be the best at what I do."

Marisol seems proud. "Beautifully said," she speaks warmly. "Turn around."

Once my back is facing her, she uses her wand to write a bold number twelve across the metal. The digits rest right underneath my last name, the reflection of all the letters glinting in the mirror. I shine brighter now. *Holy crap.* I'm the night and a star all at once. I'm blinking back tears as I struggle to catch my breath. With each cough, my chest feels like it's about to explode.

"Are you the hugging type?" Marisol asks me.

"Oh . . . Yeah, I guess."

Marisol offers me a hug and I gladly accept it. She's holding me a lot tighter than I expect.

She's holding me like Mom should've before saying goodbye.

"Thank you, Marisol," I whisper. We stay that way for a while, then I let her take me back upstairs to the men keeping secrets.

"RIGHT IN THE FRONT, LANA. ACROSS FROM HÉCTOR," NOORA instructs me.

My human teammates stand in a triangle position. Their steeds are behind them. Gabriela, Edwin, and Luis to the left. Génesis, Victoria, and Héctor to the right. They're posing with their fists on their hips, baring all their teeth. Victoria's smile is a straight line that invites the beholder to challenge her and meet their end. She's a living, breathing stop sign dressed in green light.

I take my place in the triangle. Flash after flash goes off. Noora seamlessly flows from one angle to the next. She's super gentle whenever she has to fix our hair or help us change position.

Everything is as picture perfect as President Turner wants it to be. He even claps from time to time. Maybe Andrew's right. It's useless to reason with him, but it's still worth a shot.

"Lana?" Noora lowers her camera. "Are you all right?"

"What? Oh. My bad. Just got a bit distracted there." I smile again.

Noora is flying through these shots like a pro. We leave my solo portraits for last. First, I take pictures by myself, then the dragons join me. I picture how cool it would look if they were flying across the habitat, or even if they were allowed to Fade in public. But President Turner isn't game for any action shots. He's giving me a big thumbs-up as I pretend I'm a mannequin.

Once Noora wraps up, she says, "You were wonderful to work with,

Team Puerto Rico. Expect the final results to hit the IBF website and newspapers everywhere in a few days."

"Thank you, Noora," we all say together.

She and her father start bidding us farewell, along with President Turner.

My face falls. "You're *leaving*?"

"Yes. I have a meeting with the finance committee soon." President Turner seizes my shoulders. "I'm so very happy with your progress, Ms. Torres. Keep up the great work!"

"Thank you, sir. But I was wondering if we could have a minute?"

"Oh, I'd *love* to, but I really should get going. You can always give me a call! Remember the house phone has my number saved on speed dial. Have a wonderful rest of your day!" He lets me go and makes a beeline for the elevator. "I'll see you all during the opening ceremonies!"

A phone call won't let me see how he's reacting. He could easily manipulate his voice to pretend he's telling the truth. That's if he even *answers* my call. President Turner had been so determined to remove the distance between us, and now he's shoving a fence in my path.

So I let him get into the elevator. Cornering him had been both a failure and a mistake. I need to get his attention with a different tactic. Something he won't be able to ignore.

And I know the perfect way to do it.

AFTER SIX UNANSWERED PHONE CALLS, I GIVE UP ON TRYING TO contact the president.

He could really be at a meeting. I don't have time to keep waiting, though.

I hang up the house phone and head back to my room. It takes me twenty seconds to whip up a private message to Andrew:

Hey! I saw the president today. He slipped away before I could grill him, but he said I could call him later. He never picked up the phone, though.

I have a proposition for you.

He replies twenty minutes later:

interesting. what's your proposition?

I'm in, Andrew. Let's protest the Cup together.

The screen shows me he's read the message, but he's not typing.

Not that I blame him. He could think this is coming out of left field.

This is the best way to force President Turner's attention on me. I don't want to cancel the Cup. Andrew doesn't have to know that. Neither does President Turner. He'll be forced to pull me aside so he can reprimand me. Maybe even ask me to take back my words in a public forum. I'll only do so if he comes clean. Whatever he demands, my ultimatum remains the same.

Andrew finally writes back:

excellent life choice, lana. we'll be in touch.

I send him a smile emoji and log off. I'm practically skipping on my way to the gym. Maybe this will be another failure, another mistake, but it doesn't feel like it right now.

It's the end of the game I never signed up for.

Dragon Knights originated long before the Sire had even been born. Countries like Thailand, China, Japan, Mongolia, Zimbabwe, Kenya, and Russia have been reported as having the highest number of shrines built in honor of their respective dragons. However, most of these shrines exalted dragons without advocating for the slaughter of humans. It was only when the Sire famously broke his Bond with Edward Barnes that the rise of Dragon Knights as soldiers in the war against non-dragons came to pass. Although the majority of Dragon Knights are Regulars, such as the notorious Headhunter of Alabama, Grace Wiggins, some members of the magical community have also chosen to spill the blood of their brethren to appease their master.

—*Excerpt from Edna Clarke's* Magical History
for Regulars, Twelfth Edition

CHAPTER FOURTEEN

S O THE WHOLE WORLD KNOWS I'M PUERTO RICO'S RUNNER NOW. Four days before the opening ceremonies, the IBF released our team photo and solo portraits. Joaquín taped the group pic to our fridge. He's stared at it every morning like it's a blessed trinket from the sports gods. Even though I don't tell him, I'm happy to see him happy. Someone who's as dedicated as he is should get rewarded, even in the little ways.

Manny's glanced at the photo twice. His only response upon seeing it was, "Good thing our dragons are black. Can you imagine if they were neon orange?"

Online reactions have been much kinder. A lot of people hadn't suspected I'd be the chosen replacement for Brian Santana. Jeffrey Hines did a whole segment praising me on his show. It has forty million views on BlazeReel already.

Then there's the other video with sixty million views.

"Welcome to *The Wright Report* on the Flash News Channel. I'm your host, Martin B. Wright," says the black-haired American man in a drab gray suit. He's lanky enough to pass as a wannabe Count Olaf. I'm in Training Room E, watching him on my phone instead of paying attention to whatever my teammates are gossiping about. "Lana Torres has been confirmed as the Puerto Rican Runner for this year's Cup. We know she can run thanks to the Waxbyrne video. What's up for debate is whether Torres belongs on a team representing a country she hasn't lived in since she was five years old. This is what I like to call the Convenient Latina. She remembered she's from Puerto Rico when the Blazewrath World Cup came knocking. And let's not kid ourselves. She's only been named Runner because she's famous."

I hit pause on the fifty-six-minute video. This guy has dedicated a whole episode to tearing me down way worse than Victoria. Do they hate me simply because I haven't gone back to the island? Am I supposed to yell out "Boricua pride!" whenever a camera's in front of me and tweet about tostones every day? Martin B. Wright isn't even Latino. He's all high and mighty over something that doesn't concern him just to get more ratings.

Joaquín has advised me not to acknowledge the video publicly. Samira and Papi have told me the same thing. I'd messaged Mom to ask her not to give him the time of day if he comes fishing for an exclusive. She still hasn't replied. Not that I'm surprised.

"Please tell me you're not watching that crap again." Héctor covers my phone's screen with his hand. "That stuff's bad for your mind."

"Actually, it helps me stay motivated." I quickly glance at Victoria.

"I want to prove my haters wrong." It's like Marisol told me: Don't burn yourself away, but dabble in the fire long enough to stay hot.

Victoria nods. "Using the hate as fuel. I like it."

Of course you like it.

"All right, gather round," says Joaquín. He's holding up a tablet with the Round of Sixteen groups that were announced this morning. This is the Cup's first phase. Teams get lumped into four different groups, each of which consists of four teams. One of the three other teams in our group will be our first opponent. The other two teams will battle each other in their first match. That winner plays against us during quarterfinals, if we win the first match.

Each Cup day is reserved for two matches from the same group. One in the morning. One in the afternoon. Hopefully, our match will be in the morning. I wouldn't want to run up a mountain in the dead of night because the morning match went on for too long.

The group brackets are zoomed in on Joaquín's tablet:

GROUP D

Guatemala versus France

Argentina versus Pakistan

GROUP C

Venezuela versus South Korea

México versus Sweden

GROUP B

Scotland versus Portugal

Spain versus Egypt

GROUP A

Zimbabwe versus China

Puerto Rico versus Russia

Yep. We're going up against the Zmey Gorynych. Not the biggest dragons in the tournament, but they have three heads. *Three.* That means three different sets of flames aiming for me at the same time. Also, the Zmey Gorynych are *so fast.* I'll get blown off the mountain before I can see the first Block Zone. And then there are the Volkov twins. Kirill and Artem are trained in martial arts, of course, but their tactical skills are out of control.

"We are all going to die." Luis is on the verge of hysterical tears.

"¡No digas eso!" says Edwin. "Vamos a estar bien, así que cálmate."

"That's right. We'll be fine," Génesis says, even though she's staring at the tablet like the devil's dancing on top of corpses on-screen. "It's just . . . that's a hard group to beat."

Victoria could cut through metal with her glare. "Puerto Rico is counting on us. My *mother* is counting on me. We've both been treated like trash, but that's never happening again. This is *our* Cup. We're winners."

I'm so taken aback I can't even hide it. This is the first time I've heard her speak of her mom like this. The first time she's admitted to being something other than the greatest. I can't imagine what it's like to endure years of physical abuse, let alone admit to it.

Victoria doesn't seem to realize how big of a deal this is. She watches us like she's waiting for confirmation. Everyone nods in agreement.

"Así es," says Héctor. He's upbeat as he hugs us all one by one. "We're going to win."

I let him hold on to me. He has no idea what Andrew and I have been secretly planning. Will he call me a traitor after he watches me protest? Will he finally tell me how much he's doubted me all this time? Will the others join him?

My nerves grow tenfold with every reassuring tap on the back Héctor gives me.

"You got this, Lana," he says. "You hear me?"

"Loud and clear, Captain." I stand on the Runner's mark as he rushes off to where Titán awaits, bracing myself to fly up the mountain harder than ever before.

The opening ceremonies are tomorrow, but it definitely feels like the Cup has already begun.

SIXTEEN BLACK SUVS ARRIVE AT 7:00 A.M. SHARP THE NEXT DAY. Each team gets its own car, complete with tinted windows and license plates that read WRATH. They're here to take us in a caravan to the Blazewrath stadium.

The whole team is suited up and waiting for Manny in the living room.

"Don't you think that's too much highlighter?" a disapproving Marisol asks Gabriela, who's touching up her cheeks with a fan brush. Victoria, Génesis, and I are all set with what Gabriela calls the Laidback Drama look, which is a mix of nude tones and big eyelashes.

Gabriela looks offended. "Marisol, there's no such thing as too much highlighter." She's also sporting nude lips like me, but I have no idea how she's pulling off neon pink and robin's egg blue on her eyelids and not looking like a clown. "Does anyone need retouching?"

"I'm good, thanks," says Héctor. "Marisol, are you coming to the stadium?"

"Oh, no, no. You're on your own, papito. But before you abandon me"—she pulls out her phone—"selfie!" She waits for us to squish together behind her, with Luis and Héctor throwing peace signs at the camera. We all break apart after the photo's been taken.

Manny bursts out of the double doors. He's in a suit jacket and unironed pants. His tie is loosely hanging around his neck. "Let's hit it, mi gente."

Sunlight warms me on the way to the SUV. Most teams are already inside their cars. There are three choppers above us. They've been sent to broadcast live footage of the teams' drive. It's so weird seeing them from this perspective. I'm used to bouncing on my bed as the sixteen SUVs trail behind one another in a single file, exiting the Compound as one long snake dipped in oil. I'd figured it would be more exciting from this angle. It would be such a rush to climb into that passenger seat, knowing reporters from all over the globe were waiting for me.

But all I feel is the weight of the world's eyes chained to me.

I hear Martin B. Wright's rant again. After today, there will be more of everything. Good *and* bad. The protest will be worth it, though. How can President Turner ignore me after something so blatantly disrespectful? Unless he's too pissed off to face me. What if he sends someone else over instead? Or worse, rips my contract to shreds? Would he be capable of kicking me out of the Cup this close to the start? Am I making a huge mistake?

Chill. The hell. Out. You're starting to burn too much again.

"When you get there, we'll already be waiting at the entrance," Manny says as I buckle my seat belt in the car's last row. He and Joaquín aren't coming with us in the car. A wizard clad in security black is supposed to Transport them and the dragons right after we depart. The red carpet is meant for the players alone. It's tradition to keep the dragons from flying on camera until the opening ceremonies start. "Don't pay any attention to whatever it is that you see when you get there. And don't speak to anyone that's not your teammate, ¿me entienden?"

Everyone says "Sí" except for me.

"You mean fans?" I ask Manny. "They're waiting outside the stadium?"

"You walk into that stadium without stopping for anyone or anything."

Manny slams the door shut.

While he heads back to Joaquín and the security guard, our driver turns on the ignition. We don't go anywhere, though. The car sits idly in the middle of the sand.

"Waiting for something, sir?" Luis asks him politely.

"Scotland," Victoria says. Their house's doors are wide open. Since the cars move as one, no one can drive off until all the teams are inside.

Five minutes later, Team Scotland exits their house. Four boys. Three girls. They're wearing sky-blue leather uniforms with pale-white armor. Andrew leads the charge, sporting aviator sunglasses and messy bedhead, but he lets his teammates get into the car before him.

meet me by my team's greenroom before the ceremonies start, he'd texted me last night. i have something we can both use when we fly onto the field.

I'd replied within seconds: *Count on it.* I don't know how Andrew will be able to sneak anything into the stadium, but he's crafty.

Our driver hits the gas. The invisible shield flickers a bit as we exit the protected area. The helicopters move with us. As the car goes deeper into Pink Rock Desert, weaving through dune after dune, they descend to capture better shots.

"There!" Gabriela says out of the blue. "There's the stadium, you guys!"

I search past the windshield. The Blazewrath World Cup stadium is a circular, roofless building triple the size of a football stadium. Its walls are made of glistening white marble, same as the dozens of sculptures that have been placed around the edges. Each sculpture is a Fire Drake in a different pose. Some are breaking out of their eggs and spreading their wings. Others are crouched with their fangs exposed, ready for a fight. And a few are ripping out their invisible opponents' throats with their claws. And few more are using their tails as spears. Only one dragon breathes fire at the wind— the one that's right above the stadium entrance.

"That's not the paparazzi," Génesis whispers.

A crowd has gathered outside the stadium's entrance. About a hundred people hold up homemade signs. Security guards block their way to the doors. Their messages are written in bloodred paint: CANCEL THE CUP! A few have blown-up pictures of the late Hikaru.

Sayuri Endo stands at the head of the group.

She's a short wisp of a woman, with chin-length black hair that frames her deep frown and a short black dress. Her sign is the smallest, but it's a giant among ants: NO MORE BLOOD.

"Cancel the Cup! Cancel the Cup! Cancel the Cup!"

The chant erupts as the cars approach the red carpet. This is what Manny warned us about. Protesters. Here in Dubai, right where we have no choice but to face them.

"Cancel the Cup! Cancel the Cup! Cancel the Cup!"

After parking the car, our driver opens the door for us. I'm the last to leave the vehicle. The protesters' chants whirl me around until I can't think straight. I'm stuck in my seat, hurting for Hikaru—the dragon the whole world misses—and for those of us who once loved Takeshi Endo. His mother might still think he's good like Andrew. She might be protesting for his safe return more than the lives that will be lost thanks to his master. I can't walk up to her and ask, and maybe I'll never know, but I want this woman to find the peace she's seeking.

"Lana?" Héctor says. "Are you okay?"

"We need to *go*," Victoria says spitefully.

I suck in a shaky breath, then exit the SUV.

"Cancel the Cup! Cancel the Cup! Cancel the Cup!"

My teammates lead me farther away from the bloodred words.

"THE DRAGONS ARE WAITING FOR US IN THE STADIUM'S HIGHEST level, getting harnessed to the Runner's chariot as we speak," Manny informs us in our greenroom. "Once we're cleared to leave, follow me in single file so we can get you all ready for the march."

Calling it a march feels silly. We'll be *flying* around the stadium. My rider teammates get to show off their steeds while I wave our flag behind them. The Runner's chariot is usually designed to fit the dragons' colors, so mine will be black.

I'm squished between Edwin and Génesis on a velvet couch. Luis and Gabriela are attacking one of the fruit bowls, with Luis snatching a fistful of grapes. Héctor and Joaquín hover close to a flat-screen TV, which is showing a news recap of the red-carpet entrances. I see myself with pale cheeks avoiding Mrs. Endo and looking like I'm about to cry. None of the other teams paid the protesters any mind. Their managers must've warned them, too. The SUV carrying Team Scotland is last in line. I wait for Andrew to show his support for the protesters.

He disappears inside the stadium without acknowledging his best friend's mother.

Smart man. Don't let them suspect anything.

I should meet up with him now. We don't have long before showtime.

"Manny, I'm going to the bathroom real quick," I say.

He gives me a pointed look and says a gruff, "Hurry up."

I walk briskly to the greenroom door.

Someone opens it first.

"Hello, hello!" A giddy President Turner barges inside. "Pardon the intrusion, but I have a few people here who'd like a word with our wonderful talent!"

There are three people behind him. I immediately recognize Agent Horowitz and Director Sandhar, but it takes me a second to place the man in the cherry-red suit. His glasses are round and horn rimmed, just as dark as his hair. He has a slight, lean build, like that of a swimmer who trains often, but the closer he walks toward me, the more I remember all the cupcakes he ate from his husband's plate when he served as guest judge on that baking show.

While my teammates all stand to greet our guests, President Turner says: "Everyone, this is Nirek Sandhar, director of the Department of Magical Investigations at the bureau."

Director Sandhar nods. "Just wanted to assure you I'm committed to protecting you at all costs. The Department of Magical Investigations is more than qualified to keep you safe."

"Thank you," most of the team replies. A soft-spoken Edwin says, "Gracias."

"Have any other Dragon Knights been caught, director?" Joaquín says. Bless his soul.

"Not yet, but Ravensworth Penitentiary will be filling up soon," Agent Horowitz replies. She waves to the team. "A pleasure to meet you all. Agent Sienna Horowitz at your service."

While my teammates say hello, I point to the man in the cherry-red suit. "Who's this?"

President Turner wraps an arm around him. "Last but not least, this is my darling husband, Corwin Sykes, headmaster of Foxrose Preparatory School for the Magically Gifted."

Headmaster Sykes waves hello. "Good morning! It's an honor to stand in your presence." His voice is a deep, velvety sound that belongs in voicemail greetings.

"You're the Foxrose Prep headmaster?" a wide-eyed Luis asks.

"I am, yes." Foxrose is the same school he studied at with President Turner, which means Headmaster Sykes once knew Edward Barnes, too.

He once knew the Sire.

"What's it like? Your school?" Gabriela asks.

"Loud. I'm afraid magic and children can be a cacophonous combination."

"Try combining dragons and teenagers. You won't sleep for years!" President Turner starts to laugh. Then he coughs four times in a row. It sounds as if he's just been plucked from underwater, but the poor man's still drowning at the same time.

Joaquín pours him a glass of water. "Here you go, Mr. President."

"Thank you . . . so much . . ." President Turner reaches for the glass, but his knees buckle.

He crashes to the floor.

I'm a breathless, useless pile of nothing while President Turner sinks into a seizure. He arches his back as if he's mercilessly being whipped over and over.

"Russell!" Headmaster Sykes holds him in a bear hug. Despite his efforts, President Turner is still twisting, sweating, and coughing. "Russell, hang on, love!"

"We have to move him!" Director Sandhar tries to lift President Turner, who keeps writhing, as if he's tethered to the spot, an invisible magnet dragging him against his will.

Manny pulls me back like I'm a ragdoll. The whole team is shielded behind him.

"*Damn* it," he mutters.

The TV screen flashes that static, no-signal snow.

Darkness replaces it, drifting forward, farther and farther away from the screen.

I bite down hard. The darkness is the back of a leather trench coat, and when its bearer turns around, a man made of stardust scales beams at the camera.

"The last time I addressed you, a man died," says the Sire. "His death is the fault of those who choose to challenge me. Those who foolishly defy the gods."

The camera pans out even more. It's not a mansion this time. The walls are built from stone that's been scratched in all sorts of ways. Shrubberies and a lake fill the space behind the Sire. More scratch marks adorn the soil. Some trees have been hacked down and others singed to ashes. The industrial lights have been dimmed, the area is vacant, but I know it's a habitat for an Un-Bonded, vicious dragon. He's at a sanctuary again.

"The International Blazewrath Federation is currently trying to distract you with their opening ceremonies. They have not canceled the Cup. The bureau has not freed the Fire Drake from captivity. Today you shall see what happens when my commands are ignored."

The Sire darts off deeper into the sanctuary. The camera follows him, but it's not shaking. It's gliding forward in a straight line.

Magic.

President Turner's coughs subside. Now he's huffing up a storm. He's trying to say something, but he keeps choking on air.

The Sire halts in a clearing. There's another black trench coat joining him—Takeshi. He's still clutching that claw dagger, trailing behind the Sire like his lapdog.

Something roars into the sky. It tears down the surrounding trees, smashing them into splintered wood. A wall of flames erupts behind the Sire and Takeshi. They wait as the dragon creeps through the receding flames, a crown of lava-orange feathers framing its face. Its feathery mane ruffles with each step. It hides the dragon's red scales underneath. The dragon's tail is also covered in feathers, but the spikes are still visible, sharp enough to poke their way through steel.

This dragon is a Pluma de Muerte.

There are three dragon sanctuaries in México. They're in one right now.

"We have a message for those who wish to challenge the gods," Takeshi speaks. "Do as the Sire tells you. Or watch a different city burn down every week."

"Oh my God . . ." I whisper. They won't take one life this time. Hundreds. *Thousands.*

Including my father. Nausea washes over me as I picture his lifeless body, the Sire and Takeshi Endo towering over him with an air of victory. I don't care about his precious Violet #43 or his commitment to helping Un-Bonded dragons. I don't care how many more Silver Wands the bureau plans on sending for their protection. I need Papi out of that sanctuary ASAP.

"This is a promise," says the Sire. "Play this wretched game, and the world turns to ash."

The Pluma de Muerte roars again, lifting its fanged mouth as high as it can.

The Sire laughs. "I agree. I think it *is* time you all met our cameraman. Randall?"

A third black coat comes out from behind the camera. It's still propped up high, but it's slightly turning to the supposed cameraman, then zooming in on his face, which confirms magic is moving it. The boy named Randall is blond and tall, a little over six feet, and much thinner than Takeshi. He's as pale as those vampires Samira loves to read about in paranormal romance books. When he faces the lens, I can see he's just as beautiful, too, but there's a sinister glow in his electric-blue eyes. The camera zooms out again. Randall takes his place between the Sire and Takeshi. He has the stance of a general riling up his soldiers for war.

"Nirek . . ." comes Agent Horowitz's cracked whisper.

Director Sandhar is a lifeless Polaroid of a once-brave man. He's gaping at the screen like nothing else in the world exists.

"Anything you would like to say to our dear Director Sandhar?" the Sire asks Randall.

Randall's smile is dripping poison. "Hi, Dad."

No matter how many times I search for answers in Director Sandhar's expression, he's not giving me any. He's twisting the TV into knots with his unforgiving gaze, no doubt wishing he could destroy something with sheer willpower alone.

"Most of you don't know me. That's my dad's fault, but it's okay. I'm the Headhunter's legacy. Let me make sure none of you forget." Randall fishes something out of his coat's pocket. It's a long, thin metal rod. No gemstones. No decorations of any kind.

And it's bright, glowing gold.

I cover my gaping mouth. Randall is a Gold Wand. He must've been the one giving Takeshi those magical orbs with spells inside. And he's *related* to Director Sandhar.

Takeshi is a silent snake. He peeks at Randall, then at the Sire, until he finally glances back at the camera. His grin is salt to my fresh wounds.

"Randall?" the Sire proudly calls out. "Show them what will happen if I am defied again."

"Yes, Sire." Randall raises his wand high. He brings it down in a swift thrust.

BOOM!

The sanctuary walls explode. An avalanche of dust and debris hurtles toward where the Sire, his two human lackeys, and the Pluma de Muerte watch in awe. A golden shield encases them entirely. It flashes to life upon contact with the myriad of objects bursting all around the sanctuary—lake water, rocks, tree trunks, branches, claw-stabbed dirt. Where once there was a home for a dragon, now there's ground zero. Its attacker remains unbothered, ripping it piece by piece with magic that's mightier than anything I've ever witnessed.

The Sire seems about two seconds away from breaking out into song. He's flaunting his greatest weapon against the whole damn world, and he's *so* pleased with himself.

"Remember who your master is," he says.

The screen fades to black, then shows the red-carpet footage again.

In a hushed, weakened voice, President Turner finally speaks, "Ciudad Juárez. Hurry."

He collapses into his husband's arms.

Magic is might,
But so is the heart.
Beware the desires of others,
They'll tear you apart.

—Famous last words of Eldritch Vaughn, renowned
American painter/Silver Wand

CHAPTER FIFTEEN

DIRECTOR SANDHAR HELPS HEADMASTER SYKES TURN THE unconscious president on his side. They say it's safer to wait for him to wake up on his own than to use magic after his seizure.

I'm leaning against the wall in an attempt to stay upright. What just *happened*? And why did the president mumble about a specific region in the same country the Sire is currently in?

How does he know exactly where to find him?

After Director Sandhar makes sure President Turner is comfortable, he whips out his wand and glances over at Agent Horowitz with a ferocious grin. "We need to get to México right now." He then turns to the rest of us. "Nobody leaves this room until I return."

He and Agent Horowitz are out the door in a flash.

Manny's gaze keeps darting from President Turner to the door. In Spanish, he implores everybody to stay calm, but he's as jittery as ever, pacing like he's trying to burn off calories.

I look from him to the president to him again. "Why can't we leave?"

"Because we just saw something we weren't supposed to," says a tense Joaquín.

"Are you talking about the video or the president's collapse?" I say. "Or is it *both*?"

Joaquín has eyes for his father alone. "What will Director Sandhar do to us, Pa?"

"Don't worry about that. We have to stay calm for Russell."

"We're all calm except for you." Joaquín positions himself in front of Manny, forcing him to stop pacing. "Is he erasing our memories?"

"What? No!" My breakfast somersaults in my stomach. "He can't *do* that."

"Please tell me this is a joke," Génesis says.

"No one is erasing my memory," Victoria tells Manny. "I don't give a damn about what you're afraid of us knowing or seeing. I won't say anything. None of us will."

"¿Por qué necesitan hacernos esto?" Edwin asks why they need to do this to us.

Lying to the public is one thing, but we've just witnessed something we deserve the answers to. This illness shouldn't be such a threat for a man as rich as President Turner. He could afford the best medical care in the world, and yet he's hiding a condition that causes him pain at the most inconvenient times. Why would he willingly endure this constant attack on his body?

Unless it's not treatable . . . or maybe . . .

It's not an illness.

"Oh crap," I whisper.

"What?" Victoria says.

Great. Everyone is looking at me now.

I zero in on Headmaster Sykes. "Is he taking any meds?"

"Thank you for your concern, Ms. Torres, but my husband's health is a private matter," a red-cheeked Headmaster Sykes says.

"I'll take that as a no. I go to a public school that's open to Regulars and magically gifted people. We learn about magical maladies. When a witch or wizard is sick, it can be a treatable illness like a Regular's flu"—I take a step forward —"or it can be a curse."

Headmaster Sykes's eyebrows shoot up. His silence is the dreaded confirmation I need.

Magic is what's hurting President Turner.

Someone gasps.

President Turner sits up ramrod straight, clinging to Headmaster Sykes. He's a fish fresh out of water, gulping for air and comfort. His unfocused eyes finally seem to register our collective presence. He takes out his wand. "You all need . . . to keep this . . . to yourselves . . ."

"Then tell us what the hell's going on," I say.

Manny could peel off my skin with his glare. "Lana, do as he says. *All* of you"—he points at my teammates—"can never speak a word of this."

"Okay!" Victoria raises her hands like she's being taken into custody. "We'll keep quiet."

"*No!*" I shout. From the way her eyes grow a million sizes larger, this could be the first time *anyone* who isn't her stepfather has yelled at Victoria. I turn my back on her, even though that's probably a bad idea. My beef with her isn't as important as the one I have with President Turner. "How do you know where the Sire is, Mr. President? Is it because you're *working* with him?"

The room falls dead silent. Not even the president's labored breathing is audible.

"Ms. Torres," he says, "I swear I will explain everything in due time, but right now you—"

"Tell me the truth, and I won't say anything. Otherwise, I'm walking out of this room and confessing to every news outlet in this stadium what I just witnessed. I'm sure they'd *love* to hear about how the president of the International Blazewrath Federation is in cahoots with a terrorist.

And before you think you can stop me"—I shake my head—"remember what my job here is."

All of my teammates, along with Joaquín, are watching me with a mix of admiration and terror. Protesting the Cup pales in comparison to this.

A flustered Manny is about to say something. President Turner cuts in. "Very well, Ms. Torres, but I need you all inside my Other Place." He motions to the door. "No one else can overhear what we discuss."

Manny and Headmaster Sykes both gape at him.

"What are you doing, Russell?" Manny demands.

"Something that's going to make Director Sandhar very angry."

Without warning, President Turner flicks his wrist and blinds us in a flash.

I'm back in his Other Place.

Instead of arriving in the corridor, I'm inside the opulent living room, where the fireplace is home to a small, flickering flame. There's dessert everywhere, too. Trays of pies and cakes surround the main sitting area. A glass bowl is filled with the president's cherished red apples.

"Take a seat, my dears," President Turner tells the team as he plops onto a chaise.

Headmaster Sykes is quick to fetch him a glass of water. He drinks it in slow bursts.

Manny's right next to the bar, scowling at President Turner. He fixes himself a brownish drink, then chugs it down in one gulp. He fixes himself another, but this time, he doesn't drink it. He's silently holding it while my teammates settle on the chaises and the demilune sofa.

I'm the last to sit down, choosing a chaise all by myself. "Are you working with the Sire?"

President Turner leans against Headmaster Sykes, his face pinched like he's chewing on something sour. "The truth is far more complicated than a simple yes or no. It's like you correctly guessed earlier. The Sire cursed me when I was seventeen years old."

I almost fall off my chaise. How's that even possible? No dragon has been able to use their magic to curse humans. Then again, the Sire's the only dragon to shatter the Bond with his rider.

"What does this curse do to you?" I ask.

"Another complicated answer, I'm afraid. You see, months after my best friend Bonded with a dragon, I woke up alone in a clearing one night. It was a few miles from our school. The last thing I remembered was falling asleep in bed. As I tried to make my way back to the dorm, the Sire swooped in to stop me." He pauses. "That was the first time I heard his voice."

I'm on the edge of my seat now. "A Bonded dragon let you *listen* to his voice?"

"Indeed."

"What did he tell you?" Gabriela asks.

"*You are my anchor, and I am yours.*" President Turner quivers. "Then he sank the tip of his tail through my heart. The pain . . . it was unbelievable . . . I was dead. The Sire left my lifeless body in that clearing. And still I woke up the next morning. There were no wounds or scars. I convinced myself it was a nightmare. I Transported home and went about my day."

I stiffen. The picture I found of him with the Sire and Edward Barnes had been taken in a clearing. He'd been the only one not smiling. Maybe that had been the same clearing where he died and came back to life, where the Sire spoke to another human he wasn't Bonded with.

"So you're . . . undead?" Héctor asks gingerly.

"We don't really have a term to classify him," Headmaster Sykes says, frowning. "As an academic, I specialize in obscure magical folklore and enchantments. None of the sources I've come into contact with have mentioned a dragon killing and bringing a human back to life. Much less binding him in the ways the Sire has bound my husband. This case remains an anomaly."

That's one word for it.

"What happened after you returned to school?" I ask.

"Everything went on as usual. Eddie didn't have a clue. The Sire found us playing cards by the Foxrose main steps. When Eddie excused himself to go to the bathroom, I started cutting the deck, but my hand froze. I couldn't move it no matter what I did. As I was about to call for help, the Sire spoke to me in my thoughts again. He confessed to killing and reviving me, and he said the words I've never stopped hearing since: *Remember who your master is.*"

That's the same thing he said on camera a few minutes ago.

He hadn't been talking to the world. He'd been talking to the president.

"The curse works like so," he says. "I am responsible for some of my actions. My life has been a series of choices both mine and not mine. And, most important, I'm alive because the Sire is alive. Our bodies, our very souls, are intertwined. I believe he's anchored himself to me as a form of self-preservation. If I'm hurt, or if I die, nothing happens to him. He would grow stronger through my suffering. Eddie cursed the Sire into an immortal body, but if he died, I'd die, too. Whenever he's injured, he quickly recovers, but I feel the aftereffects of his pain long after he's healed. He hurts me both of his own volition and whenever something hurts him."

I let out a gasp. "So *that's* why Edward Barnes didn't kill him twenty years ago! He knew killing his former dragon steed would kill you, too."

"Yes. Eddie discovered my curse after the Sire broke the Bond."

"But you still haven't explained how you can track him," Luis says.

"Well, it was my husband"—he taps Headmaster Sykes's thigh—"who suggested my curse could provide information I never thought possible. He's currently teaching me how to infiltrate the Sire's thoughts. Today was the first time I could actually read him in full, though, and after Lana *demanded* the truth, he chose to show you. I'm so sorry, my dears."

Héctor is barely breathing. "Sorry for what, sir?"

Crickets.

Then the president says, "Teaching has always been my passion, but the Sire had other plans. I climbed up the IBF's ranks, always hearing his voice in my head. When I became president six years ago, his biggest dream for me had been achieved."

I only know I'm still alive because my heart's beating super fast. My theory had been sort of right. The president of the International Blazewrath Federation isn't willingly working with the Sire. He's the Sire's puppet. He's not even fully *alive*. I try to keep my breathing stable, but I'm shaking, and the room is shrinking, and everything is a blur.

The Sire still lives. Edward Barnes cast a blood curse, which allowed his death to seal the Sire's fate. From what Samira has told me, that's the only curse there's no way of reversing or breaking. Whatever happened to the president, it must have a cure.

"Yours isn't a blood curse, Mister President," I say. "The Sire would have had to die performing the spell in order for it to be forever binding. You can totally break this."

Headmaster Sykes says, "We've tried everything. The Sire's magic remains."

My shoulders drop. Of course the Sire would find a way to ruin someone's life so epically, but what kind of magic carries this much weight even after the one who cast it doesn't have powers anymore? And what kind of bloodless curse is strong enough not to be broken?

"You do whatever he tells you, but you haven't canceled the Cup yet," Joaquín says, totally horrified. "He doesn't actually *want* you to cancel it, does he?"

I wait for the president to shoot down his theory as nonsense.

Instead, he says, "The Cup is part of the Sire's domain. It has been for the past six years. This is where he keeps the world's most ferocious Bonded dragons and their riders, right where he can watch their every move. It also helps him gain more allies like Mrs. Endo and the other protesters. They might not condone his acts of violence, but they're choosing to stand against the IBF and the bureau for failing to stop his murders. All this time, he's the one moving the pieces." His eyes start to well up. "Your careers, your *lives*, belong to him."

He conjures scrolls from thin air. They're long and a little faded, but I recognize them.

Our contracts.

President Turner flicks his wand. The endless black ink disappears. Our signatures stay at the bottom of the page, but the text above them is in deep scarlet. The erratic, barely legible handwriting features words I hadn't seen upon signing:

I hereby agree to participate in the twenty-seventh Blazewrath World Cup in accordance with the Sire's wishes. I shall obey his commands, as well as comply with my duties as a member of my country's team. This agreement is bound by magic As such, the consequences I face upon breaking it shall be swiftly communicated to the Sire and implemented by those loyal to him. Disobedience and/or failure to accomplish what is required, including divulging the true nature of this contract should I discover it, shall be punishable by death.

The chaise where I sit is sand. I'm being swallowed into the deepest pits of the underworld, tumbling into frigid darkness, too stunned to fight against gravity.

The Sire controls the president *and* the Cup.

We're all his playthings. Prisoners, like Andrew believes.

Of all the things I could think of, I think of my mother. She'd been right to question this whole thing. So had Papi, but Mom had been the constant voice of dissent. I'd been so angry with her I never wondered if something bad could happen. Now the worst has happened instead.

I don't know when I start crying, but I don't know how to stop.

"So we're . . . He's . . . in charge?" Luis struggles with every word.

President Turner can't even say it again.

"Mister President," I choke out, "did the Sire make you recruit us?"

He offers me a heartbroken frown. "Your stories are not the same. The Sire wished for your teammates to be in the Cup because he was curious of their dragons' magic. He wished to see what they were capable of in a controlled environment, where he could study them with greater care. But he wanted to kill you for what you did to Takeshi. He'd even planned a televised execution. Something changed his mind, though. He chose to monitor you instead."

I'm a batch of ashes and dust. My dream coming true is the result of a cursed dragon wanting to use me for his master plan. The president is a puppet, and so am I. No amount of talent matters. I'm here because I'm famous for thwarting my forever favorite. I'm here because I hurt the Sire's feelings and messed up his endgame with that crystal heart.

This isn't my dream come true. This is his punishment for me.

But I still have questions. "Why does the Sire need to monitor us? How does studying the dragons and their magical skills fit his agenda?" I pause. "What exactly *is* his agenda?"

"Maybe he's looking for ways to defeat us in case we riot?" Génesis offers.

"We can't riot, thanks to our contracts," Héctor says.

"Exactly," says Victoria. "We can't do anything other than what we came here to do, which is to win. You think I want that bastard acting like he owns me? *Nobody* owns me. But I came here to bring the Cup home, and that's all I care about. Everything else is a distraction."

I'm glaring at her with all my might. She's *seriously* putting a trophy over our rights and well-being. A trophy that means nothing because this tournament is a sham. I get that she once felt like a loser. She's here because of her mom. I crave that trophy, too, but not like this.

And here I thought not being Puerto Rican enough was the biggest blow to my ego.

"Victoria . . ." Joaquín's tearing up as he looks to the side, away from prying eyes.

It's only now that I remember Manny's here. He leaves the bar and his drink behind, approaching us with caution. "Victoria's right, mi gente. We have no choice." His indifferent tone finally takes on a logical shape in my head.

"This is why you're not invested in us," I say. "You knew about the Anchor Curse and the Sire's hold over us all. You don't care about the Cup because it's not real." The frustration I once felt for Manny's attitude evaporates into nothing. Now I understand him.

"It *is* real," says Victoria.

"You're pawns. We all are," Manny barks at her. "When I found out, Russell showed me *my* contract. I'm bound to that asshole, too."

Realization dawns on Génesis's face. "Was this when you went to London?"

Of course: Brian Santana's firing. Manny went cold after that incident.

He nods. "I was there to discuss next steps after we kicked out Brian."

"*Don't* say his name!" Victoria is a thunderstorm in a petite frame. With a sniffle, she reaches for Edwin's hand. With a tender smile, he accepts hers.

Héctor's brave enough to speak. "Don't punish yourself for missing him. He doesn't deserve a second of your time, but if you feel like you can't—"

"Stop talking about him!" She's full-blown crying.

Edwin pulls her into a hug.

"The point is," Manny continues, unbothered, "I met with Russell at his home. It was a terrible time to visit him. I left knowing more than I bargained for."

President Turner says, "The Sire was venting his rage on me for losing a Runner."

"And the bureau? Do they know about this curse?" Joaquín asks. "I'm assuming at least Director Sandhar is aware of it, since he allowed you to be present during Lana's interrogation."

Damn it, he's right. I hadn't connected those dots until now.

"Only Nirek and Agent Horowitz know. They have similar contracts, swearing them to secrecy and requiring them to fulfill the Sire's demands. The bureau is still free to try to catch him, mostly because the Sire is confident they never will. And after so many years together, it was impossible to hide this curse from Corwin."

Manny claps his hands. "This has been enlightening. Can we leave now?"

Joaquín finally speaks again, "We can't talk about what happened here, or in the greenroom, to anyone. We all understand this quite well. Don't we?"

We all nod in silence. Victoria's no longer crying, but she seems utterly depleted.

So does Joaquín, despite being the picture of calm. "Then let's get back to the stadium."

Somehow I find the strength to get up. I'm still crying, still drawing the shape of my mother's face the day she abandoned me, hoping I'd go with her instead.

The blinding flash of the Transport Charm engulfs me, sending me back to a world that's been built on blood and lies.

"Andrew has always been a friendly bloke. I don't know a single person who dislikes him! He shines brightest when speaking to others. However, in all my years in this sport, I've never come close to witnessing the kind of brotherhood he shares with Takeshi Endo. Those two are inseparable. From the moment they crossed paths, it was like watching long-lost twins find each other. Not many Blazewrath athletes can sway their supporters to root for another team. Yet Andrew has managed to get Scotland chanting for Japan during their matches. Japan's supporters have even started chanting for Scotland, too! That is the power of Andrew Galloway."

—Transcript from 2015 radio interview with
Russell Turner, IBF president

CHAPTER SIXTEEN

Director Sandhar doesn't come back to the stadium. He calls President Turner instead.

After a long conversation in which they discuss our new knowledge of our contracts, President Turner hangs up and tells us, "He got away."

Nobody speaks. I'm still in the greenroom with my team, which currently consists of crushed spirits, save for Victoria. Some of the IBF staff freaked out once they noticed we were missing. There'd been a bunch of security guards in the room when we returned. After the president calmly sent them away, he'd gotten the call from Director Sandhar, who relented to let us keep our memories. Now I want him to take every damn thing in my pounding head.

He got away.

Just like he's getting away with controlling the Cup. I need to figure out why we matter so much to him. This can't only be about making us the villains of his story. There has to be *more*.

I dab at my eyes, drying up leftover tears. Am I the Sire's prisoner? Yes. That doesn't mean I'm *staying* his prisoner.

President Turner is in the dark about his master's real plan, so pressing him will be useless. I need to get craftier if I want to figure out what the Sire wants. Grinding his ultimate desire to dust might be the only way I can save Blazewrath. This competition matters too much for it to be tarnished like this. We just need our freedom back.

He got away, but I'll make sure he doesn't get what he's after.

First, I need to stop Andrew from protesting. If I beg hard enough, hopefully I can save him from making himself the Sire's next target.

A male IBF employee arrives to take us to the dragons. We cram inside the elevators in the most uncomfortable silence ever. Even Manny, who's a little buzzed, keeps his mouth shut. By the time we get to the wait zone, a whole lifetime has seemingly gone by.

Chaos welcomes us once the doors slide open. There are Blazewrath players and IBF staff members everywhere, but there are also heaps of security guards lining the walls. They're monitoring the players' every move. Some guards stationed near the dragons' wait-zone entrance are escorting them inside. The procession is in alphabetical order.

"Follow me." The employee beckons us forward.

On the way, I spot Andrew, with his head down and his arms folded, in one of the corridors. He has three guards watching him from a distance, but no one's bothering him. It's like there's an unspoken agreement to let him grieve in peace.

I slip away from my team and head straight to Andrew. He doesn't look up at me, but his gaze flickers to my boots. "Hey," I say as softly as I can. "You need to cancel the protest."

I might as well have spit acid on his uniform. "Are you hearing yourself? We're all being herded onto that field, dismissing a horrifying threat from a terrorist, and you want me to *cancel* the protest?" Andrew shakes his head. "Not a chance."

"Listen to me, okay? You could cause more harm than good, especially to yourself."

"Is Turner paying you an extra seven million to say that?" Andrew says icily.

I tip my head back with a hopeless sigh. I can't tell him the truth, but I don't know what works as the perfect lie, either.

"Are you thinking up a convincing load of dung for me?" Andrew's grin is cocky as hell. "What's this harm you're referring to? What unspeakable evil will come to pass if I protest?"

His mocking tone would've pissed me off any other day. Right now, all I can dwell on is how to keep this stubborn boy from testing the Sire's patience. The last thing I want is for him to get hurt because *I* couldn't dissuade him from acting recklessly.

"Earth to Lana?"

I look back at him. "Remember what I said about betraying our countries?"

Andrew rolls his eyes. "Vividly."

"Well, it's the truth. We *would* be betraying our countries. I can't live with that guilt."

"But you can live with the Sire murdering people left and right? That would be bearable to you in comparison?" Andrew looks like his brain is frying up from trying to understand me. Then his eyes go wide. "Something happened before this conversation, didn't it?"

"No," I say too quickly. Damn it.

He tenses. "You're lying."

"Of course not."

"Tell me what happened, Lana."

"Nothing happened."

"Stop lying to me."

"I'm not lying." I retreat a few steps. I can't protect him without compromising my contract. "You know what? Forget it. You're going to think what you want, but trust me, protesting is useless. The Cup won't get canceled. And like I said, it could seriously backfire."

Andrew gives me a pitying look. "I'm not backing down because someone won't do what I say. I'll keep going because I believe in something greater than me. Let the Cup go on if it must, but I won't be silenced." He pushes away from the wall. "Thanks so much for pulling out at the last second like a coward. Don't concern yourself with what I do anymore. We're done."

"I'm trying to help you!" I whisper-yell. "You're making this harder than it should be." I raise a hand to his chest. "I don't know what it's like to be in your shoes, but it must suck to go through this alone, so please don't shut me out. And please don't pick fights you can't win."

Andrew leans down. He's bridging the gap between us, acting like he's about to hug me. Instead, he whispers in my ear, "Thanks, but I'm choosing to resist in other ways."

Wow. He's using *my own words* against me.

Andrew walks away before I find a suitable way to respond.

"There you are!" Gabriela seizes my arm. "Our chariot is ready!"

I follow her out of the corridor, hoping against hope Andrew comes to his senses.

EACH TEAM GETS A PRIVATE WAIT ZONE, WHICH IS A HUGE CHAMBER identical to a hangar. There are sliding panels to the front and back.

Pakistan is in front of us, with Russia settling behind. The panels will open once the procession starts. Each team will be flying out one by one.

The six Sol de Noche dragons have been arranged in pairs. Titán and Esperanza are first, followed by Puya and Daga, then Rayo and Fantasma. They're tethered to thick straps the color of their dark scales, which are all hooked to the chariot that's been built for me.

Not that I'd call it a chariot. It's more like a replica of the Sol de Noche's skull.

Its frontal horns, eye sockets, and fangs are there, but instead of bone white, the skull has been painted black. Its mouth is wide open, as if it's about to devour everything in its path. A podium is nestled between the horns, and a leather strap has been placed at the top. I have to tie it around my waist so I don't free-fall to my death. I shudder. No other Runner has had to step foot in a contraption like this. Everyone else gets Roman-style chariots. There's either been a change in protocol, or I'm the only Runner getting a different design. Either way, it's clear the Sire's trying to keep the press's attention on me. Is he expecting them to drag me for this over-the-top stunt? Or does he want to see how they react? Why would he even care?

And here I thought I couldn't loathe him more.

I walk into the skull chariot. Staff members secure the harness around my waist while my teammates mount their steeds. None of the dragons show signs of discomfort. It's as if they're unbothered by the Sire's latest message. Once the harness is set, another employee hands me a thin white pole with the Puerto Rican flag at the top. It's much lighter than I feared. The red, white, and blue above me is a sight to behold, but I can't look at it for long. I swallow down the boulders stuck in my throat and keep the tears at bay. This isn't the time for a meltdown.

"Puerto Rico ready for takeoff," I catch an employee saying into his mic.

"You look really powerful up there," Joaquín says, trying his best to cheer me up. He then looks at the rest of my team. "You all do.

Remember that. You are *powerful.*"

No. We're prisoners.

Twenty minutes later, the international livestream begins with drums. Their booming, spine-jolting sound engulfs the whole stadium. A television screen appears on the sliding panel ahead, showing a procession of two hundred men from Dubai spilling onto the field. They are all dressed in their white kanduras, cotton robes that reach their ankles. The first man in line beats the biggest drum of all. The ever-posh Jeffrey Hines, who's working as this year's Cup announcer, calls the big drum the Al-Ras and the smaller ones the Takhamir drums.

"We're about to be treated to a special performance of the Al-Ayyala!" he boasts. "Please welcome Dubai's war dancers to the Blazewrath stadium!"

Applause quickly ensues. At first, I think the men are holding long, thin blades, but they're actually camel sticks. They break into two lines, a hundred men on one side, the other hundred on the opposite side. All the men face one another while striking their camel sticks onto the sand and thrusting them into the sky. The men are chanting lyrical snippets in unison, a lovely blend of singsong voices, even though they're pretending to challenge one another in battle. It's such a pulsating, joyous performance that I don't notice the fire dancers coming up behind them.

Once the Al-Ayyala ends, though, the war dancers part ways on either side of the field, allowing a fresh batch of both men and women to toss and twirl fiery batons. It's a seamlessly woven frenzy of flames, acrobatics, and vibrant music. The field almost looks like it's made out of spinning gold. An equally large group of singers appears next, each one gripping a small version of the United Arab Emirates flag: a lone vertical red stripe, along with the horizontal green, white, and black stripes. Singers belt out the IBF's anthem, which is too long and convoluted, but the final verse has always been my favorite: "Bring home the gold, take home wherever you are." It's a reminder for players to proudly share their cultures regardless of which country is hosting the Cup. Growing up, that had been the one line I would sing along to. I prayed for the chance to sing it on the field. Now that the day has come, I can't bring myself to celebrate my culture or anyone else's.

First I have to rip this tournament from the Sire's clutches.

Once the dancers and singers disperse to the sides, President Turner, Ambassador Haddad, and a slew of IBF representatives walk out. They pass right through the middle of the action, smiling and waving at the rowdy fans, then climb on a stage at the end of the field.

"And now the moment you've all been waiting for!" an ecstatic Jeffrey Hines says. "Folks, here are this year's Blazewrath World Cup competitors! First up, Argentina!"

One by one, each team exits the wait zone. None of their chariots are as over the top as mine. This is what I get for standing up to the Sire's little lapdog, Takeshi. How lucky am I.

The sliding panel in front of us rises. I can no longer see Jeffrey Hines or the stands.

"Up next," says Jeffrey, "our newest competitors from Puerto Rico!"

The building is about to collapse. There are whistles and screams and stomping feet and that high-pitched noise that can only come from a horn. I hear an overwhelming amount of panderetas, too, which are similar to tambourines save for the jangling discs on their outer rim. A crew of musicians plays their loudest plena for the world to hear. It's the kind of upbeat music I used to indulge in during weekends at my grandparents' house. Music I haven't heard in *ages*.

So many people from the island have flown to Dubai to watch us play.

So many people have come to witness history.

A tainted, cheapened moment thanks to the Sire.

Titán and Esperanza move forward as one. The rest of the dragons are synchronized to their every motion, flying out of the hangar with ease. It's as if the skull chariot weighs less than an ant. I'm rocked forward but manage to regain my footing seconds before the dragons soar into the sky. I hold the flagpole as high as I'm able to and wave the flag side to side.

"Puerto Rico! Puerto Rico! Puerto Rico!"

Everyone seems to be chanting our country's name. The whole stadium is losing its cool as we get in line behind Pakistan's chariot, slowly circling the stadium.

I keep flaunting our flag, pretending everything is fine. At least no one is booing me. No one demands I prove how Puerto Rican I am or calls me out for abandoning the island. I really am their flag bearer. Their Runner. And yet their cheers don't cross out the words in my secret contract. My fake smile gets the crowd cheering louder. My teammates are doing a better job of appearing excited. Luis is even blowing kisses at the fans. He *almost* makes me crack up.

Russia's announced next, followed by Scotland.

Boos come hard and fast. A few people throw popcorn at the field, shouting gibberish I can't quite make out, but most simply carry on with their incessant booing.

I search for Andrew on the jumbo screens. He's inside his chariot, which is gilded to match the Scottish dragons' intimidating horned heads. While the Golden Horns are all flying in formation, sunlight bouncing off their ice-blue scales with every flap of their spindly wings, the Scottish flag stands tall *beside* Andrew. In its place, he's holding up a large sign with words in bold red: No More Blood. The same words painted on Sayuri Endo's sign.

Andrew's head is lowered, his eyes shut tight. No one from his team is openly protesting. No one else in the *tournament* is openly protesting. Whether he never approached the other players or if they rejected him like I did, Andrew's choosing to be a lone wolf in the woods.

He holds his sign until the very end of the procession, where all the dragons descend onto the creamy sand field. Noora Haddad discreetly snaps him from different angles. The crowd's boos roar like an ocean hurtling toward shore. They subside once a massive Rock Flame lights up onstage. It's about forty feet high, ascending in slow motion. The Rock Flame cracks in half to reveal the Blazewrath World Cup, that golden beacon of hope I've dreamed of holding.

President Turner says, "On behalf of the International Blazewrath Federation, I welcome you all to the twenty-seventh Blazewrath World Cup!"

An assortment of bright-red fireworks set off from all sides of the stadium. Boos are replaced with bursts of light and cheers from the people onstage. The audience joins in with cheers of their own, but Andrew never does.

Neither do I. No one will be reporting about my chariot after Andrew's protest. He'll be the talk of the town, a huge target plastered on his back for the Sire to see. I couldn't protect him.

But I'm still going to stop the Sire from claiming anything else I care about.

Dragon studies experts once believed the Bond could only end with the death of a dragon or its rider. However, this belief was obliterated with the Sire's rebellion. His Bond's rupture has been considered undeniable proof of the choice theory. A dragon can willingly destroy that which links it psychically and emotionally to a human rider. And yet the Sire remains the only dragon to have achieved, or even desired, this outcome.

—*Excerpt from Carlos Torres's* Studying the Bond Between Dragons & Humans

CHAPTER SEVENTEEN

"I'M CONTACTING THE PRESIDENT AS SOON AS I GET OUT OF these burned clothes."

Papi's uniform has been singed at the seams. His hair sticks up like he's survived a windstorm. He'd been conducting a social-skills experiment with Violet #43, which went south when his phone rang. Either the sudden disruption angered her, or she's not a Luis Miguel fan.

"You're not contacting the president, Papi."

"Oh, trust me. You're coming home with me."

Man, I wish I could come clean to him. Things would be easier to explain with the truth. "Director Sandhar promised us everyone in the Cup is super protected. They have a guaranteed lead on the Sire's next steps. I believe him, Papi. He dropped the ball on the Méxican sanctuary, but that was the Sire's lucky break."

Papi rubs his face from either exhaustion or frustration or both. "This isn't something we're going to debate. You're getting on a plane. Period."

"No. I can't get out of my contract. I don't *want* to get out of my contract. And like I said, Director Sandhar has this under control. See?" I flash him my phone's screen, which is open on a news article. The headline reads "Two Dragon Knights Captured in México Attack." While most of the bureau agents remained at the sanctuary site, Agent Horowitz had tailed two Dragon Knights deeper into Ciudad Juárez, both of whom she brought into custody. Director Sandhar granted a press conference minutes ago to confirm the arrests.

"I somehow find it difficult to believe a man who refuses to talk about his son," Papi says dryly. He opens a news article of his own, which shows Randall's smug face.

"Randall's lying. Samira texted me research she did on Director Sandhar after the sanctuary attack. He *did* have a son, but he was a nine-year-old boy who passed away three years ago. Hari Sandhar died of sudden heart complications. Randall was never part of this family."

"Lana . . ."

"And look at this." I pull up the page I'd stumbled on before Papi called me. It's a profile *The Weekly Scorcher* did on Grace Wiggins, the Regular who beheaded three witches. "He called himself 'the head-hunter's legacy.' Grace Wiggins is known as 'the Headhunter of Alabama.' If you look at her and Randall's photos, you can see a resemblance. Fair hair, vampire-pale skin, electric-blue eyes, super tall." I shrug. "I'd bet you anything this boy is Grace Wiggins's son."

Papi isn't impressed. "And a wizard is his father."

"Well, yeah, but it's not Director Sandhar. I'm pretty sure it's someone at Ravensworth Penitentiary. Grace has been locked up all this time, so that means she got pregnant *and* had her baby there." I run a hand through my hair, which is still wet from my too-long shower.

"I just don't know how they managed to keep Randall's birth, his whole *existence*, from the press."

"Because the father is a public figure with a wife and a now-deceased son."

Ugh, I give up. "Whatever, Papi. Can we talk about something else?"

Papi leans in closer to the screen, as if he's about to tell me a secret. "How's Andrew?"

Not exactly what I meant by something else.

"I haven't seen him since the ceremonies ended six hours ago. Hopefully, he's okay."

"Did you see anyone from the IBF or his team's management berating him afterward?"

"No. It was like nothing had happened." I'm not sure if Papi can see my confusion, but I'm not trying to hide it. Maybe Andrew is being scolded behind closed doors. Maybe the president's warning him of the dangers in standing out. He could be learning about the Anchor Curse.

"Maybe everyone is in favor of what he did?" Papi says.

I roll my eyes. He's making this so much harder than it needs to be. "I'm staying in Dubai, Papi. The Cup starts in two days. And I need you to promise me you're leaving the sanctuary."

Papi has the gall to laugh. "Come on, mija. You know I'm not doing that."

"The Sire is attacking sanctuaries. Yours might be next. While you stay there, I won't be able to focus on anything else. Please, Papi. Get out of there. Get *everyone* out of there."

He stops laughing, at least. "Want me to leave the sanctuary? Okay. Drop out of the Cup."

I groan so loudly I could wake the dead. "Papi. Enough. You need to protect yourself."

"We're perfectly protected here. Besides, I'm not abandoning these dragons. I'm so close to helping them trust humans, Lana. *So* close.

If I leave them, all of that hard work will be lost."

"You're no good to them or any dragon dead."

Papi looks about ready to hang up. He ruffles his hair without glancing at me. "Well, Lana, it's been fun, but I—" He fixes his gaze on me again, his expression alert, as if something's electrifying his whole body. "I forgot to tell you! I found some information on the Fire Drake that was living in Waxbyrne. According to the bureau's Public Dragon-Rider Registry, the last Fire Drake with a crystal heart to have officially Bonded died fifty years ago. There's no record of this female or her rider. So I used my credentials to dig around in other sanctuaries' databases. No sign of the dragon yet again, but Glenda Hammersmith's signature appears twenty times on the visitor's list for the largest sanctuary in England." He smiles. "Does the name ring a bell?"

"That's Madame Waxbyrne's real name," I say. "What do you think is going on?"

"The sanctuary was hiding the Fire Drake before it was moved to Waxbyrne. Since Director Sandhar knew about the transfer and refused to answer your questions about the dragon's rider, I suspect their identity is tied to the bureau or one of its enemies. I also think her rider is either dead or missing. This person might've been an undercover bureau agent, hence the secrecy, and I suspect Madame Waxbyrne had a personal relationship with them."

My head buzzes louder than a bee. If any of this is true, that poor dragon has been through so much. I can only hope she's happier wherever the bureau is currently hiding her. And that this enemy, be it the Sire or someone else, is stopped soon.

Someone wails.

It's a shrill, high-pitched sound. It happens again, louder and louder.

"Papi, I have to go. I'll call you later, okay? And please get out of the sanctuary."

I log off before he tries to fight me.

Then I dash out of the bedroom as the dragons' cries grow even more.

SOMEHOW, I'M THE LAST PERSON TO REACH THE HABITAT, EVEN though I'm the fastest runner here.

I stop to Gabriela's left. Joaquín and the whole team are deep within the habitat, facing the dragons. They lie side by side in a straight line. Daga is the only one on her back, her claws in the air. She and the others cry up at the coal outline of Puerto Rico. Their song is an intolerable squeal in parts, a low hum in others, coming and going in waves. The closest thing I can compare the melody to is a lullaby, but one where the singers are incredibly wasted.

"What's wrong with them?" I ask.

Gabriela says, "We thought it was an emergency at first, but they're fine. Well, *physically* fine, but they're . . . sad. It's like they're in mourning."

"What are they mourning?"

"No clue," says Héctor. He taps the side of his head twice. "They're not letting us in."

My eyebrows shoot up. "A psychic block?"

"Yes. We've been cut off," Victoria grumbles.

An equally sad Edwin crouches, studying the dragons further. "No nos dejan tocarlos tampoco." They're not letting us touch them, either.

Joaquín is Crickets Central right now. He's focused on the way the dragons sway with each note in their sorrowful song, watching them as if they're babies at the edge of their cribs. Manny's also quiet, but he's not as intense in his focus as Joaquín.

Esperanza holds her cries four seconds longer than the others. She sends a longing look to the map she made with her flames. She's definitely the saddest of the group.

"Do you think they're upset about today's México attack?" Génesis asks.

"Maybe. I also think they're missing home," Victoria says. "A lot."

I squint at these six dragons, scratching the back of my neck. This could be about missing the island, but it feels heavier than nostalgia. "Do they know about the Sire?"

Victoria looks seconds away from ending me. "Yes."

"They could be heartbroken about that."

"We can't conclude anything yet," Joaquín says. "We won't know what they want until they're finished with their song. Hopefully, that's before we're scheduled to leave for the stadium tomorrow." He rubs his forehead, his eyes closed. "The president called. We're playing in the afternoon slot. And we have strict orders from the Sire to win the first match. Puerto Rico will advance to quarterfinals."

"Obviously," says Victoria. She's not the slightest bit unnerved by the fact that we're being pushed around. "We're the team to beat."

I glower. "Until the Sire asks us to lose. Will he still be a distraction to you then?"

Victoria angles her body toward me, a brick wall in my path. "He won't."

"Because you know him *so* well."

"Stop!" Héctor slides between us. Somehow he seems more like a disappointed father than Papi. "The dragons are having a tough time. We're not going to make it worse for them *or* for one another. Now let's give them some space."

I walk away before Victoria pisses me off more. Besides, I have better things to do.

Not even my own team can stop me from figuring out what the Sire really wants.

"IS THAT NOT THE MOST DEPRESSING SONG YOU'VE EVER HEARD?"

I'm speaking to Samira through my Whisperer. I've locked myself in the bathroom. If the girls come in, they won't be able to pry into my business.

Samira coughs as if her entire body is coated in phlegm. "It sounds like they're having a really rough time, Lana. I can picture that jam at a funeral." She coughs again.

"What the hell, Samira? You said you went to the doctor."

"I did! My meds are crap, though. I'll have to get checked out again."

"Samira. It sounds really serious." After learning about the Anchor Curse, I can't help but picture the worst, even if it's just coughing and sneezing. "Can you go to the doctor today?"

"Girl, it's *fine*. I just need stronger meds. I'll get them first thing tomorrow morning." Samira sighs like she's been condemned to a lifetime without *Law & Order*. "Back to your team's dragons. What could make them so sad?"

"No idea," is all I can say. God, I hate the Sire so much for forcing my mouth shut.

"This might be a long shot, but maybe it's about the sanctuary attacks? Look at the Hydra and the Pluma de Muerte—each has specific abilities that make them dangerous to the Sire's enemies. I bet they're being used as soldiers." She blows her nose. "That's gotta be heartbreaking to watch for any Bonded dragon."

I lean back against the wall. Samira's right. Each of those dragons has powers that could devastate entire nations. The Hydra has nine heads. If one gets cut off, two more pop up in its place. Then there's the acid. A Hydra's breath can melt skin upon contact. Imagine having to fight a dragon that can either burn you with nine heads or poison you into a puddle of mush. The Pluma de Muerte is no better. This dragon species has a thing for flesh. Whenever it emits a specific sound, its opponent's bones break free from its body. All that's left is a meat sack. Sometimes the Pluma de Muerte will leave the flesh behind to intimidate other enemies. Mostly, though, the dragon collects it as a prize, storing it inside a hidden pouch in its chest.

The Hydra hasn't been spotted since being freed. Wouldn't the Sire be cocky enough to flaunt his new weapons together? Randall and the Pluma de Muerte had been a terrifying sight to behold, but why hadn't the Hydra been at their side? Could it be out on a special mission? Hydras aren't exactly smart or tactical. They're all brawn. If the Sire did send it on a special mission, news of a massacre would've broken out already.

What if these Un-Bonded dragons are the keys to finding out what the Sire wants?

"You okay over there?" Samira says.

"Yeah. It's just . . . the Sire's targeted two sanctuaries in different parts of the world. When he first started his killing spree twenty years ago, he went from country to country, along shared borders. Now he's jumping around without a clear pattern."

"He's trying not to be predictable?" Samira suggests, but she doesn't sound confident.

"Could be, but *one Hydra* and *one Pluma de Muerte* stayed with him. He either picked them specifically from the Un-Bondeds he's freed, or they stayed because he made them all promises and they were the ones who fell for it. Everyone assumes they're just soldiers."

"Yup. And badass ones at that."

I nod. "Or they could be useful in ways we haven't even imagined."

Samira falls silent. Then she says, "You think he *chose* them for something?"

"What if he did? Can you picture anything other than killing that they could be useful for? Like, their powers are unique enough to help him out with a super-special mission?"

She whistles. "That's a whole lot of speculation, but yup, I can brainstorm some potential uses for each dragon and run them by you when the list is ready. Maybe even make charts!"

Well, that escalated quickly. "You don't need to make charts, Samira."

"But they're sooooooo fun."

"Literally no one else thinks that."

We both laugh together, then she says, "I'm going to pretend I work for the bureau already and help you figure out what the Sire has up his sleeve with these dragons."

I wish I could hug her. "Thank you so much, Samira. Go see a doctor again. Love you."

"Love you, too."

I leave the bathroom and hop on my bed, ignoring the dragons' song. I want to save the Cup at all costs, but I've been missing a strategy. Samira is in charge of figuring out how the Hydra and the Pluma de Muerte serve the Sire's true purpose. I'm in charge of following the Sire's orders and kicking Russia's ass. But as I lay flat on my back, I think about how the Hydra and the Pluma de Muerte don't seem to have *anything* to do with the Cup. The Sire only cares about breaking Un-Bonded dragons out of sanctuaries, and if he wanted the dragons competing here to be free, he would rip their contracts apart and send them back home with their riders.

Their riders . . .

I sit bolt upright. The Sire is the first dragon in history to break his Bond. Every dragon in this tournament is Bonded, though. *The Sire wished for your teammates to be in the Cup because he was curious of their dragons' magic,* President Turner had said. What if this is about more than magic? What if the Sire's also studying the strength of the dragons' loyalty to their riders?

What if he wants to break *their* Bonds, too?

I fall on my back again. I don't have any proof to back this theory up. I don't even know how to start collecting it. All I have is a sad dragons' song echoing around me, and a death threat looming over my team's heads if I lose the first match.

Nobody is going to die because of me.

On a dreary winter's night in 1962, Perry Jo Smith had a dream about dragons battling one another for a golden cup. He's described it as "a cinematic experience in which riders and their steeds performed tricks, scored goals, and breathed fire so hot I actually woke up sweating!" Smith was on the verge of announcing his retirement from football, but the thought of spending his days sipping tea on his porch left him disillusioned. This prompted him to brainstorm further, ending up with what would later become the most daring sport in world history. "I wanted to watch magic happen," Smith has said, "but no one would require a wand for it. Young athletes are magic themselves. They are far more powerful than most people give them credit for."

—*Excerpt from Harleen Khurana's*
A History of Blazewrath Around the World

CHAPTER EIGHTEEN

TEN MINUTES BEFORE THE IBF ESCORTS ARRIVE, THE DRAGONS stop singing.

They've spent the past two days belting out their sad song. None of the riders get a straight answer as to what happened, though. Since the dragons are too young to string sentences together, they flash images in their riders' minds, but most are of total darkness. When probed as to what they represent, the dragons don't even have their usual one-word replies. It's like they don't have the magical strength yet to explain what's going on. Their emotional states are back to their peaceful norms.

Daga even tries to play fetch with Luis as a warm-up.

These steeds are ready for our match in the afternoon.

"What are you watching?" Luis asks as he sidles up next to me in the SUV. We're both decked out in the black-silk tracksuits Marisol designed for us. She's placed our uniforms in garment bags in the trunk. "More stuff about the skull carriage?"

"No. It's all Andrew this and Andrew that."

I hide my phone in my pocket. Since I can't tell Papi or Samira about my Bond-breaking theory, I'm Googling on my own. The same info on the Sire keeps appearing. Nobody knows how he destroyed his Bond with Edward Barnes. The leap from inviting a human to be his rider and seeing him as the enemy is a long one, with no connecting bridge in sight. And there's nothing on whether a Gold Wand can rupture the Bond, either.

What if I'm overreacting? What if that's not why the Sire's monitoring us?

We arrive at the stadium to the usual rabid fanfare and silent protesters. I'm swept inside too fast again, but I catch Mrs. Endo with her same sign from before. IBF staff escort us to the box seats on the left side of the stadium. Glass walls wrap around the room in a 360-degree view, locking spectators in chilly air-conditioning. Endless food platters and refreshments have been placed on tables at the far end. The seats are plush white leather with gold trimming; a cup holder that could easily fit two water bottles is available on every single armrest.

Athletes get the first few rows of seats to themselves. The rest are reserved for VIPs, press, and select staff members. Headmaster Sykes is chatting it up with a group of adults wearing Foxrose Academy blazers. Probably professors. Ambassador Haddad is also fraternizing with people wearing MEDIA tags. Noora Haddad is sneaking pictures of everyone without bothering them. I don't see President Turner. Hopefully, he's in a meeting or greeting people elsewhere. The thought of him suffering any form of Sire-inflicted pain makes me want to smash the glass walls.

As the teams start filing in, I throw a quick glance behind me. Andrew is at the head of Scotland's line. He doesn't seem the least bit tense. Hopefully, that means he hasn't suffered the Sire's wrath. I keep walking and saying hi to total strangers. Lots of people talk to Andrew, too, but he's not as enthusiastic. He mostly listens and nods. Maybe he's dead tired, or he's not in the mood to socialize. Once he's left alone, he heads for the first available seat.

He ignores me just as much as I ignore him.

President Turner shows up ten minutes later. He greets everyone with a handshake, and when he gets to me, his smile is smaller than ever. I try to convey that I'm going to destroy the Sire's whole life with my own smile, but the president silently saunters off to the next person.

At 9:00 a.m. sharp, the match between Zimbabwe and China kicks off.

The sand-colored Pangolin dragons from Zimbabwe and the bur- gundy-scaled Shăndiàn dragons from China are going berserk on the field. Their abilities are even more impressive live than on television. Shăndiàn dragons have two propellers: one for fire, one for lightning. They alternate between flames and bolts throughout the game, singeing and zapping their opponents. The Pangolin dragons are way smaller and can't shoot lightning, but they are *amazing*. They curl their whole bodies into balls mid flight, slamming into the Shăndiàns on their sides. Nine times out of ten, the Chinese team gets knocked off course and loses control of the Rock Flame.

Wataida Midzi is a sight to behold. He charges into his opponents and snatches the Rock Flame without fear. But Onesa Ruwende and Aneni Karonga are on another level of awesome. The Blockers fight like they have everything to lose. Not once does Onesa let Mei Wang, the Chinese Runner, get past her. Two hours later, Team Zimbabwe unleashes the dragonfire into the sky first. Confetti explodes all over the stadium as Zimbabwe gets crowned the winner.

"Damn it," Luis says. "If we beat Russia, we're playing Zimbabwe in the next match."

"*When* we beat Russia," Victoria corrects him.

I clap as if everything is fine. I grab lunch at catering, mingle some more, and celebrate when Team Zimbabwe reenters the room. I congratulate Team China on a great game, too, and try super hard not to smile when I notice Kirill and Edwin sitting next to each other.

At 3:00 p.m., Manny tells us to hit the locker rooms so we can change into our uniforms.

"Remember your instructions," he says. "Leave it all on the field."

I exit the box seats with my teammates, ready to show the world what I'm made of. Regardless of what the Sire has asked me to do, I have to remind myself how huge this moment is for those who are looking at me. It's still huge for me, too, but for more reasons than just having my only dream come true. Today my first Cup victory won't be a wild, faraway hope.

It'll be the only thing I can guarantee.

MARISOL MAKES SURE OUR HELMS AND PADS ARE SAFELY IN PLACE, complimenting us every five seconds. She even retouches our makeup. Manny oversees the process like a bored fly on the wall. Joaquín, on the other hand, checks us a million times and asks how we're holding up.

"We're all right," Héctor tells him with the ease of a seasoned champ. "We have every reason to be all right. It doesn't matter why we're here. We're still making history today." He puts out a hand in front of us. "This isn't for the Sire or anyone else. This is for *us*. For Puerto Rico."

Victoria rushes to place her hand on top of his. "For Puerto Rico."

Génesis, Gabriela, Luis, and Edwin all do the same, so of course I mimic them. They yell out, "For Puerto Rico!" as if they're all one voice, but I whisper it instead.

I don't want to win for the Sire, but I'm not losing and getting us all killed. Or worse: tortured to live another day with a reminder of who's in charge. I have to make it to the top of the mountain first. This isn't only for Puerto Rico anymore. All our lives are at stake.

Staff fetches us a few minutes later. We're taken to a smaller wait zone on the first level. Our team's dragons are back at the upper level. We're arranged in a specific order for our march onto the field. Héctor is first. Victoria, Luis, Gabriela, Génesis, then Edwin. I'm last in line. Team Russia is waiting on the opposite end of the stadium.

At 4:00 p.m., Jeffrey Hines's voice booms from the loudspeakers.

"We welcome you all again to the twenty-seventh Blazewrath World Cup! The Round of Sixteen continues with two of this year's most *lethal* teams! First to enter our field is the veteran of the two. This team placed third in the previous Cup, but they're back to bring home the glory. All the way from Eastern Europe, let's hear it for Russia!"

The applause is deafening. While a raucous chant of "Russia! Russia! Russia!" sweeps the stands, I see the human players in their single file. The captain's Zmey Gorynych steed flies out behind them, followed by the other five dragons. All three heads roar and bite at the air. Each head is the same length and the same width, with matching eyes that can melt steel with their intensity alone. Their emerald scales are a spectacle under the sun, glinting just enough to make me question whether they're actual scales or gems superglued to their skin. Team Russia halts once they get to the referee, with the dragons hovering above their respective riders.

Jeffrey Hines says, "Next up, the International Blazewrath Federation is proud to announce this team's debut! They're the first Caribbean team to compete in a World Cup. At just two years old, their dragons are the youngest in Cup history. Put your hands together for Puerto Rico!"

A staff member gives Héctor the cue to walk out. We all follow him to the field.

Titán glides out of the building with the kind of roar that stops hearts.

I trip on my own feet. He's never roared like that before. Esperanza mimics him, then Daga and Puya and Rayo and Fantasma. All six are lapping it up.

The applause at the opening ceremonies is nothing compared to this. There are more panderetas today, more Puerto Rican flags, and flashing lights. The crowd starts off chanting my country's name, but it's soon replaced with another chant: "¡Boricuas! ¡Boricuas! ¡Boricuas!"

Héctor raises his fist as a show of solidarity and gratitude. Luis blows kisses and throws the occasional peace sign, but the rest of us are stoic soldiers, marching as one.

Kirill has the silliest smirk on his face as we approach the referee. I catch him winking at Edwin before he faces the stands. I also catch Edwin blushing up a storm.

The Zmey Gorynych dragons glare at the Sol de Noches during their descent. Each Sol de Noche positions itself behind its respective rider, tucking its wings in upon landing.

The referee says, "Riders, on the field. Runners, wait by the starting line. When your team's Striker tosses the Rock Flame through the goal, you may race up the mountain. The game ends when the Iron Scale reaches the top. Questions?"

No questions.

"Captains, shake hands!"

Héctor and Kristina Ivanova do as he says.

The ref then gives me an Iron Scale. This is my first time holding the real thing, and even though it looks just like the replica I've trained with, this one feels a little heavier. It shines a bit brighter, too. Or maybe I'm not thinking straight from all the chanting and flashing lights? Either way, I'm holding an official Iron Scale because I'm an official Runner, and I've never been more tempted to immortalize any moment in my life with a selfie. My heart's going a mile a minute. If Papi's watching, I know I've finally made him proud. I'm proud, too, even though my circumstances suck. With a deep breath, I attach the Iron Scale—*my* Iron Scale—to my belt.

"Runners, to the starting line! Riders, mount your steeds!"

While my teammates go to their steeds, I head to the starting line. The Russian Runner, Ziven Belinsky, matches my pace with five feet between us. We bend our knees, angle our bodies to the foot of our mountains, and keep our traps shut while twelve dragons soar to the sky. Titán and the others have stopped roaring, but the intensity in their eyes hasn't dimmed.

This is their battleground. This is the end of whoever tries to beat them.

Get to the top first, Lana. Your team is counting on you.

The referee stays on the sand, but he's holding up the Rock Flame, aiming it between Esperanza and the Russian Striker dragon. With a blow of his whistle and a wave of his Silver wand, the Rock Flame shoots up like a rocket.

Kristina Ivanova grabs it before Victoria.

Crap!

Just as Kristina pivots her dragon toward the goalpost, the Russian Chargers sweep in front of Luis and Gabriela. Puya slams into the two Zmey Gorynych at once. He and Gabriela are sacrificing themselves already. They're locked in a dance of wills as Puya rams into them, first one Charger dragon, then the other, narrowly missing their fangs every time. Luis and Victoria hunt down Kristina, but they're too slow. Kristina hovers in front of Héctor within seconds. A complicated series of dives and swerves ensues. Once the Zmey Gorynych has managed to trick Titán into diving, Kristina tosses the Rock Flame to the goal.

Héctor races down the length of Titán's tail, then vaults himself into the air.

He grabs the Rock Flame.

I raise a fist in the air. "Yes!"

Titán's back cushions his fall, and Héctor throws Victoria the Rock Flame. She zips past the Russian Chargers while Luis and Gabriela keep them at bay. Victoria makes it to the goalpost. Puya and Daga are clobbering the Russian Charger dragons, despite having fewer teeth and less firepower. It's a bloodbath without the blood. The Russian Keeper is on high alert as Esperanza weaves her way toward him. She dives, teasing the Zmey Gorynych to follow her, but only two of its heads try to bite her. The one that remains upright is squaring off against Victoria. She swivels as if to toss the Rock Flame.

One of the Russian Charger dragons knocks Esperanza off course.

Victoria loses her footing, dangling on Esperanza's side, latching on to her saddle for dear life. The Rock Flame falls from her grasp. With a quick jerk, Esperanza pulls Victoria back up, but it's too late. She's lost the Rock Flame to Kristina again.

Come on, come on, come on!

Kristina swerves back to Héctor, faster and harder than before. This time, she's successfully evading Luis and Gabriela, who both are deep in battle with their Charger opponents. Victoria's too far away to stop Kristina, so she's a free agent all the way to the goalpost. Héctor and Titán brace themselves for a second Kristina attack. She's making her dragon do all sorts of twists and turns to get Héctor out of the way, but Titán is frozen in place.

Kristina's dragon whips its tail under Titán's legs, scooping him away from the goalpost.

Héctor gets tossed to the side, but not hard enough that he falls off his steed. Just hard enough to get separated from where he's supposed to be.

Luis and Gabriela are getting their butts—maybe even their souls—kicked. Victoria's gaining speed, but she's still too far. At long last, Kristina has a clear shot. I'm standing on my tiptoes, clutching both hands under my chin. Kristina throws the Rock Flame toward the goal.

CRACK!

Esperanza materializes right in front of the goalpost.

Her tail has been set ablaze. Smoke clings to her scales and horns. She's Faded inside the stadium.

Victoria is still in her saddle, grabbing onto the Rock Flame.

Oh, my freaking God! She can Fade with her rider on top now!

"It's a miracle! Esperanza has Transported herself and her rider to the opposite end of the stadium!" Jeffrey screeches. "What is this magic?!"

The clapping and screaming won't let me listen to my own thoughts. I can't do anything other than watch Kristina and her Zmey Gorynych cower before Esperanza, diving out of her way as she whips her burning tail and weaves her smoky body forward. I'm a shaking mess while Esperanza barges through the Russian Chargers, rolling them away like bowling pins, then reaches the goalpost for the second time. She and Victoria work together to coax the Russian Keeper out of his station, mixing it up between tail whips and harsh pummels. With one final shove, the Zmey Gorynych is bumped out of the way, and its rider goes along with it.

Victoria tosses the Rock Flame through the goal.

"Puerto Rico runs the mountain first!"

Jeffrey might as well have yelled the entire audience just won a billion dollars.

The referee blows his first whistle for me. I get into position. The fact that I got the head start makes me question how the Sire will react to Esperanza's Fade. Did Joaquín tell President Turner about it? Does the Sire know? What if he ordered Esperanza to use her ability as a way of testing the Bond? To see if these dragons would do something that excludes their riders?

The second whistle goes off.

I run up the mountain. Thankfully, this sand is heaven under my boots.

Wings flutter to my left. Kirill's dragon appears from behind a boulder. All three heads spray fire at the same time. I've never been to hell, but this must be a billion times hotter. I'm sweating from every pore as I bolt harder than ever. The fire nips at my heels. Once the flaming shower ends, I stick to the path, which is sloping into sharp, narrow curves. Artem's dragon is waiting for me farther ahead. Yet again, all three heads attack. More sweat. More panting.

The rain of fire ends about a foot before the first Block Zone. I plow right into it. When Kirill drops to the sand, blocking my path, I have no choice but to stop.

"Good afternoon, Bullet!" Kirill says with that contagious smile. "Let's dance, shall we?"

"Come and get it, Blueberry."

I'm about to run past him when I seize my chance to throw a punch.

Kirill evades me. He grabs my arm, then hammers his fist down hard on my shoulder.

"Ugh!" I plummet onto the sand then roll over.

Kirill steals the Iron Scale at once, then throws it back to the beginning of the path, where I'll lose my advantage recovering it. "That was a shorter dance than I expected," he says. "Let's make a deal. I'll save you the next one so we can spend more time together."

He mounts his dragon and blows me a kiss goodbye.

I run full speed back to the base of the mountain.

"Russia scores!" Jeffrey Hines shouts into the mic. "The first half of the match is over!"

Ziven Belinksy zooms up his mountain. I swear it takes him five seconds flat to get to the first Block Zone. Edwin is his opponent. There are punches and kicks thrown everywhere. I grab the Iron Scale, clip it to my belt again, then keep my speedy momentum on the journey to the top. Kirill's dragon is coming at me with less mercy than before, an explosion of fireballs shadowing my every move, but I escape. When I step onto the first Block Zone again, Ziven has already defeated Edwin. He's fleeing farther up his mountain, holding a solid advantage.

Keep. Going.

Kirill greets me in the first Block Zone. "You really need to stop following me. People will start getting ideas."

The jerk makes me smile. "You did promise me a second dance. I'm here to collect."

I'm back to full combat mode. Kirill and I spar longer than the first time, with Kirill using those hammer fists over and over, but I don't expose the Iron Scale to his grasp again. I dodge one of his blows, then kick his legs out from under him. Kirill lands flat on his back.

I bolt out of the first Block Zone. I don't even have time to celebrate my victory over a Volkov. Ziven is sparring with Génesis in the second Block Zone. My heart sings in the highest notes as Génesis yanks the Iron Scale from Ziven's belt. She throws it all the way down to the foot of the mountain. He has to start the entire path again.

OH MY GOD. YES, I LOVE YOU, GIRL.

As I enter the second Block Zone, Artem drops in front of me this time, stopping me dead in my tracks. "Hello, Lana," he says with a curt nod. "Pleasure to finally fight you."

"The pleasure is all mine."

I wait for him to strike first. He doesn't. So I take my chance to outrun him. He kicks my legs from under me, tripping me in the process, but I don't fall. I pull on Artem's arm, then send an elbow to his chest. He barely retreats. I don't even think he's hurt. Despite my numerous efforts to clock him, he keeps evading me like the pro he is. Artem's doing everything he can to make this last an eternity, never hitting me first, never blocking my blows, but instead deflecting my fists and kicks only to punch me in return. Even though I'm keeping the Iron Scale away from his reach, he never tries to grab it, either. It's like he doesn't even want to steal it.

I stop. I'm a panting, sweating blob of a human being, but I haven't stopped because of my exhaustion. I stopped because I have no idea what Artem Volkov is trying to do.

"You could've taken the Iron Scale already," I say.

"I could have." Artem is also frozen in place.

Then he drops us both to the sand. He snatches the Iron Scale and rushes off.

I tackle him from behind, then pry the Iron Scale from his grasp. He chases me, but he never catches up. I zoom past the second Block Zone. At some point, Artem mounts his dragon. I lose count of how many fireballs I dodge. Kirill's dragon is no better. My boots pound the hardened sand without pause. I'm a wreck of even mightier rage than ever before.

I make it to the third and final Block Zone. Artem drops into the combat area.

"Give me your all, Torres," he says, "because that's exactly what I'll give you."

He's not lying. Our fight starts the same way as the last one, with me hurtling onward, and Artem avoiding every blow like he's made of water. I can't shake him off. He's not grabbing at the Iron Scale. Then Artem kicks me in the shin and slams his shoulder into me, so I fall.

On the way to the ground, I drive my fist with all the power I can muster to his nose. There's a loud *crack*, followed by a smattering of blood droplets. I push myself up as he doubles over. Ziven is still sparring with Génesis in the second Block Zone. I'm free to win the match.

The mountain ends on a peak so high, I can almost touch the dimming sun. I jog to the stone platform. After unhooking the Iron Scale from my belt, I drop it where it belongs. It clicks into place.

A beam of the hottest flames shoots out of the stone and into the afternoon sky. It remains in a rigid straight line, as if it's conjuring up a Bat-Signal to send for help.

The match is over.

"Puerto Rico wins!" Jeffrey boasts to thunderous, never-ending applause.

I don't know when my team swoops onto the mountaintop. I don't know whose arms crush me first, but soon, more are crushing me even tighter. "¡Ganamos!" They all yell that we've won.

I flash a huge smile for the cameras, but it's not nearly as big as it would've been had I won without the Sire threatening to kill me. This day will be remembered as the day I sent my team to quarterfinals. The history books won't mention the Sire as one of the reasons why. They won't talk about how he's promised to burn a random city if the Cup continues, even though he's the one who can cancel it. That he's making himself look like a hero while he pulls our strings.

But I'll always know.

Now I just need to know what he's planning.

"How do you define power? It's a simple question, but most people answer it incorrectly. They think it means telling others what to do. Control over someone's actions isn't enough. You need to make sure everyone knows what you're capable of. My rivals on the Blazewrath field are well aware of my talent. But I don't speak to them. All I do is show up, and they cower before me. Power is nothing more than a promise. Don't cross me, and I won't hurt you."

—Transcript from 2015 paparazzo footage of Antonio Deluca exiting a nightclub in Milan, four months before Hikaru's murder and Deluca's disappearance

CHAPTER NINETEEN

WE'RE ALL HUDDLED CLOSE IN THE LOCKER ROOM, ABOUT TO head to the showers, when Joaquín shuts the door behind us and says, "Tell us everything that happened when Esperanza Faded."

He's speaking to Victoria. Like me, her smile flickers on and off, available only when someone is paying attention. But unlike me, she's shivering.

"V? You okay?" Luis asks.

"I think my suit's broken. It stopped cooling me right after I got back."

No one speaks, but we're all in the same "What the hell is going on?" boat. Even Manny looks like he's been slapped. He's stationed close to the wall, far away from the team. I can't blame him. As if the thought of watching a city get scorched down tonight isn't terrible enough, now we have to deal with whatever's happening to our dragons' magic, too.

"What do you think is making your suit malfunction?" I ask.

"I'm not sure, but that Fade was intense." Victoria sits on a bench, hugging herself. "Whenever I've been Transported, there's been a crack of white light. This time, there was just black sand for miles and miles. There were small puddles here and there but no ocean. It was like a half-formed beach at the end of the world."

What. The. Hell. Could the dragons be getting stronger? Or at least Esperanza? She's the only one capable of Fading with her rider mounted on her back. Then there's Victoria's suit. Can Esperanza's magic mess up other spells? Or did something else make the suit go haywire? The timing of Esperanza's reveal kills me more than anything. Why not wait until we were back at the Compound house? This isn't our secret anymore.

"Once you were inside this half-formed beach," Joaquín says, "what did Esperanza do?"

"She kept flying across the sand. It was like she knew the way all along. She never acted surprised by what happened. Then we were back here."

"And there was no white light?"

"No white light."

I pipe in. "Do you think this . . . dark island place . . . is real? Like, an actual place on a map that she took you to. Or do you think her magic created it?"

"This." Joaquín points at me. "I have my theories, but I want to hear you first, Victoria."

"I don't think it's real," she says. "I think Esperanza created it like an Other Place."

"But dragons aren't known to create Other Places," Gabriela says. "It's never been recorded in history, has it?"

Edwin shakes his head. "Nunca."

He's right. This is unprecedented.

"Maybe dragons *have* done it before," Génesis says. "It's just not in the history books."

Héctor exhales long and hard. "Something tells me this really is the first time."

"Why?" I ask.

"Call it a gut feeling. Besides, Esperanza didn't wait to be alone with us to do it. She waited until the cameras were on her." Héctor nudges Victoria softly. "I think she wanted everyone to know how strong you both are."

But wouldn't that piss off the Sire?

I turn to Joaquín. "Did the Sire order the dragons to Fade during the match?"

"The people in this room are the only ones who know about the Fade, Lana," he says. "Esperanza acted out of her own free will."

The room is quiet save for our breathing. I watch my teammates revel in Joaquín's words, sharing the same shy smiles, as if they've achieved a secret victory. I'm the only one drifting closer to the wall. What if Esperanza's choice to flaunt her Bond with Victoria leads the Sire to punish us despite the fact that we won the match? Would his anger prove he really *is* after the Bond's rupture? Or would it simply teach us not to do anything he hasn't ordered us to do?

"What is it, Lana?" Manny says. "You look like your brain is melting."

"I'm just wondering what happens next. Do you think the Sire will retaliate against Esperanza for using magic he didn't know about?"

"Not if we all pretend we didn't know about it, either," Joaquín says. "And we won't publicly call it a Fade. There will be no mention of the Dark Island. Esperanza Transported. Period." He backs up from the bench, making his way to the door. "Hit the showers and meet me outside when you're done. The conference room must be filling up with ravenous reporters."

Manny says, "You heard the man. Clean up. You all smell terrible."

So we shower. Afterward, we get dressed again, this time in our team tracksuits, then parade out into the conference hall, where dozens of reporters and photographers salivate over our arrival. We sit onstage, say hello into the microphones, and smile our best smiles.

"Victoria, what can you tell us about your dragon's newly revealed magical talent?"

"Victoria, did you plan that move with Esperanza beforehand? Or was that spontaneous?"

"Victoria, walk us through the moment your dragon vanished from the field."

"Victoria, why is Esperanza the only one who can perform this kind of magic?"

I tune most of her answers out, but I hear her confirm that Esperanza Transported. After the press conference, we get our picture taken with the Puerto Rican flag in the backdrop. We're filmed staring up at the scoreboard in the stadium lobby, which proclaims us the second winners of the Round of Sixteen. When we're finally whisked back to the Compound, I sink into a nap.

This is the only time I'm allowing myself some rest tonight.

I have to stay awake for the news.

I have to see which city burns.

ANDREW'S LEFT ME SEVEN MESSAGES IN MY BLAZEREEL LIVE APP INBOX.

That was *after* he tried to Live Video Call me.

The app's notification alert must've been going off while I napped. I go through his messages. They're all some variation of "Your dragons can *Transport*? Call me ASAP!"

My shoulders drop. *Why* did he have to contact me? Talking about

Esperanza's Fade means keeping secrets again. But if I don't call, he'll know something's up. He's even forgotten all about his pride and called *me*, so this is probably something he won't let go. Hopefully, I'll be convincing enough to kill his curiosity.

I hit the Live Video Call icon under Andrew's avatar. A yellow circle pulses around it.

He picks up on the second ring.

"And here I was starting to think you'd run off to join the Rockettes." Andrew's face fills up the whole screen. He squints at the camera as he leans in closer. "Did I just wake you up? How can you even sleep at a time like this?" Andrew shakes his head in slo-mo. "Unbelievable."

I roll my eyes. "Are you done? 'Cause I can hang up if you want."

"Hanging up is punishable in a court of law." Andrew backs away from the camera. He's ruffling his hair with both hands. "How long have you known about Esperanza's power? Can the other dragons Transport, too?" He says it all in one breath, his eyes wide and expectant.

I look at the wall across my room. "Esperanza showed us she could Transport during the match. She's the only one who can do it."

"For now," Andrew says. "The other dragons didn't seem surprised. That means this kind of magic is part of their evolution. Maybe they can't all perform it right now, but they'll be able to soon. They must feel their magic changing."

"Mm-hmm." I stretch my back, even though I don't need to. "Maybe."

"Which means they could potentially cast other spells down the line." Andrew chews on his bottom lip, lost in his thoughts. "Walk me through Esperanza's Transport step-by-step. How did it happen exactly? I'm trying to see if something provoked it."

"Nothing provoked it." I don't want to talk about the Fade anymore, though hanging up would be such a bad look, and I can't have him hounding my teammates for information or snooping around on his own. "Tell me about yourself. How've you been since your protest?"

Andrew's face falls. He's the one looking away now. "Mum reached out," he whispers.

"What did she say?"

"Doesn't matter. She's overreacting. But I guess all good mums are like that."

A Warheads candy ball is nowhere near as sour as he sounds. Maybe his mom gave him the best advice in the universe, but from the way Andrew looks like he's been shot through the heart, I'm guessing Ms. Galloway must've told him something he didn't want to hear.

I slouch, rubbing my face in exhaustion. I can't freaking believe I have to open up about my own mother to see if it'll make him open up about his. I'm already cringing, and I haven't even spoken a word about Mom yet. "You're lucky. My mother would never have called me. She doesn't care about my safety. Not anymore."

Andrew's so close to the camera again. "What do you mean?"

I take a long, deep breath. It does nothing to soothe me. "She signed my contract and said that was all the support I was getting from her. Mom's hated dragons since I was five years old."

"Because of the Pesadelo? Or did she hate them before the attack?"

I gape at him. "Wow. I didn't know you'd been Googling me."

"News channels have been going wild with facts about you. Not my fault you're everywhere." Andrew's smile is tight. "Tell me about it, though. How it went down."

"You already read everything that went down."

"Tell me anyway," he says with a soft, considerate tone. He urges me on with a nod.

Everything comes rushing back as if a dam has been blown apart in my brain. Reliving it all out loud makes me squirm and scratch the back of my head, even though it doesn't itch. Mom doesn't deserve to be spoken of like this. But from the way Andrew stares at me like he's on the verge of jumping through the screen and tackle-hugging me, I know my distraction is working.

"And then Violet #43 tried to kill me after I invaded her habitat."

I explain how Violet #43 had been asleep when I broke into her home. How the guards assigned to watch her had been playing cards in a broom closet. Papi and Mom had been busy with something on his computer. They didn't notice me slipping out of his office. I'd wanted to memorize her huge violet wings; her long, thin snout; her tar-black claws. I wasn't counting on waking her up. I remember the flames darting around me in a storm of heat and certain death. In my panic, I'd headed deeper into the habitat instead of bolting for the door. My short legs helped me soar past trees while the Pesadelo hunted me down. Her roars almost tore the building apart. Papi barged into the habitat along with six other staff members.

The way my mother screamed that night . . . I had no idea anyone could scream like that.

A tear slips down my cheek, then another. *Damn it.* I wipe them off, lowering my head before more tears tumble out of me. First, Marisol catches me off guard and coaxes me into talking about stuff, and now this crap happens. My team just won a historic match, and *this* is how I'm celebrating? *Come on, girl. Get it together.*

"Don't do that," Andrew says.

"Yeah, I know. I'll stop crying in a minute."

"No, no, no. You *should* cry. I mean don't force yourself *not* to cry. Let it all out." Andrew shrugs. "I can't assume to know your mum's thought process, but I think she still loves you regardless of how she treated you after Waxbyrne. Do I think she's in the wrong? Of course, but the thing about people is they tend to love us *their* way, not the way we'd want them to love us. We can tell them loads of times. We can draw them a bloody map. Sometimes their way is the only way that makes sense to them. Our voices are just white noise."

"Then I'm tired of being white noise."

"So am I . . ." Andrew's voice drops along with his shoulders. He perks up again in a flash, showing off a toothy smile. "Wait. Did we just talk *without* wanting to kill each other?"

I'm laughing way louder than I should. "Miracles do happen." An even bigger miracle would be for Andrew to redirect his energy into stopping the Sire the same way I'm trying to. Not only could I use more help in finding out the Sire's real plan, I can also keep Andrew from carving a bigger bull's-eye on his chest by openly protesting again. And if he's even more focused on stopping the Sire, he'll have less brain space for the Fade. "You know how you offered me the chance to protest with you? Now it's *my* turn to offer you something."

"What is it?"

"I might have a lead on how to stop the Sire *without* protesting the Cup. Think of it as a behind-the-scenes mission. Nobody can know about it." I offer him a half smile. "Are you in?"

He considers me for a moment. "Will it actually work?"

"Maybe. I'm still figuring out the details, but it looks like I'm onto something."

Andrew nods. "Okay. I'm in."

There it is. Our second truce. Hopefully, this one lasts way longer. I'm not sure if this qualifies us for official friendship status. Today, Andrew is someone who's helping me remember how good life can be even when you feel powerless.

"I'll be in touch," I tell him. "See you soon, Andrew. And thank you."

"You're most welcome." Andrew smirks as he ends our first Live Video Call.

I fall onto the bed like a snow angel, relishing my victories on and off the field, wondering whether I'll get to have another decent day like this ever again.

AT 8:00 P.M., THE DRAGONS START THEIR SONG AGAIN.

It's in a more stable pitch now. There are less screechy wails and more streamlined notes delivered with grace. It's pleasant yet still weepy.

"Aww, man." I touch my chest, right where my heart is. "This is the worst."

The longer the dragons sing, the more I crave to console them. Besides, what if their song sounds better because they're leveling up? Esperanza created something close to an Other Place after their first time singing. Tonight's song could mean something bigger is coming.

I put on my Adidas slides and head for the elevator. My teammates should either be at the habitat already or on their way. Hopefully, the dragons will now be capable of spilling the beans.

The elevator doors open.

Manny and the whole team barge into the corridor, right behind Headmaster Sykes. He's in his pajamas, covered in a navy blue silk robe that looks like water when he moves. His blue velvet slippers glide across the corridor until he's standing before me.

"Good evening. Forgive my intrusion at this hour," he says breathlessly. There are dry tear tracks on his flushed cheeks. "My husband is demanding your presence at our estate, Ms. Torres. He needs to discuss an important matter with you at once. If you could please follow me, we'll Transport to London together. I promise to have you back home in no time."

Whoa. Never saw *that* one coming. "The president needs me in London?"

"At once, yes."

"Why won't you *tell* me what this is about, Corwin?" Manny asks him.

"Because it's a private matter between Russell and Ms. Torres."

Headmaster Sykes is on the brink of tears, sniffling and blinking rapidly. "And it needs to be addressed this instant."

Joaquín says, "Why does it have to be at his home?"

"Exactly," Génesis chimes in. "Why can't the president come here instead?"

Headmaster Sykes keeps his desperate gaze on me. "He's currently indisposed. However, he *needs* to speak with Ms. Torres right now, and I'm not returning home without her."

He's been crying. He's come to fetch me in his pajamas. And his hair looks like it hasn't been brushed in weeks. Manny's grim expression confirms something is wrong. The last time he visited the president, he'd witnessed the Sire hurt him through his Anchor Curse. What if what happened in London then is happening again?

What if the Sire is actually *in* London this time?

"Okay. Take me to him," I tell Headmaster Sykes. Meeting the Sire could be a good thing. I can squeeze information out of him. I just have to be slick about it.

"I'm going with you," Manny says.

"No." Headmaster Sykes puts a hand on his shoulder. "You stay here with your team, Manuel. I will bring her back soon. Just wait for us, all right?"

Manny is about to pop a blood vessel, but he gives him a quick nod.

I peek at him again after getting into the elevator. As the doors close, Manny slips a hand into his jeans' pocket, which is where he keeps his phone.

HEADMASTER SYKES WAITS UNTIL WE'RE DEEP IN THE COMPOUND outskirts to Transport.

When the white light vanishes, I'm in the middle of a cozy living room. An explosion of gleaming wood furniture hits me. Bookcases, end tables, cabinets, TV, and DVD units have all been carved out of mahogany. There's a half-empty glass of wine and Harleen Khurana's *A History of Blazewrath Around the World* on the sofa, but not a trace of President Turner.

"Right this way. He's in the library." Headmaster Sykes gently places a hand on my back, then steers me to the narrow corridor on the left. He's shaking. His breathing is slowing down. I don't make a sound as I move forward. Butterflies fling themselves inside me at breakneck speed; they're even stronger than a Silencing Charm. I might be dying to know what's going on, but this is the Sire. I'm headed straight toward a murderer. That's never going to be in my Top Ten Things I Want to Do Before I Die. It's more like the number-one way to actually die.

I stop dead in my tracks.

Five Dragon Knights stand by the walls.

Three men. Two women. The men and one of the women have Silver wands out. That would mean only one is a Regular, though, and most Dragon Knights are Regulars. Why has the Sire brought more magical bodyguards this time? Is Randall taking a personal day?

"Library's just a little farther ahead," Headmaster Sykes says as he pushes me ever so slightly. I'm only moving because he's moving me. For a split second, I wonder if he's tricking me at the Sire's request. Is he putting up a desperate front so that I feel bad and comply with whatever he says? Then I remember how lovingly he'd treated President Turner back at his Other Place. How he's been trying to help him access the Sire's thoughts. He's just as trapped in this dark web as I am, so why would he play mind games with me?

None of the Dragon Knights try to hurt us. I ball my fists as I walk past them, anyway. Headmaster Sykes takes me to the first door on the right, which is wide open. There's even more mahogany in the shape of bookshelves, wrapping around the entire room.

Takeshi Endo stands near one of the high windows, leaning back into the drawn curtains like he owns the place and boring holes into my skin with his intense gaze.

The boy named Randall is sitting on the very edge of a desk. He's sucking on a peppermint lollipop and reading the first pages of Diana Gabaldon's *Outlander*.

President Turner sits behind the desk. He's also in his black pajamas and a moss-green robe. His eyes are no longer their natural blue. They're icy silver, mimicking the Sire's scales.

He's pressing the tip of Takeshi's claw dagger to his neck.

"Lana Torres," the Sire's voice comes out of the president's mouth. "We meet at last."

My insides turn to dust. President Turner's body has been hijacked. Wherever the Sire's hiding, he's too cowardly to be here in the flesh.

"Thank you for being here." The Sire flashes me a smile on a face that doesn't belong to him. He props the president's feet up on the desk. "You have already met Takeshi, but let me introduce Randall. Say hello to our special guest, Randall."

Randall takes the lollipop out of his mouth as he acknowledges me. A burst of peppermint wafts across the room. I wince. Now I'll never be able to smell peppermint again and picture anything but his stupid face. "Hi, Lana. Welcome to Chateau Turner." He kicks his dangling leg back and forth, back and forth.

"Why am I here?" I ask the Sire.

"Straight to the heart of the matter! Good." He sinks the tip of the dagger into the president's neck, just a few inches above his collarbone, but not enough to prick blood.

Headmaster Sykes squeezes my shoulder. He's cringing as he watches his husband's body suffer even the slightest of injuries at the Sire's hand.

I put a hand on top of his. The headmaster's grip relaxes, but he's still holding me tight.

"Tomorrow morning, you will hold a press conference outside of the Blazewrath stadium," the Sire says. "You will read a speech I have written for you, in which you will extend your support to the International Blazewrath Federation. You will ask the world to do the same."

He says it with a straight face, too, confident in his cruelty.

But I refuse to bend so easily.

"You've been so vocal about canceling the Cup, yet you're also the one who's keeping it going. Why is that?"

"Don't change the subject."

"Don't you have more important things to worry about than choosing who wins the Cup?" I let out a dramatic gasp. "Are you living a double life as a bookie?"

"Keep it up." The Sire pushes the dagger deeper into President Turner's neck. He's a breath away from drawing blood. "People could get hurt."

I gulp down. "Please leave him alone. I didn't mean to—"

"Did you hear my instructions?"

Taunting him won't work. He'll murder the president before he hints at what he's really after. "Loud and clear. But why does it have to be me?"

"I need someone to counter Andrew Galloway's protest. Tomorrow you will stand with my enemies and denounce what Andrew did during the opening ceremonies. You will serve as both his political foil and the world's distraction." The Sire glances at Takeshi like a proud parent. "Consider this the alternative to killing you for standing in Takeshi's way back at the wand shop. You can thank him for the suggestion."

Takeshi bows his head to me. "You're welcome."

Clenching my fists has never hurt this much. Neither has standing in place when I wish desperately to charge the Sire and punch his lights out. But that's not him. It's President Turner. Saying no means watching President Turner die. I can't risk his life so carelessly, much less when his husband is almost in pieces next to me.

"Do you agree to my terms, Lana?" the Sire says.

My mouth tastes like rotten fruit. "Yes . . . I'll do it . . ."

"Excellent. Your speech will be ready in a few minutes." The Sire rises from his chair. He lowers the dagger at last, leaving it on the desk. He's walking over to one of the bookshelves.

Randall goes back to reading *Outlander*.

Takeshi won't quit staring at me. I can't read him. He's a book that was written with broken quills in the dark. I don't care if he convinced the Sire to keep me alive. He's still trash.

"Andrew thinks you're a good person," I choke out. "That you're a hero."

There's a cold indifference in his once-beautiful eyes. "Do I look like a hero to you?"

BANG!

The library door flies across the room, along with one of the male Dragon Knights.

Headmaster Sykes pulls me to the floor. He shields me from the storm of magic spells flying all over the place, destroying everything they touch. Blown-up bits of book covers and pages are scattered everywhere. "Stay down!" the headmaster yells.

I cover my head but risk a peek at the library's entrance.

Agent Horowitz is shooting a spell at one of the female Dragon Knights while also kicking a male Dragon Knight square in the jaw. He tumbles into a pile on the floor. Agent Horowitz blocks spell after spell. She punches the female Dragon Knight in the gut and slams her knee into the chick's head when she doubles over.

She's out cold immediately.

"Boys, get yourselves out of here at once!" I hear the Sire's plea, followed by a sudden thud on the floor. President Turner is unconscious a few feet away from me.

"Russell!" Headmaster Sykes tries to get up, but I pull him back down.

Randall and Takeshi abandon their respective corners. Takeshi grabs the claw dagger. Randall takes out his Gold wand. They both stand side by side, even though Randall keeps a little distance. Takeshi reaches for one of the golden orbs attached to his belt.

"Drop your weapons, gentlemen. That's not a request," Agent Horowitz says, but she's aiming her wand at Randall. I get it. He's a Gold Wand, but Takeshi's still a legit threat.

"Randall, let's go," Takeshi says shakily. If I knew him better, I'd say he's scared.

Randall stays where he is. "Not. Quite. *Yet.*"

Director Sandhar charges inside with ragged breaths. "Do what she says." His voice is shaky, but it doesn't sound like he's nervous. More like his rage is eating all of his patience.

He's pointing his wand at Randall, too.

"Hi, Dad!" a peppy Randall says. "It's so good to see you again. I've missed you."

"Don't speak to me. Both of you, drop your weapons now!"

"Haven't you missed me? Not even a little bit? After everything we've been through?"

"SHUT YOUR MOUTH!" Director Sandhar fires a spell at him.

SWISH!

Randall Transports himself and Takeshi out of the house.

Director Sandhar's spell hits a section of the opposite wall, blasting it into pieces.

I let go of Headmaster Sykes. Tearful and deathly pale, he rushes to his husband's side, while I crumple into nothing where I lie. President Turner was held hostage in his own body.

Tomorrow morning, I'll be the next hostage.

The Sire might not be able to hijack me, but as soon as the sun rises in Dubai, he'll be secretly pulling my strings yet again.

Meet me in the forest,

I'll be cloaked in black,

Hiding in the shadows while you sing.

Meet me in the forest,

You're never coming back,

Locked away without your precious wings.

—*Poem written by Randall Wiggins, age seven*

CHAPTER TWENTY

Pᴇsɪᴅᴇɴᴛ Tᴜʀɴᴇʀ ɪs sᴛɪʟʟ ɴᴏᴛ ᴀᴡᴀᴋᴇ.

It's been forty-three minutes since the Sire fled. Headmaster Sykes and Director Sandhar are by his side in his bedroom, waiting for him to finally open his eyes. Agent Horowitz has shipped the five captured Dragon Knights back to the bureau with other agents.

I've refused to leave until I know President Turner's okay. I'm sitting in his living room with Agent Horowitz, who now busies herself with a luxury-car magazine. For a woman who's just kicked major ass, she's so put together and relaxed, even though her hair's a bit ruffled and her dress could use a good ironing. She's the one who told me about Manny. He'd called Director Sandhar the minute I left the Compound. Headmaster Sykes has apologized for not alerting them, but considering his husband's life was in danger, Director Sandhar let it slide.

"What are you thinking?" Agent Horowitz says, never looking up from her magazine.

"Not much. Just want to know how he's holding up."

"Me, too. Hang in there." She flips the page. "You did amazing, by the way."

"What? I didn't do anything."

"You were calm under pressure. You didn't endanger yourself or anyone else by acting recklessly. I could see you through the walls. The X-Ray Charm let me witness everything in the building before I Transported inside. Nirek and I are pleased with your poise."

"Pfft. *You're* a force to be reckoned with. Those Dragon Knights will be sore for weeks."

She giggles. "Let's hope so."

Director Sandhar drags his feet into the living room. He's clutching a sheet of paper as he sinks into the sofa across from me.

I shoot out of my seat. "Is the president awake?"

"Yes. Drained of energy but stable." Director Sandhar offers me the paper he's holding. "He just wrote this for you."

I snatch the paper and read it at once:

It's an honor to address you all today. In the wake of recent events, I've asked my friend and mentor, President Russell Turner, to let me use my voice for good. To unite our Blazewrath family before one of us shatters what's left of it. This isn't the time to stand against one another. This is the time to put our faith in those who seek to protect us. Today I wish to express my complete loyalty to the International Blazewrath Federation. I wish to offer my sincerest gratitude to the heroes in the Department of Magical Investigations. And most important, today I denounce those who doubt and oppose these great groups of people, who all are working tirelessly to ensure our safety. Resistance isn't the answer. Canceling the Cup isn't the answer. I don't believe in bending to the will of a terrorist. I believe in the people who strive to see his reign of terror end once and for all.

The threats posed against our world will be stopped, but if we don't support the ones risking their lives for us all, we're giving the Sire what he wants. Support the men and women in badges. Support the men and women of the IBF, as well. Don't waste your breath on hate, for it accomplishes nothing. Thank you, and I wish you all a blessed day.

I sink back into my seat. This is my speech for tomorrow morning. Nothing in this message feels like me. Well, I do support the IBF and the bureau, but not in this super-fanatical way. I crinkle the paper into a ball. With a harsh shove, it gets buried inside my pants' pocket.

"The press conference is scheduled for eight in the morning, Dubai time," says a deflated Director Sandhar. "You have to give your speech in front of protesters. Do you have any questions?"

I need some good news before I smash something. "Did President Turner manage to track the Sire tonight?"

"No. Since he was unconscious, he couldn't use the curse to his advantage in time. We're hoping to try tracking him again when the president is feeling stronger."

I'm dying to unleash a flurry of swear words. This is a lot of pressure on President Turner. And he can only locate one of the bad guys. Granted, it's the Big Bad, but his lapdogs would still be free. There's nothing the president can do to find Takeshi, much less Randall.

"Director," I ask, "who really is the boy named Randall?"

He grows a sickly shade of pale within seconds. He's fidgeting, too. His discomfort makes *me* uncomfortable, but I don't regret asking him. It's time I got my answer.

"I'm afraid we can't discuss that at this time," a soft-spoken Agent Horowitz says.

"And when would be a good time? Should I make an appointment?" I turn to Director Sandhar again. "I know he's not your son. My best friend told me about Hari's passing, and as sorry as I am for your loss, I also deserve to understand why the hell that vampire wannabe keeps calling you 'Dad.' *Especially* since he's working for the dragon who's trying to manipulate me."

Director Sandhar whispers, "You know about Hari?"

If he's trying to make me feel bad, it's not working. "Yeah. Now who's Randall?"

"Lana. *Enough.*" A blizzard would be warmer than Agent Horowitz's tone.

"She's right, Sienna . . . She's right . . ." Director Sandhar sits back, inhaling like it's his absolute last breath. "Randall Wiggins was born nineteen years ago in Ravensworth Penitentiary. He's the son of inmate Grace Wiggins. Are you familiar with her?"

"Edward Barnes's last arrest before his death," I say.

"Yes. Her arrival to the prison was rather uneventful, but after a standard physical evaluation three months later, it was discovered that Grace Wiggins was pregnant."

So he really isn't Randall's father. Good. "Why wasn't her pregnancy ever on the news?"

"Because of the circumstances surrounding it. Despite being imprisoned for three months, Grace's pregnancy was six days old. She'd been locked in solitary at all times, except for medical evaluations. She wasn't allowed visitors. Her child's conception remains a mystery."

Okay. Weird. "Did you do a DNA test on Randall after his birth?"

Director Sandhar lowers his head. "He has no traces of his father's genetic makeup. He has only his mother's. Randall was born a Gold Wand wizard from a Regular's womb."

That's impossible. Regulars can't have magical children unless they mate with a wizard or a witch. I don't know which is scarier: the fact that Randall appears not to have been fathered by anyone or that he was *born* a Gold Wand instead of leveling up like the rest of his kind.

"So . . . why does he keep calling you 'Dad'?"

Director Sandhar is even paler than he was a few minutes ago. "We waited six weeks before bringing him to the department. Our mission was to study him. Randall was kept in a sealed chamber, watched and cared for at all times. Our previous director assigned me to the case. The other agents in charge of Randall's care and observation would hand me notes on his progress, from crawling to walking to talking in full sentences, and I'd sign on the dotted line to ensure the work was being done. For six years, this went on without a hitch."

My jaw falls. "You kept him locked up for *six years*?"

Director Sandhar nods to Agent Horowitz. "Show her."

Agent Horowitz pulls out her Recorder. She activates it with her voice. "Access granted." Instead of breaking apart, the Recorder's shards become a screen.

A six-year-old Randall is in a white room. There's no furniture except the metal chair he's sitting on. There are dark circles under his eyes. Despite his angelic face, he's giving the camera the kind of look that suggests he'd like to pour flesh-eating acid on whoever crosses him.

"When is my dad coming home?" he asks someone off camera.

"Your dad?" a woman answers him. "Who's your dad, Randall?"

"The man who brings me flowers."

A beat, then the woman says, "Randall, no one brings you flowers."

"My dad brings me flowers. He leaves them for me in the vase outside. I see him through the glass walls."

There's a sigh of disappointment, as if the female agent had been expecting Randall to confess something entirely different. "The man who changes the flowers after they're dead?"

"Yes. He's my dad."

"No, Randall. That's not your father. That's Agent Sandhar."

"Can I talk to him?"

"I'm sorry, Randall. You can't." The woman jots something down with a sharp pencil.

Randall watches her without blinking. Now it's the look of someone skinning their victim alive, keeping them awake through the whole process, living for their screams.

A golden shimmer flashes in his eyes.

POP!

Blood splatters Randall's shirt, the bottom of his chin. He doesn't wipe it off.

The woman's shrieks ring out across the chamber. There's a loud thud, as if she's fallen to the floor. Despite her agony, Randall is the epitome of inner peace.

"He performed such strong magic *without* a wand?" I whisper.

"Yes." A squirming Agent Horowitz freezes the image on a bloody Randall. "He gouged her eyes out. She died before we could heal her."

I have a sudden need to take five hundred showers. "Jesus Christ . . ."

"Our previous director didn't want to punish Randall. Instead, he thought we could use him to our advantage," Director Sandhar says. "Randall was supposed to be the bureau's secret weapon. I opposed this plan, but I started visiting Randall at the director's request. I'd stay with him for hours, playing with his action figures, talking about the world I thought he'd never see. Randall continued to call me his father. It didn't matter how many times I corrected him. He stopped using his magic for terrible things . . . at least he did for the next ten years."

This is wild. "He worked for you until he was sixteen?"

"He helped whenever he was needed. Most of the time, he tracked criminals and their lairs. He would design traps for them, too. Complicated, intricate traps built from the strongest Gold magic on record. Randall used to call them his 'skullpits.' Those were his specialty."

"And when did he go full regalia against you all?"

He falls silent.

Then he tells Agent Horowitz, "Please show her the last day."

She taps her Recorder twice, which makes the image warp into fast-forward. There are several glimpses of Sandhar and Randall together in the white chamber. Randall gets taller and less baby faced with each frame. The one constant is his smile. I see them coming and going from the chamber, probably to those secret missions and traps Randall helped the bureau with.

The footage stops on a sixteen-year-old Randall towering over Director Sandhar:

"Why are you abandoning me like this?! Why can't I go *with* you?!"

"Randall, please stop yelling. I'm not abandoning you. This is just a brief trip. There are things I must take care of back in New Delhi. Like I said, I'll be back in a few months."

"You're taking *him*, aren't you? He gets to go with you while I rot here!"

Director Sandhar furrows his brow. "Whom are you talking about?"

"That stupid little boy!" Randall circles the chamber once, pulling at his hair, kicking at the walls. He's in full-blown meltdown mode. "He's the one you really love, isn't he? You *never* cared about me! I'm just some weapon to you!" Randall turns his back on Director Sandhar. "You're abandoning me because you don't care!"

"Please calm down, Randall. Can you do that for me?" Director Sandhar retrieves his wand from his coat. He aims it at Randall's back. "Everything will be all right."

Randall whips around and looks at the wand. He screams out in blind rage.

The glass walls shatter into a storm of knives. Director Sandhar crumples onto the floor, losing his grip on his wand. The world around him is chaos.

The image fades to black.

"Randall broke out of the bureau," says Director Sandhar. "Eleven agents lost their lives that night. When I regained consciousness, I wondered why he'd left me unharmed. Then I saw the missed calls from my wife." He's deep in thought. "Have you heard of Dragonshade?"

Papi's taught me all about this. "That's a poison, right?"

"It is. Do you know where it comes from?"

"It's dragon's blood. *Sick* dragon's blood. Two Un-Bonded Fire Drakes had been fighting in England back in the 1800s. The one who lost sustained tons of bite wounds. One of the wounds got infected, creating a sort of self-destructing virus. The dragon died five days later. Its corpse is preserved in a British lab, but smugglers stole batches of its blood years ago."

"The bureau recovered most of it," says Director Sandhar. "A small portion fell into the hands of Grace Wiggins. She used Dragonshade to paralyze her victims. That's how she was able to behead three witches without retaliation. Dragonshade strips magical beings of their abilities prior to killing them. Dragons die in five days. Humans last three. Randall had stolen a vial of Dragonshade from one of our evidence vaults. No one knew it was missing until he escaped. And they knew it because I told them." He clears his throat as if he's keeping tears at bay. "When I arrived home, my nine-year-old son, Hari, was lying on my living-room floor. He was paralyzed from multiple stab wounds. All were dripping with Dragonshade."

His confession sends me spiraling. It was cruel of the bureau to keep Randall in captivity and use him as a weapon for sixteen years. What kind of law-abiding organization snatches a six-week-old baby from his mother and turns him into a soldier? Then I remember how Hari Sandhar is dead because of Randall. Dragonshade has no cure. It kills without haste. Randall chose to end a little boy's life. He acted out of spite instead of running away in search of a better future.

"Did you have to end Hari's suffering?" I ask.

Director Sandhar gives me a simple nod.

I'm as speechless as he is. His son never deserved to die like this, but Randall never deserved to live the way he lived, either. Somehow, though, I manage a soft, "I'm sorry."

"Randall disappeared after that day. Completely off the grid for three years," Agent Horowitz says. "He hadn't been seen until the incident at Ciudad Juárez."

And now I can't unsee him.

Headmaster Sykes joins us with a tired smile. It doesn't erase the deadness in his drooping eyes. His steps are snail slow, the floorboards creaking as he plods along. "Russell wants you all to know he'll be at the press conference tomorrow morning." He sits beside me. "He's getting some much-needed rest, but he's determined to stand at your side for what you must do, Ms. Torres. I'd also like to apologize for bringing you here under false pretenses."

"Oh no, I understand. I would've done the same."

"That doesn't make it right," the headmaster insists. "Please get home safely, Ms. Torres. Russell and I will see you at the press conference. Thank you for being here."

After he hugs me goodbye, Agent Horowitz preps my Transport back to Dubai. I need to get out of this place drenched in nightmares. Deep down, I know it's useless. Tomorrow I won't just belong to the monsters.

I will become one of them.

Prior to his flourishing career as an agent for the bureau's Department of Magical Investigations, Edward Barnes had been an aspiring dragon anatomist. He'd begun to pursue his degree at the University of Cambridge, but he dropped out after one year. He then signed up for the bureau's Special Agent Recruitment Program and passed their rigorous examinations. Barnes spent the next ten years of his life hunting down the world's most dangerous criminals until his own steed betrayed him. Or had Barnes somehow betrayed him first? The cause for the Bond's disruption is unclear, but one thing is certain: No one does revenge bloodier than the Sire.

—Transcript from a TV episode of The Bureau Files: Unsolved Magical Mysteries

CHAPTER TWENTY-ONE

THERE'S A STAGE FOR ME OUTSIDE OF THE BLAZEWRATH STADIUM. It has a glass podium with dozens of microphones and a stage banner in the back. The banner is covered in a delicate white sheet, with the IBF logo plastered on its upper half.

Scotland's match against Portugal will take place after my press conference. Reporters have been settled into a cordoned section with folding chairs. They're close enough to hear what I'm going to say, but they won't block the protesters' view of me. No one has been told what my press conference is about. My teammates spent the whole night by my side in comforting silence. Director Sandhar told them everything except for Randall's past. I filled them in after he left, though. This morning, they sit with me in the living room, waiting for our car to arrive.

"How are you feeling, Lana?" Héctor asks.

All I do is shrug. The Sire's speech is still in my pocket, weighing me down.

"This is so messed up," Luis says. "Can you imagine if Lana's only the beginning? You think he'll make the rest of us talk to the press, too?"

"So what if he does? We talk to the press and move on," Victoria says.

Héctor's less charmed by the thought. "That doesn't mean we can't hate doing it."

"What does it matter how you feel? It won't make a difference to the Sire. Besides, none of us came here to get political. We're here to *play a game*. It's very important not to lose sight of that." Victoria nods to me. "Say whatever he wants you to say."

I pretend I haven't heard her. If I open my mouth, the prospect of yet another tone-deaf rant from Victoria is high. The last thing I need is her slamming me off the rails with her ridiculousness. Whether I hate the speech or not, I still have to give the stupid thing.

Génesis speaks on my behalf. "Victoria, some of us give a damn about the people dying out there. Some of us care about Lana's free will, too. This speech is gross. Not because she's siding with the IBF and the bureau. She's being manipulated into giving her support."

"She doesn't *have* a choice," Victoria says through gritted teeth.

They keep going at it, with Héctor and Edwin joining in. The people who thought I'd been dragging them down are now worried about me? Or maybe learning the truth about the Cup desensitized me to hypocrisy. I guess it's for the best. Something bigger than team drama has taken up residence in my headspace, and that's how it should remain.

Victoria's right. I don't have a choice.

Once again, I think of my mother. She'd rather have me betray my morals than watch the Sire rip my insides out. Papi and Samira would say the same thing, too.

But what if there's a way I can still belong to myself?

"Good to see you all." President Turner walks into the house. I hadn't noticed that he and Headmaster Sykes had arrived. His white suit is as posh as ever. His salmon-pink tie matches his pocket square. That salesman-of-the-month smile is still intact, but his eyes are sunken and tinged red. "Forgive my appearance. Rough night at chess club."

We are all rendered speechless. Not even Victoria says a peep.

"Mr. President, should you be attending this press conference?" a worried Joaquín asks.

"I should not, but I still have to be there," the president replies. He takes a shaky step toward me, still putting on his fake good mood. "Shall we, Ms. Torres?"

"Let's go."

I rise without meeting his weary gaze. When nobody's looking, I yank the Sire's speech from my tracksuit's pocket and toss it at the trash bin. The page lands a couple of feet away.

I pick it up again, shoving it into the trash bin before leaving the house.

Sayuri Endo holds up her No More Blood sign as I'm led to the side of the stage.

While other protesters cut me into pieces with their hardened glares, she's trying to crack my code. I wish I could tell her what her son did last night. How he stood by while an innocent man was held hostage and almost killed in order to bribe me.

"I'll introduce you in a few minutes, Ms. Torres," says Ambassador Haddad as he shakes my hand. "Is there anything else you need for this mystery speech?"

I ponder his question while Noora snaps pictures. Reporters love quotes. Newspapers love blowing up quotes into headlines and captions. The Sire's expecting a speech, but the most important thing is the message itself.

"Do you have a black marker I could borrow?" I ask.

"We can certainly arrange that." He leaves to speak with a staff member, who makes a black marker appear with his Silver wand. The ambassador then hands it over to me.

After I thank him, he escorts me to Noora, who asks if she can take solo shots. I pose with my fists on my waist. President Turner, Headmaster Sykes, Manny, Joaquín, and a newly arrived Director Sandhar chat a bit farther away from the stage. They're too busy checking up on President Turner to notice the black marker in my hand.

At 8:00 a.m. sharp, Ambassador Haddad introduces me to the crowd. I walk onstage with my head held high. Flashes go off as I shake Ambassador Haddad's hand again. He leaves me to join the others on the ground. I get to the podium, but it's too bright to make out any shapes other than dancing stars. The protesters are silent. So are the reporters. Then the flashing lights stop.

I uncap the marker and face the huge stage banner behind me. It's a white backdrop with the IBF logo on the upper right corner. Everything else is blank. I make each letter big enough for the crowd to see. Then I face the cameras again, resolute, as everyone reads my message:

TO THE SIRE:
YOU ARE NOT MY MASTER.
THE BLOOD YOU SPILL IS ON YOUR HANDS.
BUT THE CUP WILL BE IN MINE.

Camera flashes blind me again. The crowd's murmurs multiply to deafening heights.

I take it all in without blinking or wincing. My posture is even straighter. But as the photographers immortalize the words behind me on film, a part of me wonders how the Sire will handle my tiny rebellion. What if I'm making a huge mistake?

No. This isn't a mistake. Now walk away with poise.

I read the message one last time, then strut offstage like a champion.

"CONGRATULATIONS. YOU'VE JUST SENTENCED YOURSELF TO DEATH."

Manny kicks a metal chair in our greenroom. This is the first time I've seen him so passionate about *anything*. The fact that it's in regard to my safety is blowing my mind.

Joaquín and Director Sandhar are also in here with us. At the director's request, President Turner is in his private office with his husband. A small army of bureau agents watches over them. My teammates are settled in their box seats, but even without them, this room feels too crowded. Scotland is playing against Portugal in thirty minutes. That hasn't stopped Director Sandhar from quarantining me like a criminal who has the secret code to deactivate a bomb.

"Calm down, Pa. This isn't helping," Joaquín says, disconcerted.

"You know what's not helping? Pushing a killer's buttons," Manny scoffs.

"I can't believe I'm saying this," Director Sandhar says, "but Mr. Delgado is correct. Your stunt represents an open act of war on the Sire. You've broken the agreement you signed."

"I haven't broken the agreement," I cut in. "He told me to condemn him. I did that."

"Technically, yes, but the Sire wanted you to read a *specific* speech."

"Well, he can be pissed about me discarding his speech, but *I did what he asked.*"

Telling him I did this so I could belong to myself won't get me in his good graces. I need to convince him I'm also helping him catch the Sire. That I did it to protect President Turner.

"Why would you discard the speech?" Joaquín seems like he's fitting pieces into the wrong puzzle. He steers his wheelchair closer to me, shaking his head.

I retreat a few steps. "To distract him from the president. If he's focused on me, he'll have fewer chances to block President Turner from locating him. We'll catch him faster."

Director Sandhar knits his eyebrows together. "We?"

"Yeah," I say. "I'm as much a part of this as the rest of you."

"Are. You. *Serious?*" Manny swears in Spanish and English, a tennis match against the two languages. "You're not a bureau agent! Acting like one could piss off that bastard even more! What if his best Dragon Knights are outside this room, ready to kill you on sight?!"

"I'll take care of that," Director Sandhar says confidently.

"Okay." Manny draws nearer to him, his nostrils flaring. "Let's say he doesn't kill her. What if he goes after her family instead? Or her best friend? She modified *his* rules. Big whoop. So can he, especially since he's had it out for her since that Waxbyrne shitshow."

I'm flatlining and bursting to life all at once. Andrew hadn't already been on his bad side before he protested the Cup. Neither had Esperanza before she Faded. I, on the other hand, almost got killed for fighting Takeshi. What if delivering the Sire's message hadn't been a replacement punishment for me? What if it was a test to see if I behaved?

A test I've failed.

"But he won't be angry . . ." I whisper breathlessly. "He won't hurt them . . . right?"

Joaquín says, "This is the Sire. He's capable of many things."

No, no, no, no, no.

I almost lunge at Director Sandhar. "That Fire Drake at Waxbyrne . . . Is she still safe?"

He nods. "And will remain safe for the rest of her life."

"Then hide my loved ones like you hid the Fire Drake. President Turner can keep working on his locator abilities. You'll catch the Sire if he tries anything."

"*When* he tries anything," Manny says.

I flinch as if he's spat on me. I'm not sure how Samira and her family will take it. My parents are going to flip. But if it means keeping them alive, I'd rather they hate me forever.

"We need to act fast," Director Sandhar says. "The Jones family, Carlos Torres, Leslie Wells, and Todd Anderson could be his next targets."

My stomach twists at the mention of Todd. "Why do you think my cousin is a target?"

"You saved him back at Waxbyrne."

Right. Guess he *should* be protected, too. "Okay, but don't put him with Samira."

He nods without asking why, which makes me like him ten times more. He then pulls out his phone and rapidly texts someone. Probably Agent Horowitz. "You all should get to the box seats. Don't answer questions about the press conference. I'll have further instructions soon."

I'm out the door before Manny and Joaquín.

Andrew stands across the corridor.

I trip as if I'm learning to walk for the first time. My brain hadn't been ready to bump into anyone right now, let alone the guy I've been keeping secrets from. "What are you doing here? You have a game coming up in a few minutes. Shouldn't you be getting prepped?"

He marches over to me. "What in the name of Odin have you done?"

"Ugh. Not right now, Andrew." I walk away.

"Wait!" Andrew matches my pace. "I just want to understand. Was that stunt part of the plan you told me about? Or did the president ask you to do it for him?" I walk faster, but he catches up to me. "You begged me not to protest, Lana. Now *you're* taunting the Sire in front of the whole bloody world." Andrew entwines his hands behind his head. "Why?"

He's chosen the wrong career path. He'd be better off working for the freaking bureau.

"This *is* part of my plan, but I can't explain it right now."

Andrew cuts in front of me. "You asked what my mum said. She told me not to protest. That it's like slapping a bull's-eye on my forehead. The Sire could hurt the ones I love most."

I cringe for a split second but recover quickly. "Your mother's a smart woman."

"She's the only family I have left. And she knows better than anyone what the Sire's capable of."

Right. I'd forgotten Ms. Galloway had studied at Foxrose. She'd been in the same class as Edward Barnes and President Turner. What if Ms. Galloway knows what the Sire wants?

"You keep changing sides like it's nothing." Andrew bends his knees so we're eye to eye. "One day, you're this, and the next day, you're that. How am I supposed to trust you?"

His words are worse than a slap. How dare he act all high and mighty? Thinking I'm some confused, shady person with no regard for the lives of those she loves. Trying to make amends with him is exhausting. I still have Samira. She and I can crack the Sire's code together.

I don't need Andrew Galloway. I never did.

"I'm sorry I disappointed you, Andrew. Best of luck on your match today."

I don't look back on my way to the box seats. Andrew doesn't stop me, either. Maybe this is another mistake. I should keep him on my good side in case I have to rely on him later.

Or maybe it had always been a mistake to trust a Dragon Knight's best friend.

When Regulars first discovered the magical community in 1743, reactions were mixed. There were those who feared the rise of an oppressive regime, but with the bureau's numerous efforts to create all-inclusive policies, these fears were assuaged. Magical-history and dragon-studies classes became mandatory in the Regular educational system, along with more dedicated magical-study programs at the university level. Regulars could study and work alongside magic users. However, it would be unwise for Regulars to believe there are no more secrets being kept from them. Of course, we still have secrets. So do dragons. I suspect theirs are much more exciting.

—*Excerpt from Edna Clarke's* Magical History for Regulars, Twelfth Edition

CHAPTER TWENTY-TWO

"I'M FINALLY LIVING MY DREAM OF REENACTING AN EPISODE OF *Law & Order: Magical Crimes Unit,* but without the car chases and sexual tension." Samira zooms her phone's camera in on her silly grin, then zooms out to show the box of Kleenex and the new Copper wand resting on her lap. Her wand is a little thicker than her previous victim, lacking any other adornments.

"What time's Director Sandhar picking you up?" I'm lying in bed with my phone aimed overhead. Everyone else is at the habitat or the gym while I'm seizing my chance to talk to Samira before she disappears to a mysterious location courtesy of the bureau.

"He told Mom he'd be here in an hour, but there are a couple of agents stationed outside my house." Samira grins even harder. "I'm going to a *hideout*, girl."

"So you're not mad at me?"

"Not really. Daddy and Shay aren't too happy with just up and leaving everything, but they understand why it's important." Samira blows her stuffy nose. "Hopefully, this hideout will have healing powers and get rid of this dang cold already."

I sit up, slouching. "Those meds still aren't working?"

"Oh, they were, but the cold came back out of nowhere like an undead creature. Zombie colds are the *worst*." She turns serious all of a sudden. "You should know I'm absolutely terrified for you. You've poked a really dangerous bear, Lana, and you still haven't told me why."

"Don't worry. What matters is you and your family will be safe. The bureau's done an excellent job at hiding the Fire Drake. It'll do an excellent job at hiding all of you."

"Yep." Samira wiggles her eyebrows. "Can we talk about dragons now? I don't know how much time I've got left here."

I could kiss the screen. "Be my guest."

Samira runs to the dry-erase board on her bedroom wall, grabs her blue marker, and taps a list scribbled in the center. "Behold!"

Regeneration
Body
Magic
Blood

I don't see any correlation between those words. "So, what's your theory?"

"What happens if you cut off one of the nine heads on a Hydra?" Samira says.

"It grows back."

Samira taps the word REGENERATION on the board. "Hydras are the only dragon species that can restore their bodies after a serious injury. They can regenerate in no time."

"Which is why the Sire may or may not still have one in his army."

"Oh, I don't think the Hydra's a soldier. You were onto something." Samira flips the phone back to herself. "It hasn't been seen by the Sire's side since the Athens attack, has it?"

I shake my head.

"Exactly. Now tell me which dragon species keeps the flesh of its enemies."

"The Pluma de Muerte."

"And what does this creature do with skin?"

"Well, they claim it as a prize after battle. Others just leave it behind as a scare tactic."

"And what else?" Samira waits in vain for me to speak, but I'm drawing a blank. She sighs in frustration. "What did we learn about, like, one percent of Pluma de Muertes in our dragon-studies class? Specifically in regard to the sound they use for bone removal?"

I almost drop my phone. "It can also mold flesh into any shape."

Samira taps the word BODY on her board. "The Pluma de Muerte creates. The Hydra restores. All these years, the bureau thought—"

Someone knocks on Samira's door.

"Ms. Jones? This is Agent Sienna Horowitz with the bureau. We've come to escort you to your new living quarters. Are you set for Transport?"

"Just a minute!" Samira power-erases everything on the board. When her words are gone, she says, "Stay safe, and keep your guard up at all times!"

"Got it. I love you, Samira."

"I love you, too. Don't die."

After we hang up, I'm still racking my brain for what Samira's theory could be. *The Pluma de Muerte creates. The Hydra restores.* She'd been seconds away from saying something about the bureau, but what do they have to do with these dragons' powers? And how do these powers benefit the Sire? He's immortal, so the Hydra's regeneration is useless. Same goes for the Pluma de Muerte's ability. The Sire doesn't need human flesh.

I slap both hands to my cheeks.

Regeneration. Body. Magic. Blood.

Edward Barnes used his blood to create his curse. His magic as a Gold Wand had made the spell possible. And he'd forced the Sire into a human body that can regenerate.

The Sire doesn't need these dragons as soldiers. He needs them as *ingredients.*

"Oh my God. He's trying to turn back into a dragon."

Time slows to a stop. I'm in some sort of other dimension, where I'm getting punched to the core endlessly. Of course the Sire would want to become a dragon again. It never occurred to me it would actually be *possible.* The Sire freed those dragons so he could manipulate them. He risked everything to spring them from their sanctuaries. Now they owe him.

He can't have Barnes's blood to complete his spell. Barnes doesn't have any family left.

I think Takeshi needed to bring the crystal heart to a Gold Wand working for the Sire, Samira told me right after the Waxbyrne incident. *Maybe they're strong enough to force the heart to perform magic.* What if the wish granted by the Fire Drake's crystal heart was never intended for Takeshi? Could the wish's power replace the blood needed to break Barnes's curse? Randall seems a whole lot stronger than Barnes ever was. He could be strong enough to bend the heart to his will. *He's* the Sire's magic for the counter curse.

All the pieces line up. The Sire is only missing the crystal heart.

I sigh in relief. He's never getting it. Just like he's never finding my loved ones.

I should check on Papi. Maybe the bureau hasn't picked him up yet.

He's not answering. He doesn't reply to my texts, either. For a split second, I start breathing a little faster, then I remind myself he could be with the bureau already. I'm obviously not calling Todd. He's probably going to the same hideout as Mom, seeing as Todd's a minor.

I shouldn't do this, but the least I can do is let her know I really do want her to stay safe. I dial my mother's number before I can regret it.

She doesn't pick up, either. I try four more times. Nothing. That could just mean she's busy moving to her hideout. It could also mean she's refusing to talk to me. As understandable as that is, she really can't drop her ego for just one second? Is she still that pissed at me? Whatever.

I take my phone to the gym, where I hope to forget about hearts and gold for a few hours.

HISTORICALLY SPEAKING, BLAZEWRATH QUARTERFINALS ARE where the most upsets occur.

My favorite one is still Venezuela versus Ireland in 1973. I've lost count of how many times I've watched that match on BlazeReel. European teams remained the popular choice to move on to the semifinals, even though Venezuela's upcoming debut was as talked about as my team's. But the Irish Spikes had been no match for the Furia Rojas. This dragon species can eject spears from their bloodred tails. These weapons are as sharp as they're fast, capable of piercing through any Regular or magical material. By the time Colin McGrath, the Irish Runner, had entered the first Block Zone, half of it had been demolished.

But the biggest quarterfinals upset to date is the 2013 Japan versus France match. Takeshi's debut had drummed up some excitement, seeing as he's the youngest dragon rider to have Bonded with his steed, but it was Hikaru who stole the show. It took him ten and a half seconds to reach the goalpost. That's the fastest dragon to fly in a Cup match on record. Takeshi scored a second later. Haya Tanaka, the Japanese Runner—or as everyone calls her, the Ghost of Shibuya—unleashed the winning stream of flames in ten minutes. The French Blockers couldn't catch her.

Everybody's A-game is kicked up a thousand notches during quarterfinals. I don't think this year will be any different. The teams moving on have been divided like so:

GROUP D
Argentina versus France
GROUP C
Venezuela versus Sweden
GROUP B
Scotland versus Egypt
GROUP A
Puerto Rico versus Zimbabwe

Quarterfinals matches will only last two days, with two matches each day.

We're playing first.

And we've been ordered to win again.

"You'll advance to the next round," President Turner tells us in our greenroom.

"And if we don't?" I ask.

"We will," Victoria says. She's as pleasant as a thunderstorm on a beach day.

President Turner nods. "But if you don't, the Sire will order your deaths by burning."

Everybody but Victoria is slack jawed. She looks at President Turner as if the thought of us losing a match is the most outlandish thing she's ever heard.

"Awesome," I say dryly. "Thanks for the heads-up, Mr. President."

"I'm so sorry, my dears. He wants you to understand what's at stake."

"Oh, we understand it quite well," Gabriela says. She's hugging Edwin and Génesis with her head down. "We're going to win."

"Absolutely," Héctor says. "There's no other option."

My teammates put their hands on top of one another and pretend to be enthusiastic about what's about to go down. I can't tell if ordering us to win again means the Sire is happy with me. He hasn't summoned me again. He hasn't burned anything since the Cup started. President Turner hasn't been tripping or shaking. My friends and family have been safely delivered to Director Sandhar's secret lodgings. Samira and her family are together. Mom and Todd are together somewhere else. Papi is alone. Director Sandhar said he had put up a fight, pleading to stay with the Pesadelos. He's reportedly livid with me, but he's safe. That's what matters.

We get called out to the field before Zimbabwe. I'm at the back of the line, marching on the sand with the rest of my teammates. The Sol de Noches fly out faster than they did during our Russia match. Maybe because there are triple the amount of Puerto Rican flags today. With each dragon's roar, the flags get higher and higher, raised to the skies as an offering of hope and pride.

When Héctor gets to the referee, Jeffrey Hines calls forth our rivals.

"Put your hands together for the first African team to compete in the Blazewrath World Cup! This is their fourth time in the tournament! Let's hear it for Zimbabwe!"

I almost clap, too. I *really* have to train myself not to be such a fangirl.

Six girls and one boy hit the field. They're all dressed in their bright-red leather suits, their golden chest plates and helms. Onesa is the first to walk out. Aneni Karonga, the team's other Blocker, is right behind her. Wataida is second to last. The Pangolin dragons come out once their riders are halfway to the ref, flying in a synchronized, wavy line, showing off their wondrous wings and super-tough scales for the world to marvel at.

The ref goes through the rules. Héctor and Onesa agree to them.

"Runners, to the starting line! Riders, mount your steeds!"

I make it to the starting line before Taona Mawere, the Zimbabwean Runner, gets to hers. This is off to a promising start. I just need Esperanza to Fade again and stop Zimbabwe from scoring first. We have to show the Sire what we're made of. We have to win for Puerto Rico.

We have to win in order to live. I'm not about to screw up and get us all killed, least of all in a quarterfinals match. We're staying alive, *and* we're going down in history.

The Rock Flame is tossed into the air.

Kunashe Hatendi, the Zimbabwean Striker, catches it before Victoria.

A frenzy of flapping wings, fireballs, and body slamming ensues. Wataida and his steed are careening toward Luis and Gabriela, forcing them to take turns pushing him back. The other Charger protects Kunashe from Esperanza's attacks. She's not Fading, though. She's flying and fighting like any normal dragon. The Charger dragon shoves her back hard enough to clear Kunashe's path to the goal. Héctor guides Titán down to block Kunashe's shot, but the Pangolin pulls up suddenly, and Kunashe makes a quick toss.

The Rock Flame sails through the goalpost.

"Kunashe scores!" Jeffrey Hines freaks out. "Zimbabwe runs up the mountain first!"

I stomp my foot on the sand. Esperanza could've easily Faded by now! Has she not read Victoria's mind? Does she not know about us getting burned to death if we lose?!

Taona hits the mountain. Edwin and Génesis swarm her at once, but she's a rocket.

"COME ON!" I yell. "SOMEBODY STOP HER!"

Héctor grabs the Rock Flame from Kunashe.

I jump, fists high like a boxer who's won the title belt. *"Pass it to Victoria!"*

Esperanza flies close enough for Victoria to fetch the Rock Flame, then shoots toward the opposite goalpost, where Gabriela is still fending off Wataida. Puya's mouth is wide open in a roar. He clamps his teeth down on the Pangolin's neck to prevent him from moving. As the Keeper dragon inches forward to help, Esperanza zooms by, faster than a bullet. Victoria is standing on her closed mouth. The Keeper dragon rushes to meet Esperanza halfway.

Before they collide, Esperanza blows out a cloud of fire onto Victoria's back.

Victoria flies past the Keeper's clutches. With a twist of her body, she tosses the Rock Flame through the goalpost.

I scream my head off. "YES!" Even though Taona's already inside the first Block Zone, winning is in *my* hands now. I don't have to count on anyone else to save us.

My two whistles blow.

I get out of the base faster than I did during the Russia match. The Pangolin dragons are on me before I can take a breath. They're assuming positions, one to the left, one to the right.

Grab something, grab something, grab something.

As I lunge at the wall, the Pangolins curl into balls, then crash into the mountain. This is their modus operandi—slamming their bodies like boulders sent straight from the underworld. I've been such a huge fan of this tactic for the past four Cups, but being on the receiving end has drained me of all the fangirling I've ever done.

BOOM!

The mountain quakes. I'm latching onto a rock that's jutting out of the wall, but my boots keep sliding back. The edge is about three feet from me. If this rock slips out, I'm done for.

The Pangolins retreat with open mouths. Fire might be next.

I dart forward. The first Block Zone is so, so close.

The Pangolins hit the mountain again.

I'm thrown to the edge. Sinking my fingers into the sand, I strain every muscle in my arms while my lower body dangles off the side of the mountain. The Pangolins are hitting the mountain over and over. I'm slipping, grunting, and gasping for air.

Puerto Rico is watching you. Show them how strong you are.

My boots scrape stone without finding a good-enough hold, but I'm digging my fingers deeper into the sand, fighting for my teammates' lives as much as mine. Losing isn't an option. So I kick up, raise myself an inch, and repeat until I can drag myself forward. The mountain is still rocking as I land on the path. I break into a run, then make it to the first Block Zone.

Aneni drops into my path. "Hello."

"Hi. Please don't kill me."

"I make no promises."

She sprints at me.

I dodge her jab-and-upper-cut combo. She tries to grab the Iron Scale. I kick her in the shin. Even though she yelps, she's not crumbling. She's not getting out of the way, either. I launch a roundhouse kick to her gut. Aneni blocks it with both arms. As she holds my ankle, I drop to the ground, then sweep her feet with another kick. She's down at once.

I'm out of the first Block Zone before she can get up.

The earthquakes come back on the left side of the mountain. The dragon to my right is shooting fireballs at me instead. It's a combination of super-unsteady ground and a super-hot shadow of death following me at every sharp turn. These Pangolins mean *business*.

Taona is racing up to the third Block Zone. She's dodging Fantasma's fireballs with ease.

I blast through the second Block Zone just as Aneni's about to land inside it. I'm an unstoppable force, with even more speed than Haya Tanaka against the French Blockers in 2015. With an enraged cry, Aneni eats my dust. The quakes and the fire return on the way to the final Block Zone, where I'll for sure meet Onesa instead. I'm pouring out more sweat, and my whole body's throbbing even faster than it did the last time I ran this course. My gas is running low, but I don't stop.

Onesa greets me inside the third Block Zone. "This is where your journey ends."

She blows me a quick kiss goodbye.

God, I wish I could hate her, but I still have to beat her.

I check the other mountain. Taona is also on the last Block Zone, facing Génesis. I have to get past Onesa *right this second*.

"All right," I say. "Let's finish this."

I rush toward Onesa, but she evades every blow. I even try faking her out with a double punch. She reads me before I can land a hit. She's not lunging at the Iron Scale, which makes me think she's tiring me out. And she's not letting me gain a single inch forward, either.

Taona flips Génesis over her shoulder, launching her to the sand a few feet away.

She sprints up the last patch of mountain.

"No!" I'm striking Onesa with as much power as possible, but she's a human wall. Génesis gets back on Rayo while I'm trying to tear down the unbeatable Blocker before me.

SWOOSH!

Onesa and I stop fighting, checking the skies at the same time.

The Sol de Noche dragons are gone. They've all Faded away with their riders.

"Folks, Puerto Rico's dragons have disappeared from the stadium!" Jeffrey Hines announces. "They've Transported outside of—"

SWOOSH!

The dragons are back. Right where I last saw them—Blockers on Taona's mountain, the rest hovering on the field, but they're wrapped in flames from horns to tails. Even their *riders* are covered in fire. Esperanza roars first, then Titán, Rayo, Fantasma, Puya, and Daga join in a raging chorus. They're ejecting flames from the sides of their bodies and connecting with one another until their flames form a circle. All six dragons are tied together in a broiling ring.

Taona isn't moving. She's transfixed by the ring of fire covering the field.

Onesa's transfixed, too, gasping in awe. The Pangolins have also been lulled to a stop.

"What are they doing?" Onesa asks.

I don't know what to tell her.

So I run out of the Block Zone instead. I fly up the final expanse of land, then slap the Iron Scale to the stone dais. Firelight beams up like a cannonball.

"Puerto Rico wins the match!" Jeffrey Hines yells.

Panderetas, güiros, and drums go off from all sides of the stadium. People chant, "¡Puerto Rico!" like it's a Top 40 hit.

The ring of fire fizzles out, and my teammates fly to my mountaintop. Victoria tackles me to the ground, screeching in wild abandon. The rest of my teammates raise their fists at the crowd, chanting "¡Puerto Rico!" but there's restraint in their cheering, a forcefulness to their smiles. Maybe the ring of fire freaked them out. Or did something else spook them?

I have no idea what just happened. I know the Sire's seen it, though. He threatened to burn us if we lost, but the only thing that burned today was a team of six dragons flaunting their power for the world to marvel at. They burned so we could live. Their magic is our salvation.

I never want the Sire to forget.

Dragon mothers are the fiercest creatures on Earth. A dragon mother's love for her egg makes the rider-dragon Bond seem trivial. A mother will fight to the death against her own kind in order to protect her unborn offspring, which makes her subsequent disappearance upon her baby's hatching contradictory. The mother ensures her egg cracks at the right time, but she has no need to ensure the baby's life continues past its incubation period. Every dragon grows up alone. Whether they would've made excellent mothers or not, their children will never know.

—*Excerpt from Carlos Torres's* Studying the Bond Between Dragons & Humans

CHAPTER TWENTY-THREE

I'M STILL REELING FROM THE RING OF FIRE WHEN MANNY DRAGS us into the locker room.

None of the riders are shivering. They keep glancing at one another with concern. Victoria's the clear exception, burning with an effervescent thrill. She glides into the room, then catches her reflection in a mirror. Her smile is brighter than the sun on a summer's day. When the rest of the team sits on the benches, she remains standing, as if she's too wired to take a seat.

Manny simply says, "Start talking."

Génesis takes the lead. "Our uniforms' magic deactivated when we entered the Dark Island. I could hear it fizzle out once we landed inside.

When we returned, the dragons must've restored their magic, because it protected us from that fire."

At first, I think I've heard wrong, but when I check on Manny and Joaquín, they also look like someone's given them an unsolvable trigonometry test. The Sol de Noche dragons can take magic away *and* give it back? That makes them more powerful than anyone in this locker room suspected. And their unprecedented magic has just been revealed to the whole world.

"What did you see this time?" I ask Victoria.

"The sand was still there, but now there are black palm trees and a black ocean and a *throne.*" I've never heard Victoria speak this fast or this high-pitched. "A freaking throne."

Okay. I really need to sit down. I settle on the bench next to Héctor. "Victoria, I know you don't have a sense of humor, but please tell me you're joking."

"Nope. I saw it, too. We all did," Luis makes quick eye contact, as if he's too stressed out to focus. "The dragons flew around the throne for a minute, but there was an invisible shield blocking it. We couldn't get too close."

What. The. Hell.

"The throne was built out of dragon-claw bone," says Génesis. "Full-blown ivory. Each bone curved inward, as if the throne was designed to trap whoever claimed it."

"No se olviden del pit," Edwin cuts in. "Esas torres se veían brutales."

Gabriela nods. "There was a square pit a few feet away from the beach's shore, and these endless skyscraper claw-bone towers surrounding the pit."

"Aiming straight for the stars," says Héctor.

I put my hands in prayer form. Dragons who can build impenetrable thrones and bone towers are a little out of my league. They're also out of Joaquín's and Manny's leagues, as they're both totally spaced out.

Not even Victoria snapping her fingers can get them to talk.

"Earth to adults. Hello, adults?" she says.

Joaquín comes to his senses first. "Did you all experience the Fade like Victoria had?"

Luis shakes his head. "There wasn't silence or surprise. I could *hear* Daga singing in my head before she Faded." He dabs a clean towel on his forehead. "Did y'all hear a song, too?"

Everyone nods.

Génesis says, "It was the same song they sing at the habitat, but I only had Rayo's voice in my head. About five or six notes in, we Faded."

"Igual yo con Fantasma," says Edwin.

"Same here," Héctor and Gabriela say together.

Joaquín blinks with heavy eyelids. "Then what happened?"

"We came back here, and the dragons went off with those flames," Luis replies. "Daga wasn't blocking me, but I couldn't hear anything except for the roars. It gave me goose bumps."

He lets those last words hang between us, waiting for the other riders' reactions.

They're all dreadfully quiet.

Then Joaquín says, "I think we can conclude the dragons' song isn't really a song. It's a spell, and it's getting stronger. So are your dragons. I just don't understand *why* they keep Fading into the Dark Island during matches. They can secretly perform this magic in the habitat, but they're choosing to do so in front of the whole world. Have they shown you why?"

"No, but they're singing in our heads, and we can all Fade together now," says Gabriela. "It could mean they're almost capable of communicating more clearly."

"They already are," Héctor says. "That roaring was the angriest I've ever heard them. I don't think it was an intimidation tactic for Zimbabwe. This was *real* rage. It was like they were out for blood. Like they were ready for war."

"Oh, don't be melodramatic. They just wanted to scare Taona." Victoria is squatting down next to me, fixing her scraggly ponytail. "It was all strategy to stop her, and it worked."

Gabriela rolls her eyes. "I felt it, too, Victoria. The rage. It was intense."

"Like their wrath wanted to break free from its cage," Génesis says.

Victoria's good mood is dead and gone. Her arms crossed tight, she's looking at everyone like she's plotting their murders. "Because it was *supposed* to look scary."

"You really think this was about winning a match?" Héctor raises his voice with every word. He stands up, towering over Victoria. "You're really gonna tell me that's all this was?"

"Obviously. Our dragons have sent us to the semifinals. Now we wait to see who wins the next game in a couple of hours and figure out how we can beat them in two more days "

Héctor's eyes are a silent plea for Victoria to see reason. "This was a call to arms, Victoria. You saw how the Pangolin dragons watched them in total awe. How mesmerized they were? Whatever our steeds did out there today, it wasn't for us. It was for others like them."

My heart's speeding up. Esperanza's first public Fade had been such a wild card. This show of magical strength has been bigger, bolder, harder to ignore. If it really *is* a call to arms, then that means the dragons don't want to be here. But they don't want to go home, either.

They want to fight the Sire. They just don't want to do it alone.

My thoughts flash back to the Sire's counter curse. He only needs a Hydra and a Pluma de Muerte, and even though México is competing in the Cup, he rescued an Un-Bonded dragon instead of using one from the tournament. If the counter curse requires a willing sacrifice, the Cup isn't where he's getting his ingredients. It's just where he's picking soldiers. What if he tries to break the Sol de Noches' Bond first? He could use them to fetch the Fire Drake's crystal heart.

Victoria's yelling brings me back to the locker room. "I told you to stop being ridiculous, guys! Our dragons used their fire so other teams would fear them. And they were *successful.*"

"Enough!" Joaquín's cheeks are bright red. "There are reporters waiting for you as we speak. The Dark Island stays between us. Now let's head out."

I hang back so that everyone else can exit before me. Joaquín, Manny, and I are the last ones in the locker room. I edge closer to Joaquín. "Do you think they want to fight?"

"Go to your press conference, Lana. We can discuss this later."

I'm tempted to demand that he answer the question, but he already did.

I perk up for the cameras. From the side of the stage, President Turner watches us like a hawk. My team and I stick to the Transport angle, seconding Victoria's claims that the ring of fire had been a strategic attempt to distract Zimbabwe. I get a few questions about my demonstration yesterday. Specifically, if I think the dragons were protesting, too.

"The Sol de Noche dragons are gifted at many things. One of them is winning matches." I smile like I'm a born winner. "Just like the six people joining me on this stage."

Ten minutes later, President Turner announces the end of the press conference. I'm whisked offstage alongside my teammates. President Turner and Manny whisper something to each other, probably about the Fade or the ring of fire. Then the president tells us, "Congratulations on advancing to the semifinals!" He leads the way back to the box seats.

My team's victory is the talk of the town when we arrive. Even Onesa comes over to hug us one by one, congratulating us with more grace than I'll ever have. "You were smart to run when I wasn't looking. You wouldn't have won otherwise," she says with a wink.

"That's the truest thing anyone's said to me in my whole life," I say.

"I'm glad. Remember that forever."

She moves on to Héctor. They start chatting while I scoot away to the staircase.

Andrew watches me from the room's topmost area, where the catering tables have been placed. He's snatching a bottle of water without breaking eye contact, like he's egging me on. We haven't spoken since our post-Sire-message conversation. When his team won their Round of Sixteen match against Portugal, Andrew had high-fived everyone except for me. He's also been MIA from BlazeReel Live. I don't know if I'm to blame, but all signs point to probably.

He takes a swig of water and looks past the glass, where the field is being prepped for his match in a few hours. There's something heartbreaking about the way he's forcing his gaze elsewhere. How he's ignoring the girl who promised her support and ended up shunning him.

Sorry, Andrew. I have bigger things to worry about than your bruised ego.

His team gets called to the field, along with Team Egypt.

He runs off to play a game he doesn't even want to play anymore.

AFTER THREE AND A HALF HOURS, ANDREW PUNCHES THE IRON Scale onto the stone dais.

"Scotland is moving on to the semifinals!" Jeffrey Hines says.

The Scottish Golden Horns swoop down on Andrew at once. Their riders tackle him the same way I've been tackled during my past two matches. Andrew's lifted onto their shoulders and shown off for the stadium to shower him in adoration. Some people are booing. The Scottish fans are properly celebrating with all sorts of chants, but one is louder than the rest.

"Galloway! Galloway! Galloway!"

His mother's family name echoes across the field. If she's watching, she must be thrilled.

"So we're playing Scotland next." Victoria claps with a cocky grin. "Should be fun."

I focus on the boy who doesn't want to play this game. He's just won for his country, and he's smiling like he meant to. In two days, we'll be rivals on the field.

That is, if the Sire doesn't come after our dragons.

"Yeah," I tell Victoria, my hands limp on my lap. "Should be a lot of fun. . . ."

THE MAP OF PUERTO RICO IS STILL CHARRED ON THE HABITAT'S ceiling.

The coconuts are new, though. There's a pile to the left side of the habitat. A few cracked shells are scattered here and there, but most remain whole.

Gabriela and I are the only humans here. We're not being serenaded with a nighttime singing session. The dragons are in the large rock pit filled with water at the end of the habitat. They're playing a game of "Who can splash more water at your face?" with impressive zeal.

Puya and Daga are the current MVPs. They're scooping mouthfuls of water and spitting at their opponents in lightning-fast streams. Titán uses his wings to shield Rayo, Fantasma, and himself, while a swift Esperanza spits water back at them. On occasion, Titán flies as high as he can, then drops back to the lake in a perfect cannonball. Puya and Daga squeal in melodramatic angst. Esperanza huffs out the closest thing I've heard to a dragon laughing.

I'm far removed from the splashing. Gabriela sits next to me, searching for a Slovakian fashion designer's runway show on her phone. Joaquín had asked her to look after the dragons while he Skypes with his family. I'd volunteered. Whether the Sire makes an appearance in President Turner's body, or if he sends word to hand over the dragons, nobody's touching them. I can convince him to use me for another mission. As long as President Turner and these dragons remain unharmed, as long as I can distract him from the Fire Drake, I'll do what he tells me.

Part of me wants to share my Bond theory with my teammates. But without proof, Victoria would launch into one of her spiels about how I'm overreacting. I'm not in the mood to be told I'm wrong. Or to disturb what little peace we achieved after the ring of fire.

"Oh, cool," says Gabriela. "Andrew's finally posted on BlazeReel again."

"Good for him," I grumble.

Gabriela clicks on Andrew's avatar, which has a red circle wrapping around it. The screen shows Andrew sitting on a couch at his Compound house. He's still in his uniform, but his hair is a disaster. I hate myself for laughing as Andrew pulls his hair up high.

"Lovely to see you again!" he says. "I figured I'd provide you with quality content today, hence the new look. This is what happens when you let a Golden Horn comb your hair."

Gabriela sighs. "So sad to see him in uniform. Those shoulders deserve cashmere."

Andrew picks up an acoustic guitar from the floor. The guitar is midnight blue with a black swirl looping all around it. There's a sticker on the left side that says WORLD'S BEST SON. The handwriting is slanted yet delicate, as if his mother scribbled it herself.

She knows better than anyone what the Sire's capable of.

Andrew is still joking about his hair when I pull out my phone. I open the search engine app and type in "Lucy Galloway Foxrose Prep."

Most of the articles that pop up are related to her achievements as a young musician representing her school abroad. One article is about a Foxrose professor and author named Edna Clarke. It's a tribute from a former student who collected quotes from other students. Ms. Galloway is one.

So are President Turner and Edward Barnes.

There's a picture with the three of them outside of the school library. They're showing off a huge yellow book titled *Regular History & Customs for Magic Users*. Edward Barnes is the carbon copy of the boy in that clearing photo. President Turner is also the same, but he doesn't have dead eyes and a silent scream choking him. Ms. Galloway had been rocking bangs.

I fly through the rest of the photos. The last two are group shots. Every student featured in the article poses outside of Foxrose. Edward Barnes and Ms. Galloway are partially hidden in the back. She smiles for the camera. He's tilting his head toward her, sneaking a glance in her direction. In the last photo, the same students are talking, dispersed into different subgroups. President Turner is busy with three other students. Barnes and Ms. Galloway are barely visible among the crowd, but I zoom in on the way they're meeting each other's gaze. His dreamy eyes aren't a figment of my imagination. Neither is that shy smile. She's giving him one back.

This could mean absolutely nothing. I could be blowing things out of proportion.

But it seems to me Edward Barnes and Lucy Galloway had a thing for each other.

I search for "Edward Barnes Foxrose Girlfriend." Eight different articles state he never dated a fellow student. He didn't date anyone in college, either. Hundreds of users in gossip forums have left theories about his dating life, ranging from midnight picnics with a tap-dancing freshman to raunchy escapades with a chess player, but their only evidence is that Barnes shared breathing space with those girls. Ms. Galloway's name is nowhere to be found.

I lower my phone, eyes wide in horror. Edward Barnes had died twenty years ago.

Andrew had been born a year later.

No. *Three months* after his death: March 12, 1998. A boy born without his dad's name.

A stiff hand finds its way to my lips. What if Edward Barnes is Andrew's *father?*

This could be why his mom warned him to stop protesting. Andrew's the missing link to breaking the Sire's curse. He's the *freaking heir of Edward Barnes.* Whether Ms. Galloway knows about the other ingredients or not, she's been possibly hiding the most important one.

Now I have to help her save him.

Dragons of all species are remarkably self-sufficient. When they break out of their eggs, they're physiologically programmed to adapt to their environments and hone their survival skills without the aid of other dragons. According to rider testimonials, their steeds know the identities of their parents. They leave a magical imprint on their newborns. Dragons can also sense when their parents or offspring die. Their mourning process varies from species to species, but it's never quite as volatile as the one observed in humans, since the latter can either grieve in harmless ways or they could endanger the lives of others.

—*Excerpt from Carlos Torres's* Studying the Bond
Between Dragons & Humans

CHAPTER TWENTY-FOUR

I HATE THE BUREAU FOR TAKING SAMIRA'S WHISPERER.

I'm hiding in the bathroom again, desperately trying to speak to the only person I trust to help me with this heir theory. The bureau must've taken off her Whisperer so she couldn't be tracked if mine were compromised. So I try calling her on my phone. Nothing. Wherever she is, it's the safest place on the planet.

Maybe it's for the best. I shouldn't bother Samira with wild theories when her life is in danger, thanks to me. I should be bothering the bureau. Go directly to the people who can actually *do* something. They can't possibly know about Andrew, or else they would have protected him, right? Unless they're pretending *not* to know to throw off the Sire's scent?

I dash out of the bathroom and search for the card Agent Horowitz gave me the day we met. Luckily, there's nobody in the kitchen. I fetch the house phone and dial Agent Horowitz's number. She'll probably be quicker to answer someone calling from the Compound.

She's not picking up.

"What is it with people ignoring me tonight?" I leave her a message so she'll call me the second she gets it.

When I hang up again, I can only think of one other person to contact. If President Turner knows and my heir theory is true, he's been lying for years. And if someone like me can connect the dots, the Sire won't be far behind. We have to work together to guarantee Andrew's safety.

I press number three.

After four rings, the president picks up. "Good evening, House Puerto Rico! With whom do I have the pleasure of speaking?"

"It's Lana, Mr. President. So sorry to bother you, but there's something I need to discuss. I tried contacting Agent Horowitz, but she's not picking up. And I don't have Director Sandhar's number. Could we all meet up tonight somehow? I'd rather talk in person."

"Right. I see." President Turner's cheerfulness is dead and buried. "Well, my dear, I'm afraid Nirek will be a little hard to reach."

I press my back against the wall. "What happened?"

"I'll call back tomorrow, Ms. Torres. I've got a lead on the Sire and his Dragon Knights. Nirek and his squadron are in Sweden right now. I'm supposed to hear from them soon."

The weight of his words pummels me into silence. I'm left open-mouthed and numb in the empty kitchen, a smile slowly creeping onto my face.

Then I whisper, "You found the Sire?"

"We don't know for sure. But I'll call you back."

"Why would he be in Sweden? Is he at another sanctuary?"

The president is quiet. Then he says, "Perhaps."

Well, that was a cagey response. What else would the Sire be doing so far from his last-known location? The only other thing he cares about is the crystal heart and—

"Oh my God," I say. "Is the Fire Drake in Sweden?"

"I don't have that information, Ms. Torres. We'll speak soon. Good night."

President Turner hangs up.

How convenient. The Fire Drake *has* to be in Sweden. The president might be lying to keep me out of more trouble. I place the phone back on its perch. After so long, the Sire could be hours, maybe even minutes, away from getting caught. But he might not be in Sweden by the time the bureau locates his hideout. He could flee with the last ingredient for his counter curse.

Either way, Andrew is still in danger. If I'm going to protect him, I have to do it alone.

I pull up the BlazeReel Live app. Andrew's online. I click on our message history and start typing:

Hey. Just wanted to see if you are available to talk today. Would that be okay?

He replies five seconds later.

depends. will you kidnap me and take me to an EDM festival so I'm driven utterly mad and am incapable of playing tomorrow?

Damn it. How did you know?

i'm a genius.

Debatable. ☺ *So are you free to chat?*

sounds horrible. see you in half an hour?

Half an hour it is.

ANDREW IS ALREADY INSIDE THE WHITE TENT WHEN I GET THERE. It's the same tent we had our welcome party in. Most of the decorations are still here, but the stage, the chocolate fountain, and the photo booth are gone. Andrew is playing a song I don't recognize on his black-and-blue guitar. He seems to be on another plane of existence, eyes closed and head tilted back, as he jams out on the same couch my team had claimed.

I walk up to Andrew. "Is that an original?"

Andrew cracks an eye open. "Did you just ask me if a Garbage song is mine?" He whistles. "I don't know if I should feel flattered or disappointed in your lack of Garbage knowledge."

"Oh, I've heard of them. Just not that song. What's it called?"

"'Lana Torres Doesn't Know Who We Are.' Massive hit in Europe right now." Andrew grins. He strikes one more chord, then hugs his guitar close. "This is 'Happy Home.' I'd recommend it, but you don't listen to fantastic music, so it would be a waste of my time."

"Dramatic as usual, I see." I sit next to him. "How've you been today?"

"Spent. We've been training even harder to beat your lot tomorrow. You?"

"Same," I lie.

I can't wait till the day I won't have to make stuff up for Andrew's sake. Right now, though, it's all about getting the information I need in order to keep him safe, which includes some more lying. His mother must've spoken about Edward Barnes at some point. If she never did, that's a huge red flag. How could you never mention going to school with the most important wizard in history?

If she spoke negatively about him, my theory could still be correct. Bad-mouthing Edward Barnes could make it seem like she'd never be caught dead having a child with him. But if she's said only *good* things, that reduces the odds. Ms. Galloway would have to be the most reckless liar in the world to speak highly of someone she's trying to distance her secret child from.

"You look like your head is about to explode from thinking so hard," says Andrew.

"I'm fine. It's just that I've been meaning to apologize for the way I treated you the other day. I was really rude, and I'm sorry if I hurt you, Andrew. We don't have to be on the same page, but we do owe each other respect." I hold out a hand. "Truce?"

Andrew's gaze softens. He looks from me to my hand. "I don't get many apologies, so I should relish this one a wee bit longer. Keep your hand like that for about six more hours."

"Andrew."

"No, no. Talking ruins the moment." He breathes in like he's in paradise.

I playfully punch his shoulder. "Come on, man. Truce or no truce?"

With a quick strum of his guitar, Andrew nods. "Truce." He shakes my hand.

Get in his good graces? Check. Now on to the next step.

"So how've you been?" I ask. "And how's your mom? Did she see your winning match?"

"She did. I called her right after I got to the house. She just kept crying from joy." Andrew taps his guitar in sporadic bursts of energy. "I always feel better after I talk with her."

Here goes nothing.

"You know, I remembered what you said about her growing up with the Sire around. It got me thinking about Edward Barnes's reputation and how he was so beloved."

Andrew stops tapping his guitar. "Mum's told me how kind he was. No bad vibes there." His expression turns sour. "Wish she could've had better judgment when it came to my dad."

He's talking about his dad as if he's not Edward Barnes. As if they're two different men.

"What has she told you about your dad?" I dare to ask.

Andrew balks at my question. He places his guitar on the couch in one slow movement. "She didn't have to tell me much. I've met him."

I can hear the wind rustling the sand outside, but it feels like the commotion is happening inside me, flinging me in all directions. This is the boy who told Jeffrey Hines that his father had left his pregnant mother and never looked back. Now he's telling me he's actually *met* the guy?

And it's not Edward Barnes.

Andrew isn't the missing key to breaking the Sire's curse. His bloodline isn't tied to the most important wizard in history. Besides, Andrew's a Regular. Since his mother is a witch, his father must've been a Regular, too. Some Regulars are born from a pair of magical parents, but it's rare. I'd been too caught up in my theory to even *remember* that. The Sire's been pining for the crystal heart, like I suspected, not an heir that doesn't exist.

"You . . . you've met him?" I whisper.

"Yes, we've had a chat," Andrew admits. "But you can't speak of this publicly."

I nod. "This stays between us."

"Thank you." Andrew picks at a loose thread on the couch's armrest. "Mum told me the basics. He's a Regular from Aberdeen who'd moved to Glasgow for a graphic-design job. He used to play the drums in his spare time. They met at a pub where he was performing. Dated for a few months. After she got pregnant, he got fired for drunken behavior, got banned from loads of pubs for picking fights, fled back home, and wanted nothing to do with me."

"Wow. Sounds like a real winner."

He tries to smile, but he gives up midway. "She said I could go look for him once I turned eighteen if I really felt like it, but that I shouldn't get my hopes up. I should've believed her." His laugh is mirthless, hollow. "I drove all the way to Aberdeen alone. That had been my birthday wish. To meet the man who abandoned me. I didn't expect much, just to take one good look at his face and tell him I forgave him. It had already been a year since Hikaru's murder and Takeshi's disappearance. My ex-girlfriend and I had been fighting a lot, too, so I was in a really bad place. All I wanted was to center myself. Let go of as much of the hurt as I could."

He ignores the loose thread in favor of stroking his guitar strap. "I found him at the address Mum gave me. He reeked of whiskey and mumbled like he'd forgotten how to use his own mouth." Andrew smiles for real this time. "But he recognized me. Said I looked just like my mother." The smile is dead and gone. "Then he punched me and tried to steal my wallet."

I jolt back as if I'm the one who's been punched. "He did *what?*"

"He was hammered, lass. And broke. I'm embarrassed to admit he actually knocked me to the floor. Kicked me a few times, too. My instincts only surfaced when he lunged for my wallet. I was too shocked to even move before then." Andrew raises his fists, admiring them. "He was too pitiful to knock out, but he got what he deserved. I thanked him for staying away all these years. For letting me live a happy life without him. Then I left."

I lay my head on his shoulder. I bet it's not a huge comfort for him, but it's a start. "I'm so sorry, Andrew. You didn't deserve to be treated like that."

"And yet I'm grateful. I got exactly what I wanted. I met the man who abandoned me. Turns out I hadn't been missing out on anything, but I wouldn't have believed it unless I saw it for myself. I've never told Mum what really happened. She still thinks he wouldn't answer the door and I gave up trying. But I'm never the one who gives up trying." He takes his sweet time before speaking again. When he does, his voice is feeble. "Everybody leaves me, Lana. That's just how my life works. I'm not the one people fight for. I'm the one fighting for people to stay, to support me, to believe in the things I want to achieve."

I clutch his hands. "Well, that stops now. I'm not going anywhere. Your mother's not going anywhere. Your teammates, your fans: They're all here for you. You're worth fighting for, Andrew. You always have been, regardless of those who chose not to stay." I don't know how I would've reacted if our places had been switched. If Papi had been the one to abandon me before I was born, then tried to rob me when I knocked on his door eighteen years later.

Andrew isn't the heir of the most important wizard in history, but he still matters.

He's the hero I should've believed in instead of Takeshi Endo.

"I refuse to trust someone who doesn't listen to fantastic music," he says with a smirk. "Thanks, Lana. You're a good egg."

"Same. Now play some more of that 'Happy Home' song."

Andrew loses himself in the melody again, taking me along with him. I'd been wrong about the heir theory, but at least Andrew's not in danger.

All I ask is for the bureau to *finally* catch the Sire before he steals the crystal heart.

I brought you a basket of apples,

Why don't you take a bite?

Go to sleep, my little princess,

You won't wake up after tonight.

—*Poem written by Randall Wiggins, age nine*

CHAPTER TWENTY-FIVE

TWO YEARS AGO, I SAT IN SAMIRA'S LIVING ROOM AND WAITED FOR the twenty-sixth Blazewrath World Cup to start. Samira commented on the absurd questions male reporters asked female players. Shay commented on the jaw-dropping stunts. I focused on everything in between. Mrs. Jones fed us pizza and curly fries. Mr. Jones popped in for the occasional joke about teenagers acting tough in tights. Mom texted four times to check up on me. We'd told her we were researching colleges. I texted back to say I still hadn't died.

Two years ago, I was dying to be where I am today. The farther I go into the stadium's box seats—the more I say "hello" and "how are you"—the more I grapple with the fact I'm actually playing in the semifinals. Sure, my team was forced to be here, but the crackling energy in the air has nothing to do with the Sire. It permeates every handshake and bow, the endless compliments, the euphoric fan chants. Today, I'm a winner without a trophy. I can bask in the glory of being right where I'd wanted to be all my life. I still love this game.

Now I just need to know if I'm free.

Once the team greetings are over, I walk up to Manny. He's decked out in a crisp gray suit and perfectly arranged tie. He's even brought out some leather shoes instead of sneakers. And his posture is way straighter. For the first time, he actually looks the part of team manager, and oh my God, does he look like a different person. Maybe he's better dressed because it's the semifinals? Or is he finally starting to believe in us? Either way, he's a sight for sore eyes.

"Will President Turner be here soon?" I ask.

Manny's blinking in that slow way that suggests he's either exhausted or I'm irking him. My money is on the latter. "Of course."

Good. I lean in closer, dropping my voice to a whisper. "Any updates on Sweden?"

"I got nothing for you, nena," he whispers back.

It's been thirty minutes, and the president's still not here. I'm double-checking my phone to see if it's really been thirty minutes or if I'm imagining the clock speeding up. He should be here by now, right? Unless something's wrong? I'm tempted to ask Manny to call him, but he's too busy mingling with the other team managers to notice me.

Five minutes later, President Turner finally arrives. He and Headmaster Sykes walk straight for the Foxrose professors near the entrance. It would be rude to interrupt, but I can't wait thirty more minutes. The match is scheduled to start soon. Besides, my head won't be fully in the game if I'm wondering whether the Fire Drake is out of harm's way. I jog down the stairs. By the time I reach the president, he's already turning to face me.

"Ms. Torres! Good morning!" He shows off his pearly whites as he hugs me. "My apologies for not returning your phone call. It's been a little hectic."

"Not a problem, sir." I hold him as tightly as possible. "Has he been caught yet?"

"Team Puerto Rico! Team Scotland!" an IBF staff member calls. "Game time!"

My teammates rush downstairs along with Andrew and the Scottish players. I'm still holding on to the president, but he's backing away.

"We can chat after the match," he says. "Best of luck out there!"

I don't let him go. "It's a yes-or-no question, sir."

His forehead creases as he inches away from me. Maybe he thinks I'm being pushy. Okay, so I *am* being pushy, but why can't he just be honest with me? It's not that hard!

Someone taps me on the shoulder. "Lana, let's hit it." Manny. "Now."

"But I need to know if he's been caught."

"Like I said," says the president, "we'll discuss this later. Have a great game."

Manny whisks me away before I can insist any further. Andrew high-fives me as we march next to each other, oblivious to how confused I am. Why wouldn't President Turner just say yes or no? Is the truth more complicated than that? Does that mean the Sire is *still* free?

"Ready to lose?" Andrew jokes.

I force a smile. "Keep dreaming . . ."

He laughs. "See you out there, lass. May the best team win."

Andrew and the rest of Team Scotland are led to their side of the stadium.

I join my teammates in our wait zone. The dragons are already stationed above. Joaquín is checking in with everyone, asking if they're okay. When he gets to me, I gasp. I totally forgot about what I'm supposed to do on the field. What's happening here is just as important to the Sire as whatever's happening in Sweden. "President Turner hasn't told us if we're supposed to win again." My words come out like a strained cry for help.

Joaquín shakes his head. "He didn't have instructions for us today."

Chills run through my whole body. Does that mean the Sire is stuck in bureau custody? Or that he's too busy dodging spells from agents? I *hate* not knowing what's going on, especially when I'm about to play the most important match of my Blazewrath career!

"So what do we do?" Héctor asks cautiously.

"We win," says Joaquín. "That's what we came here for, right?"

"Right." Victoria is smiling the way she does when I reach the top of the mountain.

Héctor nods. "We're moving on to the final, guys."

Gabriela jumps up and down, almost knocking Edwin off his feet, but he doesn't seem to mind. Génesis and Luis are high-fiving with both hands.

Héctor rallies us in a circle. We put our hands on top of his. "Today will belong to us. Whatever happens, we leave everything on that field. We do what we can for our country. I love you all. Even you, Luis." We laugh as one. "Thank you for everything."

"Thank you," Gabriela says.

"Mil gracias a todos. Los amo demasiado," says Edwin.

"I love you, too, Edwin. I love you all." Génesis tearfully winks at us.

I watch as my teammates take turns thanking one another, welling up with every word. *This* is what this tournament should've been about all along. *This* is the kind of happiness I should've felt since the beginning—what I never thought I'd feel after learning the truth about my contract, a distant dream wrapped in a nightmare. Feeling it now, at this point, is both awful and awesome. Right now, though, it's definitely more on the awesome side of the spectrum.

I gulp down the boulder in my throat. "You all took a huge risk and let a total stranger into your family. Even if we had some differences"—I sneak a glance at Victoria—"I think we were meant to be a team. It's an honor and a privilege to wear the black uniform alongside you."

Before we can raise our hands in the air, Manny swoops in and slaps his palm on top. "The honor and privilege is mine. I've gotten to see seven greats do what they were born to do. I'm sorry, mi gente, for not supporting you more. Thank you for making history on behalf of our little island. But above all, thank you for helping me *believe* again." Cranky and standoffish as he's been, it means the universe that he's trying. Hopefully, he'll keep it up forever.

"Get in here, mijo," Manny says to Joaquín, who's already leaning closer.

When Joaquín's hand joins our little pile, Héctor yells, "¡Por Puerto Rico!"

"¡Por Puerto Rico!" we echo him together, raising our hands high.

We position ourselves in a single-file line. A staff member tells us we'll be outside in three minutes. I jog in place, pumping myself up for the showdown of my life. Those Golden Horns won't be easy. They might not have three heads or the ability to rattle mountains, but being chased with fire *and* a spear-shaped horn? No, thank you.

The jumbotron flashes a snowy, static screen.

I cringe at the earsplitting noise. "What the hell?"

Whenever the static appears, the Sire follows. I wait for his ugly mug to pop up on-screen, but the snow is still blocking the field from view, and the Sire has yet to make his cameo. Why would he be drawing this out? Is he trying to fry everyone's brains from dread? Mine's about to burst. Whatever this stunt is, I hope it ends quickly.

My father's face is broadcast to the entire stadium.

He's lying on his office floor, both hands tied behind his back. His mouth has been gagged with a white cloth. Dust flies down from the office's ceiling, along with a few pieces of cement, as if something exploded before the transmission. Flames lick the edges of the screen.

"Oh my God! Papi!" My voice quivers. The whole stadium is blurring into white spots save for the jumbotron. I'm trying to take a step forward, but my boots are superglued to the floor, which is where my heart is also dropping. "That's my dad!"

A new face comes into focus.

"Hi, everyone," Takeshi says in the flattest tone. His claw dagger is aimed over Papi's neck. "I have a message for Lana Torres. What you did at the press conference was unacceptable. My master has chosen your father's death as punishment. We can't be stopped, Lana. We're everywhere. *Especially* in the safest places you can imagine."

My teammates say something, hold me close, and say something again.

It's all white noise to me. I'm shaking so, so hard. "Don't hurt him . . . please . . . just don't hurt him . . ." I whimper, even though he can't hear me. I don't know what else to do.

"This is my master's message for you." Takeshi tilts his head. "Welcome to the doom."

He ends the transmission before I can beg again for my father's life.

*It is never easy to predict how a group of strangers will get along,
especially when there are dragons involved. There have been instances
where riders know one another prior to being selected for the Blazewrath World Cup, but this rarely comes to pass. Players are ordered
to live together while they train in an effort to cultivate trust. Their
chemistry is just as important as their athletic skills. Respect is also
crucial. Anyone who enters the Cup must agree to be mindful of their
teammates' needs. The suffering of one becomes the suffering of all.*

—*Excerpt from Harleen Khurana's*
A History of Blazewrath Around the World

CHAPTER TWENTY-SIX

"**T**AKESHI HAS MY DAD! HE'S GOING TO KILL HIM!"

I black out everything except for Manny. This is the closest
thing to dropping from the tallest skyscraper on Earth, sinking into a
dark hole that leads to another dimension, but realizing I'll never get to
see what it looks like because my heart will stop long before the crash
landing. I fly to Manny, almost knocking him down. "He's in Brazil! You
have to do something, he has my dad, *he's going to kill him!*" I'm yelling
so, so loud. The air in the room is thinning to the point where I can't
even breathe. "You have to call Director Sandhar and tell him to leave
for Brazil!"

Manny turns ghost pale. He fidgets with his phone. "Let me contact
him . . ." He waves Joaquín over while he dials the director's number.

After a few seconds, he hangs up and tries again. He hangs up for a second time. "*Balls*. He's not answering."

Damn it. "Do you think the bureau could be ambushing the Sire right now?"

"Anything's possible at this point, nena."

"Then Director Sandhar will be unreachable. My dad . . . he won't . . ."

I lean into Edwin's chest, a storm of heaves and tears. I'm shoving my fists into my eyes, trying to keep it together, but it's all a waste of energy. It doesn't matter how tight Edwin holds me. It doesn't matter how he rocks me side to side to soothe me.

Takeshi Endo is going to kill my father.

"She needs a medic!" I hear Andrew say. I don't know how he got here, but he's also holding me up. "Let's sit her down."

He and Edwin gently place me on a nearby folding chair. A witch shows up, and she's asking me questions I can't understand. I bend over, head hanging between my knees, and her voice sounds light-years away. Teardrops splatter my boots, the floor. More voices fill up the space around me, but none are loud enough to distract me from myself. Takeshi waited until minutes before the start of my match to destabilize me. I'm stuck here, unable to save Papi.

A cold breeze washes over me. It's about two or three seconds' worth of shivers, but once it's over, there's only the strongest, most soothing warmth I've ever felt. Something blooms in the middle of my chest, like a seed growing into petals. A sturdy stem, anchoring me to myself again. I straighten up. The medic witch has her Silver wand pointed at me. She says something about the Calming Charm being a temporary relief.

"I'll keep trying to get in touch with Sandhar," Manny reassures me, but he's wasting his breath. "Russell can contact the IBF's antiterrorism unit, too, to see if they can help." He looks like a demon fresh out of the underworld, glowering with the kind of intensity that could silence even the most talkative person. "He *has* to postpone the match."

"Our contracts are still binding," says Joaquín, throwing a cautious glance at Andrew. "I'm sorry, Lana."

He says it like Papi's in a coffin already. Like there's no other choice.

All I feel is the fire Marisol had told me to control before it burned me away. The flames carve out a path straight to my shattered shell of a heart, refusing to die out. Maybe President Turner and Manny will be able to get in touch with the bureau. Maybe they'll Transport to Brazil just in time to save my father's life and stop the vomit pile that is Takeshi Endo.

But I don't want to wait for them to do something. I don't want to play a game while Papi's dying. I want to save him *myself*.

"Lana?" Joaquín calls for me. "We need to get back in line."

"No," I say.

"You have to—"

"NO! I won't go out there until someone helps me save my dad!"

"Calm down!" Victoria yells. "You're no good to us in this state."

She's lucky Andrew and Edwin are in front of me. Otherwise, I would've clocked her. "Oh, I'm sorry, Victoria. Does my father's kidnapping *inconvenience* you? How rude of me!" I'm trying to close the gap between us, but Andrew and Edwin won't let me go. "Why can't *you* be of some good and think of a way to stop my father from being murdered?!"

The Sol de Noche dragons roar as one in the hangar above us.

They're unleashing a fury unlike any other, six apocalypses all devastating the earth in a single sweep, making the hairs on the back of my neck stand. All of my team's riders slap both hands to the sides of their heads. They scream and sink to their knees.

Then the roaring ends.

"What the actual hell was that?" I ask.

At first, all I get is silence.

Then a startled Génesis says, "They showed us the truth . . . I could see it so clearly . . ."

"See what clearly?"

"War," Gabriela and Luis say together.

Andrew leans forward. "Did you just say *war*?"

"Sí," says Edwin. "Los dragones quieren salvar al papá de Lana."

I lean back, hands raised in surprise. The dragons *want to save* Papi. They can get to Brazil using the Fade. It's the fastest anyone can get there without a wand. My best bet.

"Are you sure that's what they said?" Joaquín asks.

"The dragons have been desperate to use their powers for something greater," says Héctor. "It's like I told you—the ring of fire was a call to arms." He stops long enough to take a breath. "But they're begging us to go with them. They don't want to fight alone."

I'm rocked to the core, shaking again. There's not a single spell in the history of magic that can get rid of the jitters this time. They're not from stress or pain; they're an electric jolt of hope coursing through all that I am. "Then hop on!"

"*No!*" Victoria is on the verge of tears. "Saving people from terrorists is the bureau's job. The dragons belong in this stadium. You're putting our safety at risk by asking us to leave."

With a swerve, I get past Andrew and Edwin, landing so close to Victoria that we could slow dance. "You play the most dangerous sport in the world! You've faced the Zmey Gorynych and the Pangolin dragon, and you're afraid of *one* Dragon Knight? Are you kidding?!"

"There could be threats we don't know about," says Génesis. "This is clearly a trap."

I wish I could contradict her. This reeks of a trap. But this is also my father. I refuse to do nothing just because I'm scared. I'd rather get hurt than see him suffer because of me.

"Don't forget about our contracts," Génesis says. "Victoria's right regarding our safety."

Luis holds up a hand to her. "We need to think about President Turner, too. His safety's on the line just as much as ours. Maybe even more."

"What do you mean?" Andrew says.

"We can't piss the Sire off without risking Turner's life." Héctor tries to play it cool with a shrug. "You know how much the Sire hates the IBF, right? The president is a likely target."

He's right. If we go after Takeshi, President Turner could be tortured or killed. He's the only one the Sire can hurt without relying on his cronies. Of course he'll be the first to suffer.

"Do you think the dragons can Fade other people into the Dark Island?" Joaquín says. He pays no mind to the way Andrew's leaning closer to him as if to check he's hearing correctly.

"Oh yeah. They're stronger now than ever before," Gabriela replies.

"Then hide President Turner inside the Dark Island." Joaquín ignores everyone's raised eyebrows. "Magic doesn't work there. Your contracts will be null and void. They might not even carry any magical weight once the president is brought out. You'll be protecting him from magic that could threaten his life. Magic that can't be undone, like those contracts."

He doesn't say the words "Anchor Curse," but I can read them all over his face.

I've never wished to hug anyone as much as I do right now. This is the missing piece. "Joaquín . . . you're a genius. An actual, honest-to-God *genius!*"

"Hang on, lads." Andrew butts in. "What's the Dark Island?"

"Shut up!" Victoria snaps at him, then zeroes in on Joaquín. "This is way too risky."

"I would never put you at risk. Neither would your dragons. They know you're prepared, even if you haven't accepted it yet," Joaquín says. "Go ahead. Ask them if my plan will work."

Victoria doesn't move.

Héctor closes his eyes, though, as if reaching out to Titán.

The dragons roar again, but this time, their riders aren't bent over in excruciating pain.

"That's a resounding yes," says Gabriela. "They're ready."

"They're ready . . ." Luis repeats with less enthusiasm.

Edwin pulls him close, smiling, and Génesis grabs Luis's hand. "I get it. I'm terrified, too, but maybe the only way we'll know if we're ready to fight the Sire is to just do it."

"Okay, but *how* do we get out of here without being stopped?" Luis asks.

"Act like you're playing the match," Joaquín says. "Then go find Lana's father."

Takeshi could have a battalion of Dragon Knights protecting him, with Un-Bonded dragons guarding the sanctuary. I could be sending myself off to my death. My teammates could be, too. But if their dragons feel this is the way to go, I trust them. There's no greater guarantee against the Sire's pawns than those six majestic creatures from the Caribbean.

"I'm in," I say.

Then I turn to Andrew. He's frothing at the mouth to find out what we're talking about. Or maybe he's eager to beat the crap out of the boy who was once worth believing in. I know I can save my father without Andrew. I just don't want to. If anyone deserves to witness Takeshi's downfall, it's him. Maybe *this* is how he lets go for good. How he heals and moves on.

"Come with me, Andrew. The more fighters we have, the better, especially if they're as fast as you. Besides"—I press a hand against his chest—"we both know the Cup isn't your dream. Let's fight for something you *do* care about, and let's fight for it together."

Andrew nods like he's been waiting for me to say that. "He was my best friend," he says firmly. "He's hurt me, too. I'd like the chance to spit on his face—to see me standing against everything he's become." He turns to my teammates. "Now whose dragon am I hopping on?"

Holy. Crap. I wouldn't have guessed this moment would ever come. Andrew Galloway is no longer a Takeshi Endo apologist. Better late than never.

"You can ride with me," Héctor says.

"Thanks, mate."

"I hate you all," a red-cheeked Victoria whispers. She's made of tremors and crackling rage. "Esperanza and I are staying behind. You can go ruin everything without us." She's glaring at me now. "Your dad's probably dead. Now you're killing my hopes, too. Thanks a lot."

"*Victoria.*" Héctor stands between us. "Don't."

A dragon's shrill cry fills up the stadium, a song of the heaviest misery and grief.

Esperanza. She sounds . . . destroyed.

Victoria winces but recovers just in time for the staff to pull us all into position again. As Andrew disappears to rejoin his team, a sharp pang hits me hard. I despise Victoria for not letting Esperanza, the strongest and largest dragon in the lineup, come fight with us.

But Victoria can hate us all she wants. Her dragon hates her more.

We're called out to march, despite Esperanza's cries. The crowd is as welcoming as ever, cheering for us and waving that beautiful Puerto Rican flag high. I try not to focus on them for long. I can't watch them hope for something that's not going to happen. The Scottish fans are also lighting up the stadium with their flags and chants while their team files out.

"Captains, shake hands!" the referee commands.

Andrew and Héctor do as they're told.

"Runners, to the starting line! Riders, mount your steeds!"

Andrew and I jog to the starting line. A sourpuss Victoria is the slowest to mount her steed. Esperanza is still weeping, but no one checks what's wrong. I'm hoping no one can see how bad my knees are shaking, how hard my chest pops up and down from the frantic heartbeats pounding inside. All six dragons are flying high. While the Scottish Striker positions himself near the referee, Héctor nods to the teammates who've chosen to help me. They all nod back.

Five Sol de Noche dragons shift their bodies toward the box seats. They leave Victoria and Esperanza to face the ref, who's holding up the Rock Flame.

The ref blows his whistle. "Everybody back in formation! The game's about to start!"

All five dragons face a confused President Turner. To be fair, *everyone* inside the box seats is super confused except for Joaquín, who's beaming. The dragons roar at the exact same time, lifting their heads, closing their eyes. Black smoke swirls around President Turner, slow at first, then faster and faster until he's smothered in the darkest cloud.

He's gone.

"Now!" Héctor yells.

The five dragons descend. I sprint to Gabriela and Puya, who both dive down to fetch me. Whistle after whistle goes off. A few poorly aimed spells fly past me. While Andrew's jumping onto Titán with Héctor's help, Gabriela yanks me up onto Puya's back. The saddle is only big enough for one rider, so Andrew and I sit on the dragon's scales. Thankfully, our suits protect us from discomfort or injury. Once I'm settled behind Gabriela, she tells Puya to soar high. The wind slaps the crap out of me on the way up. I can't hear anything but the flapping of massive, glorious wings and a dragon's battle cry.

I do see one thing, though. A tearful Victoria bent low atop her steed, ignoring our escape, and a wailing Esperanza watching her brothers and sisters disappear from the stadium.

Then the black smoke returns, and I can't see them anymore.

The Weekly Scorcher: *How would you describe your Bond, Mr. Barnes?*

Edward Barnes: *Enlightening. My steed has taught me so much about his species, as well as what it takes to be a better rider. I'm constantly fascinated with the way his mind works.*

The Weekly Scorcher: *What exactly makes it fascinating to you?*

Edward Barnes: *How vast it feels. There's an infinite amount of thoughts blasting toward me. It's like stepping into a maze, and it can be easy to feel like you're never getting out.*

—Excerpt from a 1988 interview with Edward Barnes, on his one-year bureau anniversary

CHAPTER TWENTY-SEVEN

S O FADING IS *NOTHING* LIKE TRANSPORTING.

First, there's the whole matter of riding a dragon. Puya is very much used to being in the air, while I'm not. Even though he flies like a dream, without any rough dives or death-defying turns, it still takes me a minute to get comfortable. I shift from side to side as a mighty wind whips my face. With every sudden tug on the saddle, my heart hammers to the rhythm of an electric drill breaking into cement.

Second, my suit's magic is fizzling out. The fabric might as well be cooking burgers from how much it's sizzling. And it weighs more than usual. The magic that makes it an airy, cozy fit is no longer helping me breathe or move with ease. I feel so, so naked.

Then there's the tunnel. Fading is like being stuck in a cylinder-shaped highway, but instead of seeing concrete walls as you fly past them, you see these white tendrils that span forever on either side. You're swept into a void of matching ivory farther ahead, peering beyond the tendrils to catch a glimpse of the vast darkness that sweeps everything outside.

My teammates had been right about the Dark Island. It's a deserted beach, blanketed by the night sky, where scorpion-dark palm trees sprout from the blackest sand. Even the ocean water is black, with waves crashing into one another instead of reaching the shore. That giant pit with the claw towers is there, too. So is the bone throne right at the beach's center.

President Turner is standing a few feet away from it, yelling something with all his might. I can't make it out. A shimmering light flickers on and off around the throne. It must be the shield my teammates told Joaquín about.

"Hang tight!" Luis yells. "We'll be back after we kick Dragon Knight ass!"

"How's it going back there?" Gabriela asks me.

"Still alive and still not puking!"

"Awesome. We'll be there in a few seconds!"

Leaving the tunnel is like walking through fog. There's a slight shift in how my eyes perceive what's around me, but the rest doesn't feel any different. My suit's fabric no longer sounds like it's cooking burgers. It's not squeezing me, either. I'm once again wearing a snug uniform that fits like a dream. My suit is slowly being repowered, so the feeling of being naked fades.

A crescent moon hangs in the São Paulo sky. Despite the darkness, I scour the area. Perfectly round copses of trees dot every square inch of the grounds below. Some stand tall, while others have fallen into scorched heaps. Flying spells strike the area where the trees have been torn down. The majority are coming from the left side, where an army of Dragon Knights casts its vicious magic.

Eight Pesadelos, all Un-Bonded escapees, shoot flames across the forest at the handful of surviving sanctuary guards. Their wings serve as shields from spells, keeping them and the Dragon Knights safe. They bite at the air after each fireball throw, which is their way of menacing opponents. Violet #43 is nowhere to be found.

"We *have* to get down there. Those guards are going to die!" Gabriela says. She leads Puya closer to Titán until they're next to each other. "Héctor! What's the plan?"

"Get Lana and Andrew to the sanctuary! Once they're dropped off, the four of you turn around and fight these bastards! Titán and I will stay with the Runners!"

Gabriela nods, then tells Puya to soar onward.

The forest stretches farther and farther, until there it is, right at the center of burning green—The São Paulo Sanctuary for Un-Bonded Dragons. It has five separate buildings, which all are connected by metal bridges in the shape of dragon tails. The eastern wings are offices and meeting rooms. The western wings are observatories and labs. Habitats are located in the middle. One western wing has been laid to waste, smashed and scorched and useless. Half of the other western wing is still there. So are both of the eastern wings.

I point to the left building in the east. "My father should be there!"

Gabriela gives Puya the command to drop. There's no sign of Dragon Knight activity near the mechanical doors. Still, when Puya hovers close to the dragon-tail bridge, I wait for Héctor's signal before jumping off. He nods at me, then at Andrew.

We get down at the same time.

The bridge is as steady as I hoped. The only commotion is miles away, where the guards are slowly losing the battle. Luis and Edwin shield us on either side while Héctor dismounts Titán. Gabriela and Génesis stay a little higher than the boys, looking out for airborne threats.

BOOM!

"Take cover!" I duck and shield my head with both arms. Even though the explosion went off right in front of me, there's no debris flying around. No sparks, no smoke. There is, however, a pair of recently polished Nikes. And they're camel colored.

Samira Jones, BFF extraordinaire, has Transported to Brazil.

She holds up her Copper wand, decked out in black Nike sweatpants and a pink hoodie.

I almost faint. "Oh my God! *Samira?* Is that really you?"

"Yes, dummy! I wasn't about to let you run off to fight Dragon Knight trash without my help this time." Samira stares at her wand, terrified that it's going to break in half. "Please don't embarrass me, baby. I love you. Please don't fall apart right now. Pleeeeeaaaase."

The wand doesn't fall apart. It's as sturdy as ever.

"*It didn't break!* Yessssss!"

"How did you know I was here?" I ask.

"Bureau agents came to take us to another Other Place. President Turner alerted them of your dad's kidnapping. They wouldn't say where he was or who took him, but I hung around close enough to overhear them talking about Takeshi and this sanctuary." Samira backs away from me. "I watched your team disappear from the stadium as we were abandoning our Other Place. I knew you'd come here. I couldn't let you face danger by yourself, girl."

"So now we have a witch on our side?" Andrew says with a huge grin. "Brilliant."

Samira gapes at him. "You're Andrew Galloway . . ."

Héctor claps his hands. "Can we get back to the mission, please?"

"Yes. Sorry, Héctor Sánchez." Samira fawns over him, too. "Carry on, team captain."

Héctor blushes as he looks up at the other riders. He clears his throat. "Um . . . Get back to the battleground! I'll join you as soon as I can, but if you need more help, call out for us!"

"Got it," Génesis says. She zooms out of view with Rayo. Luis, Gabriela, and Edwin trail behind with their steeds, boldly hurtling themselves into the thick of the Sire's war.

BANG!

Blasts of magic strike the bridge.

Three Dragon Knights barrel toward us from the opposite building.

Titán launches himself in front of us. He blows a cloud of flames at the Dragon Knights. When the fire clears, all that's left are dark cloaks and the bones underneath. Holy freaking crap, the Sol de Noches can incinerate humans in a *snap*. Not that I feel bad for these guys. It's one thing to know your team's dragons are strong, and it's another to actually witness their strength.

Héctor signals for us to run, so I bolt to the mechanical doors.

They're jammed.

"Let me try," says Samira. She uses her wand to lift a piece of concrete into the air, then magically slams it against the doors. They shatter at once. "Okay. Go time."

BANG!

More Dragon Knights scurry in from the opposite building, along with the level below, scattered everywhere like ants.

"Inside now!" Héctor mounts Titán. Samira takes aim at the Dragon Knights on the bridge, but Héctor shakes his head. "I'll handle it! *Run!*"

I grab her at once. We disappear into the building, along with Andrew. The corridor ends a few steps before it should, since the stairwell's been smashed to bits. Flickering electric lights surround us. I shudder. I've never walked into a haunted house, but this place is giving me VENGEFUL GHOSTS LIVE HERE vibes. Samira manipulates each chunk of concrete to make a staircase. I'm the first to jump up, careful not to lose my balance. I make it to the third floor.

My breath hitches. Papi's office door has been blown away. There's clutter of metal and glass all over. It's too dark to tell anything apart inside the office. He could still be in here. When I turn to help Samira up, another flash of magic flies past me, then another.

"Get down!" Andrew lunges, shielding us from the oncoming spells.

Samira peeks over Andrew's shoulder. "They're coming up the steps!"

She pushes Andrew off. As the Dragon Knights are about to reach the landing, Samira summons a giant metal door. She hurls it at the first Dragon Knight, who topples down to the first floor. While he's falling, Samira scatters the concrete steps, sending the other four Knights flying. They Transport up to our landing before I can blink. Soon enough, we're surrounded, wands pointed at our chests. Four men. One woman.

Andrew and I share a look. We nod at each other.

Then we throw ourselves forward.

He goes left. I go right. I kick a Silver wand out of the woman's hand, then a second out of a dude's. They beckon for their wands to return, but I'm too quick. I knock the woman out cold, then elbow the dude's throat. He squeals as I pick him up and toss him onto his back. Knuckles slam into my rib cage. I let out a yelp as a Dragon Knight tries to hit me again.

Samira clocks him with a candlestick, and it's lights out. She turns to where Andrew's still fighting three Dragon Knights. "Now to save our boy."

But Andrew's fine. Granted, Knights are armed and shooting at him, but he's dodging with grace, speed, and a hell of a smile. He kicks the Dragon Knights' legs out from under them, and their heads smack the floor. Their wands roll away from their unconscious bodies.

Samira and I throw each wand into the darkness below.

"Guess our warm-up is over," says Andrew. "Let's go get Mr. Torres."

"He's supposed to be in there." I point to his obliterated office.

Andrew motions for me to follow. Samira takes the rear. I hold my breath as I enter the darkened room and scour Papi's entire office. His usual stuff is here—copies of his bestselling book, photos of me as a kid racing down the streets of Cayey—but his shelves have been destroyed. The folders where he keeps all of his Pesadelo notes are either charred or torn apart. His desk has been split into halves, one in each corner of the room. At least there's no blood.

"Do you think they Transported out?" Andrew asks as we return to the corridor.

"Why would the Dragon Knights still be here?" I say.

"To protect the sanctuary dragons? Maybe to give Takeshi time to run off?"

"The Dragon Knights kept coming from the habitats." Samira looks around, her eyebrows raised. "Can you still hear Titán?"

"No . . ." I whisper.

Samira makes another staircase out of blown-up concrete for us, then races down like there's a fire behind her. I'm only slower because I don't want to fall and break something. Once I touch the floor again, I'm off at full speed, blasting through the shattered mechanical doors.

Héctor and Titán are gone. So are the Dragon Knights.

Andrew yells at me to take it easy, but I can't stop.

I'm inside the habitat building. Most of the lights and walls have been torn down here, too. Debris litters the entrance level, but I slip over to the open elevator. I stall while Andrew and a breathless Samira hop inside, then punch the button with a large number three. The elevator doors stay open as we're whisked to the third level, home of the smallest habitat. The same habitat I invaded when I was five years old.

A *ding!* goes off when we get to our destination.

Most of the habitat hasn't changed in twelve years: There are trees and fruits and a lake in the middle. Violet #43 has flown the coop, and there's a spotlight at the edge of the lake, shining down from a magic source high above the habitat.

It illuminates Takeshi pressing his claw dagger to Papi's neck.

My father kneels in front of his captor, both facing the elevator. Only Papi gasps when he sees me. His eyes are tinged red and swollen from crying.

But that's not why my body goes cold.

"Wonderful. I'm *so* happy you could all make it." The Sire stands right next to Takeshi, with a smirking Randall a few inches away, twirling his Gold wand for all to see. The Sire's cold sneer will haunt my nightmares for as long as I live. "Let us start the show."

Edward Barnes's legacy as a bureau agent pales in comparison to his final act of selflessness. While some deem his sacrifice a noble act, others refuse to acknowledge it as anything other than a tragedy. Despite several attempts to decipher his dragon's curse, not a single living witch or wizard has been able to do so. The secret, it seems, is lost to us forever. What's not lost is the memory of a man who saved the world. Neither is the hope that comes with knowing his dragon's curse can never be broken.

—*Excerpt from Julissa Mercado's article*
"A Cursed Life: How a Gold Wand Saved the World"
in The Weekly Scorcher

CHAPTER TWENTY-EIGHT

R ANDALL CASTS A PARALYSIS CHARM ON ME BEFORE I CAN CHARGE forward.

He also hits Samira and Andrew. His spell clings to me like a vine, coiling around me until it's too tight to move. I can breathe just fine, but it's definitely uncomfortable.

"No!" Papi yells. "Please don't hurt them!"

"Don't worry, old man. It doesn't hurt," says Randall. "Not yet."

I grit my teeth as I try to shake off the spell. Randall flicks his finger. A wild gust of wind shoves me across the habitat. The glass walls that wrap around the enclosure have been smashed to smithereens. Shards are scattered all over. Even though my suit protects me, the glass still pricks at my legs. I yelp upon contact. Then Randall's magic drags

Samira, Andrew, and me all the way to where my father and his three captors are. With a jerk, the spell roots me to the spot, forcing me to my knees. Samira and Andrew are kneeling beside me.

"Excellent." The Sire walks in front of us, hands behind his back. "Disarm them."

Samira whimpers. While Randall searches her pockets, she squints hard, as if trying out charms in her mind, but nothing works. He's too damn strong. Randall pulls out her wand and stares at it like he's found trash.

"Oh, you poor little girl," he mocks, with a dry laugh. "You brought a knife to a gun fight." Randall tosses her wand over his shoulder. It rolls away onto the lake's shore. He searches me and Andrew next, finding nothing, then returns to his original spot next to Papi.

"Do whatever you want to me," Papi begs the Sire. "Just let my daughter go."

"*No*. I'm not leaving without you."

The Sire halts. He laughs in a grave voice, but it still rattles my bones as if it's coming from loudspeakers at a music festival.

"What are you doing?" Andrew shouts. He's not looking at the Sire. He's looking at Takeshi.

"I thought you were still one of us. Not after this, mate." Smoke might as well be coming off Andrew's body. He's hardened his expression into steel, unyielding in his rage. Andrew winces as Randall's magic coils tighter around him, but he recovers quickly. "That man's done nothing to you. And you're about to slit his throat!"

Takeshi says nothing. He's as poised as ever.

"How is *this* avenging Hikaru?" Andrew's raising his voice now. "In what world is this what he would've wanted? Tell me right now!"

The Sire paces from side to side. He stops to Andrew's left. "The boy you used to be friends with is long dead." The Sire looks over his shoulder. "Am I mistaken, Takeshi?"

His reply is swift. "No, Sire."

Andrew looks like he's just been shot. He's struggling to speak again, but his silence isn't because of the spell. It's like he doesn't have words left.

"As I was saying"—the Sire steps closer to me—"now we can start with today's activities. I can no longer feel my Anchor's presence. I can't punish him nor can I force him to punish you. This would upset me if my original plan hadn't worked."

"And what's that?" I growl.

"I needed you here, so here you are." The Sire turns to Takeshi. "Escort Mr. Torres to the forest. Do you still have your magic?"

Randall scowls at the question, but it lasts only a second.

Takeshi nods. He shows off two golden orbs clipped to his belt. "One is a Death Charm."

"And the other?"

"Freeze Charm," Randall cuts in. "It incapacitates whatever it touches by cloaking it in frost." He glances at Samira. "Can *you* do that?"

Samira doesn't speak. She's not even looking at him.

"Didn't think so," Randall says triumphantly. The Sire chuckles, and Randall practically floats with delight, until the Sire shifts his attention back to Takeshi.

"Do you understand your orders?" the Sire asks.

Takeshi pulls my father to his feet. "I won't fail you."

"Don't do this!" I plead, still writhing in vain. "Punish me any other way, but please let my father go. He's done nothing to you!"

The Sire shushes me. "Your hysterics will accomplish nothing. Besides, he won't die just yet." He looks at Papi. "Outside, Mr. Torres. I'll see you soon."

Papi hangs his head low. He's not crying anymore, but his eyes are far too wide and alert, as if he's terrified of what could happen to me with him gone. Takeshi grips him tightly and ushers him along, dagger still pressed against Papi's throat.

"Te amo, mija. Stay strong, okay? I'll be with you soon." Papi's voice is trembling.

"Te amo . . ." I don't promise to stay strong. I don't know what that looks like anymore.

"Hikaru's memory deserves better than this. Your mother deserves better, too!" Andrew yells. "You're a disgrace, Takeshi. You were once everything to a lot of people, and I regret ever being one of them. Rot in hell." He's ripped the words right out of my heart. They sound sharper, colder when Andrew says them.

Takeshi guides my father to the elevator, as if Andrew had spoken to the wind.

They disappear in total silence.

The Sire walks closer to me. He reaches down to my hair, removing a lock from my face. I tremble despite his leather glove's warmth. I can see him just fine. This jerk is only trying to make me squirm. He says, "My Anchor was slimy enough to attempt to enter my consciousness undetected. But I allowed him a glimpse so he could locate me. I gave him just enough to set a trap for those bureau worms." He glances at the floor, standing even taller, a king surveying his court. "You have brought me precisely what I desired, Lana."

I furrow my brow, no longer writhing. "What the hell have I brought you?"

The Sire drifts toward Randall. He slips a hand into his coat's pocket, then pulls out something white and glimmering.

The Fire Drake's crystal heart.

So he *was* in Sweden searching for his missing ingredient! The thought of that poor dragon injured and deprived of something so valuable wrecks me. She wasn't as protected as the bureau wanted me to believe. Neither was my father. This has all been a colossal failure.

"Did you kill the Fire Drake?" The words are glass in my throat.

"Takeshi retrieved the heart while I led the bureau on a wild-goose chase."

"That's not what I asked."

The Sire pinches my cheek, winking. I'm seconds away from emptying a whole week's worth of meals onto his shoes. "Do you know why this object matters so much?"

"It has powerful magical properties," Samira replies. "It can grant wishes but only to its rider." She hesitates. "Who isn't you."

"That's where he comes in." I narrow my gaze at Randall. "He'll force the crystal heart to help you get what you're after."

The Sire smiles. "What am I after, Lana?"

Samira recites, "Regeneration. Body. Magic. Blood. You want to break your curse, but you don't have all the ingredients."

I nod. "The crystal heart will replace the blood you need."

The Sire raises his eyebrows. "Randall, look at them! Such smart girls, are they not?"

Randall is the least excited I've seen him. He's hunched over, his weary gaze glued to me. "Yes, Sire, but she's wrong," he snarls.

"She is." The Sire steps closer, hiding the crystal heart behind his back. "Regeneration. Body. Magic. The Hydra and the Pluma de Muerte I rescued were kind enough to offer me their hearts. A small sacrifice for what I did to save them."

"*Small* sacrifice?" Andrew scoffs. "Unbelievable. You killed two dragons. Or, I should say, your loyal dog over there killed two dragons with his Gold magic."

"Wrong again," Randall fumes. "Both dragons volunteered their hearts to my master."

So Samira and I were right. The rescued dragons were just supposed to be sacrifices.

"You're still killers. Both of you," Andrew says. "You saved those dragons only because you needed something from them. Same thing with you." He motions to Randall. "Your master doesn't give a crap about you, mate. He's using you."

"Andrew, stop." I can't say more; everything in my head is an expletive. I'm half expecting Randall to blast him dead right there. Instead, he keeps that foul glare aimed at Andrew, casually showing off his wand from inside his coat.

"He's your magic," Samira says. "He'll perform the reverse curse."

"A favor I will reward him for," says the Sire.

"Then where is Lana wrong? You don't have the blood, so the crystal heart must act as a substitute through your wish."

The Sire taps the tip of her nose, which makes Samira wince. "No."

She's as confused as I am, but I do the talking this time. "So if the crystal heart isn't for the reverse curse, why go through all the trouble of stealing it?"

The Sire backs away from Samira. He's doing that side-to-side walk again. "Blood is forever binding. Not even a wish from a crystal heart can break it. I mourn the misguided dragons who gave my former master their hearts. They were fooled into his deluded efforts to end me." He stops, admiring the pale stone. "Just like the mother of his child."

"Edward Barnes never had children," Samira says with great confidence.

"He did. A single child." The Sire tosses the crystal heart into the air. It hovers a few feet above him, rotating in slow circles, glowing brighter and brighter. "Randall kindly bent the crystal heart to my will. My wish was simple. I didn't know whether I would see anyone, but I had to try. So I said the one thing I have been waiting to say for the last twenty years. Allow me to share my findings with you." He speaks to the stone. "Show me the heir of Edward Barnes."

The habitat fills up with the whitest light, forcing me to shut my eyes. The brightness dies down, and when I check the stone again, it's projecting a thin, golden screen.

Edward Barnes hugs a woman in front of a quaint cottage overlooking the sea.

There's a winding road behind the cottage, but no traffic or pedestrians. There aren't other houses nearby. The ocean's waves are dead, too, and the sky is a faded pink with no clouds in sight. This is an Other Place. Edward Barnes seems to be the same age he was when he died. The woman's back is to the screen. He's much taller than she is, which makes her seem even frailer. They cling to each other as if this is the last time they'll meet.

"I will always love you," he whispers in her ear, "but I have to do this."

He kisses her cheek goodbye, then vanishes with the Transport Charm.

The images blur together, then rearrange into another scene. The woman's back is still turned. She tilts a bit. Even though her face is obscured, her baby bump isn't. She must be five or six months pregnant. Behind her, a TV shows the breaking news of Barnes's death and the Sire's defeat. The woman sniffles in her living room, cradling her baby bump as she cries.

Another whirlwind. Another scene. I still can't see the pregnant woman's face, and it's even worse because of the pitch darkness of the night. She lurks in the shadows at the edge of an alley, the sound of punk-rock music blaring from the building to the left. I catch the heavy thud of footsteps drawing closer to the darkness, then the flick of a cigarette lighter. The woman pulls out her Silver wand as a broad-shouldered figure stumbles toward her. His lighter illuminates the lower half of his face, showing off the patchy brown stubble on his chin, then the red-rimmed eyes of someone who's been drinking for hours. They widen when he spots the tip of a wand aimed at him. The cigarette falls from the white man's lips. He's about to shout when a blinding flash shoots out of the woman's wand. The spell hits him in the chest, shocks him into trembling.

"He is my son," the man says hoarsely. "But I hate him. I must stay away forever."

Then he face-plants to the ground.

As the woman leaves him unconscious in the alley, the scene changes yet again.

Now she's sitting on a rocking chair inside a living room with seashell-white walls. I can see that dead ocean and the faded pink sky from the windows. She's back at the Other Place. The woman holds a pudgy bundle of white blankets in her arms. Her baby. As the little one cries, the woman's face is finally visible, as if I'm looking up at her from the baby's vantage point.

"You've nothing to worry about, my beautiful boy. I'm going to keep you safe. He will never find you. This is my promise," says a smiling Lucy Galloway.

She's smiling down at a baby Andrew.

No, no, no, no, no.

I had been right. Andrew Galloway *is* the heir of Edward Barnes.

I'm heaving what little air I can, but the habitat feels drier and drier. My lungs fail me completely when I glance over at Andrew. He's a paper-white version of himself. He must recognize that cottage by the sea, that seashell-white living room. He must've seen endless pictures of himself as that baby. He must remember that broad-shouldered drunk as the man he confronted in Aberdeen. A stranger who had been charmed into thinking he was Andrew's father when his defenses had been at their lowest.

The crystal heart flashes its white light twice, then the screen disappears.

The stone descends back into the Sire's grasp. He hides it in his pocket while Andrew presses his eyes shut. "Rest assured, young man. Your father died before he ever knew you were on the way. I doubt he would've been much of a father, had he known. You dodged a bullet, Andrew Galloway. Or I should say, Andrew *Barnes.*"

The way he says it makes the truth sound colder, crueler. My tears come back, falling faster. A headache drills into my skull. Still, nothing hurts worse than knowing how powerless I am. I'm not a Gold Wand. I can't get Andrew the hell out of here.

This shouldn't be how he dies. This *can't* be how he dies.

If I stall long enough, my teammates will arrive before the Sire lays a hand on Andrew.

"The man your mother cursed had been in her sights for months," the Sire continues. "Everything she told you about their relationship was a lie. They were never together." He nods to me. "And you, Lana Torres, are the one I wish to thank for today's victory. I could have used Lucy Galloway as my hostage to lure Andrew here, but she's been in hiding ever since her son's protest. I suspect she's in her Other Place. Plan B had been simple enough—tell my Anchor to bring Andrew to me. Then I saw how close you two were getting." The Sire bends over until our eyes are level with each other's. "Ask me why it had to happen this way, Lana."

Stall as long as you can.

I whisper through my tears, "Please don't kill him. *Please.* Maybe Randall can make the crystal heart finish the spell for you. It could replace the blood and—"

"Ask me why it had to happen this way."

Andrew still has his eyes closed. Why isn't he begging for his life? Maybe the truth has stunned him into silence? I refuse to believe he's accepted his death so easily.

"He doesn't have to die. There's another way you can break the curse," I say.

"I could help you find an alternative," Samira offers tearfully. "I'm not as strong as Randall, but I'm smart. I swear I'll help you. Just don't hurt Andrew."

"Yes!" I say. "She's the smartest person I've ever met. Let her—"

"Ask him the bloody question, Lana," Andrew says. There's an emptiness in his voice. Like his fighting spirit has been buried miles-deep in snow. He's convinced I won't be able to save him—that today is his last day on earth.

"Shut up, okay? Just let me handle this."

"You're not handling anything," the Sire says coolly. If he's irritated, he's hiding it behind a smirk. "Now ask me why it had to happen this way."

Stalling has worked. I should keep baiting him. "Why are you controlling the Cup?"

Samira's jaw almost hits the floor. Even Andrew is finally looking at me, tears drowning those beautiful hazel-green eyes.

"What?" he asks.

"The Sire has been playing both sides for years," I say. "He bound President Turner to his every whim when he was still a dragon. He bound *us* the moment we signed our contracts."

Andrew blushes furiously, but I suspect it's more out of rage than shame. He's sizing up the Sire, as if he's readying himself to beat his ass. "Prisoners," he says. "All along."

With a sigh, the Sire taps me on the forehead twice. "Such an inquisitive mind."

I'm as unmoving as the marble dragon sculptures on the Blazewrath stadium walls. "Are you trying to break every competing dragon's Bond?"

The Sire's hand freezes in midair. He laughs humorlessly. "You clever girl." He drops his hand with a flourish. "Every dragon deserves to be free. Even if they can't see a better life without their humans, I will make them accept it. They'll join my army once they see the light."

So my theory's right. "You only want soldiers? Or will you use them in other ways?"

"Ask Master the right question!" Randall watches me like he's desperate to dip me into a vat of frying oil.

"Now, now, Randall. Let the clever girl speak." The Sire steps back without looking away from me. "I don't fully understand your team's dragons yet, but I know they're not Transporting. If my Anchor were in a normal Other Place, I could still feel him in our world. But it's as if he no longer exists. No Other Place can *remove* magic. If that is indeed what the Sol de Noches are doing, then their abilities could play a critical role in destroying others' Bonds."

No. My teammates are going to roast him and Randall any second. He won't win.

"I answered your questions," the Sire says. "Now ask mine."

Fine. "Why did it have to happen this way?"

The Sire spreads his arms wide. He exhales like he's been offered a lifetime of free vacations. "*You* had to be involved in Andrew's death. This is your punishment, Lana—living with this memory."

This sick bastard's right. If Andrew dies here—which he *won't*—his blood will be on my hands. I'm the one who asked him to come.

"'Takeshi . . . he agreed to this . . . '" Andrew's voice quivers. He's staring at the floor with those drowning eyes. Every ragged breath seems like a challenge for him.

The Sire pauses to drink in Andrew's quiet despair. Then he waves Randall forward. "Our time with our guest of honor has ended. Kill him."

"*No!*" Samira and I are one voice, but it doesn't matter.

Randall whips out his wand. He conjures a metal cauldron as dark as his cloak. The cauldron lands inches away from Andrew. Randall then conjures the dragon hearts. Both are faded crimson, as if their vibrancy lessened after removal from their hosts' bodies. Randall moves his wand in a complicated pattern, aiming it at the cauldron. A cloud of red smoke billows out of its edges. He tosses the hearts into the cauldron, which makes the smoke grow thicker.

The air reeks of fresh blood.

"Don't hurt him!" I try to launch myself at Randall. The Paralysis Charm's grip is relentless, even though he's distracted. Each attempted thrash sends a sharp pain into my ribs, my shoulder blades. I'm screaming and crying and hoping my teammates can hear me.

But they don't come.

Randall holds out his wand to Andrew.

"Do everything you can to get yourselves out of here," Andrew says, his tearful gaze fixed on Randall's wand. He might speak firmly, but his expression is as heavy as a soldier who's lost the battle for his whole regiment. His hopelessness is tenfold now. "This isn't on you, Lana. Forget what he said. This will never be on you. Just tell my mum that I—"

A golden lightning rod hits Andrew in the chest.

"ANDREW!" I roar till all I know is the incessant stabbing at my sides from trying to reach for him, the weight of his blood on my hands, the ashes of memories we'll never make.

He's doubled over, screaming as more lightning pours out of the wand's tip. Andrew's whole body shakes. His suit's magic is no match for Randall's powers. The golden lightning shifts to red, seeping out of Andrew as if he's being drained of blood. Randall shapes the lightning into a steady stream of crimson tendrils. He spills them into the smoking cauldron, which hisses upon contact. The bigger the red cloud grows, the fainter Andrew's screams get. I pray for him to fight this, to keep living, but he's shrinking into a ghostly pale shell of himself.

The crimson tendrils stop coming.

Randall dumps what's left into the cauldron. It bubbles and hisses as the cloud thickens.

Andrew lands with a thud on the floor. He's facing me. Both eyes are pressed shut, with tears running down his sallow cheeks. No matter how hard I beg him to move, he doesn't.

The heir of Edward Barnes is dead.

I'm a thunderstorm of cracked wails. Andrew should be meeting with reporters right now, talking about my team's disappearance.

He should be boasting about us being too afraid to play his team. He should be nagging the IBF to cancel the Cup. He should *still be alive*.

A dozen little explosions spark. The red smoke flies out of the cauldron, swirling up to where the Sire floats in midair. Limbs sprout from the back of his coat. His silver scales elongate on either side of him, a much frailer netting piecing them together. He has his wings back. He unfurls them as his face morphs. He keeps getting bigger and bigger until he's the largest dragon I've ever seen. His hands are claws, and a tail grows out from behind him, whipping side to side. He aims his fire propeller at the ceiling.

There's a diamond-covered dragon where the Sire once was.

He's burning a crater into the ceiling. As soon as the hole's big enough for him to fit through, the flames disappear. The Sire flies away, announcing his return as a dragon with a mighty roar.

Your glass coffin awaits,
It's calling out your name,
So say goodbye,
To everything you love,
Now it will all be mine.

—*Poem written by Randall Wiggins, age thirteen*

CHAPTER TWENTY-NINE

"I DID IT!" RANDALL SPINS IN PLACE. THEN HE JUMPS WITH A FIST in the air. He sprints and jumps once, twice. He's getting farther and farther away from us, too excited to glance in our direction.

Samira grunts. She's squirming hard again, sweating up a storm.

"What are you *doing*?" I whisper-yell. "You're hurting yourself!"

"Be quiet!"

"He's going to see—"

"Be *quiet*, Lana. I need to concentrate."

Randall's laugh stabs through whatever's left of my heart. He clicks his heels together in a ridiculous display of euphoria. His back is turned to us as he faces the lake. "*I did it!*"

Samira's shaking so much, I think she's about to pass out. "Just . . . a little . . . more . . ."

"You have to stop. Whatever you're doing, it's hurting you."

She keeps pushing herself to the brink, doubling over with her eyes pressed shut.

Then she stops. She's huffing out in exhaustion as she straightens back up. Randall's magic is still gripping her as hard as it's gripping me.

"My master rules the skies again." Randall walks back over to us. When he's close enough for me to touch, he points to the hole in the roof with his wand. "Your worthless friends are about to regret their defiance. And they will—"

Samira bulldozes into Randall.

She pins him to the ground with a battle cry. Randall loses his grip on his wand.

The stabbing pressure on my body washes away in a steady stream. I lean to the left. No pain. The Paralysis Charm is no longer trapping me!

I jump to my feet. "What . . . how did you—"

"I don't know! I just felt the need to charge him, and I could!" Samira kicks Randall's wand away. It lands about four feet from where he lies. "Let me fetch my wand real quick!" She rushes off to fetch her wand, while I launch myself at Randall. Then I beat him over and over.

He slams his head against mine.

I'm knocked off of him. Even without his wand, this jerk's strong enough to paralyze me yet again. At least he's not gouging my eyes out like he did to that bureau-agent lady when he was a kid. "Ugh!" I'm lying on my back. The pain in my ribs and my shoulder blades smashes into each bone like a wrecking ball. Randall's magic returns even worse than before.

He towers over me. "It feels good, doesn't it? Your rage? It makes you think you can do anything." Randall wags his finger. "Rage is a liar, Lana. So is hope. Your friends at the bureau taught me that. The first thing I did when I freed myself was act on rage. It didn't make me happy. It just fanned the flames, but Master showed me true power. Revenge hurts more when it's calculated." He shrugs. "Too bad you'll never avenge stupid little Andrew."

I try to lunge at him, forgetting about the Paralysis Charm. Invisible knives slice into me. My scream could shatter an entire building made of glass. "Don't you dare say his name again!"

Randall smiles. "Andrew. Andrew. Andrew."

"SHUT UP!"

"What a great name, isn't it? *Andrew.*"

A boulder rushes toward Randall from behind.

Randall raises his clenched fist. The boulder disintegrates. He magically yanks Samira across the habitat, and drops her directly between me and him. Samira tries to summon a fallen tree, but Randall cracks it into splinters. He laughs as he lowers her wand. Then he marches to the spot where the Sire flew outside of the habitat, twirls his wand, and aims it at us.

"I don't know how you got free, but it doesn't matter," he says. "Lights out, little girls."

A golden lightning bolt shoots out of Randall's wand.

I thrash to no avail. "Samira, get out of the way!"

She summons a lightning bolt, too. It's as copper as the humble weapon she wields.

BOOM!

The two lightning bolts clash, spreading outward and engulfing the two wizards in a giant ball made of magic. Part of the ball is made of copper lightning; the other half is gold. While the copper lightning flickers, the gold lightning is steady, and devours its rival inch by inch. Punishing heat swarms the habitat. Samira's barely able to keep her wand from breaking. She shakes and sweats and doesn't let go of the metal rod. It's seconds away from bursting.

Randall's the picture of poise. He's still smiling.

"Samira, just run!" I yell. "You're not going to die for me, too!"

"I'm not going to die, and *nobody's* killing my best friend!"

She lets out an earth-rattling scream. Her wand quakes harder. The coppery color fades, as if the wand's turning itself off. The magic ball keeps getting dimmer and dimmer. It grows smaller, too, leaving Randall out of its lightning walls. Only Samira is stuck inside.

Even if I could move, chances are I'll get fried if I touch that ball. But I can't have Samira's blood on my hands, too. One loss has already ruptured my soul. I need her out of that magical prison ASAP. "Samira, get out of there right now! He's going to kill you!"

She doesn't listen. Her copper lightning is three inches away from her skin.

Randall blows her a kiss, leaning forward as if he's about to jab his wand in her direction.

The lightning stops.

It's frozen about a breath away from Samira, shaped in an electric outline of her body.

Randall jabs his wand. His lightning doesn't move.

"What the hell?!" he spits out.

Samira's wand doesn't have any color left. The metal rod is translucent, worn-looking, and dead. None of us make a sound. It's like the whole habitat has been stripped of life, along with the wand's magic. Then the whole thing bursts into light, but it's not copper anymore.

Samira's wand shimmers bright gold.

"Oh my God . . . Samira, you . . ." I can't even finish my sentence.

Samira throws all of herself into the counter spell, her screams rising as the copper lightning bolt shifts to the same gold that's filled up her wand. It's gold against gold now.

The ball leaves Samira behind. Now it's traveling back to Randall at an even quicker pace. No matter how hard he tries to shove it toward Samira, the ball keeps barreling toward him. His eyes are bulging out. He's heaving frantically, shaking his head like he's in disbelief. "How are you doing this?! Stop!" Randall wails.

With a jab of her wand, Samira rips the ball apart in a flurry of crackling sparks.

BOOM!

Randall's wand explodes into dust particles.

He's in the middle of a scream when Samira strikes him in the chest with a lightning bolt. He's launched ten feet deeper into the habitat, landing spread-eagle on the other side of the lake.

"Yes!" I haven't laughed this hard since God knows when. Who cares if my sides are exploding with each prick of those invisible knives? Samira has to be the first witch in history to evolve from Copper to Gold. To *change her wand* from one level to another. Magic users can't change their wands even when their wand level evolves. Their wands just stop working. Instead, they have to buy a brand-new wand for their brand-new status.

Samira pants like she's been running a marathon nonstop for a week. She waves her Gold wand at me. I can move again. My ribs and my shoulder blades aren't begging for mercy.

"Are you okay?" Samira asks, watching Randall intently. He moans, so I know he's still alive. Though it's taking him forever to get up.

"Forget about me." I let her help me stand. "Are *you* okay? That looked like it hurt a lot."

"Not as much as he's hurting right now. I mean, it was just a Shield Charm. I didn't mean to do any damage." Samira risks a smile. She lets out a soft giggle, as if she's excited yet a little guilty about what she did to Randall. "But I guess some jerks get what's coming to them."

Randall is back on his wobbly feet, bleeding from his nostrils. "You . . . stupid . . . Regular-loving . . . Gold wannabe!" He's closing his fist, as if he's about to conjure a spell.

Samira yanks me behind her and raises her wand.

WHOOSH!

A white object flies past me. I don't recognize it until it finds Randall's stomach, stabbing him in a clean, swift blow.

Takeshi's claw dagger.

Randall doubles over with a grunt. He unclenches his fist and pulls the dagger out. It falls to the floor with a clang. The dagger's tip isn't smeared in blood, though. It's coated in a viscous liquid the color of tar—the same color Randall's veins are turning. He stops bleeding. Randall grunts then drops on his side, hugging himself.

"Dragonshade," Samira murmurs. "He's been poisoned. His magic is gone."

"He'll be dead in three days," someone behind us says.

I wheel around.

Takeshi exits the elevator alone. His eyes are glued to Andrew's body. And. He's. *Crying.*

His is a silent, lonely kind of devastation. He makes it to Andrew without sparing us a glance, even though Samira's pointing her wand at him. Even though I'm ready to knock his teeth out and demand to know what he's done to Papi. He kneels on the floor and puts a tender hand on Andrew's shoulder, as if he's made of glass.

"I didn't know," Takeshi whispers. "I'm so sorry, Andy. I didn't know it was you."

I wait for him to stop acting—to pounce on me with a hidden Death Charm orb, but he stays where he is, quietly draining himself of tears for a boy he just said he didn't care about.

I don't give a damn about how sad he seems. Not only did he betray Andrew, he also took my dad. He's not getting out of this building without telling me where Papi is.

"What have you done with my father?" I ask.

"He's safe," he replies quietly. "Sienna is Transporting him to New York headquarters."

Wait, what? Agent Horowitz is here? And he's on a first-name basis with her?

"Takeshi!" Randall yells, zapping me back to reality. "You *filth!*"

Takeshi finally releases Andrew. He lingers beside him for a bit longer, eyes unfocused, then he rises. "Could you please bring Randall over here?" he asks Samira.

"No way," I cut in. "Why should I listen to a thing you say?"

"Because I think he saved your dad's life," Samira says. "Also, he just poisoned the strongest Dragon Knight of all time. Maybe I'm wrong, but I feel like he's not all trash, Lana."

"He also stole a Fire Drake's crystal heart. He *killed* a bureau agent!"

"I didn't kill him. He's not dead," Takeshi says, firmly.

Oh, you've got to be kidding me. "So that whole throat-slitting thing was all an act, huh? Agent Robinson is pretending to be dead?"

"No. Yes. It's quite complicated, but I can explain later."

Samira uses her magic to drag Randall across the habitat. He lands at Takeshi's feet. His veins are even darker now, bulging and slithering like snakes in a frenzied search for prey. "Here's the garbage you ordered."

Takeshi nods at her, then stares at Randall. He's no longer a boy-shaped disaster without a course. Now Takeshi is a tempest that's found its target. "My name is Agent Takeshi Endo with the International Bureau of Magical Matters. Randall Wiggins, you're under arrest for multiple murders, including Andrew Galloway, Hari Sandhar, and my steed, Hikaru."

Samira and I gasp at the same time.

I take a shaky step back. "What? You're a . . . and he's . . . *what?*"

Randall twitches, but his eyes are unblinking. "You knew this whole time?"

Holy. Crap. He's admitting it!

"I've known for a while," says Takeshi. "I just don't know what you've done to Antonio Deluca. You either killed him or kidnapped him. Which one is it?"

Randall's silence unnerves me, even more than Takeshi's accusation. Then there's the whole separate matter of Takeshi Endo being an *undercover bureau agent.* How come they couldn't catch the Sire with an agent in his midst? Director Sandhar's been relying on President Turner to locate the Sire, when Takeshi could've easily given them his whereabouts. He could've stopped his transformation. Turned Randall in. He could've saved Andrew's life.

I glance at the Dragonshade. Director Sandhar never would've given Takeshi that poison. He never would've approved of Takeshi's actions since becoming a Dragon Knight.

"You've been playing both sides," I say. "Just like the Sire. You did this for Hikaru."

He's about to speak when Randall asks, "How did you figure it out?"

"Six months after Hikaru's murder, I found another Fire Drake with a crystal heart. He granted my wish after I did him a favor. I saw you and the Sire in Hikaru's quarters. I saw him give you the order. And I saw you obey. Three months later, I joined the bureau in order to get Dragonshade. Then I joined the Dragon Knights in order to get to you and the Sire. In all this time, I've had only one question." Takeshi's eyes narrow into vicious slits. "Why?"

Randall winces, the poison eating him from within. "Akarui dragons can scramble their opponent's senses by emanating a blinding light from their scales. Master suspected that power had been used in his curse to restrain his magic. Hikaru wasn't a total waste, though. His death broke you. It made the most beloved Blazewrath player go rogue." Randall winces again. "Does my father know you've stolen Dragonshade from his vaults?"

"He's not your father, and once he sees you like this, I don't think he'll mind. Now tell me what you did to Antonio Deluca."

Randall's expression hardens even more. "You'll never find him. And I'll tell Hikaru you said hi when I get to hell."

"He won't be there." Takeshi gets up, then draws nearer to Samira. "Remember our faces, Randall. Remember our names. Samira took your wand and your dignity. I'm taking your life. And if the Sol de Noche dragons haven't beaten me to it, I'm taking your master's life, too."

"You'll never do it!" Randall's yell could rattle the habitat's walls. He's red-cheeked despite the black seeping into the rest of him. Snot hangs from his flaring nostrils.

"I joined his army to help him return to his dragon form. Do you know why?" Takeshi says with an unnerving calmness. "So that he would be able to *die* again. As of right now, the Sire is a mortal dragon. I will end him today."

"No!" I say. "The Sire's life is tied to someone else's."

Takeshi nods. "I know about the Anchor Curse, Lana, but this is the plan. I have to see it through." His tone is so final, so heartless, it makes me want to throw up.

I give him my most defiant scowl. "You want to take petty to a whole new level, I get that. But enough people have already died. *We both* have to accept responsibility for that. So before you go on about *more killing*, ask yourself if revenge is worth another person's life."

Takeshi looks like his brain is about to burst. He's not happy, but he's not exploding, either. Like his grayed mind is filling with colors he's never seen before.

Finally, he says, "What do you suggest?"

My spine tingles. There's only one thing that could end this war. One prison the Sire will never be able to escape from.

"We'll lock him inside the Dark Island."

Samira and Takeshi stare at me. "The what?"

"Just trust me." I turn to Samira. "Get us to the roof. We'll signal for my teammates."

"You'll never win! None of you will see the end of this war!" Randall spits out a gob of black blood. He's coughing like his lungs are already failing him. As much as I despise him, this is a horrible way to die, and he looks like he's aware of it. I wonder if he's also realizing he never had a fighting chance in the poor excuse of a life he's been given.

He's better off unconscious. That'll help him suffer less.

"Lights out, little boy." I kick him in the face.

He's knocked out immediately.

Samira uses her magic to tie his arms around the sturdiest tree she can find. Then she says, "To the roof!"

"Wait." Takeshi runs to fetch his claw dagger from Randall's gut. He tucks it into his pocket and frowns at Andrew. "Are you sure this Dark Island will hold the Sire for good?"

"Definitely. He won't even have his fire."

Takeshi blinks slowly, as if he's both exhausted and on the verge of crying again. He bows his head. "Then to the roof it is."

Most Likely to Eat, Sleep, and Breathe Blazewrath
over Anything Else:

Definitely Victoria.

Most Likely to Bake You a Cake on Your Birthday:

Héctor. Our team captain and a wonderful soul.

Most Likely to Have Your Back in a Fight:

Oh, honey. It's us seven against the world.

—*Excerpt from Gabriela Ramos & Edwin Santiago's
interview with* Sworn Magazine

CHAPTER THIRTY

WHEN THE TRANSPORT CHARM'S WHITE LIGHT FADES FROM VIEW,
I'm standing a few inches away from the rooftop's ledge, gazing
down into the charred hole the Sire used to escape. Randall is still out
cold, back inside the habitat. Even if his Dragon Knight buddies arrive,
he's not going anywhere.

Dragon roars split the sky into pieces.

All eight Un-Bonded Pesadelos are unconscious on the forest floor.
Bureau agents have surrounded them, wands out in case they wake up.

The Sire, however, is very much awake. He's headed straight toward
a wall of five black dragons, all baring their teeth in defiance. The Sire
rams himself into them, but they don't relent. Rayo and Fantasma whip
their tails against his sides. Puya and Daga blow fire at his face and neck.

Titán bites down on his spine, holding him in place.

The Sire breaks their wall. He sends them flying in different directions.

"He's getting away!" Takeshi yells.

"Samira," I say, "do you think you can help me communicate with Héctor?"

"I can Transport my Whisperer to him, then he can talk to you through yours."

Crap. "I left mine at the Compound!"

Samira conjures my Whisperer out of thin air. Her own Whisperer disappears from her wrist as she hands mine over. "He's wearing it!"

"Héctor? Are you there?" I speak into my Whisperer. "It's Lana. Can you hear me?"

"Why am I wearing a Whisperer, and why is your voice coming out of it?!" Héctor is barely audible amidst the roars surrounding him. "I'm *very* busy right now!"

Titán launches himself at the Sire, blocking his flames from the others. Then he fires back flames of his own. The streams meet in the middle like Samira and Randall's lightning bolts. A deafening crackle comes from the Whisperer.

"The Dark Island could take his magic, right?" I ask.

"We're *trying* to get him there," Héctor replies. "But this silver bastard is tough!"

The Sire shoots a thick stream of fireballs.

Héctor and Titán dive out of the way, but the Sire's flames travel with them. While he's distracted with Titán, the other four Sol de Noches scramble into their circle formation, trapping the Sire in the middle. They spread their wings wide and rattle the earth with their roars. Flames edge out of their scales.

They're going to cast a ring of fire again.

The Sire whirls around, shooting fireballs like a cannon.

He knocks the dragons away one by one. While they cry out, the Sire spews more flames, darting from one dragon to the other in blinding chaos.

I almost go bald yanking my hair. He's too strong. How are we supposed to beat him?

"Takeshi," Samira says, "do you still have that Freeze Charm?"

"Right here." He points to one of the golden orbs on his belt.

"Lana, tell Héctor to lead the Sire over here. Takeshi and I will hit his fire propeller with Freeze Charms." Samira aims her wand at the sky. "Once we strike, Randall's Gold magic won't let him burn anything ever again."

Brilliant. I quickly relay it into my Whisperer. "Héctor, bring the Sire over to the habitat. Samira's going to take his fire away with a double Freeze Charm!"

Crickets.

I'm about to call for Héctor again, when he yells, "Okay! Let's do it!"

Takeshi carefully removes the Freeze Charm from his belt. At his touch, a little frost-white light blooms at the center. "Bring that coward over here."

For the first time in a long time, Takeshi Endo makes me smile.

It doesn't last long, though.

The Sire is pummeling, burning, and biting at the five dragons determined to stop him. Titán takes the beating of his life, shielding his brothers and sisters from the silver dragon's fury. Puya and Daga angle themselves at either side of Titán. Rayo and Fantasma are hovering a few feet below the Charger dragons.

Then Titán shoots up higher. The Sire makes the mistake of looking at him. Puya and Daga zoom forward, crashing into the Sire's lower body. Rayo and Fantasma slam into his shoulders, then clamp down on the Sire's wings. The four Sol de Noche dragons move simultaneously, jostling the Sire across the forest sky. His shrieks are music to my ears.

"Lana, I need you to back up!" Samira says as Takeshi stands next to her.

I run farther away from the ledge but not too far. While Samira keeps her wand raised, Takeshi holds the golden orb behind him like a baseball he's about to pitch.

My teammates finally make it to the habitat and pin the Sire against the ledge where Takeshi and Samira await. Titán glides toward the roof, and a vengeful Sire follows his every move, mouth open and ready for retaliation.

His propeller is in plain sight. It doubles in size as he preps to blow out the flames.

Then the Sire's eyes find Takeshi.

"Now, Samira!" he yells.

The Sire rolls forward. His brute strength knocks Puya and Daga away from him. Rayo and Fantasma are dragged down as they cling to the Sire's wings. With a sudden jerk, he flaps them so hard they're thrown over his head. Free at last, the Sire drives his tail into the building.

It lands right between Samira and Takeshi.

They're knocked off-balance. Takeshi drops the Freeze Charm, and the orb makes a beeline for the floor. I dive for the orb, just managing to catch it in my outstretched fingertips before it becomes shards. With a grunt, I cradle it close and search for Takeshi and Samira.

They're not on the roof.

"No, no, no . . ." I race to where they fell. They're sinking into a giant cloud of rubble and dust. A bluish light wraps around them like a halo. Maybe a Shield Charm?

"Lana, come on! He's going to hit it again!" Héctor pulls up beside me and waves for me to hop onto Titán. "Hurry!"

"We need to help them!"

"And *you* need to get out of that building!"

The Sire's tail comes whizzing down again.

I jump onto Titán's back. By the time I'm settled, the Sire's destroyed most of the roof and the side of the building. He's sending more pieces of concrete, dust, and smoke raining down on Samira and Takeshi. I hold on tight to Héctor and the Freeze Charm. "Let's go get them!"

"He'll take us out easily if we turn our backs!"

I hate that he's right. Fantasma and Edwin creep up on the Sire's left. Fantasma swipes with his claws. Puya, Daga, and Rayo pummel the Sire with fiery battering ram–style attacks. It's a frenzy of fighting dragons and teens sweating from heat and terror.

My heart speeds up. Samira could Transport with Takeshi, right?

Unless she's unconscious.

The Sire bashes his head against Titán's, sending us spinning like we're stuck on a hellish Ferris wheel. I scream and squeeze the life out of Héctor. When Titán regains his balance, we're out of the Sire's range. His brothers and sisters rain down flames. Daga cries out. No matter how fast Luis steers her away, the Sire's fire finds her.

For a second, I think I catch the Sire smiling.

"You okay back there?" Héctor asks, panting.

Sparks light me up from within. My best friend and the world's greatest Striker are in danger. Or maybe they're just out cold? My teammates and their steeds are also in danger. I'm not a Striker. My aim is probably in the top-five-worst category in the whole world.

And yet I'm the one who has to end this.

"*Lana?*"

"Get Titán closer to the Sire. I'm going to throw this orb at his propeller."

Héctor looks at me over his shoulder. "Are you sure?!"

"He'll be easier to strike if I drop it from above. Can you force him to look up at us?"

Whether Héctor believes in me or not, he nods. "We'll attack right over him. When he opens his mouth, do what you need to do."

"Yes, Captain."

Héctor taps Titán. "¡Vamos!"

Titán obeys with a roar. Rayo is fielding off the Sire's fire with her own, but her stream is getting smaller, the Sire's flames blasting hers away. Puya, Daga, and Fantasma hit the Sire's body over and over, then he twirls in the fastest whirlwind of limbs. His tail is a loose weapon. The Sire slams it into everything in its path. Once again, all four dragons are sent flying away.

Titán charges. I keep my breathing steady, ignoring the breakneck speed at which my heart is pounding, and hide the orb behind me. Titán swoops close enough to taunt the Sire, then pulls up. I lean to the side, angling myself so I can see down. The Sire stays below us as expected. He watches us glide above him with his shiny, narrowed eyes.

He headbutts Titán in the stomach.

Titán is thrust upward. He loses control of his wings, doubling over from the blow.

"Ugh!" Héctor and I rock back and forth. I'm losing my grip, but I hold on just in time to see the Sire's teeth bared. He's opening his mouth to burn us. I need to get closer *now*.

The Sire aims his wide-open mouth at Titán.

"Get down!" I unhook my arm from Héctor's waist. I jump to a standing position and use Héctor's shoulders to steady myself. He leans forward low enough so that I can leap over him. He yells something, but it's white noise to me.

I run down the entire length of Titán's neck, his head, until I get to his nose. The Sire's propeller expands as if he's bracing for a full-blown explosion.

This is it. I'm going to die.

And everyone I care about will live.

My heart's in my mouth, but I push the words out anyway. "Héctor! I'm really sorry for everything. Please tell the others I'm sorry, too. And thank you for helping me!"

His whole face is a question mark. "What are you . . . Wait, no! LANA, DON'T!"

I'm skydiving right into the Sire's line of fire.

Please don't miss, please don't miss, please don't miss.

I put everything I have left into my throw. The white light at the golden orb's center shines even brighter as it shoots out of my hand. Flames erupt from the Sire's propeller. The orb and the fire crash into each other.

BANG!

Ice blasts out of the orb. It travels the length of the fiery stream, freezing everything it touches. The ice grows and grows until it bursts into sharp bullets, shooting out everywhere. I drop a few inches past the Sire's lips. He lets out a strangled cry and tries to blow out more flames. He's lurching and spitting, but no matter how hard he tries, the flames never come.

His fire is gone.

"Yes!" I pump my fist in the air, even though I'm still falling to my death.

Then something breaks my fall.

"Ugh!" I lurch forward as the wind's knocked out of me. Whatever's cushioning me is hard and soft at the same time, a bed made of jagged rock and supple skin. My whole spine is a throbbing extravaganza. Still, I look down at what's beneath me. I sigh in relief—black scales. I've landed on a Sol de Noche's back.

"Nice shot," Victoria says behind me.

No. Freaking. Way. Am I hallucinating? Or did Victoria Peralta really save my life?

"What are you doing here?" I whisper breathlessly. "You said—"

"I know what I said. Now, hold on. This is gonna get rough."

I rush to sit behind her, still making sense of what just happened. Victoria went against her word to rescue me. She's steering Esperanza higher and higher. The Sire is trying to flee before she gets him. He's still crying out, but the jerk is strong enough to fly away.

Five Sol de Noche dragons appear all around him. They trap him in a circle again.

"Do you know the plan?" I ask Victoria.

"Obviously! Hang on!"

The Sire turns around just in time to meet Esperanza face-to-face. When he roars at her, I can see what was once his propeller caged within ice. It's cracked and dented from the Sire's attempts to burn the ice away. Drops of blood splatter the ice cage's roof. He still attempts to burn Esperanza, but his efforts only slow the rest of his reflexes down. Esperanza sinks her teeth into his neck, which causes him to growl in fury. Then she buries her claws into his wings.

Esperanza rips the Sire's wings out.

They soar down into the smoke and debris. They're a pair of gleaming silver petals sinking into a thick, gray cloud—worthless reminders of a dragon without flight and fire.

The Sire cries louder than Daga ever did. He's trapped in Esperanza's claws, which she attaches to his wingless sides. She shoves him down and falls with him. For a few seconds, the world remains the same. We're hurtling toward the smoke and debris.

Then it's all night and black sand. Esperanza launches us into the Dark Island. The other Sol de Noche dragons are hot on her trail. President Turner is right where we left him, his jaw dropping when he spots us. Esperanza shoves the Sire into the pit with the claw towers. While the team's dragons hover around the pit, Esperanza pins the Sire with a victorious roar. Then she flies out, leaving the rest of the dragons to bend the towers forward with their claws, curving them into spikes aimed at the Sire. He can't move without getting stabbed.

I half expect myself to smile. It's over. He's not hurting anyone else ever again. The only company he'll keep is his tortured roars. But seeing him stuck does nothing to ease the pain of losing Andrew. It doesn't wash away the bitterness of how I played a part in that loss.

I helped him win.

"What's up with you?" Victoria surprises me with a soft, almost motherly tone, and I realize I'm crying again. "Cheer up. This is a happy moment."

I give her a single nod, wiping my tears away. "Yeah . . . it's just . . ."

I can't even say he's dead.

Victoria frowns but doesn't try to coax details out. She calls to everyone, "Let's hit the road. We're still needed outside. That includes you, Mister President! We have to go!"

Farther away from the pit, President Turner is as still as a corpse. Then he reaches out in the Sire's direction. His hand lingers in midair as if he longs to confirm what he's seeing. I can't imagine how it must feel to see the dragon that cursed him in this state. From the way the president's shaking his head, I don't think he fully accepts what's happening. Tears pool in his heavy-lidded eyes. "His wings are . . . His fire . . ." he whispers. "He's . . . nothing."

"You can thank us later!" Luis smiles. "Hop on with Gabriela!"

President Turner can't stop staring at the Sire as Gabriela helps him onto Puya's back. It's like he's committing his weeping to memory. So I do the same. The Sire's wails won't bring Andrew back. Or erase the terrible things he's done. But I'll know he hurts because of us.

Six black dragons fly side by side with their triumphant chorus still ringing in my ears.

Then the darkness spits me back out into another sky made of night.

"You can do great things with this opportunity, but it's easier to be careless. It's easier to act like the world's laws don't apply to you. It's all about remembering what matters most. The Cup itself doesn't make you a winner. How you handle yourself in the spotlight does."

—Excerpt from a 2015 interview with Takeshi Endo,
seven days before the Cup

CHAPTER THIRTY-ONE

THE SMOKE'S BEEN CLEARED FROM THE SÃO PAULO SANCTUARY. Magic holds the top half of the habitat in place.

Twenty-two Dragon Knights kneel with their arms behind their backs in the courtyard. They've all been bound with a Handcuff Charm. Dozens of bureau agents surround them, wands aimed at their chests. Samira waves up at me as Esperanza descends. She's standing next to Takeshi and an awestruck Director Sandhar.

Takeshi's in handcuffs, too. He's perfectly still, watching me dismount.

"Are you guys hurt?" I run over and ask.

"Not at all," Samira replies. "I cast a Shield Charm before we hit the ground." She gives me a big hug. "What about you? I saw you *jumping at the Sire!*"

"Yeah." I let her go. "The Sire's locked up without his fire."

"So it worked?"

"It worked."

President Turner draws up behind us. He seems stuck in a dreamlike state, his gaze, weighed down and gleaming, drifting from person to person. "I can still hear his voice. The Sire is trying to make me threaten the dragons' lives, but I can resist him without feeling any pain. He can't hurt me." He points to the Sol de Noches. "Their magic is weakening the Anchor Curse."

"And the contracts?" asks Director Sandhar, gripping his wand a little too tight.

The president's face scrunches up. "Let's see." He pulls out his wand, then conjures a contract from thin air. "He's screaming at me to stop," he says with a coy smile. President Turner aims his wand at the contract. With a flick of his wrist, a silver line appears at the center of the scroll, spreading out in the shape of a snowflake. Every inch of the contract glows in starlight as it crystallizes. The edges start to crack little by little.

BOOM!

I cover my head as a shower of silver sparkles falls all around us. They're already pretty, but they're even prettier when I remember what they used to be. How the Sire's words have exploded into nothing. At long last, we're free.

"His will isn't mine anymore," a relieved President Turner declares. He brushes off a few sparkles from his suit jacket. "How did he break his curse? He couldn't use Eddie's blood."

I glance down, biting hard so the tears stay away.

Samira says, "He used his son's blood."

President Turner gapes at her. He's scratching the back of his head, as if he's struggling to understand what he's just heard. "Eddie didn't *have* a son."

"He didn't know," Samira says. "Neither one knew about the other. Andrew's mother found out she was pregnant after Barnes cursed the Sire. She kept his father's identity a secret to protect him. Andrew only found out minutes before his death."

President Turner is paler than he'd been under the Anchor Curse. "Andrew was . . . his son?" So he had no idea, then. He's frantically searching for a place to sit. Héctor and Gabriela grab his hands. They lead him to one of the few benches that hasn't been smashed to bits.

"Galloway is dead?" Victoria presses a hand to her rosy cheek, her brow furrowed.

I can only nod.

"Oh no . . ." Génesis covers her mouth. She lets Edwin hug her, even though he's shaken as well. Luis tries to speak twice, but nothing comes out.

This is the worst part of losing someone. It's not when you realize they're never coming back. It's when you're reminded of the moment, over and over again. It drains me to watch President Turner and my teammates grapple with the news. The Sire might be our prisoner, but he's made sure we'll never forget we were once his.

Director Sandhar clears his throat. "Andrew's body has been found. I have agents prepping him for Transport at the moment." He lowers his head. "We're taking him and Randall to forensics in New York once we corroborate the Sire's location. Samira here explained what she could, but I need to see it for myself. I need to know he truly has been put away."

"Wait. Randall's already dead?" I say.

"He's still agonizing," Takeshi says, remorseless. He turns to Director Sandhar. "Get him to confirm Antonio Deluca's whereabouts. As one of the few Gold Wands alive, his rescue should be a top bureau priority, especially if he's spent the past two years with Dragon Knight captors. He also has sensitive information on another of your most pressing cases."

"Don't speak to me about *priorities*." Director Sandhar seems seconds away from yelling. "Killing Randall wasn't your mission, Agent Endo. Neither was cutting off all communication with me, stealing bureau property, or kidnapping your colleague for public execution."

"*Agent* Endo?" President Turner peeks up at Takeshi, his posture ramrod straight.

Director Sandhar sighs in exasperation. "He joined the bureau a year ago, Russell. He's been undercover for the past eight months. Though it appears he only wanted access to our intel and Dragonshade." He looks like a disappointed father. "A thief, a liar, and a traitor."

Takeshi isn't the slightest bit interested in defending himself.

Part of his plan involved the dragon hiding in Sweden. "What happened to the Waxbyrne Fire Drake after you stole her crystal heart?" I ask.

His grin should be illegal. It makes him seem five years younger, canceling out the bags under his eyes, the dark gleam haunting his irises. "I didn't steal it. She gave it to me, just like the male I found six months after Hikaru's murder. It took me longer to gain her trust. She didn't believe me when I promised to protect her rider, but after I video-called him to confirm he's alive, she gave me the crystal heart and accepted my help in fleeing Sweden. She's with a friend of mine now. You all know her as the Ghost of Shibuya, but I just call her Haya."

Gabriela gasps. "Team Japan's Runner?"

"Yes."

I shake my head. "Why would she be with Haya Tanaka? What about her rider?"

Director Sandhar steps forward. "That's classified informa—"

"Agent Robinson is her rider," Takeshi says. "His death was faked. I chose him for the execution because someone other than the Sire is hunting him. It was the perfect excuse to send him into hiding. Agent Robinson will reunite with the Fire Drake soon. They're safer with Haya than with the bureau."

"*Takeshi*." Director Sandhar spits out the word. "You're not cleared to speak of this!"

I walk around the director, facing Takeshi. "But if Agent Robinson is the Fire Drake's rider, couldn't he have created an Other Place to hide her? Why was she left at a wand shop?"

Director Sandhar waves me off. "Like I said, that's classified informa—"

"He was Madame Waxbyrne's lover," Takeshi says. "The person who's trying to kill him is one of the most dangerous murderers the bureau has ever faced—a former wand-making student of Madame Waxbyrne's, and Antonio Deluca's ex-girlfriend."

"TAKESHI!" Director Sandhar is inches away from Takeshi's face. "Enough!"

So the rider *had* been linked to Madame Waxbyrne like Papi thought! Whoever this former student is, she doesn't sound like a walk in the park, especially if she once dated a guy who punched another athlete out of envy. I hope Takeshi's right about the Fire Drake being safe with Haya Tanaka. I hope this murderer never lays a finger on that poor dragon.

"I helped expose a Dragon Knight in your department," says Takeshi. "Agent Grant West led me to the Fire Drake and Carlos Torres. Your agents found him unconscious next to my Recorder, which secretly captured our conversations." He pauses. "You're welcome."

Director Sandhar slaps both hands behind his neck. His nostrils flare as he inches even closer to Takeshi. "Listen, you—"

"Takeshi helped us stop the Sire," I say. "He saved my friends. He's with us." My chest tightens. Andrew would've loved to hear me admit that. He'll never know his best friend was a bureau agent. He'll never know Hikaru was avenged. That *he's* been avenged, too.

"Ms. Torres, I'm Transporting you and Samira to bureau headquarters ahead of everyone else," says Director Sandhar. He's so fed up it's not even funny. "Your father is waiting for you there. Neither of you are to leave until you've been properly interrogated. Is that clear?"

Samira says, "Yes, Director."

I remain silent.

Director Sandhar cocks his eyebrow at me. "Ms. Torres? Is that clear?"

"The same boy who killed your son killed Takeshi's dragon steed. He killed Andrew. I'm not defending what Takeshi's done. He *did* commit crimes. He *did* betray your trust. But he's not like them." I motion to the handcuffed Dragon Knights. "He risked his neck to get you intel."

At least the director's not scowling. His eyebrows hang low, along with his shoulders. He reminds me of what I used to look like when I started running—frustrated and spent.

Bureau agents wheel two stretchers into the courtyard.

On one lies a body covered with a white blanket from head to toe. Andrew. I pretend to care about the clouds while the agents walk away. When I look back down, more agents file out with the second stretcher, which has been left uncovered. Randall's arms and legs are strapped tight. His eyes are wildly unfocused. His darkened veins pop out even more.

His gaze finds Director Sandhar's. "Father . . . don't let me die like this."

Director Sandhar studies his veins from afar. He gulps down hard, taking his sweet time drinking in the boy he helped raise. "I'm sorry," he says. "I should've done more to save you."

Randall wails. This boy has always been a tool. He grew accustomed to being used long before the Sire tricked him into believing he was free. Now he'll never know what freedom is.

Director Sandhar turns his back on Randall. "Get them both to headquarters," he says to the agents. "I'll meet you there soon."

"Father, please . . . Don't let me die alone. . . ."

SWISH!

Randall disappears along with Andrew's body.

Director Sandhar then turns back to Takeshi. He bumps his fists against each other, then hides them behind his back, as if he's tempted to crush Takeshi into powder.

I wedge myself between them. "Arrest Takeshi. Charge him for his crimes. Just remember there are *real* Dragon Knights still out there. Remember what we're fighting for."

Director Sandhar's eyes go wide. He's smiling at me. "We?"

I lift my chin. "Yes. We."

"I'll make sure never to forget that." He nods to his wand. "Now will you please join Ms. Jones so I may Transport you to New York together?"

"Wait." I turn to Takeshi. Given all he's endured, I never would've been capable of planning such a detailed, vicious payback. Now his freedom is gone, and he didn't even get to kill the Sire, because he listened to me instead. "Thank you, Takeshi. I'm sorry for everything you've been through. I'm sorry you lost Andrew, too. He believed in you more than you know."

I walk away before he can respond.

"Lana?" he calls out.

Of course I stop and look at him.

Takeshi smiles like someone who's been crushed under the weight of their sorrow, unsure of how to make it stop, but is trying their best. "I once told you to believe in the world that's coming. That was a mistake. The world I wanted to live in was filled with anger, but your heart and your courage gave me hope. I watched you run and fight and stand up to the Sire, but when you stood up to *me*, I saw that the world worth believing in is the one we're in now."

Whoa. Takeshi Endo is *complimenting* me. I never expected to mean anything to the person who once mattered most to me. My mouth is too dry to speak, so I give him a quick nod. I ignore Samira's dramatic throat clearing and focus on Director Sandhar.

"Ready?" he asks.

"Ready," we answer together.

I wave goodbye to everyone as the courtyard drowns in the whitest light.

THE INTERNATIONAL BUREAU OF MAGICAL MATTERS IS JUST A FANCY thing to call a bunch of gilded elevators in a circular, marble-tiled chamber. There's a painted mural in between the elevators at the center. It features a wizard raising his wand, a Regular woman carrying a book, and a gray dragon calmly posing behind them. They represent everyone under the bureau's protection. All three stand on a cliff's edge. Dark clouds float above them, along with black-and-white tendrils of smoke that reach down for their necks. They appear unfazed by the shadowy threats.

Agent Horowitz is already waiting for us by the mural. "Ladies! I'm happy to see you both in one piece." She greets us with a simple nod, but she sounds stoked.

I throw my arms around her. "Thank you for bringing my dad here."

"You're welcome. He's unharmed and desperate to see his daughter. Shall we?"

"Absolutely."

She takes us through the brightly lit lobby, where employees are filing in and out of the elevators. There aren't any signs to let people know which elevator leads to where. There isn't even a screen hanging over them to let people know which floor they're on. The doors just open at random like a game of Whac-A-Mole. Agent Horowitz makes a beeline for the nearest one. She pushes the Magical Investigations button while Samira and I settle inside. Some people point at us, whispering like we're the hottest gossip in town. Have they heard about what went down in Brazil? I'm sure they know about my team ditching the semifinals match.

After a quick elevator ride, we exit onto a carpeted corridor. There are red doors on both sides. Agent Horowitz stops beside the third one on the left. The sign above reads INTERROGATION ROOMS. Once inside, Agent Horowitz unlocks another door.

Papi sits alone at a metal table. "Lana!" He rushes over to me, sweeping me in a hug. He holds me as if I'm made of the most fragile glass. "Did the Sire hurt you?"

Only my heart.

"No, Papi. I'm okay. I love you."

"Te amo más, mija." Papi hugs Samira, too. "What you did was incredibly reckless, girls. You could've died."

"Director Sandhar will arrive soon with more details and further instructions. The interrogation will begin once he's here," says Agent Horowitz. "Lana and Samira will both be interrogated, as well as the Puerto Rican team, so I suggest getting comfortable while you wait. For now, I'll let you all catch up." She addresses Samira, "Your family will be here soon, too."

Samira says, "Thank you."

Agent Horowitz exits the interrogation room, closing the door behind her.

I use my sleeves to wipe the tears away. After we're all seated, Samira does most of the talking with Papi. She explains everything that happened after Takeshi took him. He flashes her a look that's a mix of pain and disgust and mumbles Spanish insults for the Sire and Randall.

"Andrew's dead?" Papi says. "He's really gone?"

I wince. My sudden tears answer Papi's question.

"Dios mío. That poor boy," he whispers.

Once Samira's done, I fill in the blanks of what went down on the Dark Island. I keep the president's curse a secret, vaguely insinuating he needed to be protected from the Sire.

"Your turn," I say to Papi. "What happened with Takeshi?"

"Oh, I thought he was going to kill me. But after he dragged me outside, he told me he was an undercover bureau agent. He told me to find Agent Horowitz in the forest and that he'd go back to save the three of you. I've spent these last few weeks hating that boy, and there he was promising to bring my daughter back alive from the monster he pretended to serve."

Yeah. And now he's in handcuffs.

The door bursts open.

"Samira?" Mrs. Jones barges into the room. "Oh my Lord! There you are!" She's a blur as she races toward Samira, scooping her up in her arms. "Julius, here she is!"

"Yes, I can see her just fine from here, sweetheart." Mr. Jones swoops into the room and wraps both Samira and his wife into a bear hug. "You almost gave us a heart attack, Samira! Nobody gave you permission to go to Brazil!"

"They told us you'd been fighting against the Sire and his Dragon Knights!" Mrs. Jones sounds even more alarmed. "And what's this I hear about you knocking out a Gold Wand?"

"She did just that, Mrs. Jones," I say as Shay enters the room and gasps. She dives for her family, squeezing herself into their embrace. "Samira crushed him in a duel."

Mr. and Mrs. Jones back up first, letting Shay cling to her big sister. They all look like they've won the lottery.

"You Ascended to Silver today?" Mrs. Jones asks.

"No, ma'am." Samira takes out her wand and holds it up. "I'm a Gold Wand."

Her parents are too dumbfounded to speak. Mrs. Jones clutches her husband's sleeve, pulling down on it like she's trying not to collapse.

"Where did you get that?" Shay asks.

"It's my Copper wand, Shay. Only it's not Copper anymore. I still don't know how, but when my magical status changed, the wand changed, too."

"That's amazing," someone by the door says. "Congratulations."

Agent Horowitz has returned, but she's not the one who spoke. It was the woman to her left. She's wearing that blush-pink satin shirt I bought her three Christmases ago, a gray tweed skirt, and a white doctor's coat with DR. WELLS embroidered on it.

My stomach drops. "*Mom?*"

"Hi, Lana." That's her voice. Her nervous gaze and stiff posture and clasped, sweaty hands. "I, uh . . . I don't mean to bother you, but I wanted to see if you were okay. I was watching the game when you disappeared along with your teammates and the Scottish boy. Then the agents took Todd and me to another location because Carlos's hideout had been compromised. Now that we're safer, I had to come see . . . if you were okay," she repeats.

I listen to her every word, but only a few stick with me: *I was watching the game.*

She broke her promise. I don't care why. I don't care whether she regrets being furious at me for living my dream. All I care about is I've just survived the worst day of my life, and she's here to see if I'm okay. It's impossible to delete the bad memories, but I'll never forget how my mother chose to be with me when I needed her most.

"You must be exhausted, so I'll . . . I'll just wait outside." Mom starts for the door.

I push my chair back. It hits the table with a clang, the noise startling Mom.

I launch myself at her. Fresh tears poke at my eyes. "I love you, Mom," I choke out.

She's holding me closer than ever before, sniffling into my hair. "I love you, too."

One cannot hope to tame dragons. This doesn't mean a Bonded dragon will betray their rider. It means the Bond is never about subservience. A dragon has a voice, too, and it's a rider's duty to listen with careful consideration of their steed's feelings. When a dragon expresses what it most desires, with either words or actions, it's essential we don't take it for granted. Believe dragons when they tell you their truths.

—*Excerpt from Carlos Torres's* Studying the Bond Between Dragons & Humans

CHAPTER THIRTY-TWO

MOM HASN'T LET GO OF MY HAND IN THE PAST THREE HOURS.

We still haven't discussed what our reunion means for the future. She *did* mention Todd was escorted back to Aunt Jenny's at his unbearably insistent request. The fact that she was present during my interrogation with Director Sandhar, sitting right next to Papi in respectful silence, gives me the slightest bit of hope that all's well again.

She even waits with me while my team endures the interrogation. Since Manny and Joaquín are serving as our guardians, Edwin's grandparents and the others' parents aren't required to join them, but they've been texting and calling frequently. They're waiting to see what happens with the Cup in order to decide if they'll fly out to Dubai, too. None of my teammates come out to the waiting room with negative feedback. Héctor mentions how easy it was to take Director Sandhar and his agents into the Dark Island and show them the Sire's cage. After the director approved keeping the Sire there, he sent the dragons to Dubai and beefed up their security detail in case of rogue Dragon Knights.

Victoria's the last one left. She's been gone thirty-five minutes.

Ten minutes less than Samira and her family have been stuck in the Department of Magical Artifact Permits and Regulations. Since her wand had originally been certified and sold as Copper, Samira needs government approval before she can legally use it. That's just the first step. According to Director Sandhar, even if she does get her wand approved, she'll have to undergo a series of tests and interviews to further study her Gold Wand status.

Only Samira Jones could ever be ecstatic about something that draining.

"Would you like some soup, honey?" Mom offers me her cream of broccoli.

"No, thanks. I'll eat later."

"But you must be starving."

"Not really." I slide closer to her seat with a yawn. "I'm just tired."

Papi yawns, too. "You'll be able to rest soon, mi amor."

Luis's snores are getting louder. He's asleep on Génesis's shoulder with his mouth wide open, unleashing the sounds of the underworld.

"I wish I had my phone right now," Gabriela says through a fit of giggles.

Stoically, Héctor replies, "I apologize for the disruption. But if it's okay with everyone, I can wake him up with my best rendition of the Celine Dion classic, 'My Heart Will Go On.'"

"No!" Gabriela, Edwin, Génesis, and I say together.

Luis is startled awake. "What happened?! Whose ass are we kicking now?"

"Yours if you don't stop snoring," says Héctor.

More laughter. Luis pretends to be offended, while Edwin does a flawless reenactment. The whole time we're bantering, Mom smiles.

"They're wonderful," she whispers.

"I know," I whisper back.

"V! About time!" Luis stands up as Victoria approaches him. They fist-bump each other. "These fools have been accusing me of things I haven't done."

Victoria grins. "If it's snoring, then you did it."

"Boom." Héctor gives her a high five.

Luis groans. "Y'all suck."

"You know what sucks more? Sitting in those freezing metal chairs." Manny stretches his arms. He and Joaquín are right behind Victoria. "We should get going, mi gente. Director Sandhar's given us the all clear to go home and prep for tomorrow's press conference. The IBF is planning Andrew's public memorial service. That'll be two days from now."

I close my eyes. A public memorial service for Andrew is both great and terrible. Family, friends, and fans around the globe will honor his life as it should be honored. But there'll be a billion cameras there. It could easily become more of a spectacle than anything else.

"Have you heard anything about the Cup?" Victoria asks. "What's gonna happen now that Andrew's gone? Our semifinals match is forfeit, isn't it?"

Manny flashes a deep frown. "Russell texted me with an update. The staff in Dubai said the other dragons caused major commotion in their habitats after you Faded to São Paulo. According to their riders, they wanted to join the fight in Brazil. It would've taken them longer to reach the country without magical help, and since the IBF wouldn't allow them to leave, they kept on squealing." He nods to my team's riders. "They were rooting for you all."

My heart swells as I picture all those wings flapping and fangs bared for my country's team. They were willing to go to *war* for us.

"Are they calm now?" I ask. "Do you think they still want to finish the Cup? What happens if they refuse to continue? Will the Cup get canceled?"

Joaquín says, "President Turner will speak at the bureau's press conference tomorrow morning, which we all are attending, too. He'll address our next steps then."

That doesn't give me any hint of what to expect.

I try again. "What happens to us if the Cup is canceled?"

Manny squeezes Joaquín's shoulder tight, smiling weakly. "We go home."

For a brief second, I catch Victoria glancing nervously at me. It's so quick I almost think I imagined it. She'd be going back to a life without her coveted trophy. So would I, but that wouldn't be the worst part. I'm supposed to start senior year soon. My teammates will be swarmed with agents hired to fend off Dragon Knights. I'm also at risk of being attacked, but I'm not the one with access to the Sire's prison. I won't feel at ease knowing my teammates' lives are in constant danger. Plus, I'll just plain miss them.

What do I even want anymore?

"Okay. Ready to go?" Manny asks.

"Wait." I look at Papi. "You're going back to São Paulo, right?"

"Yes and no, mija. We recovered eight of the Pesadelos, but Violet #43 flew away. I'll help my colleagues with the ones that stayed behind, and once they're all settled again, I'm hoping to search for her." He sneaks a peek at Mom, as if he's waiting for an atomic bomb to go off, but she just nods in approval. He smiles at her. "I'll get her back soon."

"I'm sure you will, Carlos," Mom says. "Just be careful out there."

My eyes almost pop out of their sockets. Mom is *totally okay* with the fact that my father is going to find the dragon that nearly killed me. I have no idea what prompted her to start watching Blazewrath matches and support Papi's job, but I'm sure as hell not complaining.

"Lana? Is everything all right?" Mom asks.

"Yeah." I smile so, so wide. "Papi, listen to Mom. Please be careful."

"Always, mi amor," he says.

I hug my parents tight. I ask Mom to please tell Samira to call me later, and she promises to do so. Manny and Joaquín shake their hands and exchange kind words with them both.

Then I'm led back to where Agent Horowitz is waiting to Transport us to the Compound.

VICTORIA ISN'T EATING. SHE'S NOT SPEAKING, EITHER.

She stares at the bedroom ceiling with vacant eyes, as if she's lost the will to live.

I'm the only one here with her. Joaquín has told us all to rest, but my teammates are in the habitat with him and Manny. I'm supposed to fetch Gabriela's favorite compact and bring it back to her. Apparently, saving the world makes you want to retouch your makeup.

"Hey," I dare to say. "Do you need me to get you anything?"

Victoria shakes her head.

"Are you sure? Because I can—"

She shakes her head even faster.

"Cool. I, um . . . I'll head out now."

Victoria slow-claps.

I walk to the door, but each step slams more guilt into my conscience. Once upon a time, I would've chosen to swallow burning coals over having a heart-to-heart with Victoria. I don't even know if a heart-to-heart with Victoria is *possible*.

My body winds itself into knots.

"Okay, listen." I turn to the bed. "You're not the only one who's dreamed of holding that Cup. I don't know what's gonna happen at that press conference. My mind is a mess right now. But I *do* know that I'll never know pain worse than losing a friend."

Victoria presses her eyes shut.

"I mean, I'm not comparing how bad *you* feel to how bad *I* feel. This is super hard for me, too. You're not the only one who fears what's next. You're choosing to cope this way, and I respect that, but don't forget there are others who can help you process what you're feeling." I bump my fists together. "That's all I want to say. I'll go now."

I head for the door again.

"I'm sorry for the way I treated you, Lana," Victoria says.

Her apology hooks itself into my chest, stopping me dead in my tracks. "No, I . . . I'm not trying to get you to feel sorry for me. I just wanted to—"

"There was someone else before you." Victoria sits up as if an anvil is pulling her down, each movement heavier than the last. "I trusted Brian more than I should have. I *loved* him. But he was just nothing wrapped in pretty packaging. When he revealed the real him, he hurt people I care about. That was horrible enough. Then he hurt me, too." There's a grim shadow cast on her expression. "Do you know what his last words to me were?"

Of course I don't, and I'm not sure I want to hear them, either.

"'You've never been a winner and you never will be,'" she says. "The same words my fucking stepfather said for years. I shared them with Brian in secret." His name sounds foreign in her throat, as if she's out of practice. That scum bucket used her abuser's words against her. He used her trust as a weapon, right after disrespecting Edwin and Gabriela.

I'm so happy he's thousands of miles out of my fist's reach.

"I didn't trust you as a person or as a teammate because I didn't think you could help me get what I want, Lana. I thought you were here to bring us down. That you'd end up embarrassing our country." Victoria rubs her sleepy eyes. "I lied about the others feeling the same way. I'm sorry for that, too."

Ugh, I should've known. "Water under the bridge."

"No. I put you through some bullshit. You proved yourself the minute you saved that Fire Drake. And again when you demanded the Iron Scale for practice, then again when you froze the Sire's propeller. That fire in here"—she taps her chest where her heart is—"that's all Puerto Rico. You might not have strong memories of the island, but it will never forget *you*."

I flash her the smile I never thought she'd deserve. Whether we play again or not, she finally respects me. Hearing it tastes much better than the president's no-calorie cake.

"Thanks, Victoria. That's really sweet."

"Oh, there's nothing sweet about me." Her grin is a devilish treat.

We both love Blazewrath with everything we are. Blazewrath was supposed to make us *matter*. That's what I told Mom. The thing is, we matter with or without trophies and medals.

We matter whether the people we love believe in us, support us, or not.

"Marisol told me not to burn away," I say. "If you let hate get the best of you, the best will be gone. You're too important to lose, Victoria—for your mom, for your fans, for *yourself*." I sit at the edge of her bed. "We might not play Blazewrath again. That freaking *sucks*, but we matter wherever we are." I put my fist on top of hers. "And I'd like to add that we matter without things that make us feel important. Including fancy Gold Cups."

She's nodding weakly. "Including fancy Gold Cups . . ."

"That's right. Let's see what tomorrow brings, okay?"

Victoria puts her sneakers on. We leave the room together, smiling like we've been friends this whole time. Maybe we could've been friends earlier, but the past is the past.

We're bigger people than the girls who met in the kitchen.

THE NEXT MORNING, I'M OUTSIDE THE BUREAU'S MAIN ENTRANCE, where reporters are waiting for Director Sandhar's press conference to start. I've had two hours of sleep. My team stayed with the Sol de Noches last night while they acclimated to their bodyguards. Daga was the fastest to get used to them. She even tried to play catch, but to her dismay, they remained professional.

I returned to my room to talk to Samira. She told me about the Department of Magical Artifact Permits and Regulations as if she'd gone to Disney World. She has to stay in the bureau to start her tests, but they've given her clearance to attend Andrew's memorial service.

Joaquín and Manny are chatting to the left of the stage. Headmaster Sykes plants a delicate kiss on President Turner, then joins Joaquín and Manny in the crowd. Director Sandhar motions for my team to walk onstage. The seven of us are shining brightly in our uniforms.

Director Sandhar goes straight for the podium. He recalls how he and dozens of other agents stormed off to São Paulo yesterday. Though he doesn't reveal the Anchor Curse, he mentions President Turner had been a target, and so he was kept in a secret location created by the Sol de Noche dragons. I nod along as he confirms the Sire is trapped. It's reassuring to hear him say it with such confidence.

"We owe our lives to the seven young heroes on this stage," he says. "We owe them to Samira Jones, the young witch who couldn't be here with us. But there are two other names I must mention today. Two young boys who are crucial to understanding yesterday's events—Takeshi Endo and Andrew Galloway."

Murmurs trickle over from the crowd.

I block them out as Director Sandhar continues. "A year ago, Takeshi

Endo asked to become an undercover agent assigned to infiltrate the Dragon Knights. His role was to serve as our informant, but he'd been secretly plotting to help the Sire become a mortal dragon again. For his counter curse, the Sire needed the living blood of Edward Barnes. Or, as it happened, the living blood of Barnes's heir. Agent Endo failed to discover the identity of Barnes's heir in time to prevent his death."

At first, I think something's wrong with Director Sandhar's microphone, but it's just that he stopped talking. He lets a few camera flashes go off before speaking again. He mentions Andrew's murder, his true identity.

"Randall Wiggins has confessed to capturing Antonio Deluca in 2015 with the intention of framing him for Hikaru's murder. The bureau will continue their search for Deluca with the information Wiggins provides after his interrogation."

"What about Takeshi?" a female reporter asks. "Is it true he's also been arrested?"

"Yes. Agent Endo broke the terms of his contract. He withheld information and stole from the bureau in order to commit murder. He kidnapped Agent Michael Robinson and has refused to disclose the whereabouts of the Fire Drake. He was also willing to let the heir of Edward Barnes die so he could enact his revenge."

But he chose to spare President Turner's life instead.

"Agent Endo will be tried for his crimes in the coming days."

Does that mean Takeshi will rot in a cell while the world celebrates Andrew one last time? Regardless of what Takeshi's done, this is cruel. He won't celebrate and say goodbye to his best friend. I won't spend another day in the presence of the boy who was once my favorite.

The boy who's slowly becoming my favorite again.

"That will be all from me this morning. Mister President, if you please."

President Turner wastes no time getting to the podium. He's

slumped over and yawning, but he has enough energy for whatever he's about to do. "Good morning. I'd like to start with acknowledging the brave young people of Team Puerto Rico behind me. Without them, none of us would be here. It's because of them that I come to you today with the truth."

Wait. What is he doing?

"Many years ago, the Sire cast an irreversible spell on me. It bound my life to his. I've served as his Anchor to this world ever since. This means I obeyed his every command against my will." He leans closer to the mic. "He's owned the Blazewrath World Cup since 2013."

The crowd gasps as one. Some people exchange wide-eyed glances, but the majority can only look up at the man who's confessed the devastating truth about the Cup.

President Turner goes on to detail how the Sire orchestrated his ascent in the IBF ranks, how he demanded the Cup never get canceled despite the ongoing protests, and how the president couldn't scheme behind his back without him retaliating.

"I was unaware that Eddie Barnes had a son," he says in a low voice. "Andrew Galloway lived and died a hero. He stood up to injustices and fought to end them. So have the other dragons competing in the Blazewrath World Cup. Their desire to fight the Sire overpowered their will to play, and there are still Dragon Knights roaming the world. Therefore, the International Blazewrath Federation has decided to cancel the Cup and announce our organization's dissolution. This year marks the official end to the sport of Blazewrath."

So that's it. No more Cups. No more Blazewrath.

I wait for the heartbreak to swallow me whole, but the longer I think about it, the better I feel. I love Blazewrath. I always will. But this game stopped being what I imagined. Part of that is the Sire's fault. The other part is what the Sol de Noche dragons have shown me since they started building the Dark Island. Dragons aren't born to battle one another for a trophy. They're here for their riders. For their countries. For *themselves*. President Turner has chosen to let them do what they were meant to.

He continues, "To the aspiring Blazewrath players who hoped to qualify for future Cups, I apologize. To the teams participating in this year's Cup, your achievements will be properly rewarded and remembered.

"The Sire has been imprisoned. However, those who are loyal to him are still at large. I urge you to return to the people you love most. I urge you to *live your lives*. And when the time comes, I urge you to fight."

Smiles pop up on my teammates' faces, except for Victoria, who's tearing up next to me.

I grab her hand. "There's life beyond the gold, Victoria. Find it." I bump my shoulder to hers. "You're worth much more than a trophy."

Her hand grabs mine, too. She whispers, "So are you."

President Turner thanks us again and requests applause for our bravery. Manny claps the hardest out of everyone. He waves at us as we're led offstage. We all wave back. Six guys and girls dressed in my same black uniform. All six making sure nobody trips while flashes go off all around us. Six people who chose to save my father over winning an international tournament.

They're not my teammates. I don't have a *team* anymore.

I have a family.

The Weekly Scorcher: *Lastly, how would you like to be remembered?*

Edward Barnes: *The fact that I might be remembered is good enough, but I'd like to become a father someday and raise my children to defend the same things I do. I'd love to build a home that stands for justice, equality, and the belief that we all deserve to live alongside one another without hate. Most of all, I want to be a father who loves his children with all his might.*

—Excerpt from a 1988 interview with Edward Barnes, on his one-year bureau anniversary

CHAPTER THIRTY-THREE

I'VE NEVER SEEN MORE SCOTTISH FLAGS IN MY LIFE.

Fans from all around the globe have been filling the Blazewrath stadium since before the crack of dawn. Some have been camping out there since President Turner announced the memorial service. They carry small and large versions of Scotland's flag. I've caught hundreds of T-shirts with Andrew's face on them, too. Those who bought tickets for the finals are lucky enough to keep their seats. The rest are being treated to the service via a massive screen outside the stadium walls. Black banners and ribbons adorn them today. A giant billboard featuring Andrew's solo portrait has been erected near the entrance, too.

President Turner invited Mom, so now she's in the box seats along with Samira and her family. I'm down in the field. The Runners' mountains are gone. So are the Keepers' rings. A black carpet covers the whole stadium floor, with matching folding chairs on either side of the runway, where all the Cup's former players are being seated. The dragons have a section reserved for them behind the players' seats, too. All fourteen bureau bodyguards escort the Sol de Noche dragons to the area. Some of the Zmey Gorynych dragons smell the bodyguards' suits and shoes. They lose interest minutes later and focus on their fellow dragons.

Onesa's the first person to greet us. She hugs me with reddened eyes, then moves on to Gabriela behind me. I go down the row of chairs. Aneni and Wataida take the longest to release me. Artem and Kirill are at the end of the row. Kirill heads straight for Edwin, giving him a sweet, lingering kiss. They hold each other's hands as they claim their seats side by side.

As I sit next to her, Onesa says, "How are you feeling?"

"Better but still wrecked, if that makes any sense. You?"

"Grateful." She nudges me. "Very grateful for all of you."

I thank her with a nod, then distract myself with my surroundings. Our side of the field fills up pretty quickly. The Scottish team is the only one not here yet. On the other side of the black carpet, staff and team management file in little by little. Manny and Joaquín have already settled in the first row, right across from me. There are two empty seats beside Manny. A lone bureau agent is guarding them. Maybe it's for the president and Ambassador Haddad?

I still can't believe Takeshi's not allowed to attend the funeral. Scratch that. I can believe it. It just stings more than salt to a fresh wound. The thought of him staring at his prison cell's walls with no chance of bidding his best friend farewell cracks my heart in half. Would he have handled seeing Andrew's casket with his usual poise? Or would he have cried again?

The crowd breaks into earsplitting applause.

Takeshi and his mother are walking down the black carpet.

I'm gripping the edge of my seat way too tight. *He's really here!*

Mrs. Endo grabs onto his arm, elegant in her black dress and shawl. He's not in handcuffs anymore. He's not in his Dragon Knight outfit, either. Takeshi's been allowed to wear a crisp black suit and tie for the occasion. His cropped hair is gelled down. He looks fresh off a menswear catalogue instead of a Ravensworth Penitentiary cell.

Seven bureau agents tail him. They become his shadows as he helps Mrs. Endo to her seat, then takes his own next to her. Joaquín avoids him. Manny dares to say something to Takeshi. I can't quite read his lips. Takeshi bows his head quickly, but he doesn't look at Manny.

He looks at me.

Neither of us smiles or says a word. This is the first time I've seen him in days. This might be the last time I see him until his trial. This might be the last time I *ever* see him.

He's looking at me like he knows it, too.

It's been three days since he poisoned Randall Wiggins. Even though the bureau hasn't confirmed anything publicly, he should be dead by now.

It's also been three days since Takeshi told me that I gave him hope.

Scottish bagpipes start playing in the distance. Musicians march down the carpet, wearing traditional Scottish attire. Andrew's closed mahogany casket floats right behind them. My heart constricts. Ms. Galloway is clutching a tear-stained napkin, her gaze to the floor. Team Scotland marches a few feet away from her. Two boys and one girl are crying already. Their dragon steeds approach with heads held high, but wrecked with deep frowns and tear-filled eyes.

President Turner, Ambassador Haddad, and Director Sandhar round out the procession. While everyone goes to the stage, Ms. Galloway heads to Takeshi. He sweeps her into a hug. She cries quietly into his shoulder, then he whispers something that makes her smile.

Ms. Galloway pulls away first, giving Takeshi a soft kiss on the cheek, then she embraces Mrs. Endo. They hold each other close for a while. It's only when Ambassador Haddad speaks into his microphone that Ms. Galloway leaves for the stage.

Ambassador Haddad and President Turner give tender speeches about what Andrew meant to them. Director Sandhar thanks him for his courage and reiterates how he'd been a hero off the field. Andrew's teammates also take turns speaking about his humor and unparalleled love for his country. The musicians play more songs. A singer croons about heaven and angels.

Ms. Galloway is the last to address the audience. "My son would be so touched to see how much you all love him. *I'm* touched to see it. There are many things I wish I could've told him. So my wish for you all is to speak your truths. It's a difficult task, but it's so worthwhile. Andrew knew that better than anyone. He spoke his truth. He *fought* for his truth. Wherever you're from, however old you are, do what's in your heart before it's too late."

I'm sniffling and clapping along with the whole stadium. Once Ms. Galloway wraps up, the Golden Horns aim streams of fire into the air. Warmth trickles down to where I sit. They burn the sky while Andrew's casket floats back down the aisle with the recession. When he passes me, I press a fist against my heart, vowing to never forget his mother's words and his selfless acts. I vow to fight for my truth, too, regardless of the odds.

I search for Takeshi again.

He's already gone.

So are his mother and guards. I frown at the carpet. They must've Transported.

Onesa hugs me goodbye. I do the same with everyone else, exchanging numbers with the friends I've been lucky to gain, wishing them well in whatever they choose to do next. Then Manny wrangles us so we can get back to the van.

Victoria takes her time looking around the stadium. "This is the last Blazewrath field there will ever be," she says solemnly. "We won't get to play ever again."

"True," says Héctor. He takes a bow. "But the rest of our lives have just begun."

We all take quick bows, too, saying goodbye to the life we once knew. Then we link arms and exit the stadium for the last time.

MOM IS ALREADY AT THE COMPOUND WHEN I GET THERE.

Samira, her family, and Marisol are in the living room, sharing a giant bag of potato chips and flipping through TV channels. Noora is also there, sandwiched between Shay and Mom.

"Hi, Lana," Noora says. "It's great to see you again."

"Great to see you, too. Were you at the service?"

"Yes. I told my father I preferred not to work today. I just wanted to be someone in the stands." She pulls something out of her purse. "I came here to give you this."

She's holding out a photo of Andrew and me. We're standing by the chocolate fountain at the welcome party. He's smiling. I look confused. I had no idea Noora was at the party, let alone that she had immortalized my first conversation with Andrew in a picture.

"You're really good at stealth," I say with a laugh. "I can keep it?"

"No newspaper or magazine could ever offer me enough money. You should have it."

"Thank you." I hold on to the photo as if it were my most prized possession. Then I hug the wonderful girl who gave it to me. "What will you do after today?"

"Go back to freelancing. I was hoping to do a portrait series, but

I still haven't decided on a subject. Perhaps things will fall into place soon." She smiles. "If you ever need a photographer, you know where to find me."

"I wouldn't ask anyone else."

Noora walks over to Marisol while I plop down on the edge of the couch. Mom puts her hand on top of mine in silence. Samira offers me some potato chips, but I decline, so she gives the bag to Mr. Jones instead.

"Did everyone finish packing?" Manny asks.

"All packed," Héctor confirms. "I threatened to sing if they didn't."

We all laugh.

"You're kidding me . . . " Shay says. "You're. Kidding. Me."

"What is it?" Samira asks.

Shay points to the TV.

I notice the Flash News logo first. Then I spot the segment title flashing on the bottom of the screen: EXCLUSIVE! LANA TORRES'S COUSIN BREAKS HIS SILENCE!

Martin B. Wright sits across from the Boy King. He's as revoltingly smug as ever. He reeks of money in his brand-new Dior suit, Balmain loafers, and black Rolex.

"Welcome to this edition of *The Wright Report*. I'm your host, Martin B. Wright, and I'm thrilled to announce our guest for today, Mister Todd Anderson."

The camera pans to my sellout cousin. "Thank you for having me, Martin. It's an honor," Todd says with the inflection of a trained political spin machine.

"Let's dive right in. After Lana Torres's spectacular failure of a press conference in Dubai, you and your aunt were apprehended by the bureau and moved to a secret location for fear of a Sire attack. What are you allowed to share with us about that experience?"

Todd pretends to be pained with a grimace. "Not much. What I *can* say is that I felt appalled with how little regard for my life Lana holds. She purposely put me in danger."

"Has she reached out to you since the Sire's defeat?"

"Not a word, but my cousin has always been selfish. She even started an argument with me *on my birthday*, and it was over my justified criticism of how much the world is enamored with dragons. I'm glad she was able to end the Sire's reign. His defeat is a victory for wizards and Regulars alike. His supporters disgust me. I hope the bureau captures them all."

"So you would classify Lana and the Puerto Rican team as heroes, then?"

"They're misguided. You can't go around thinking only one dragon is a rotten egg. Dragons are dangerous. They're elitists who think this world is theirs to burn."

Just like you.

"You don't believe the Bond is strong enough to keep them in check?" Martin asks.

"There's nothing we can do to tame these monsters. They're just biding their time, playing the game until they're ready." Todd rubs his chin, then sighs. "Another Sire will emerge. Another dragon who thinks he's a god will come for our blood." He speaks to the camera. "Gold Wands, if you're listening, heed this warning. We have to end them before they end us."

My blood runs even colder than when he started speaking.

"Did he just say to *kill dragons* on national television?" Gabriela asks.

Nobody answers her. I don't think anyone has the strength to talk.

Martin seems unaffected with Todd's horrific statement. He's a stoic, dead-faced professional. Or more likely, he just agrees with Todd. "What would you tell Lana right now?"

Todd looks at the camera again, this time serious. "Open your eyes. Forget the old world you're clinging to. This is the new world, Lana.

This is the time to defend ourselves. You're scheduled to return to the States soon. Come to the studio so the people can get their answers. If you think dragons are better than us, too, you're as good as a Dragon Knight."

It's a henhouse all of a sudden. Everyone has something to say, an insult to hurl at the boy on-screen, and I'm just sitting there, letting them all vent.

Mom races to turn the TV off.

She's *turned the TV off* on her favorite nephew.

"I'm sorry you had to see that." She fixes her hands into prayer form. "While I was with him at the hideout, he just . . . became something else. He kept threatening to sue you and the bureau. He said his mentor, Mister Thompson, would help him fix everything. His rage helped me see what *I'd* become. In clinging to the past, I'd lost my relationship with my daughter."

"I'm right here, Mom," I reassure her. "Don't let Todd get to you."

"Yeah, Ms. Wells. He sucks big-time." Samira frowns at me. "I should've stood up to him whenever he ranted. Sorry, girl."

I shake my head. "Nothing to be sorry for."

"So are you gonna go on *The Wright Report* and shut that damn kid up?" Manny asks.

"He's not even talking to me, and *I* want to shut him up," says Génesis.

Marisol raises a potato chip like it's a weapon. "Disrespectful little wimp."

All these people are waiting for my response. Everyone who's watched *The Wright Report* is waiting for it. Todd's blasted me for more than ratings. He's desperate to humiliate me. He knows I'll accept his challenge. Whenever he pushes me, I push back.

There *is* an old world that should be left behind.

The one where I would've rather spent hours among dragons than one second among humans. Where I would've cried for months if Blazewrath had been canceled. Where all I wanted was to run from my life. That's not my world anymore. It's not who I choose to be.

"No," I tell Manny. "I'm going to Puerto Rico."

Mom's eyes are as big as saucers. "You really want to go back?"

"My heart calls for the island, Mom." Speaking the words fills my lungs with oxygen. My truth has always been this, but some truths take longer to spread their wings and soar. "I know we can't stay long, but I'd feel so much better knowing I can help keep my friends and their steeds safe. Even if it's for a little while, I want to protect them, too."

Mom's smile is warm. "If that's what you really want, then we can go together."

Wow. I bum-rush her into a hug. "Thanks."

"We'll be delighted to have you there," says Joaquín, smiling. He's nodding at me like he's proud. "Now let's watch something better than Flash News, shall we?"

"Yes," everyone says.

My cheeks hurt from smiling. Mom is willingly visiting Puerto Rico. She's allowing me to find a place for myself in this new world, and she doesn't want to abandon me. She and Papi are not at each other's throats. They're okay enough to put the past where it belongs.

It might be a terrible idea. This could be a nightmare greater than facing Todd.

Deep down, I know that's not the case.

There's no other place, no other people, I'd rather call home.

THE END

ACKNOWLEDGMENTS

THERE ARE SIX DRAGONS ON A BLAZEWRATH TEAM, BUT THE TEAM behind this book consists of *way* more beings of magic and might. I wish I could repay them with a dragon chocolate fountain. I'll just thank them here instead.

My agent, Linda Camacho: You emailed me on October 26, 2016, to tell me you'd been thinking about the dragon fantasy book I was too scared to write. You wouldn't stop believing in this story and my ability to write it. I finally started the first draft two months later. When I had to stop drafting after Hurricane María, you made sure that I was okay as both a creative and a human being. Thank you for being such a kind soul to me and for being the most badass advocate an author could ever have!

My editor, Ashley Hearn: You are *unreal*. I've always wanted an editor who loved my story, but I never expected to have an editor whose love made mine pale in comparison. Long before you became my editor, you kindly agreed to swap manuscripts as beta readers. Then you sent me the most amazing seven-page letter with notes that changed my life. I firmly believe that Lana's story chose us both to make it better. #TeamBlazewrath for life!

The Page Street team: How did I luck out with such a stellar group of publishing professionals? I may never know, but I sure am grateful. Thank you to everyone at Page Street Publishing/Macmillan who helped my little dragon book find its way to shelves. From the design team to publicity and marketing, you are all superheroes. And Rebecca

Behrens, thank you for being the Wonder Woman of copyeditors!

My critique partners, the Iron Keys: Natasha Heck (Commander) and Karuna Riazi (Once and Future Queen), you two deserve to win the Blazewrath World Cup for putting up with my shenanigans. Thank you for helping me become a much stronger writer and for making me feel like I'm part of a family. This Dragon Tamer loves you very much.

My first critique partner and favorite Brit, Lindsay Scott: I'm so freaking lucky to have found you when I did. You never deserved the horrible drafts I sent you, but you're a trooper for sticking with me this long. Thank you so much for your wonderful friendship, lady.

My Pure Magic gals: Amanda Lang and Sarah Shockley, you freaking rock stars. Amanda, the mock cover you designed for this book remains one of the best things I've ever seen. Thank you both for every single conversation, message, and email. The world needs your stories, and so do I.

My glorious beta readers: Maritza "Mari" Cardona, you were the very first reader to send me feedback, and I still can't believe how much you liked this book. You were also the first person to demand more scenes with Andrew, which I wasn't mad at. Autumn Krause and Bethany "Beth" Neal, you read one of my earliest drafts, which means, like the heroines you are, you sacrificed your eyeballs to read something super messy. Mia García, your feedback on a revised draft made me realize that I had to dig deeper. I owe you all the baked goods in the universe. Camryn Garrett, Nina Moreno, Alice Fanchiang, and Kelly Andrews, you were kind enough to share your enthusiasm for this book before it was worthy of being read! Your support means everything.

Sensitivity Reader Extraordinaire, Mara Delgado: When I reached out to you, I expected thoughtful notes that would help me write authentically about what it means to be Puerto Rican. I never expected the mind-blowing amount of love and good vibes you continuously give me. It's a coincidence that Team Puerto Rico's manager shares your surname, but meeting you was fate. Gracias por todo, Mara.

My Books with Bite Workshop crew: Micol Ostow and Nova Ren Suma, you will forever remain the writing mentors of my dreams. Thank you for reading my work and helping me shape my incoherent thoughts into something readable! I hope to finish that demon story someday. Thanks also to my workshop mates and brilliant people: Robyn Ford, Melissa Gould, Elena Pérez, Stephanie Feldstein, Kate Pentecost, Amanda Lang, Sarah Shockley, Alexis Karas, Aimee Payne, and Beth Neal. A cabin in the woods will never be scary with all of you around.

The Latinx book and blogging/vlogging community: I still can't believe I get to be read and reviewed by others, let alone readers who crave Latinx stories as much as I do. The hard work that goes into your craft doesn't go unnoticed, and it should never be underappreciated. Thank you so much for taking the time to read and talk about Lana's story. Special shout-outs to Adriana Martínez (@boricuareads), Marianne Robles (@bookishboricua), Cande (@iamrainbou), Carmen (@tomestextiles), Melanie Pacheco (@ashymareads), Adriana De Persia (@adrii_deper), Itzamar Peña (@lovelybookreads), Josie Meléndez (@TheJosieMarie), and Gabriela Burgos (@gaby_burgos27) for being so enthusiastic about this book long before it hit shelves! Mil gracias, mis amores.

The Bookmark crew: Paola "Lola" Nigaglioni and Melanie Barbosa, my favorite booksellers on the planet. Thank you for the countless book and music recommendations and for your friendship. You make each visit to the bookstore a total party. Melanie, extra thanks for the author photo! Keep sharing your talents with the world, queens. #IPurpleYou

Las Musas: I never imagined I'd have the chance to join such a fantastic group of Latinx authors! Thank you to Mia García for the invite and the newsletter help! Special thanks to NoNieqa Ramos, Yamile Saied Méndez, Laura Pohl, Ann Dávila Cardinal, and Nina Moreno for always being so kind to me. Also, thank you to my fellow 2020 Musas. *We did it!!!*

The #POCdebuts group: June Tan and Julie Abe, thank you for letting me be a part of this wonderful collection of debut authors! My bookshelves will be filled with even more incredible stories from #ownvoices authors, including yours. And, June, it's always a treat to support other ARMYs! #IPurpleYou

My fellow #Roaring20sDebuts: We did it, everyone! Congratulations! Rebecca "Becks" Coffindaffer, thank you for being such a great cheerleader and friend!

My friends: Apologies for ignoring you at some point, lol! Jorge, Mitchlery, Isa, and Zoeli, you are all part of my beloved Psych gang and the best weirdos I've ever met. Zoeli, you read two of the worst books I've ever written, so thank you, and I'm sorry for the torture. Jean-Carlo and Verónica, thank you for being a constant source of inspiration and support, for scolding me whenever I doubt my work, and for your shared love of all things geek. Alayra and Brenda, for putting up with said geeks and making me laugh with your mutual trolling. Amarilys and Dixie, for always telling me to keep writing despite our many tasks as college professors. To my English department lady crew and a few members of #SPNFamily: Keila "Keeks," Raisha, Mari, Kitty, Valerie, Christabel, Catilia, and Frances Z. Shakespeare would be proud of our wit, my loves. Alejandra "Aya" Zapata, cofounder of We Love Satos and animal rescuer queen, thank you for being a light in this world.

My family: The journey to publication wouldn't be half as meaningful without sharing it with you. Thank you to my parents, Wilfredo and Carmen, for raising me on a steady diet of fantasy films and TV shows, and for feeding my wildest dreams. Thanks also to Renis, my little brother and best friend, for believing in me long before I believed in myself. Los amo.

And you, for giving Lana's story a chance.

ABOUT THE AUTHOR

AMPARO ORTIZ WAS BORN IN SAN JUAN, PUERTO RICO, BUT SHE currently lives on the country's northeastern coast. Her short-story comic, "What Remains in the Dark," appears in the Eisner Award–winning anthology *Puerto Rico Strong* (Lion Forge, 2018) and *Saving Chupie*, her middle grade graphic novel, is forthcoming from HarperCollins. When she's not teaching ESL to her college students, she's teaching herself Korean, devouring as much pizza and as many Twizzlers as she can, and writing about Latinx characters in worlds both contemporary and fantastical.